"At once a cautionary tale of people caught in a web of lies and creeping terror, and a love song to the beauty and power of being different. At the novel's heart is the kind of grace Carey is known for: an illumination of the strength that lies hidden inside all of us."

—Eric Van Lustbader,
New York Times bestselling author, on *Santa Olivia*

PRAISE FOR
THE NOVELS OF JACQUELINE CAREY

Kushiel's Mercy

"Vivid...a heady mix of adventure, power struggles, and romance."
—*Publishers Weekly*

"Carey has wowed us throughout the second Kushiel trilogy, which this book sensationally concludes, leaving faithful readers feeling both deliciously sated and hungry for more from her."
—*Booklist* (starred review)

"Sensual prose and graphic eroticism make this fantasy saga particularly appealing...Highly recommended."
—*Library Journal*

"Few tales of star-crossed romance offer as much delight and satisfaction as Jacqueline Carey's Kushiel series. Sexy, tragic, and always suspenseful, these novels are notable both for their impeccable characterization and their startling plot twists. *Kushiel's Mercy*...will keep book lovers glued to the pages as this final novel in the Prince Imriel series races to its rousing conclusion."
—SciFi.com

more...

Kushiel's Justice

Kushiel's Scion

"Intelligent, sexy, heartbreakingly human...Carey at her intoxicating best...Carey continues thoughtfully and respectfully re-envisioning S&M images of beauty, power, and eroticism firmly rooted in the sacred."
—*Booklist* (starred review)

"Skillfully rendered, sensual, and thoroughly engrossing."
—*Kirkus Reviews*

"Magnificent...credible and gripping, this is heroic fantasy at its finest."
—*Publishers Weekly* (starred review)

"Evocative...Her exotic alternate earth, set in a Renaissance-like time of cultural flowering and sensual gratification, provides a lush backdrop for a cast of compelling and fascinating characters."
—*Library Journal* (starred review)

Other books by Jacqueline Carey

Kushiel's Legacy

*Kushiel's Justice**

*Kushiel's Scion**

*Kushiel's Mercy**

Kushiel's Avatar

Kushiel's Chosen

Kushiel's Dart

The Sundering

Godslayer

Banewreaker

*Available from Grand Central Publishing

SANTA OLIVIA

JACQUELINE CAREY

GRAND CENTRAL
PUBLISHING

NEW YORK   BOSTON

Copyright © 2009 by Jacqueline Carey

Grand Central Publishing
Hachette Book Group
237 Park Avenue
New York, NY 10017

Visit our Web site at www.HachetteBookGroup.com.

Printed in the United States of America

First Edition: May 2009

1 3 5 7 9 10 8 6 4 2

Grand Central Publishing is a division of Hachette Book Group, Inc.
The Grand Central Publishing name and logo is a trademark of Hachette Book Group, Inc.

Library of Congress Cataloging-in-Publication Data

Carey, Jacqueline, 1964–
  Santa Olivia / Jacqueline Carey. — 1st ed.
    p. cm.
  Summary: "A SF/fantasy novel set in the near future and featuring
a young woman with special genetically engineered 'wolf-like'
powers"—Provided by publisher.
  ISBN 978-0-446-19817-2
  I. Title.
  PS3603.A74S26 2009
  813'.6—dc22

                                                        2008038747

Text design by Meryl Sussman Levavi

SANTA OLIVIA

ONE

They said that the statue of Our Lady of the Sorrows wept tears of blood the day the sickness came to Santa Olivia. The people said that God had turned his face away from humankind. They said that saints remember what God forgets about human suffering.

Of course they said that in a lot of places during those years.

For a long time, there was dying. Dying and fucking. A lot of dying and a lot of fucking, and more dying.

There were rumors about El Segundo's forces staging raids across the wall; Santa Anna el Segundo, the rebel Mexican general. If it was true, they were never seen anywhere near Santa Olivia. But why would they be? There wasn't a hospital there. After the second wave of sickness, there wasn't even a proper doctor.

But it must have been true because the soldiers came.

The day the soldiers arrived, Our Lady's tears dried to rust in her shrine. There were bullhorns and announcements about a wall, a new wall to the north to bracket the wall to the south. A cordon to contain El Segundo's attempted incursions. People could stay or go. Elsewhere in the cordon it was different, with wholesale evacuation and reparation, but there was no help for those who wanted to leave Santa Olivia.

Some went.

Most stayed. They stayed because they were sick and dying, or because they were orphaned and confused. They stayed because it was home and they had nowhere else to go and the sickness was everywhere. They stayed because the soldiers didn't really want all of them to go, because the soldiers didn't want to be all alone in the hot, arid cordon between two countries.

But it wasn't home anymore, not exactly.

After the reservoir had been secured and the golf course seized for recreational purposes, after the bulldozers and the backhoes had chewed and leveled the terrain, after the cement trucks had poured foundations and the cinder-block walls had begun to climb, the soldiers explained. There was a meeting in the town square. It took place in the evening. There were generators to fuel the arc lights, because the power grid had been down for a long time in that part of Texas. General Argyle was there, a middle-aged man with a face like a knotted fist. His spokesman explained, bawling through a bullhorn.

"We are at war!

"This is no longer a part of Texas, no longer a part of the United States of America! You are in the buffer zone! You are no longer American citizens! By consenting to remain, you have agreed to this! The town of Santa Olivia no longer exists! You are denizens of Outpost No. 12!"

No one knew what it meant, not exactly. There was something about sickness and something about the scourge to the south on the far side of the old wall. But there was too much dying to be bothered. If the soldiers brought money and food and medicine and doctors who hadn't succumbed to the plague, that was to the good. It had always been an isolated place.

Santa Olivia; Santa Olvidada, soon to be forgotten by most of the world.

Outpost No. 12.

What Carmen Garron remembered most about that night was the humming generators and the light. She was thirteen years old, and for the past six years of her life, there had been precious little of it after nightfall. Generators were scarce, fuel to be hoarded for important matters like refrigeration. Now, here! Light, white-hot and spilled with reckless abandon, throwing stark shadows. It highlighted the general's clenched face with its incipient lines. It teased out the lurking sickness in her aunt's and uncle's faces, in the faces of their neighbors. It lit up her cousin Inez's nubile features, and her own.

And the soldiers . . . the American soldiers looked so strong and hale.

Carmen Garron liked soldiers.

After the barracks and the other buildings were finished, there were more soldiers. They didn't want to be bothered with the town's troubles, so arrangements were made. With the army's blessing, Dan Garza declared himself in charge and his men took care of security. They swaggered through the dusty streets, deferring to no one who wasn't in uniform. They weren't allowed to carry guns—no one in Outpost except soldiers were—but they carried lengths of metal pipe and weren't afraid to crack heads if they felt like it. People muttered, but what could you do? As long as they kept the peace, the general didn't care.

Old Hector Salamanca, who owned a good chunk of real estate in town, made arrangements, too. He was a shrewd old fucker, too scrawny and stubborn for the plague to take. His arrangements were made with the chief warrant officer and involved liquor and food and generators and kerosene. His businesses thrived. Bodegas turned to bars and brothels, and people could buy what they needed in his shops. As long as it kept the peace and kept the soldiers happy, the general didn't care.

Sister Martha Stearns and Father Ramon Perez also made arrangements. She was a diminutive blond woman with an intense gaze and a sense of purpose that owed nothing to divine calling; despite her nun's garb, she was in fact an orphan of the church and had never taken vows. Handsome Father Ramon, who was himself only a novice despite his priest's collar, knew this. They kept each other's secrets. It wasn't their fault. Father Gabriel, the last real priest in Santa Olivia, had caught the plague and hung himself from the bell tower before it could take him.

"Go forth, fornicators!" he had shouted before he plunged, perched on the narrow walkway, the noose around his neck. "Go forth while you may; go forth and seize the day! Fuck your mothers, your brothers, your sisters and fathers; fuck in the streets like dogs, you sodomites and whores! Why not? Death rules all! God has turned his face away!"

Then he jumped.

That explained all the fucking, in part.

What Sister Martha and Father Ramon arranged for was medical care. Once a week, a doctor from the base would hold a free clinic at the mission church, with its ancient adobe walls, and anyone could come. He taught Sister Martha enough about medicine to care for the townsfolk the rest of the time. They made those arrangements with the army chaplain, a sincere fellow who hadn't the faintest idea neither of them were true clergy. As long as it didn't interfere with the care and well-being of his soldiers, the general didn't care.

General Argyle cared about three things. He cared about his men; and they were men, all men. There was a story that once women had served in the army as officers and everything, but it was only a story. He cared about patrolling the southern wall and keeping his section of the cordon secure.

And he cared about boxing.

One thing about the general—whose full name was William Peter Argyle—was that he *loved* boxing. Loved it. It was said he'd been a boxer in his youth, a junior heavyweight of some promise, and maybe it was true. Anyway, he couldn't get enough of watching it. So the soldiers held boxing matches on the base, and on the third Saturday of every month, there was a match in the town square.

For the first year, they were mostly exhibition matches: soldiers fighting soldiers. When that began to bore the general, he made an offer. Higher stakes made the matches more exciting. If any of the townsfolk were able to defeat one of his champions, they would win a considerable purse and safe passage to the north for themselves and a companion. Out of the cordon, back to free territory in the U.S. of A.

A lot of men tried. None of them ever stood much of a chance, but they tried anyway. They put brawn and heart and sweat and blood into the effort, fighting until they were knocked down too hard to rise and lay gasping on the canvas floor. And that made the general very happy.

"Men ought to strive for what's beyond their grasp," he said once. "That's what makes 'em men."

What he thought of women, no one knew.

There were no women in the army and no women on the base, except for the local women hired on the cleaning crew, and they had to leave the premises before sundown. Married men had to leave their wives behind when they did their tours in the cordon. Single men with sweethearts were forced to abandon them; single men without sweethearts were forced to reconcile themselves to the fact that they'd not find lasting love until their tours ended. It had been declared illegal for military personnel to wed denizens of Outpost.

"Why?" Carmen Garron asked her first soldier-lover. She was seventeen years old, but she looked nineteen and had told him she was. Her aunt and uncle had passed, taken by the sickness; her cousin Inez had gotten her a job waitressing in a diner the soldiers liked to frequent. It didn't quite pay enough for her share of the rent on their apartment.

Her first lover was a clever boy from somewhere out East, with brown hair, spectacles, and a wiry wrestler's body.

"Because." He stroked her warm flesh, her skin damp with sweat. His face looked a little naked without his glasses, but his gaze was sharp and earnest. "They don't want people to know you exist. Not for certain. They don't want anyone to know. You understand that, don't you? That this used to be part of America?"

Carmen shrugged. "I guess."

His palm shaped the curve of her waist. "Trust me, they don't."

"Why?" she asked.

"Because they've told everyone there are no civilians left in the cordon." His hand dipped lower. "Everything that happens here is classified. We're not allowed to talk about it. And you're not allowed to leave."

She looked at the top of his head as he bent to follow his hand with his lips. "What about the general's offer? The boxing?"

He glanced up and laughed. "No one will ever win. And anyway, General Argyle's a little crazy."

"Okay," Carmen said uncertainly.

Her lover peered at her. "So you understand?"

A little bird in her heart uttered a single warbling note and died. "Yes," Carmen Garron said sadly to her first lover. "I understand."

He came and went, that one, after his tour ended. And then there was another who said much the same thing. He wasn't as clever, but he was fun and funny. Life settled into certain rhythms. By day there was the diner, by night—most nights—there was the soldier. Like the other, he gave her an allowance that enabled her to pay her share of the rent. Once a week, there was a visit to the free clinic in the mission. The army doctor gave her a certificate of health and a week's supply of condoms. He wasn't authorized to offer any other form of birth control to the female denizens of Outpost, no matter how hard Sister Martha argued for it.

The third soldier was different.

He was a boxer; that was where she saw him first. Fighting in the ring in the town square on the third Saturday against a young townsman named Ricky Canton. Carmen should have been rooting for the local challenger, the underdog; everyone did. Instead, her gaze was fixed on the soldier.

He was a big Minnesota farmboy with a nice, easy smile and a lazy, looping left hook that looked much slower than it was. He used it to pummel Ricky Canton up and down the ring.

"Go on!" Inez nudged her cousin.

In between the fourth and fifth rounds, Carmen Garron slipped through the crowd, made her way to the outside of the soldier's corner. Out of the corner of his eye, he saw her.

"Hi there." He slid one muscled, sweaty arm through the ropes, touched her hand with his gloved fist.

The bird in her heart warbled.

"Hi," Carmen whispered.

It took three more rounds for Ricky Canton to go down for good, but he did. The Minnesota farmboy stood in the center of the ring, tilting his head modestly as the referee raised his hand in victory. And then he went back to his corner, leaning on the ropes, lowering his head toward Carmen's.

"Can I buy you a drink?" he asked. "At Salamanca's?"

She flushed. "Of course."

She was twenty years old, still in the first flush of youth, and he was her first love—her first *true* love. His name was Tom Almquist, and on nights when she was alone, Carmen whispered his name to herself like a prayer. Like her first lover, he was earnest; like her second, he was funny, although it was humor of a slow, careful kind. But he was different.

"I'll marry you," he whispered the time the condom broke, his lips pressed to her temple. "Don't worry. Either way, I will."

"You can't!" Carmen whispered back.

His massive shoulders rose and fell. "Don't care. I *will*." He gave her a reassuring smile. "I bet we catch El Segundo in six months' time and all this will be over."

It didn't happen that way.

He would have kept his word if it had, because Tom Almquist was a determined young man, and when he found out that Carmen was pregnant for sure, it only made him more determined. He even talked to his commanding officer about Carmen. But two weeks after they knew for certain, Tom Almquist was killed when his squadron was sent to investigate a report that El Segundo's men had breached the southern wall some twenty miles away. There was a breach, but it was a small one. And there was a booby trap and a bomb.

The bird in Carmen Garron's heart went silent for a long time.

TWO

She named the boy Tom. He was a good baby, strong and sturdy, seldom fussy. By the time he was six months old, it was obvious he took after his father: blond-haired and blue-eyed, likely to be strapping.

There were no more soldiers paying an allowance, but there was still the diner, and the church helped with its widows and orphans fund, eked out from its meager coffer of tithes.

"I'm not a widow," Carmen murmured to Sister Martha Stearns. "And I'm too old to be an orphan."

Sister Martha gave her a pitying look. "Honey, we're all God's orphans and Christ's motherfucking widows. Take the money."

The tear-stained face of Our Lady of Sorrows seemed to nod in agreement. In the alcove nearby, the little effigy of Santa Olivia watched with wide, dark eyes, her basket over her arm.

"Okay," Carmen said.

The grief never went away, but after a while it faded. They got by. When her cousin Inez asked her to move out—the presence of a baby in a small apartment didn't exactly inspire the soldiers Inez dated—Carmen took a room above the diner. The owner's wife was a good-hearted woman named Sonia, crippled by severe arthritis, and she offered to watch Tom while Carmen worked.

So they got by, and Tom grew bigger, turning into a cheerful toddler with his father's sweet smile. After two years, Carmen began dating—but no soldiers. Only local boys. Danny Garza, the mayor-for-life's swaggering eldest son, took a fancy to her. He was a good-looking young tough who could be charming when he wanted to be, and for a while, he did. But he got angry when she wouldn't go to the fights with him. She hadn't been to the fights since a Minnesota farmboy beat Ricky Canton.

"No," Carmen said. "Never."

"I wasn't *asking*," Danny Garza said ominously.

Carmen shrugged. "No."

In Danny Garza's experience, women didn't say no. When Carmen wouldn't stop saying it, he hit her hard enough to blacken one eye and make the left side of her face swell, though not hard enough to break bones. Carmen wept, and her boy howled with confused horror.

"Serves you right," Danny spat. "Anyway, I've had better."

The swelling went away and the bruises faded. Danny Garza never came back, and Carmen Garron stopped dating. Years passed, one by one. In the cracked mirror above the dingy sink in her tiny bathroom, she watched her youth ebb away slowly. Her cousin Inez chided her.

"You should date," Inez said. "Find a man."

"I don't want a man," Carmen said.

"So find a woman." Inez shrugged. "Whatever. You'll wither up and die."

"I have a man. A little man all my own." Carmen gathered Tom in her arms and bounced him on her knee. At six years old, he was almost too heavy for it. He thrust his fists into the air and crowed like a victorious boxer.

Inez eyed her. "You're crazy, *mija*."

"No," Carmen said. "Just sad."

What she didn't say was, why bother? Who will protect us? Who will be strong enough to stand against the forces that have overturned our lives? Who can fight the killing sickness that comes in waves? Who can fight the menace to the south that slips through the wall and sets bombs and ambushes? Who can fight the government to the north that decided we were no longer its citizens? It was like the fights. The odds were insurmountable. She thought about her first lover, the clever brown-haired boy from somewhere out East, with a pang of distant regret.

No one will ever win.

"Whatever," Inez said diffidently. "We gotta survive."

Two weeks later, Carmen Garron met a man.

He was waiting in the street when she unlocked the door to open the diner, a dim figure in the early dawn. A soldier like any other, this one a black man in desert fatigues wearing his cap with the brim pulled low to shadow his face. There wasn't anything different about him, except that there *was*. He waited politely for her to finish turning the sign from Closed to Open, and his motionlessness was more motionless than it should be. She watched from the corner of one eye as he followed her into the diner and slid into a cracked booth. When he moved, he moved with a peculiar economy of movement.

"Morning," he said without looking up. "What do you have?"

Carmen pointed at the chalkboard. "On the wall."

She could have told him what they served—it usually paid to be polite—but she had an odd urge to see his face. He cocked his head and glanced up at her beneath the brim of his cap with a profoundly tired and utterly fearless gaze. No bird warbled, but her heartbeat quickened unaccountably.

"Eggs and chorizo," he said, looking past her. "A lot of both."

She brought a heaping plate and watched him eat steadily and methodically. No one else entered the diner.

"Hungry, huh?" she asked at length. "Long patrol?"

He looked up briefly. "Yes."

It was . . . what? Something about the eyes. Dark and unblinking as the statue of Santa Olivia, the fearless child-saint who'd ventured onto a battlefield with a basket of lunch for her soldier-papa and brought a war to a standstill over a hundred years ago.

At least that was the story.

"Yeah," Carmen said. "I've heard the guys complaining after they been out chasing the ghost. Powdered eggs on the base don't cut it. Ours are real, honest-to-God eggs. Laid by real hens."

Jesus, she was babbling. A flicker of amusement crossed his

face—or at least she thought so. It was hard to tell. "Chasing the ghost?"

"Santa Anna," she said. "El Segundo. Isn't that what you call it?"

"Ah." A flicker of something else. "Yes." He held out his empty plate. "May I have another order?"

"Sure." Their fingers brushed as she took the plate. A touch, the merest touch, but Carmen shivered. "You really *are* hungry."

"Yes."

Grady, the owner and cook, scrambled another mess of eggs and chorizo, grumbling. She watched the soldier. When a couple more patrons from the base trickled in, jocular and still half-drunk from a night's carousing, he ducked his head unobtrusively. Carmen slid the second plate before him.

"Here."

"Thank you." He ate mechanically, quicker now, fork to mouth, never spilling a crumb. She thought about how unspeakably tired his eyes had looked, and about how he didn't know that everyone in Outpost called patrolling in response to rumors of El Segundo's forces chasing the ghost. About how his uniform didn't seem to fit quite right, come to think of it. When his plate was empty, she paused beside his booth and laid a casual hand on his shoulder.

Jesus!

Muscle twitched beneath her hand, somehow denser and heavier and more fluid than muscle had a right to be. For the first time since Tom Almquist's death, desire flooded between her legs, startling and unexpected. Carmen's face grew hot and her fingers tightened involuntarily, craving more. The soldier's chin rose with a surprised jerk, his eyes suddenly wide and filled with wonder.

"Do you . . ." Acting on pure instinct, she lowered her voice until it was barely audible. "Do you have a place to stay?"

He shook his head imperceptibly.

Carmen nodded. "Come back at five."

He did. She wasn't sure he would, but he did. The bell jingled and there he was, leaning in the doorway, head lowered to shade his face, somehow more solid and *present* in the space he occupied than seemed natural. Carmen untied her apron and went to him, clearing her throat. Grady shot them an incurious glance, then went back to tending his grill.

"I'm not a whore," Carmen said.

"I didn't think you were," the soldier-who-wasn't-a-soldier replied.

"It's just a place to stay," she added. "I have a son."

He nodded. "You're a widow?"

A bitter laugh caught in her throat. "Aren't we all?"

He didn't move. "Yes."

Still; so still. Carmen reached out her hand. He took it, his fingers folding around hers. Strong and gentle. Too strong; too gentle. It felt like a promise of grace and a harbinger of sorrow. Her eyes burned with tears. He regarded her with the same weary fearlessness that he had shown before. He smelled hot and acrid, like sun-scorched dust. Her pulse beat hard, the blood throbbing in her veins.

"Why am I doing this?" she whispered.

He shook his head. "I don't know. You don't have to."

She gazed at their conjoined hands. "Tell me your name."

"Martin." The name had an unfamiliar lilt on his tongue.

"Just Martin?" she asked. He nodded. She smiled ruefully. "I'm Carmen. Carmen Garron."

She led him upstairs. The room wasn't much; there was her bed and Tom's cot, a table and a pair of chairs, and a hot plate where she cooked a little. Mostly she ate food from the diner. But it had its own bathroom, and it was clean. Martin took off his cap and hung it carefully from the back of one of the chairs. He looked younger without it, except for his eyes. "Where's your boy?"

"Down the hall with Sonia. She looks after him while I work. I should go fetch him." Carmen hesitated. "Make yourself at home. The shower works, if you like."

His lips curved upward. "I can take a hint."

She flushed. "It's not that."

"Carmen?" He stopped her as she was leaving. "Will your boy be scared?"

She paused, considering. There hadn't been a man in her quarters since Danny Garza beat her. "Maybe."

Martin nodded. "I'll wait, then."

She went to fetch Tom. He was reading a picture book while Sonia watched him, her gnarled hands folded in her lap; or at least he was turning the pages and telling stories to himself. He glanced up brightly when she arrived. "Hi, Mommy!"

"Hi, *mijo*." She kissed his cheek. "Any progress?"

Sonia shook her head. She'd been trying to teach him to read, but she suspected he had a learning disorder. "I know there are techniques, but I'm afraid it's beyond me. Mr. Ketterling might know."

Carmen planted another smacking kiss on her son's cheek. "Ketterling's a coward and a drunk. He leers at the girls and he hits the boys. I'm not putting Tommy in school until he's old enough to take care of himself. Unless he's a bother?"

"Never." The older woman smiled. "I'd miss him something awful."

"Go kiss your Tia Sonia goodbye," Carmen instructed him. "We have a special visitor who wants to meet you."

"Okay." No fear, just cheerful obedience.

Jesus, she thought as they walked down the hall. What am I thinking? He's such a good kid; he shouldn't have to see what he saw with Danny. Why did I ask some stranger—some fucking *deserter*, from the look of it—if he needed a place to stay?

At the door, she almost changed her mind. But Tom, holding her hand, looked up at her with an expression of fearless trust. Carmen opened the door. "This is Martin," she said. "He's going to stay with us for a little while. Say hello."

"Hi," Tom said.

Martin the soldier-who-wasn't dropped to squat on his heels, his hands dangling loosely between his knees. "Hi there, young fellow." They gazed at each other, man and boy. An inexplicable grin split Tom's face, widening, filled with glee. He let loose a chortle that sounded like a flock of birds taking flight. Martin laughed and shook his head, rising to his feet. "Well. I guess that's all right, then."

"I guess it is," Carmen agreed.

THREE

"Shit!" Carmen said fervently.

Martin came out of the shower glistening, a white towel around his waist. Her towel. There wasn't an ounce of superfluous flesh on him. "Sorry," he said apologetically, gesturing. "My clothes . . ."

"Yeah, yeah." She waved one hand. "I'll wash 'em."

He stepped closer to her, moving with that odd, thoughtless efficiency. "You don't have to do that."

Carmen dug her nails into her palms. "I don't mind."

Oh, sweet Jesus, she wanted to *touch* him! Wanted to run her hands over his shower-slick skin, feel those muscles surging and leaping. Wanted him atop her, against her, inside her.

"Thank you." He touched her forearm. "You're kind. I won't last long, I'm afraid."

She stared blankly at him.

"Sleep," he said. "I haven't had much."

Carmen flushed. "Right."

She found a pair of old drawstring pajama bottoms that had belonged to Tommy's father for Martin to wear, then sent Tommy down the stairs to the kitchen while she washed Martin's uniform; standard-issue desert fatigues, suitable for chasing the ghost. She hung them on the line stretched across the narrow balcony, overly aware of his presence, his goddamned *presence*. Tommy came back, trotting up the stairs, clutching a grease-stained paper sack of hamburgers.

"Eat," she said shortly.

Mother and son watched in amazement as two burgers vanished at record speed.

"Sorry." Martin crumpled the paper wrapping, then yawned, his jaw cracking. "I'm about done in." He gestured at the floor. "There okay?"

"The bed's fine if you don't mind sharing it." She got the words out without blushing. Jesus, it wasn't as though she was going to fuck the man with Tommy in the room!

Martin looked at her for a long, long time. "You sure?"

"Yeah."

"Okay," he said. "Thank you."

Five minutes later, he was sound asleep on one side of her bed. When Tommy crept over to peer at him, Martin's eyes opened like a shot, but when he saw it was just the boy, he gave a smile of surprising sweetness and closed his eyes. Tommy stayed where he was, watching the man sleep as though he were some exotic pet his mother had brought home.

And exactly what the hell *was* he, anyway?

A soldier, a deserter. Yeah, probably. Maybe. But who deserts on an army base in the middle of nowhere? The cordon was fifty miles wide, fifty miles of nothing. Maybe he'd been out on patrol and had just had enough. Walked away, walked back to town because it was the only place to go. Maybe he was afraid of the other soldiers seeing him because they'd report him.

So why didn't he look afraid?

Why didn't his uniform fit quite right?

Why did he look so damned *there*, and why did his muscles feel like they writhed under his skin like a sack of rattlesnakes? And why, oh why, had she invited him to stay with them?

"Fuck," Carmen said in disgust, then glanced at Tommy. "Sorry, honey."

Dusk came without answers. Martin slept, barely moving. Tom took to his cot without a single protest. In the bathroom, Carmen washed her face, then looked at herself in the mirror. At twenty-six, she looked worn, but she was still a pretty woman.

"What are you doing?" she asked her reflection. "What the *hell* do you think you're doing?"

Her reflection didn't reply. She brushed her teeth, put on a nightgown, and went to crawl into bed beside Martin-the-mystery.

He woke and turned toward her. In the gathering dusk, his eyes glimmered, dark and steady. Carmen laid one hand on his bare chest. His skin was smooth and cool. He shifted to accommodate her. She put her head on his shoulder. His arm came around her. Heavy; Jesus, it was heavy! But it felt good, too. Solid, protective.

She slept.

In the morning, the bed was empty. She came awake all at once with a sudden pang of loss and sat up; but no, Martin was still there, sitting at the table with Tommy, teaching him some card game.

"Mommy!" Tom's face was ebullient. "Martin's teaching me poker."

"Great," she said. "A card shark."

"He's a smart boy." Martin gathered his cards and squared the deck. "You keep these, Tom. A goodbye present."

The boy's face fell. "You're leaving?"

He glanced sidelong at Carmen. "You've been kind. But I can't stay."

"No?" A wave of anger swept over her. "Where you gotta go?" She gestured around. "You gotta hot date out there in the desert? You think you gonna run all the way north? With no food, no water? You think you gonna make it to the wall, climb right over?"

Martin's eyes flickered. "No."

"So, what?" Carmen climbed out of bed, put her hands on her hips. "*South*?" she asked incredulously. "You running *south*? You some kind of *spy*?"

And then he was there, just like that, all the way across the room, one hand on the back of her head and the other covering her mouth, and she hadn't the slightest doubt in the world that he could break her neck with one quick twist. "No. Hush."

Tommy made a stifled sound.

She hushed.

Martin sighed, his hands dropping. "Better you don't know. Trust me."

She took a deep breath. "Is someone looking for you?"

He hesitated. "No. Not exactly. Not here, not yet."

"So stay." Carmen glanced at her son. It was what he wanted, despite what had just transpired. He didn't want Martin to leave. It was written on his face. "Stay a few days. You're tired, you're hungry, and wherever you're going, you don't have any supplies to get there. I'm lonely and Tommy likes you. Stay a little while." She paused, then needled him. "Unless you're *scared*?"

Danny Garza would have punched her for those words.

Martin-with-no-last-name only smiled, sad and wistful. "Scared? No." He sighed and rubbed his eyes with the heels of his hands. "Never." He reached out and brushed her cheek with his fingertips. "All right. A few days."

Heat scalded her face. "Okay, then."

Tommy chortled.

All day long, she thought about it. Thought about him. It was a goddamned long day. After the lunch rush, she went over to Inez's and asked if she'd take Tommy for the night.

Inez raised her eyebrows. "You *met* someone?"

"Yeah. Kinda." Carmen's unruly blood rose.

"Shit, girl!" Inez laughed. "I'd about given up on you. What's he like?"

Good question. "I don't know." Carmen shrugged. "Kinda quiet. Nice," she added, not sure if it was a lie or not.

"Huh." Inez regarded her. "Well, good for you."

She worked the rest of her shift. Tommy wasn't happy about the arrangement, but he went anyway. He was a good kid, never prone to whining. She promised him he'd see Martin tomorrow. And then she went back to her room above the diner, where she found Martin waiting and the table laid with barbecue pork tortas and cool, sweating bottles of beer he'd gotten from a corner vendor.

"Aw, shit." Tears stung her eyes. "Aw, shit, Martin!"

He blinked once, slowly. "I thought you might be hungry."

"Yeah. No." She wiped her eyes. "I gotta shower, okay?"

"Okay."

When Carmen got out of the shower, he was standing before the window, gazing at the street below. His head turned slightly toward her, lowering sunlight gleaming on one cheekbone. She crossed the room on bare feet, wearing only her threadbare robe, and slid her arms around his waist from behind, laying her cheek against his back. "Make love to me," she whispered. "Please."

He turned in her arms. "You're sure?"

She began unbuttoning his freshly laundered shirt. "Yes."

It was and it wasn't like it had been with other men. The act was the same, but he was different, so different. She traced the column of his neck with her open mouth, tasting him. His skin tasted like any man's, but the flesh beneath it was too dense, too solid. When he kissed her, his lips were soft, but his tongue was alive with muscle. It excited her beyond reason.

"Jesus!" Carmen clutched him.

Martin's brows furrowed. "You like it?"

"Yes!" She yanked at his shirt. "*Yes!*"

He was gentle; with any other man, she would have said too gentle. But there was nothing gentle about his body, the stark physical reality of it, sliding over hers as sleek and deadly as a shark in dark waters. She wrapped herself around him, clung to him as he moved in and out of her, and ripples of pleasure kept surging, surging. His cool skin grew hot. His cock felt like a living thing throbbing inside her. She came and came, stifling her cries against his shoulder, until finally he shuddered and went still. For a moment, his body went slack and she felt the full, impossible weight of him on her; then he sighed and rolled over.

Carmen lay breathing hard. "Martin?"

"Yes?"

"What the fuck *are* you?" she asked. He didn't answer. "I'm serious." She propped herself on one elbow and stared at him. "*Who* are you? *What* are you?"

He shrugged. "I don't know."

"What do you mean, you don't know?" She blew out her breath in frustration. "Okay. Shit. We just fucked. I just fucked you *without* a condom. Shit. I let you come inside me. And I don't even know your last name."

"Ah." He smiled wryly. "It's all right. You're safe."

"From what?"

He ran his thumb over her lower lip. She resisted the inexplicable urge to grab his dark, sinewy hand and suck his thumb into her mouth. "Me."

"You're clean?" Carmen asked. "Yeah, well, good. Me, too. But that's not the only risk. I can't afford another kid." She shook her head, tears welling. "It's not even that, you know? It's just . . . who the fuck are you? Why am I doing this? Jesus! Tell me something; tell me anything. Make me feel better about it. Where do you come from and where are you going? Where were you even born? 'Cause I know it's not America. I can hear it in your voice, man. I've heard a hundred thousand different soldiers' accents, and yours isn't one of them."

"Hush." Martin gathered her into his arms and let her cry. "I'm sorry."

She cried harder. "No, you're not!"

"I am," he said. "You don't know."

She lifted her head and glared through her tears. "Don't know *what*?"

"You don't know what a gift you are," he said softly. "Don't know how beautiful you are. Don't know what a gift your desire is."

Carmen sniffled, inhaling snot and tears. "Well, I can't fucking help it!"

"Carmen." Martin cupped her face in his strong hands, gazed at her with his calm, fearless eyes. "Okay. You did this because you wanted to, and that's a gift I've never been granted before. I hope I accepted it with grace. Because that's what it was, a gift of grace. I can't answer a lot of your questions because I don't know the answers. Okay?"

"I guess," she murmured.

"I'll tell you what I do know." He caressed her face, his touch at once soothing and arousing. "You're okay. We could fuck all day long, and I couldn't get you pregnant. I'm sterile. A mule. So that's all right. And I know where I was born."

"Yeah?" Carmen swiped at her dripping nose.

"Yeah." Martin smiled. "It was an island. A barren island. Seems fitting, eh?"

She eyed him suspiciously. "What island?"

"La Gonâve," he said.

"Where's that?"

He shrugged. "It's part of Haiti."

"Oh, holy shit!" Carmen sat bolt upright, wide-eyed, clutching the damp sheets to her breast. "You're one of the fucking Lost Boys!"

FOUR

She got the yellowing stack of tabloids from the closet and showed him the article while they ate cool tortas and drank warm beer. Martin laughed at the photo of the feral-looking wolfman with the pointed ears and snarling face, but he didn't laugh while he was reading.

"Where did you get this?" he asked when he was done.

"Ben," Carmen said. "He was this soldier-guy I dated a long time ago. Before I met Tom's father." She shrugged. "His mother had a thing about those papers. I guess she was a little crazy. They're not supposed to have newspapers from the outside world on the base, but she used to smuggle them to him somehow. She said they printed lots of bullshit, but that secret rebels in the government used them to leak true stories. Like it was some kind of code." She paused. "Maybe she wasn't so crazy, huh?"

"I don't know," Martin murmured.

"But it's true, isn't it?" she asked. "About the Lost Boys."

"There was a facility on La Gonâve," he said slowly. "Funded by the Chinese. Yes. Haiti is a very, very poor country. For enough money, they were willing to permit things that would have been unthinkable even in China."

"Like making . . ." Carmen skimmed the article, looking for the term and pronouncing it with care. "Human genetic hybrids."

"Yes."

" 'Artificial werewolves spawned in secret laboratories,' " she read aloud. " 'An army of ravening wolf-men poised at America's back door.' She frowned. "What does 'ravening' mean?"

"Hungry," Martin murmured.

Carmen eyed the empty plate before him. "Yeah, I guess."

"I'm not a goddamn werewolf," Martin said mildly.

She eyed him. "Yeah, right."

He returned her gaze steadily. "They did a lot of experiments, tried a lot of things. When the Americans found out about the facility and raided it, the scientists burned all their records. I don't know exactly what I am. None of us ever did."

"Us." She cleared her throat. "The Lost Boys."

Martin nodded. "There were twenty of us. We were all around eight years old when the Americans took us." He smiled briefly. "Some ravening army."

"What'd they do with you?" Carmen asked.

"Studied us." He shrugged. "Or at least they started to. Then the first big wave of flu hit and everything went to hell. All the important scientists were put to work looking for a cure or a vaccine." Martin fell silent for a moment. "We grew up in laboratories," he said at length. "They didn't do any more genetic testing and no one ever told us what they learned from the first ones, but they'd have less important guys running less important tests. Strength, endurance, speed, metabolism. How much food we need," he added, seeing the question on her face. "How long we could go without it. How long we could go without sleep. Sometimes they'd talk in front of us. That's how I know we're sterile. That's how we learned about fear."

Carmen blinked at him. "What's to learn?"

"We don't feel it," he said.

"So you're all like super-brave, huh?" she asked. "Big heroes?"

"No," he said patiently. "We don't *feel* fear. You can't be brave if you can't be scared. Henri figured it out. He was the oldest; he was sort of our leader. Fear's a survival mechanism. You're supposed to be scared of danger. Henri figured out that we were missing something. And he figured out that it meant we had to be extra careful. To learn to think about what we couldn't feel."

"Okay." It overwhelmed her all at once. She got up from the

table and walked around the room, holding her robe closed tightly. "Okay."

"Carmen."

She held up one hand. "Gimme a minute."

He waited.

She breathed slowly and deeply. "Okay. I already know enough that you're fucked if I talk, and I'm fucked if you decide to be extra careful and shut me up. So you might as well tell me the rest. How'd you end up here? You bust out of the lab? And where's your buddy Henri and the others?"

"Do you really want to know?" he asked.

Carmen thought about it. "Yeah, I do."

Martin told her.

Told her how by the time they turned eighteen, the government decided they might as well get some use out of their unlikely refugees and train them to do what they were bred for. Trained them as soldiers. Used them as an elite squadron. Told her stories of what they'd done.

"We were good," he said dryly. "Too good. There were rumors. People got nervous." He nodded at the tabloid. "No one was supposed to know we existed."

"So you deserted?" she guessed.

He shook his head. "Not right away. They decided to break up the unit. Split us up." His mouth twisted. "Henri got wind of it. He said if it came to it, we should run. There were some good people, people who tried to help us, but we were the only family any of us had."

"The Lost Boys," Carmen murmured. "So they did it, huh? Split you up?"

"Yes."

"Why'd you run *here*?"

Martin smiled sideways at his half-empty bottle of beer. "It's on the way. I got turned around in the cordon for a few days. Whatever I'm bred for, it's not a good sense of direction. I needed food and rest."

"Mexico," she said. "You're going to fucking *Mexico.*"

"Do you hate it that much?" he asked curiously. "Half the folk in this town must have roots there."

"Yeah." Carmen sat down. "*Viva la Raza.* We used to say shit like that when I was a kid. Put it on bumper stickers, you know? But that was before the war. Before El Segundo." She shivered. "He killed Tommy's father. He's killed a lot of people."

"Someone has," Martin agreed.

She stared at him. "What are you saying?"

"I don't think he's real," he said softly. "I think he *is* a ghost. Something the government made up to give them an excuse to seal the border and cut off aid to a country hit worse by the flu than America."

"So who's setting the bombs?" she asked. Martin didn't answer. "Oh, shit." She shook her head. "No. No."

"I don't know for sure." His voice was still gentle. "It was Henri's theory. He was the smart one."

"And that's why you're going?"

"It's one reason," he said. "Mostly because we can't stay here. We never thought to complain about anything until they tried to split us up. Then we did. As a result, the U.S. government declared us *property.* Spoils of war. Because we aren't entirely human, you see."

"Wolf-man," Carmen murmured.

"Maybe." He laughed unexpectedly. "Maybe not. Who knows? Henri said if they bred us for strength, we'd more likely be part ant than wolf. Maybe they ought to call us the Myrmidons."

"How can you *laugh* about it?" she asked plaintively.

Martin shrugged.

Silence stretched between them. "I wish you'd never come here," Carmen said at last without looking at him. "I don't want to know this shit. Any of it."

"Do you want me to leave?" he asked.

She lifted her head and gazed at him. Despite everything, she didn't. "Did you kill some poor soldier-boy for that uniform?"

"No," he said steadily. "I stole it. I didn't kill anyone for it."

She sighed. "Okay. What's a Myrmidon?"

Martin smiled and told her.

FIVE

In the end, he stayed longer than he meant to.

It was the desire that burned between them, hot and unquenchable. Knowing what she knew, it didn't matter. Wolf-man, ant-man; whatever Martin was, she wanted him. Couldn't help the way her blood leaped at his touch, couldn't help the way her body craved his. Couldn't fucking help it.

And it was something he'd never had with anyone else.

"No one?" she whispered in the small hours of the night, her breasts flattened against his hard chest, her sweating skin plastered to his.

Martin shook his head. "No one."

Carmen groaned and dug her nails into his flanks. "Aw, *fuck!*"

So he lingered.

Days turned into a week; a week turned into a month. Except for Inez, no one but Grady and Sonia from the diner knew he was staying with her, and they weren't going to talk. No one came looking for him. Martin kept a low profile, content to stay indoors, teaching Tommy card games. Tommy doted on him, so much so that he didn't even mind splitting his nights between Carmen and Inez. And in the end, Martin stayed long enough to discover he was very much mistaken about one big, important thing.

"I'm pregnant," Carmen told him.

He stared blankly at her. "That's not possible."

She shrugged. "Well, maybe they shouldn't have left the shitty scientists to run tests on you, or maybe it's a goddamn miracle. But I went to the free clinic today and they did the test. And I haven't been with anyone else."

Martin gave a short, wondering laugh.

Carmen scowled at him. "It's *not* funny! They won't do abortions, Martin. It's against the rules."

"I'll stay with you." He said it without hesitation.

Tears brightened her eyes. "You sure?"

He gave her that surprisingly sweet smile, making her heart leap. "Yes."

Work was a problem; they couldn't all live on her meager earnings. Martin had some cash, but it wouldn't last. And it wasn't a good idea to have him do anything that would put him in regular contact with the soldiers, which was pretty much any job in Outpost.

"Talk to Salamanca," Inez advised Carmen. Carmen had told her that Martin was a deserter, though not the part about him being not quite human. "He's always looking for guys desperate enough to haul garbage."

It was the worst job in Outpost: collecting garbage and hauling it in hand-drawn carts to be burned or buried. But the garbage collectors went around in the early dawn hours, and no one looked at them.

It was a risk. When they met, Hector Salamanca studied Martin with narrowed eyes. "What are you hiding from, son?" he mused. " 'Cause I don't think you're from here. You running scared from El Segundo? Looking to desert?"

"Yes," Martin agreed. "Is that a problem?"

Old Salamanca licked his lizard lips. "Half wage. And if you get caught, I don't know nothing."

Martin nodded. "Okay."

For two months, it was good. For two months, it was like they were a family. Martin hauled garbage better than anyone had ever hauled garbage before. No one took notice of him and the grueling work didn't bother him. Carmen waited on soldiers in the diner, wondering what in the hell was growing in her womb, but glad that whatever it was, it was conceived in something that was beginning to feel a lot like love. And Tommy was just plain happy.

Fight night was when it changed.

It was Tommy who wanted to go. She'd begun to tell him stories that had been too painful before. Stories about how she'd met his father. He wanted to see the boxing, begged and begged until she relented for the first time since her first true love had died.

It was still the best spectacle in town—with free beer, too. They stood in the cheering throng, watching a hard-hitting army middleweight slugger patiently stalk an agile local boy nicknamed Fleet Ortiz. Martin put Tommy on his shoulders. When Fleet made a misstep in the fifth round and went down with a stiff jab to the jaw, the Outposters groaned and the soldiers cheered. Fleet got to his feet after the count, wobbly but defiant. Locals cheered. The general nodded in curt approval. The crowd began to thin and the lights dimmed as the generators sighed. Martin swung Tommy down.

"Hey, Martin!" Tommy gazed up in adoration. "You could of beat that guy, huh?"

"That guy?" Martin smiled. "I guess so, Tom Garron."

"Any guy!" Tommy persisted. "You could, right?"

Martin shrugged. "Lots. Most."

"Is that so?" It was a new voice, a familiar voice. Carmen's belly tightened and the left side of her face ached with remembered pain. She looked up to meet Danny Garza's gaze. He was still handsome, but he'd gotten fleshy. There was a new scar running through one eyebrow and his eyes were cold. He had his younger brother with him, hulking twelve-year-old Miguel. "Who's your invincible new friend, Carmen?"

"Martin," she muttered.

"Martin," Danny echoed. He laid one hand on his brother's head. "My brother here's gonna be a boxer when he grows up. Gonna win the prize and go to the free land. He punches like a donkey kicks, don't you, Mig? Show the man."

Miguel grunted and threw a punch at Martin's gut. "Ow!"

Martin raised one eyebrow.

"Shit!" Miguel backed away, shaking his bruised hand. "That ain't right, Danny."

"No," Danny said thoughtfully. "It ain't."

That was the beginning of fear.

Martin couldn't feel it and Tommy was too young, so Carmen carried it for all of them. Carried it with a dread certainty, carried it for a full four days before Danny Garza came to the diner and slid into a booth, accompanied by a few of his bully-boys.

"He's a traitor," Danny said conversationally.

She tensed. "Whaddya want, Danny?"

He slid a hand over hers. "You know who the general trusts in this town? My dad. And he told him something mighty interesting. Over at another Outpost, they caught a guy trying to sneak through the cordon. The general says there might be others. So I been asking around. This new man of yours, he ain't from the base. Word is he's been hauling trash for Salamanca." Danny smiled, his nails digging into her skin. "There's a reward."

She shook him off. "Whaddya *want*, Danny?"

He licked his fingers and winked at her. "Lemme think about it and get back to you in a couple of days."

That night Carmen sent Tommy to Inez, then told Martin what had happened. "You can't stay here," she said when she finished. He looked at her with his unblinking, fearless gaze. "Martin, you *can't*."

"I could kill him," he said calmly.

"It wouldn't end it." She shivered. "He knows, his father knows, the guys he runs with know. Salamanca knows, and if the Garzas know about the reward, he's bound to hear it. You want a list of the guys who collaborate with the army, that's it. You can't kill 'em all. And sooner or later, one of them will turn you in."

Martin was silent.

She took his strong hands in hers and pressed them to her cheeks, wetting them with her tears. *"You can't stay!"*

"What about you?" he asked. "You and Tommy and the baby?"

Carmen sighed. "We'll get by."

"I don't like it."

"Neither do I," she said. "But, Martin, they think you're a traitor. They've already decided you don't have any rights. If they catch you, they're gonna put you someplace where you never see daylight again." She smiled sadly. "I know that doesn't *scare* you. But you've gotta do like your Henri taught you. You've gotta think about the danger. And then you've gotta run."

He frowned. "I *am* thinking. What if it's a trap? Why would he give us time to think? Time for me to run?"

"Because Danny Garza is a stupid, fucking bully, and that's what they do." She let go of his hands and scrubbed at her tears. "Get off on having people in their power. Get off on making 'em scared. I'm scared out of my fucking wits, and he's getting off on it."

"I don't understand."

"Yeah, you wouldn't." Carmen gave another sad smile. "I guess on the inside bullies are as scared as the rest of us. Danny wasn't so bad, once. But he's scared people won't think he's a hard guy like his dad. So he acts like a shit, and it makes him feel better."

Martin contemplated her. "That's the sort of thing Henri would have said. He would have liked you."

"You think he was the one who got caught?" she asked hesitantly.

"No." He shook his head. "He's too smart."

"You've gotta be smart, too. Promise?"

He was silent for a long time, longer than usual. "There was a place in Mexico Henri chose for us. He read about it in an old travel guide. It had a funny name and a lot of fish. Huatulco. He thought it sounded nice. I'll write it down for you. If this ever ends, if they ever open the border, I hope you'll come find me."

"Thank you," Carmen said through tears.

The next day was a long goodbye.

Martin talked to Tommy about what was to come. Once the boy got over the worst of his upset, he listened well.

"You know you're going to have a little sister or brother, right?" Martin asked him. Tommy nodded. "Well, your mama's going to need a lot of help. And you're going to have to be the best big brother anyone could be."

"I will," the boy said gravely.

"You know I'm different, right?"

Another solemn nod. "You're the strongest man in the world and you're not scared of anything."

"Maybe not the world." Martin smiled briefly. "But you're right about the not being scared part. Here's the thing, Tom Garron. Never being scared is a kind of stupid. You understand?"

The boy shook his head.

"Okay." He propped his elbows on the table. "Would you pet a rattlesnake?"

"'Course not."

"Well, this little brother of yours, if he turns out like me, he might just pet a rattlesnake if he took it in his head to do so, because he wouldn't have the sense to be scared of getting bit. He's going to have to learn all kinds of things regular people just know."

"What if it's a girl?" Tommy asked.

"No difference," Martin said. "Not if she turns out like me. You're going to have to help your mama teach her to be extra careful. Especially when she's little. Teach her to recognize danger, okay? Like not petting rattlesnakes, and staying out of the street when the soldiers' trucks are coming through, and not ever getting in a fight you know you'll lose."

"You'd never lose a fight!"

"I lost one yesterday, son." Martin touched the boy's cheek. "But it took your mother to make me see it. Sometimes the only smart thing to do is run away. That's what you're going to have to teach your little sister or brother. Can you do that for me?"

"Yes."

"Good boy," Martin said.

The boy listened attentively while Martin told Carmen all the other things she needed to know, all the ways in which the child she was carrying might be different. About food, about sleep. About strength and speed. About the vast reserves of energy to be hoarded and expended, and what was necessary to replenish them. He spoke in a low murmur about a few things the boy was too young to understand.

And then there was nothing left to say.

There was the last supper. Carmen went out to fetch it. She ascended the stairs wearily, tossed a greasy, bulging sack of burgers on the table.

"No Danny Garza?" Martin asked.

She shook her head. "No."

"Good."

They ate in silence. Tommy kept his head lowered, fair hair shuttering his face. He imitated Martin, eating with steady, methodical precision. Afterward, they played a few hands of poker while twilight settled over Outpost. In the distance, they could hear the sounds of a night's revelry beginning.

"Time for sleep," Carmen told her son.

"Martin?" Tommy lifted his head. "Will you be here in the morning?"

"No," Martin said gently.

When Tommy lay on his cot, Martin smoothed the boy's hair back, kissed his brow, giving him the love he'd never have a chance to express to the child growing in Carmen's womb. Tommy sighed and closed his eyes, sinking into sleep despite himself.

Carmen shivered. "Hold me?"

"Yes."

She nestled against him, taking succor from the weight of his arms around her. Together on the big bed, they watched twilight deepen into night. When the sounds of revelry began to grow dim, Carmen sighed. "You should go."

"I know." Martin's voice deepened. "Will you do me one kindness?"

"What?"

"Boy or girl, name the child Loup. L-O-U-P." His teeth flashed in a grin, white and unexpected. "You know what they call a werewolf in Haiti? A *loup-garou*. Loup Garron."

"Lou," Carmen murmured.

"Yes. But spell it the way I told you."

"I will," she promised.

And then he stood, a dark figure in a dark room. She rose and kissed him one last time, wrapped her arms around his uncanny solidity. Let him go and gave him a shove. He left by the balcony. If Danny Garza wasn't completely stupid, he'd have someone watching the door, but he wouldn't expect a man to jump from the second story into the alley. Martin dangled from the ledge, let himself drop. He landed with a soft thud, crouching. He straightened and glanced up at her. She gave him one forlorn wave. He returned it, then began moving, swift and silent.

In seconds, the darkness swallowed him.

Gone.

SIX

So what's it gonna be, Carmen?" Danny Garza smiled brightly at her. "Make me an offer."

She filled his coffee mug. "He's gone."

His smile froze. "Whaddya mean, gone?"

"He went back to the base to turn himself in." Carmen eyed him. "What'd you think, Danny? He was just a guy who got tired of chasing the ghost. That story about a reward was bullshit to get you to turn in a deserter." She splayed one hand over her belly. "So you scared him away and now I'm knocked up, and he's gonna get thrown in the brig. Thanks."

Danny's eyes narrowed. "I don't believe you."

Carmen shrugged. "Suit yourself."

He rose, grabbing her arm and wrenching it. "Don't lie to me, girl!"

"Hey!" Grady waddled over from the grill and pointed a spatula at Danny. "I pay my dues to your old man, mister. You're obliged to keep his peace."

Danny Garza wasn't afraid of Grady, but he was afraid of his father. He let Carmen go. "If I find out you're lying . . ." He shrugged, because there really wasn't a whole lot he could do if he did. "And if you're telling the truth, sucks to be you, huh?"

"Yeah," Carmen said sadly. "It kinda does."

A flicker of something that might have been guilt crossed his face and he turned away. "Yeah. Well, I'll see ya."

"Hey, Danny," she called after him on impulse. "You ever think maybe it's *all* bullshit? Maybe they call it chasing the ghost for a reason? Maybe there's no such thing as El Segundo and we're all just stuck here to cover up a lie?"

A few soldiers lifted their heads. The diner got very, very quiet.

Danny Garza froze. "You shouldn't talk that way, Carmen," he said without turning around. "You don't wanna give comfort to the enemy. That fuckin' deserter tried to poison your mind." He left, taking his bully-boys with him.

So that was that.

She passed a dread-filled week, fearful of hearing news of Martin's capture. There was none. Instead, there was something even more terrifying and unprecedented.

There was a missile attack on the base.

It happened in broad daylight; it happened under a clear blue sky. It happened during the lunch rush, while Carmen was doing her best to sling hash and make nice with the soldiers, ignoring the ache in her heart and the morning sickness that persisted until late in the day.

It started with a hollow thumping sound and dishes rattling. And then sirens, a loud, blaring Klaxon. Everyone stared wide-eyed.

"We're under attack!" A man with a sergeant's stripes and a fondness for tripe soup stuck his fingers in his mouth and whistled shrilly. "Back to base, men! Civvies take cover!"

"Take cover *where*?" Carmen asked in bewilderment.

Soldiers streamed around her, grabbing hats and guns, boiling into the streets. Armored trucks roared to life. The siren yammered incessantly.

"The walk-in!" Grady shouted above the clamor. He stabbed one meaty finger at the ceiling. "Get your boy! I'll get Sonia!"

They did.

They huddled in the walk-in cooler, surrounded by darkness and hamburger and chorizo, while missiles pounded the base. Tommy clung to her, burying his face in her neck. Carmen did her best to soothe him.

"It's okay, *mijo*," she whispered. "It's okay."

He whimpered. "I wish Martin was here!"

She kissed him. "Me, too."

"Martin." Grady's voice was disembodied in the darkness. "He was an odd one, eh? Had that way of looking at you without blinking." He was quiet a moment. "What was it Danny Garza was saying? That he was some kind of traitor? Maybe in league with El Segundo?"

"No," Carmen said automatically.

"Hush, Grady," Sonia murmured.

In the chilly darkness, Grady's shoulders rose and fell. "It's pretty weird. This Martin fellow vanishes and a week later we're hit. Pretty goddamned weird, that's all I'm saying."

Carmen tightened her arms around Tommy. "So stop saying it, please."

After a while, there were no more distant thumps and tremors. The Klaxons went silent. They emerged from the walk-in, ventured into the streets along with hundreds of others, surveying the damage. One missile had landed in town.

"Oh, shit," Carmen said, gazing at the rubble of the building where she had once shared an apartment with her cousin Inez— where Inez yet lived. Or had lived. Her eyes burned. "Oh, *shit!*"

There were mounted arc lights and bullhorns. "*Step away, people,*" said an amplified voice. "*This is a war zone. For your own safety, a curfew is in effect. Go home and stay home!*"

"Mommy?" Tommy looked up at her, clutching her hand. "Did Martin do this?"

"No, honey." She had to believe it. "No."

Onlookers began digging through the rubble, ignoring the soldiers. They found a piece of sleeve, a limp hand, and frantically shifted chunks of concrete.

"*A disaster team is on the way! Go home and stay home!*"

No one heeded the soldiers. They formed a brigade. Two bodies were uncovered: Mark Zaltan and his grandmother Esmerelda, the oldest woman in Outpost. The old woman was still in her wheelchair, Mark draped protectively over her. Carmen watched in horror, clutching Tommy.

"He's got a pulse!" someone shouted.

"What about her?"

"No!"

"Ah, God!" Carmen whispered. "Inez."

There was a shot fired in the air. *"You are ordered to disperse! Go home!"*

"He needs a goddamn *doctor!*"

"Keep working; there are others!"

And then Father Ramon was there, his cassock swirling, confronting the soldier in charge. His eyes blazed like the wrath of God. He was magnificent, shouting down the soldiers. They stopped ordering people home and began working side by side with them. More help came from the base with earth-moving equipment and a medical team. Carmen took Tommy to stay with Sonia and went back to help, clearing rubble until her back ached and her hands were raw. If the effort brought on a miscarriage, so be it.

It didn't.

In the gray light of dawn, there were eleven dead and two survivors: Mark Zaltan and an infant no one could identify. The babe squalled.

"A miracle child," Father Ramon murmured, his face gray with exhaustion and dust. "We will take him."

Inez was dead. It was Grady who found her, working tirelessly despite his bulk. Shirtless and sweating, he approached Carmen, and laid a gentle hand on her shoulder. "I found your cousin. I'm sorry."

She looked past him. He had draped his shirt over the face of the twisted form, but she knew the dress it was wearing. Her voice caught in her throat. "Thank you."

Grady patted her shoulder. "And what I said before . . . forget it. Doesn't matter. We've all got to stick together."

She nodded. "Okay."

Out of respect, the soldiers offered to carry the dead to the church. But something had changed. A balance had shifted; a line had been crossed. The Outposters refused the soldiers' help. Aid to the living would be accepted; Mark Zaltan with his crushed rib cage was taken to be tended by doctors on the base. But the dead belonged to Outpost, and they would tend to their own.

Carmen Garron helped carry her cousin's body to the church. It was not the first time she'd seen death, but it was the first time she'd seen death by violence—seemingly random violence. She grieved for Inez and the others laid out, awaiting their coffins and a swift burial. She thought about Grady's words, unable to forget.

The sirens on the base remained silent.

She thought about Martin's words, too. She wished she'd never heard them.

She wished she'd never given voice to them. The thought that she might be responsible for provoking the attack that killed Inez horrified her to her core. Still, the doubts remained.

If it had truly been an attack by El Segundo, how was it that the army was so sure it was over?

SEVEN

Fear and grief.

That was what Carmen Garron remembered most about carrying Martin's child after he vanished. They were months of fear and grief. The army poured men into the base. Patrols were tripled, swarming the cordon. Soldiers went over the wall; soldiers claimed to have captured one of El Segundo's top men. Claimed to have found a cache of weapons.

No one in Outpost rejoiced.

There was a sullenness that had set in—a realization that they were trapped here. That they would never be a target if it weren't for the base. That the soldiers could leave and they couldn't. It made them resent both sides of the conflict in equal measure.

But only Carmen doubted the news.

As her belly swelled, the fear and grief and doubt grew. She went to church and made her confession to Father Ramon, pouring out the tale of Martin-with-no-last-name, the Lost Boys, his departure, the missiles. The fact that the child growing in her womb might not be wholly human. There was no confessional booth, just the two of them, talking. Father Ramon listened, smoking a cigarette, his dark, piercing eyes narrowed. "What do you think?" he asked when she had finished. "Speak from the heart."

"I think Martin told the truth," she whispered. "And it scares me more than lies."

The priest-who-wasn't-a-priest blew out a meditative plume of smoke. "It would explain a hell of a lot. But I think it is best if these words remain between me, you, and God, who doesn't seem to be listening anyway. Don't speak of it aloud again."

Father Ramon stubbed out his cigarette and rose with careless grace, laying a hand on her bowed head in benediction. He bent to kiss her brow, his breath smelling of nicotine. "Whatever the truth, do your best to love the child. Mercy and compassion are all the grace left to us."

"Okay," Carmen said. "I'll try."

She went into labor during the Festival of Santa Olivia. For as much as Outpost had forgotten and been forgotten, it remembered its patron saint's feast day. Orphans from the church carried Santa Olivia's effigy into the town square and placed her carefully on a dais. Townsfolk carried baskets of food in their arms in emulation of the child-saint and picnicked in the square.

Once there would have been banners and streamers and firecrackers, but the first two were too costly and the last had been outlawed. But there was food and music, and for a day, Santa Olivia remembered what it had been.

Her water broke without warning in the early afternoon. The contractions came hard on its heels, hard and fast. Too fast. Carmen stood dumbstruck and dripping, Tommy tugging at her hand. There was commotion all around her.

"Carmen." Hands clasped her shoulders; Sister Martha's intent gray-blue eyes gazed into hers. "Can you walk to the clinic?"

"No." Another wave struck, doubling her over. "It's coming!"

Maybe God or nature had some small measure of mercy left, because Carmen didn't remember much afterward except pain and the shocking swiftness of it all. Not the resurgence of the panic she'd managed to keep at bay since visiting Father Ramon. Not the humiliation of giving birth in the town square. Not the worry over Tommy's whereabouts that dogged her between the swift contractions. Only pain building and building, then Sister Martha's voice telling her yes, push; now, already.

And then it was over.

Carmen lay panting, her head pillowed on the knees of an unfamiliar girl—one of the church's orphans. A throng of others surrounded her, their backs to her, keeping the crowd at bay.

There was a single thin, angry squall, then silence. She made an effort to lift her head. "Is it?"

"Oh yes." Hands helped her sit, supported her. Sister Martha placed the baby in her arms. "I've never heard of a labor that quick. Maybe it's a gift of the saint after all. You ought to name her Olivia."

A girl. It was a girl.

"I can't," Carmen whispered. "I made a promise."

There wasn't much at first to indicate that Loup was different from other infants. She cried only when she was hungry, but then Tommy hadn't been a fussy baby either. She ate a lot and slept a lot, but so had Tommy.

"You're blessed with easy babies," Sonia observed. She'd volunteered to watch Loup along with Tommy when Carmen went back to work.

Carmen eyed the baby. "I guess."

She was a cute baby with caramel-colored skin, a thatch of black hair and black eyes like her father. At first they were as wide and wandering as any newborn's. It wasn't until her eyes began to focus that Carmen was sure. In her round cherub's face, those eyes were as steady and fearless as the effigy of Santa Olivia the child-saint, just like her father's had been.

"Loup Garron," Carmen murmured, stroking her cheek with one finger. "What are you gonna be, wolf-cub?"

The baby smiled at her with surprising sweetness.

Tommy adored his baby sister without reservation or a hint of jealousy. He seemed to mature overnight, taking the role that Martin had given him with great seriousness. And it was a good thing, too. At six months, Loup began crawling with dexterity and vigor. Tommy was far more adept than poor arthritis-ridden Sonia at chasing her down.

"No, baby!" he said, scooping her up as she nearly tumbled down the narrow stair that led to the diner. "You have to be *careful*."

She wasn't.

Given half a chance, she fell down stairs and out of cots, banged her head on table legs, burned her fingers on the hot plate. As soon as she began to walk, at less than a year old, it got worse. But Loup never cried or complained when hurt, only frowned in wounded perplexity. And because Carmen was working herself to exhaustion trying to support them all, it was Tommy who explained to her, over and over, that she had to be *careful*. And Loup listened to him with wide, grave eyes, trusting and doting on her older brother. At eighteen months, she began talking.

Life in Outpost continued. There were no more missile attacks, only the ever-present rumors of El Segundo's intentions. Soldiers went out on patrol and came back weary and thirsty. Sometimes they found bombs, traps like the one that had killed Tom Almquist. Sometimes they found them in time. Sometimes they didn't. But at least there were no more missiles. And Carmen Garron never, ever spoke of her doubts aloud again.

While Loup was between the ages of two and five, the differences that marked her grew more pronounced. She was an agile, darting child, curious and fearless; and yet when she was still, it was an unchildlike stillness.

"Tell me about my daddy, Tommy," she would ask.

Tommy never got tired of talking about Martin. "He was the strongest man in the world." He extended his arm, making a fist. "He used to let me hang from his arm. I couldn't budge it an inch."

Loup would plant her feet and tug at her brother's arm until it trembled, lowering. At twelve he was a strapping boy; but she was preternaturally strong and weighed more than appearances suggested. Tommy grinned and dropped to his knees, ruffling her thick, coarse hair.

"You're just like him, *loup-garou*," he whispered.

It was true and it filled Carmen with secret pride and hidden fear. She adored her responsible son and her strange, fearless daughter with a deep, aching ferocity. She treasured their bond—and envied it a little, too. She was terrified that word would get out that she'd borne a daughter to a man who wasn't wholly human, a man the government wanted to catch. Fearful that Father Ramon would talk, or Grady or Sonia, or that Danny Garza would unearth her secrets out of spite. Fearful that one day there would be soldiers on their doorstep to take her baby away to a laboratory.

But no one came.

Instead there came another wave of sickness, passing over Outpost like a bloody-winged angel. For once, for a mercy, it passed lightly over the children. It ravaged the elderly and took a handful of healthy adults. It left a number of others with weak lungs and racking coughs.

Carmen was one of the latter.

Sonia was one of the former.

"*Mijo.*" Carmen stroked her son's hair. "You know Tia Sonia is gone?" He nodded gravely. She sighed. "I think it's time you went to school, *mijo*. You and your sister."

Tommy knelt by her bedside, leaning on folded arms. "Let me take a job. I could work at the reservoir. Or I could haul garbage like Martin. I don't mind. Then you wouldn't have to work so hard."

"No!" Carmen coughed and spat blood.

"Mom . . ."

"No."

So they went to school, brother and sister. It had been a good school once—or an okay school, anyway. Now the halls were nearly empty and most of the classrooms dusty and abandoned. Ancient, yellowing signs hung from the walls cheering on the Santa Olivia Jaguars, but there weren't enough students to field a team in any sport, and no one to play against them if they could. All forty-odd kids met in a single big classroom, all ages grouped together. The only teacher left alive was Mr. Ketterling, a bitter drunk who'd gotten only more bitter with age. On the first day, he mocked thirteen-year-old Tommy for his poor reading skills.

"I'm trying," Tommy said calmly.

The yardstick cracked over his shoulders. "Try harder!"

"*Don't.*" Six-year-old Loup was out of her seat, standing atop her desk. She snatched the yardstick from Ketterling's hands, wielding it like a pugil stick. Her black eyes glittered. "Don't hit my brother."

Ketterling flinched.

"Loup," Tommy said. "No."

"Holy *shit!*" someone said fervently.

Ketterling grabbed for the yardstick. Loup leaned away just enough to evade him. Ketterling overbalanced, arms wheeling. Forty-odd kids of varying ages snickered. His face turned red and he lunged. Loup leaped backward, landing lightly on the floor, watching him with interest.

"Loup." Tommy got between them. "Give me the stick." For a moment, her small face turned set and mutinous; then she handed it over. Tommy turned and gave it to Mr. Ketterling. "I'm sorry, sir."

The man was shaking with rage. "Get out!" His voice emerged high and strained. He pointed at the door, his hand trembling. "Take your *freak* of a sister, get out, and never come back!"

"It won't happen—" Tommy began.

"*Get out!*" The words were shrieked.

They went.

Outside it was dusty and sleepy in the late-afternoon heat. Brother and sister sat on the school steps.

"'Sorry, Tommy." Loup propped her chin in her hands. "I didn't mean to ruin school for you."

"'S'all right." He ruffled her hair. "I didn't really want to go."

"Me neither."

They sat companionably for a while until Tommy roused himself. "Hey. You want to go someplace special? Someplace I always wanted to see?"

Loup raised her head. "Sure."

EIGHT

The faded sign read "Unique Fitness." Ten years before Tommy was born, it had been a family fitness center where men preened with weights, women sweated in all manner of contraptions, and there were special classes for children twelve and under. There were still murals on the walls, stylized athletic silhouettes rendered in uninspiring mauve and teal. But throughout Tommy's and Loup's lifetime, it had been a boxing club.

The plateglass windows were still intact; it was one place in Outpost no one dared to vandalize. Carmen Garron's children stood outside gazing in at the spectacle of half a dozen men sparring, shadowboxing, and working the bags.

"That's him!" Tommy pointed at a figure inside. He lowered his voice. "Grady says he's the man who taught the general to box. He's the only guy in Outpost who doesn't have to stay if he doesn't want."

"Huh." Loup pressed her face to the glass. "How come he's teaching *us*?"

"Get back!" Tommy yanked on her shoulder. "I dunno. The general asked him to."

She slipped out of his grasp. "Let's go in!"

He reached for her again, but too late. Her hand was on the doorknob. When Loup moved fast, really fast, you knew it in no uncertain terms; but even her ordinary movement was quicker and slipperier than it looked. A bell on the door jangled, and her slim body angled through the opening.

Reckoning it was too late, Tommy followed his sister inside.

No one noticed them at first. The place resounded with dull, slapping thuds. Tommy took a deep breath. It smelled like sweat and mildew, overlain with something sharp and antiseptic. He watched the men hitting bags, lifting weights, and knew he wanted to be one of them.

It felt like he belonged here.

It felt like home.

"Hey!" There were two young men sparring in the near ring. One of them broke off a clinch and came to lean over the ropes, his broad face caged in protective headgear and distorted by a mouth guard. "Beat it, punks."

"Miguel Garza," Tommy whispered to Loup. She nodded sagely.

"Floyd!" Garza's opponent spat out his mouthpiece. "Got some brats gawking!"

Tommy knew they should go, but he desperately didn't want to. Suddenly, unexpectedly, it had become very important to him that he be allowed to stay. The trainer came drifting toward them. His name was Floyd Roberts, and he was tall and lean and colorless, with pallid skin, white hair, and pale, watery eyes.

"Did I tell you to break?" he asked mildly, making a shooing gesture at the fighters. "Go on." They grimaced and resumed sparring. Floyd Roberts bent absently toward Tommy and Loup, repeating his shooing gesture. "Begone, children."

Tommy's heart contracted. He laid one hand on Loup's shoulder, drawing courage from its small sturdiness. "I'd like to stay, sir."

White brows rose. "And do what?"

He took another deep breath, tasting the air of the place. "Learn." Tommy squared his shoulders. "I'll work for whatever you can teach me. I'll haul your garbage, clean your bathrooms. I don't care."

The pale eyes blinked. "How old are you?"

"Sixteen," Tommy lied.

Floyd Roberts snorted. "Start as you mean to go on, boy. I don't work with liars."

"Fourteen," he lied.

"Show me what you've got." He put up his hands. Tommy jabbed at them the way he'd seen it done, shuffling his feet in an exaggerated fashion. The old coach snorted and began to lower his hands. Feeling his chance slipping away, Tommy threw an instinctive left, finding it barely deflected at the last instant.

Floyd Roberts blinked thoughtfully. "That's a funny left hook, boy. I knew an army fighter, once, threw that punch."

"Tom Almquist?"

His pallid brow wrinkled. "That's the one."

Tommy's heart swelled. "He was my father."

"Oh, well." The pale eyes peered at him. Long, strong fingers prodded his muscles. "You're well built for fourteen. You say you'll clean bathrooms?"

"Anything!" Tommy breathed.

"And leave the little one at home?" Floyd pressed.

Tommy glanced at Loup, his heart sinking again. "I can't, sir. I'm responsible for her."

"Ah." Floyd bent lower and peered more closely at Loup. She looked back at him with her odd, fearless stare. "Why isn't the child in school? Is she simpleminded?"

"No!" Tommy said in a defensive tone, then dropped his voice to a mumble. "She got kicked out."

Another slow blink. "This mite? For what?"

Tommy opened his mouth to lie, but something in the old man's watery gaze killed the lie on his tongue. He'd gotten away with one. He didn't think he'd get away with another. "Mr. Ketterling hit me with a yardstick, and Loup grabbed it from him. Then he chased her and got mad when he couldn't catch her. She's really quick."

The coach's long, wrinkled mouth curved upward like a lizard's. "Oh, indeed?"

"She won't be any trouble, sir," Tommy said desperately. He gave Loup's shoulder a shake—or tried to. It didn't move much. "Will you, Loup?"

"No, Tommy," she agreed.

"See?" Tommy held his breath.

In the sparring ring, Miguel Garza's opponent called for a halt, his nose bleeding from an unlucky punch.

"Ice it," Floyd Roberts said briefly.

Miguel came to hang over the ropes. "Floyd, don't do it, man! I don't care if you want to hire the kid, but we don't want some weird punk-ass brat hanging around the place."

The coach turned his pale stare on Miguel for a long moment. "That's three times the young man's called me sir, Mr. Garza," he said slowly. "I like his manners. If he says the little girl will be no trouble, I choose to believe him."

Miguel shrugged. "Whatever."

"Come back tomorrow," Floyd said to Tommy. "Be prepared to work hard. I'll give you a month's trial. If you stick it out, I'll start teaching you. If you don't work as hard as you say, if the little girl's a problem . . ." He shrugged. "Come back when you're sixteen."

"Yes, sir!" Tommy said excitedly.

"Good." The old man pointed at the door. "Tomorrow."

Outside, Tommy took long, deep breaths, his heart pounding. Loup regarded him. "Mommy's going to be mad," she said in a pragmatic tone.

"Yeah." He swallowed, his excitement fading a bit. "Loup . . . what if we don't tell her? She'll think we're going to school every day, and she won't have to worry. We don't want her to worry, do we?" He searched her face. "Okay?"

She shrugged. "Okay."

It was the beginning of a new life for both of them.

Carmen didn't know. Tommy begged Grady to loan him Sonia's books, then hid them in a locker at the gym. Every day, he and Loup left for school, each of them carrying a book. Every few days, he switched them around. Exhausted from work, Carmen never noticed.

"How was school, *mijo*?" she asked.

"Good," he lied.

Between the two of them, Tommy had a better imagination, but Loup was a better liar because she had no fear of getting caught. They invented stories together about their days at school, and while it was always Tommy who made up the best stories, it was Loup who told them.

Meanwhile, Tommy worked.

He scrubbed toilets and scoured shower tiles, ignoring the mocking derision of the young men who used them. He sprayed and wiped sweat-slick weights and equipment with assiduous care. He sprinkled the bloodstained canvas with a special powder that Floyd Roberts got from the army, then scrubbed it clean. He ran and fetched whatever the coach wanted: boxing tape, petroleum jelly, lunch from the torta vendor.

Loup helped him, except in the locker room and showers. She was quiet and unobtrusive and after the first week, the boxers-in-training quit complaining and ignored them both.

Together, they learned the gym.

There were two sparring rings, and access to them was a thing to be coveted. Only the serious contenders were allowed to spar. There were four heavy bags and six speed bags. There were free weights to be pressed and benches to be wiped. Coach insisted everything be kept clean. There were a few machines from the old days that worked muscles the free weights didn't. There were treadmills that went dead when the power faltered.

It was a world unto itself with its own caste system. Miguel Garza and his coterie of friends ranked at the top. There were only three of them in training, but a dozen other young men swaggered in and out at any given hour, placing bets and making crude jokes. Floyd Roberts tolerated them because the politics of Outpost demanded it and they gave him grudging respect, in part because he was the general's man and could summon the authority of the army if he wanted to, and in part because he was the coach, and no matter what else was true, the coach commanded respect.

After the Garza gang came the men Tommy called the Real

Men. They were older, in their later twenties and thirties—working men, men with families. They were reservoir workers, greenskeepers, odd-jobs men. They came later in the day and trained hard in silence. They were the men who'd trained for years, who'd fought actual bouts against the general's boxers.

None of them had ever won, of course. They kept trying because it paid; the general rewarded even the losers with a generous purse. But anyone could see that they'd long since given up hope of winning the fabled ticket out of Outpost. They trained to keep from getting hurt worse than they would otherwise, suffered their broken noses and cauliflower ears in silence, took the money, and went home. When Floyd Roberts thought they were getting close to taking one punch too many, he turned them gently away.

In between, there were the independent young hopefuls, too poor or proud to toady to the Garza gang. They had hope and hunger in their eyes. Two or three of them showed real promise, and Floyd was bringing them along slowly. This Tommy knew because when the trial month ended, the old coach dropped his first tidbit of information.

"See that?" He nodded at Kevin McArdle, a thickset redhead with pale, freckled skin. McArdle was working the skipping rope so fast it was a blur, though his feet scarcely seemed to leave the ground. "Learn it. That's your first lesson."

"Yes, sir." Tommy hesitated.

The old coach's mouth wrinkled. "You want to learn to punch."

"Yes, sir."

Floyd's gaze drifted toward Miguel Garza. "Don't they all. But it starts with footwork and conditioning. That's the key." He turned his gaze on Tommy. "I had to bring the first generation on too fast. Bill wanted his prizefighters. Well, he got 'em. But I'm not rushing the rest. You, either."

"Yes, sir," Tommy said.

The coach jerked his chin at Loup, her brother's silent shadow.

"I bet the little one can show you how. You like to jump rope, missy?"

"Don't know, sir," she said thoughtfully. "I never had one."

Something flickered behind the old man's watery eyes. He muttered under his breath, then jabbed his thumb. "Storeroom," he said to Tommy. "Get yourself a rope and find a short one for the little girl. There's some old kiddie equipment in the back."

Tommy ran to do his bidding. Loup watched Kevin McArdle with a fixed gaze. He grinned at her and stepped up his pace, doing double-unders and whipping the rope under his feet twice on one hop, first with both feet, then hopping from one to the next. And then he switched to a complicated crisscrossing motion, the blurred rope whistling. Loup cocked her head.

"Here!" Tommy returned panting, two ropes in hand.

Floyd nodded. "On the mat. Keep it low."

McArdle stopped and beckoned to them. He'd always been one of the nicer ones. "Just like this." He swung his rope in a slow, easy arc, hopping over it. "One, two, three."

They emulated him.

"A little faster now." McArdle bounced at a deliberate, steady pace. "Okay, now we're gonna run in place."

Tommy got tangled.

Loup didn't.

"Yeah?" Kevin McArdle's copper-red brows rose. "Okay, here we go!"

His rope whistled. He did double-unders, two-footed and one-footed. He did crisscrosses, arms and rope whipping with fluid precision, his feet skipping through the loops. Loup imitated him perfectly. Faster and faster, until McArdle stopped, a sheen of sweat on his freckled skin.

"Okay," he said in a good-natured tone. "You suckered me, kiddo. What are you, Outpost's jump-roping champion?"

Loup shook her head. "No."

"Loup." Tommy cleared his throat, suddenly anxious. She

gave him an oblique sidelong look. "That was a good trick, huh? You fooled everyone. Think you can teach me?"

She nodded.

"So you lied?" Floyd Roberts asked softly. "You've done this before?"

"No, sir." Loup might have lied well, but without prompting, she tended to tell the truth.

"Yes, sir!" Tommy said hastily. He took the limp rope from his sister's unresisting hands. "I'm sorry. I should have told you. Do you want me to put it back?"

The old coach's considering gaze rested on Loup. She returned it without blinking. "No," Floyd said slowly. He waved one hand in dismissal. "Go on, Tom Garron. You've had your first lesson and you've found your first teacher. Go home. Learn to skip rope. Let your little sister teach you."

"Yes, sir."

They beat a retreat. At the door, Miguel Garza moved to block their way. He was big and broad, thick with muscle, and looked older than his nineteen years. He moved heavily in the ring, but he punched harder than any man there. Tommy had overheard the coach say privately once that Miguel had as much potential as any fighter he'd ever trained anywhere, but he was lazy.

"I just remembered," Miguel said in a casual tone. "Garron. My brother Danny used to go with your mama."

"Long time ago," Tommy mumbled.

"Yeah." Miguel stabbed a thick finger at him. "She threw him over for some *chango*, some fuckin' deserter. I seen him once."

"Oh?" Tommy licked his lips.

"Yeah." Miguel nodded. "I threw a punch at him. Felt like hitting a rock." One hand shot out with unexpected speed, reaching past Tommy's shoulder to grab Loup's hair. Or at least that was what he meant to do. Even as she skipped out of reach, her slim left arm flashed in a quick overhead arc to deflect his grabbing hand. "Fuck!" Miguel rubbed his bruised wrist.

"Miguel." Floyd's dry voice interrupted. "Punching drill."

"Coming, Coach." Miguel eyed Loup dourly, but he stepped aside. Tommy reached for Loup's arm and propelled her through the doorway. She went without protest.

"Psst!"

Tommy looked back. Miguel put one forefinger on his own face, pulled down his lower right eyelid. "I'm watching you, boy," Miguel whispered. "You and your freak-ass punk brat of a sister. 'Cause something ain't right here."

Outside the gym, Tommy broke into a run. Loup followed at his heels, trotting steadily. He came to a halt in the dusty, sun-beaten town square, breathing hard. Loup stopped obediently. Parties of strolling soldiers ignored them.

"You can't do that." Tommy dropped the skipping ropes he carried and squatted in front of his baby sister. He gripped her shoulders, fingers flexing against her too-too-solid flesh. "You can't let them see what you are, what you can do. You just can't, *loup-garou*. Otherwise someone will talk. And then they'll come for you; they'll take you away. Understand?"

"You're scared," Loup observed.

He shook her narrow, rigid shoulders. "For you! *Think*, Loup. Do you want to be taken away? Do you want to hurt me that way? To hurt Mommy?"

"No," she murmured.

"So, okay." Tommy sighed and released her. "Pretend for me."

Loup dropped to squat on her own heels, her child's body folding with boneless effortlessness. She bowed her head, tracing the coils of the fallen rope with one finger. "I like it, though. Fighting. Like you do. But I'll do what you say, Tommy." Her head lifted, a shock of black hair falling over her bright, unblinking eyes. "Can I still teach you to skip rope?"

"Yeah," he said. "Of course. Coach *said* so."

She stood. "Okay. Let's get something to eat."

NINE

For Tommy, the years that followed were heaven.

For Loup, they were purgatory.

She liked the gym. She liked the smell of sweat and antiseptic. She liked the myriad rhythms that permeated it—the dull thudding of men working the heavy bags, the boppita-boppita of the speed bag, the clanking weights, the skip and scuffle of feet on the mats, the steady pace of feet running on the treadmills. It lulled her and made the tedium bearable. It was the tedium that was hard.

She liked listening to Floyd train the men, telling them over and over that boxing was a science, that a smart fighter with a box full of tools could beat a less skilled fighter any day.

Some of them believed him.

Some of them didn't.

Miguel Garza didn't and that was a problem, because Miguel was good. And Coach had refused to give him a prize match until he took his training seriously.

"They'll eat you alive, boy," Floyd said. "You know what kind of boxers Bill recruits for this?" He poked Miguel in the chest. "Olympic champions. You know what that means?"

"No," Miguel said sullenly.

That gave Floyd pause. "It means they've beaten the best amateurs in the world," he said in a gentler tone. "And if you think you're going to beat them without training until you drop, you're sore mistaken, boy."

But Miguel didn't; didn't do all that Floyd asked of him, didn't push himself. He didn't have to push himself to hold his own against the others at the gym, so he didn't. And it was disheartening to the ones who tried.

Miguel made good on his threat and kept his eye on Loup. She made good on her promise to Tommy and kept her head down. She made herself unobtrusive and tried to remember to move slowly and carefully. Careful, always careful.

A year passed and Tommy turned fourteen in earnest and had a growth spurt. He was a tall, rawboned youth and he could skip rope like nobody's business. Coach taught him to shadowbox.

"Coach!" Tommy pleaded. "At least let me work the bags."

"See this?" Floyd took Tommy's knobby wrist and held up his right hand, showing him the protruding knuckles. "You're still growing, boy. You start hitting the bags, hitting the weights too hard, you'll make your bones brittle. Sure way to ruin a fighter." He dropped Tommy's hand. "Give it a year. Sixteen's soon enough."

And so for a year, Tommy did nothing but shadowbox. Even that was a slow process. For a solid three months, Coach wouldn't let him throw anything but a straight jab, concentrating on footwork and guard positions. Step inside, jab. Step outside, jab. Circle left, circle right. Peekaboo, crouch. Tommy fought imaginary opponents, contenting himself with the knowledge that in a year's time, he'd be fifteen and a year ahead of the coach's schedule.

Except for cleaning the bathrooms, Loup took over most of her brother's duties in the gym. It helped pass the time. When there was nothing to be done, she sat in an out-of-the-way place and watched Tommy train.

She watched the long, dull regimen settle into his bone and muscle, habit slowly turning into ingrained instinct. She watched Floyd's face and knew the exact moment when he made the decision to introduce a new element into Tommy's training. Crosses, uppercuts, hooks—including the left that came so naturally to him. Bit by bit, his repertoire grew. By the end of the year, Coach began teaching him combinations.

And she watched Tommy grow away from her.

He didn't mean to. It was the rough camaraderie of the gym

that absorbed him. Tommy worked hard and trained hard. For that, he earned the coach's respect. The serious young fighters like Kevin McArdle respected him for obeying the coach without complaining. The Real Men respected him for scrubbing toilets without complaining. Miguel didn't respect him, but that was to be expected. At least he respected the coach enough not to make trouble.

Tommy turned fifteen—sixteen in the coach's eyes. He started weight training and working the bags. He kept growing, but he was adding solid muscle to his lengthening bones.

After much begging on Tommy's part, Carmen Garron eyed her near-grown son and agreed to let him attend the Saturday-night fights with Loup in tow.

"I guess it's in your blood, huh, *mijo*?" she said sadly.

Tommy squirmed. "I guess."

She stood on her toes to kiss his forehead, then bent to kiss Loup's. "Be careful."

It was a spectacle Loup never forgot. The packed square blazed with lights, all centered on the ring. There was a throng of soldiers, half of them there to curry favor with the general, half of them there for the fight. A full half of Outpost was there, some to root on the hometown underdog, most for the free beer. Salamanca's men were circulating through the crowd taking bets. No one was betting on who would win or lose. They were betting on how long the fight would last.

Loup cocked her head and considered the fighters.

Roberto Hernandez was fighting for Outpost. He was one of the Real Men. At the age of thirty-three, he worked as a caddy, lugging golf bags under the blazing sun for eight to ten hours a day for soldiers on leisure. When he was done, he trained for hours. He had a wife and three children. He stood flat-footed in plain black trunks, lean and stringy, waiting patiently for the bell.

This year's army middleweight champion was new. He was a few inches shorter than the challenger, but he sported a body thick with exquisitely conditioned muscle. He jogged in place, tossing his shaved head. His trunks were red-and-white-striped. He was already sweating in the desert air. His dark skin gleamed and his chest heaved as he breathed deeply, substantial pectoral muscles rising and falling.

Loup nudged Tommy. "Got any money?"

He looked down at her. Since he'd turned "sixteen," Floyd had begun paying him a small stipend for his work. "A little."

Loup jerked her chin. "Roberto's going to go the distance."

"You sure?" Tommy jingled the change in his pocket.

She smiled. "Yeah."

The bell rang for the first round. It was an ugly mismatch and it was obvious from the beginning, but Roberto refused to go down. He stayed on his feet and took the punishment, absorbing blow after blow, going to a clinch at every chance, swaying, but still upright. Halfway through the match, Loup turned her gaze toward the bleachers where the VIPs sat. For the first time, she saw the general. He was leaning forward in his seat, his jaw working.

In the tenth round, Roberto rallied.

He was bleeding from a cut under one eye and he'd taken a lot of body blows. But the army champion was fading, breathing hard. Roberto pressed him. The champion went on the defensive and rode out the last three rounds, content to win on points.

Loup watched the general make his way from the stands and offer cursory congratulations to the winner. He clapped Roberto's shoulder, praising his effort. His white hair gleamed in the lights. Once, he glanced her way. She lowered her head and stared at the dusty ground.

"How'd you know?" Tommy asked curiously.

"The army guy was too sweaty," she said.

"Huh."

Tommy took his chit to get paid and stood in line. Salamanca's eldest daughter, Rosa, was dispensing the cash with painful slowness, the old man peering over her shoulder. A handful of Garza's men stood around, providing security for a cut of the profits.

"Hey, kid!" Miguel Garza mimed a punch at Tommy's head. Tommy's hands rose automatically to a guard position. Miguel laughed and ruffled his hair. "I'm kidding, eh?" He looked at Tommy's chit and whistled. "You picked Berto to go the distance?"

"Loup did." The words were out before he thought.

"Oh, *Loup* did." Miguel stooped in front of her. She looked away. "Lucky, lucky little girl." He smelled like beer. "Sooner or later, that old fucker Floyd's gonna have to give me a prize match," he said conversationally. "He's gonna run out of fighters. You gonna bet on me, Lucky Lou?" When she didn't answer, he took her chin in his hand and turned her face toward him. "Huh?"

Her eyes glittered.

"Loup," Tommy murmured.

She summoned a smile of surprising sweetness. "Sure."

It startled Miguel. He released her and took a step backward. "Yeah? Okay, here." He snapped his fingers at Salamanca's daughter and claimed Tommy's winnings, peeling a few dollars off the top before handing it over. "Security fee." He tousled Tommy's hair again. "Knock yourself out, kid."

They went.

Loup trailed behind Tommy, watching his tight, hunched shoulders. "Tommy?"

He rounded on her. "*What?*"

She shrugged. "I don't know."

He sighed and led her to a quiet corner of the square. "I'm angry, Loup. Okay? Because Miguel's an asshole, and I'm not big enough to stand up to him. I wish I was, but I'm not. Not yet, anyway."

Loup blinked at him. "But that's not your fault."

"No." Tommy regarded her ruefully. "You don't really understand, do you, *loup-garou*? Being mad and scared all at once?" She shook her head. "That's okay." He hugged her. "Hey! What are we gonna do with all this money? You want an ice cream?"

Loup looked around. She pointed at a street vendor whose wares were spread out on a rough blanket. There were only a few soldiers there, haggling over gifts for their temporary Outpost sweethearts. A black plastic comb adorned with red fabric flowers caught her eye. "Let's buy a present for Mommy."

"Something pretty?" Tommy asked.

She nodded. "Yeah."

"Okay, let's." Tommy hesitated. "Loup?" She cocked her head at him. "You won't ever bet on Miguel, will you? Promise?"

Loup smiled. "Promise."

Tommy sighed. "Thanks."

TEN

Three years later, Carmen Garron was buried with the comb in her hair.

She had never fully recovered from the last bout of flu. The winter that Loup was ten and Tommy seventeen, it finally took its toll. It started as a chest cold and turned worse.

"Pneumonia," the army doctor at the clinic said.

He gave her medicine, but it wasn't enough. At the age of thirty-eight, Carmen had seen a lot of people die. When Death called her name, she knew the sound of his voice.

She spoke to Grady alone and the big man left her room in tears. She sent for Father Ramon and Sister Martha. One gave her extreme unction and the other made her promises. When that was done, she sent for Tommy.

"Mijo." Carmen gazed at her tall son with his blond hair and blue eyes. "You're going to be alone soon."

He knelt beside her bed. "Don't say that!"

"It's true." She closed her eyes briefly. "Don't worry, baby. I'm not scared." She opened her eyes and smiled at him. "Maybe I'll see your father. You know, I really thought I loved that boy. Maybe I did. Him and Martin both. They were good men." She touched his fine, blond hair. "I know what you've been doing, *mijo.* I found out a couple years ago."

Tommy flushed red.

"It's okay." Carmen smiled again. "You kept Loup safe. You're a good boy. But I don't think she ought to grow up in a gym. So when I'm gone, the church will take her."

"No," Tommy whispered.

"Yeah." Carmen coughed, deep and racking. "They're good people. And you can't do it on your own, Tommy."

"I can, too!" he cried. "I'll get another job—"

"No." She shook her head. "It's never gonna be enough. Trust me, I know. You won't be able to be there. And Grady says he's heard you're good. That there's rumors in three, four years, you might be the one to win a ticket out of here. You gotta live your life too, Tommy."

"No," he repeated.

"Tommy." Carmen took his hand. "You're not going to be able to stay here. Grady can't afford it, not without me working. It breaks his heart, but it's true. And Father Ramon knows about Martin. I told him a long time ago. Sister Martha knows, too. She was there when Loup was born. They'll keep her safe. Promise me you'll let them."

He bowed his head. "I don't want you to die, Mom."

She stroked his hand. "Me neither. But tough shit, *mijo*."

In the end, he promised.

Carmen sent for Loup, who sat cross-legged on her bed and gazed at her with those wide, unblinking eyes.

"You know, huh, sweetheart?" Carmen asked softly.

Loup nodded. "Tommy told me."

"Did he tell you about the church?" Carmen asked. Loup nodded again. "Are you mad at me?"

"No," Loup said simply.

"You don't get mad often, do you, *mija*?" Carmen smiled sadly. "I wish to hell I'd been able to make a better life for you and Tommy. And I wish to hell I could stay long enough to see you grow up."

Tears gathered in Loup's eyes and shone there without falling. Even when she'd cried as a baby, there were never tears. There was something strange and pure about the quality of her unleavened sorrow; strange and pure and oddly comforting, as though a child-saint or a fearless, untamed creature had come to keep a vigil over Carmen's death. Carmen lifted one hand and traced the curve of her daughter's cheek.

"*Mija*," she whispered. "You know you're special, right?"

Loup nodded.

"Special and wonderful. Don't let the world break you." Carmen closed her eyes. "It wasn't always like this."

"What was it like?" Loup asked. "When you were little?"

"Oh!" Carmen smiled, her eyes still closed. "Like nothing you would believe, baby. Everything was so nice. I used to ride the school bus with Inez. It was big and yellow, and the driver knew everyone's name. Sometimes he would honk the horn. Every day, after school, we would go to her house and Tia Lucia would make us peanut-butter-and-jelly sandwiches. Inez's big sister Julia was still alive then. She always had to watch her soap opera that she taped, the one about the doctors. That was when all the TVs still worked. Every time a boy kissed a girl, Inez and I would laugh and shriek until we fell down, and Julia would yell at us to be quiet . . ."

Her voice soft and drifting, Carmen talked for a long time about a world that seemed distant and unimaginable, where there were no soldiers, where everyone had cars and houses and TVs and music players, and little girls and boys dreamed of growing up to be doctors or lawyers or astronauts.

After a while, her voice fell silent.

Loup smoothed her mother's hair.

"It went away so fast." Carmen opened her eyes. "And we just let it happen."

Tommy crept into the room, opening and closing the door gently.

"Don't be like us." Carmen glanced from her dark, quiet daughter to her tall, fair son. She let her eyes close again, creased lids sinking shut. "Don't."

Tommy stooped to kiss her careworn brow. "Okay, Mommy."

Carmen smiled and slept.

Two days later, she died.

There was a funeral at the church. Father Ramon gave the eulogy. Only a handful of people attended. Danny Garza was one of them, stolid and dignified in a three-piece suit. He'd taken over a lot of his father's business. Miguel was at his side, thick and hulking. It had become a matter of pride with the Garzas over the past ten years that they attended every event of significance in Outpost.

Floyd Roberts was there, too. It was a sense of duty that drove him to attend. He stood beside Tommy, colorless and upright, his hand on the young man's shoulder.

When the eulogy was done, they carried her casket into the church's graveyard, past all the old, old markers, past the multitudes of new graves with no markers at all, only sad personal effects moldering on the ground: a tea set, a teddy bear, a ship in a bottle.

"It's all right." Sister Martha fell in beside Loup. "There's a chart in the rectory with all the plots. We know where everyone rests. No one is lost."

Loup nodded and fixed her gaze on Tommy's broad back. He was serving as a pallbearer along with Father Ramon and Floyd and Grady and two boys she didn't know—church orphans. One looked to be about fourteen, handsome and slender. The other was younger, with hard gray eyes and a mouth shut in a firm line. She'd wanted to be a pallbearer, but Tommy had been afraid it would make people suspicious.

When this was over, Tommy would leave. He'd go back to the gym with Floyd Roberts and take up residence in an unused office. He'd live and work and train at the gym, and Floyd would pay him enough money to get by.

The thought made her feel very alone. It wasn't a bad feeling, but it wasn't a good one, either. That probably meant that if Loup were normal, she'd be frightened. But mostly she was just sad.

There was a fresh hole with a big pile of dirt and a special sling beside it. The men lowered the casket into the sling, then eased it into the hole.

"Ashes to ashes, dust to dust." Father Ramon crossed himself. "May God's peace be upon her."

There were plain, ordinary shovels in the dirt. Tommy took one, shoveled a spadeful of dirt onto the casket. He dragged his shirtsleeve over his eyes, then passed the shovel to Loup.

Dust to dust, she thought.

Dirt rattled on the plain wooden casket. Someone took the shovel from her hand. Loup lifted her face and gazed at the vivid blue sky.

"You okay?" It was the boy with the gray eyes. He had a thin white scar creasing his face and a surprisingly deep voice for his age.

"I guess," she said.

"You will be." He laid one hand on her shoulder and squeezed it, then looked at her with a surprised frown. Loup moved away from him.

"Mack." Sister Martha hurried over. "Will you and Diego finish?"

He took up a shovel. "Sure, Sis."

And that was it. It was over. They turned and went back, leaving the church boys to finish the work of burying Carmen Garron. In the courtyard, Danny Garza shook Tommy's hand and offered a word of condolence. Even Miguel gave him a brusque nod. They were treating him as a man grown. She supposed today he was.

"Bye, little one," Grady said gruffly to her. He stooped and folded her in a bulky embrace, smelling of sweat and grease. "Be good. There'll always be a bite for you at the diner."

Loup hugged him back carefully. "Thanks, Grady."

"Loup?" Sister Mary led over a striking young woman with long, shining black hair. "This is Anna. She'll help you get settled here."

Anna gave her a beautiful smile. "You don't remember me, but I was there when you were born, Loup. I'm so sorry about your mother."

"Thank you."

Anna held out her hand. "Do you want to come with me and see your room? Mr. Grady and your brother had your things sent over."

Loup looked past her. "Tommy?"

He came quickly, looking stricken. "I'm sorry!" He knelt on the hot tiles of the courtyard and took her hands in his. "It's only for a little while, *loup-garou*," he murmured. "Only until Floyd gives me a prizefight. Then I'll start winning money, even if I lose at first. I'll be able to get a place for us."

"I know," Loup said.

Tommy squeezed her hands. "Then I win a ticket north for both of us, right?"

"Yeah." She smiled at him. "It's okay. It's what Mommy wanted. I know you promised."

He stood. "I'll come see you every weekend. And you come to the gym any time, okay? Floyd says it's okay. Any time."

Loup nodded. "Okay."

"You'll take good care of her?" Tommy asked Sister Martha.

The nun-who-wasn't-a-nun gave him a long, grave look. "We'll do our best."

"Okay." Tommy pressed the heels of his hands against his eyes. "Okay."

Loup jerked her chin. "Go."

Tommy went.

ELEVEN

So!" Anna said with cheerful kindness. "Here we are."

Loup cocked her head, eyeing the rows of cots. Most were empty and unmade, just bare mattresses. Only a few had sheets and blankets. One had a skinny blond girl lounging on it, reading a book. One held a duffel bag she recognized from the gym.

"That's yours," Anna said. She pointed at a row of dressers. "You can put your clothes in any empty drawer."

"Thanks." Loup sat on the bed.

The blond girl on the bed opposite rolled onto one elbow. "I'm Jane."

"Loup," Loup said.

"Short for Louise? Luisa?"

Loup shook her head. "L-O—" She had to think back to Sonia's spelling lessons, learning to write her name in careful letters. "L-O-U-P. It's French. For wolf."

"Wolf!" Jane exclaimed scornfully. "French, is it?"

"Be nice, Jane," Anna said in her melodic voice. "This is a hard day for Loup." Her brows furrowed. "Can I get you anything, honey?" she asked Loup. "You want to see the rest of the church? Or would you like a Coke?"

Loup shook her head. "No, thanks."

"Okay." Anna lingered doubtfully. "Okay, dinner's at six. If you need to talk, just come find me, sweetheart. Otherwise, Jane will show you to the hall, right?"

"Yeah, yeah." Jane waved a careless hand. When Anna left, she muttered under her breath, "Slut." She read for a moment, then peered over the edge of her book. "You know she is, right? You know the deal here?"

"No," Loup said.

"Oh, shit!" Jane hauled herself to a sitting position and closed her book. "Father Ramon? Not a real priest. Sister Martha? Same deal. Shit, they've been fucking for years, since she was like sixteen years old. You know what fucking is, don't you?"

"Sort of," Loup said.

Jane hooted. "You don't!"

Loup shrugged. "Tell me, then."

She did.

Loup listened. "Okay. So?"

"So . . . shit!" Jane scowled at her. "They're not supposed to do that, okay? I know. I read. You don't read much, do you?" When Loup shook her head, Jane hooted again. "I knew it!"

"So?" Loup repeated mildly.

"Are you, like, slow?" Jane asked. "Dense?" She lowered her voice. "Anna shares a fucking bed with them, okay? *Both* of them. That's why she's a slut."

Loup glanced around the room. "Is there anyone else here, or is it just us?"

"Ah, fuck you!" Jane opened her book.

"Hey." A boy's curly head poked into the room, his brown eyes bright with interest. "Crazy Jane," he said in greeting. "This the new girl?"

"Fuck you, T.Y." Jane hunched her shoulders.

Loup stood. "I'm new."

"Hey." The boy grinned. "I'm T.Y."

"Loup," Jane spat without looking up. "L-O-U-P, Loup. It's French for wolf. I had to teach her what fucking was. Her mother just died and Anna says be nice. Got it?"

"Got it," T.Y. said affably. "You want to see the place, Loup? I'll show you around."

She nodded. "Okay."

T.Y. showed her all the best places of the church: the rec room in the basement, the kitchen and the passages that led to it, the outer and inner courtyards. The inner courtyard had a fountain that actually worked, powered by the reservoir. "You want to see something cool?" He glanced around, then lowered his voice and pointed at a persimmon tree growing at the edge of the lower roof. "Okay, quick." He climbed agilely up the tree, Loup following, then showed her how to clamber onto the rounded red tiles. At the top, he straddled the spine and pointed again at a window. "That's Father Ramon and Sister Martha's bedroom."

"Yeah?" Loup gazed over his head. "Anna's, too?"

T.Y. glanced over his shoulder at her and blanched. "Jesus fucking Christ! Are you crazy? Sit *down!*"

Standing balanced atop the roof's spine, Loup looked from T.Y.'s white face to the drop into the courtyard below. "Sorry." She sat carefully to straddle the spine like he was. He just stared at her, his chest rising and falling quickly. "I wasn't thinking." She peered over the edge, gauging the drop. "It's not *that* far down."

"Are you *crazy?*" T.Y. repeated.

"No." She shrugged. "My mother just died, okay?"

It mollified him. "Yeah. I'm sorry. You scared me, you know?"

"Sorry." Loup cocked her head. "What about you?"

"My parents?" T.Y. picked at a cracking tile and looked away. "I dunno. I'm the miracle baby." He pried off a flake of glazed red clay and flicked it away. "You hear about the night the rockets fell? Long time ago?" She nodded. Everyone in Outpost knew that story. "I'm the bomb baby. The one they found. No one ever claimed me."

"So you been here all your life?"

"Yeah." T.Y. scooted around on his butt to face her. "It's not so bad. Don't listen to Crazy Jane."

"Do you think everyone's crazy?" Loup asked.

"Nah." He laughed. "It's a nickname. Father Ramon gave it to her because she gives him a hard time. He says it's *ironic*." He pronounced the word with care. "It's from some old poem, I don't know exactly."

"Well, she doesn't like Anna," Loup observed.

"Ah, Jane's just pissed." T.Y. shrugged. "Anna's our teacher, except on days like today when there's church business. And Jane just thinks she's smarter than everyone, including Anna. Which is kinda true, actually, except for maybe Jaime. They're both awfully smart. Plus, Anna's pretty. And yeah, Father Ramon likes her, and so does Sister Martha. I don't think Jane's gonna be as pretty when she grows up." He ducked his head, his color rising. "Not like you."

"Yeah?" Loup smiled.

T.Y. peered at her with a crooked grin. "Yeah."

"Thanks."

He cleared his throat. "We better get down. We'll get in trouble if we get caught up here."

They clambered down the roof and climbed down the tree. T.Y. went first. Loup let herself drop lightly from the lowest branch. He reached to steady her, hands grazing her rib cage.

T.Y. blinked. "Whoa."

She took a quick step backward. "Hey. Don't."

He put up his hands. "Sorry. It's just . . ."

His words trailed away. Loup looked at the sky, looked at the lowering sun caught in the branches of the persimmon tree. She thought about her mother lying in the ground. She thought about Tommy. She thought about being alone, and knew she wasn't good enough to pretend all the time. It was too easy to forget to be careful, too hard to keep people from touching her. And she didn't want to be someone who was never touched. She looked at T.Y., his face uncertain and hopeful, brown eyes bright under his shock of curls. "Can you keep a secret?"

He crossed his heart. "Hope to die."

Loup held out her hand. "Come here."

In the room with the cots, she found Jane was gone. She dug in the duffel bag that held her meager belongings and showed T.Y. her most sacred artifact, the brittle, yellowing tabloid paper with the story about the Lost Boys. She couldn't read all of it, but she knew the story by heart. It even had the name of the place in Mexico where her father was going written in the margins.

"That's what my father was."

T.Y. read avidly, eyes flickering back and forth. "Holy shit!" he breathed. He lifted his head, wide-eyed. "You're a superhero!"

"A what?" Loup asked.

It was his turn to grab her hand. "Come on! I'll show you!"

He led her to the basement, to the rec room with the Ping-Pong table and the TV with its collection of grainy, hissing videotapes and scratched, skipping DVDs, all of which had seemed a marvel to her. He bypassed the shelves of books and dug into a cabinet for a stash of well-thumbed comics.

"Here," T.Y. said reverently. "Be careful; they're really, really old."

Loup turned the limp, worn pages, perusing the colorful panels. There were men and women in crazy costumes doing crazy things, shooting rays out of their eyes, changing shapes, sprouting claws, flying.

"They're mutants," T.Y. explained. "They're like a new race." He scooted closer to her, pointing. "That's Wolverine, he's my favorite. His bones are made out of adamantium, and he has awesome claws and fighting skills, and he heals super fast. He's, like, part animal, I guess, and he has super-hearing and super-smell. Do you?"

"No," Loup said absently. "Good, I guess. Not super."

"Oh." He sounded disappointed. "I just thought maybe."

"No." She handed him the comic. "Sorry."

T.Y. took it reluctantly. "You don't want to read it?"

"I kind of forgot how," Loup admitted. "Maybe I'll read it later. Is Anna a good teacher?"

He stared at her. "You don't know how to *read*?"

"Well, I did, a little. Tia Sonia taught me before she died. I can spell my name. But then I got kicked out of school right away, and Tommy found his job at the gym . . ." Loup shrugged. "So I guess I'll have to start over."

"Don't tell anyone!" T.Y. whispered urgently. "Especially Jane. She'll make fun of you."

Loup cocked her head. "Why?"

"Because they'll think you're stupid."

"But I'm not," she said patiently. "Not that way, anyway."

His voice rose. "But they'll *think* so!"

"So?" She thought, frowning. "That's supposed to make me feel scared, right? That they would think I'm stupid even though I'm not?"

"Well, no . . . but yeah!"

She nodded. "Thanks."

T.Y. blinked at her. "Whaddya mean, thanks?"

She'd never had to explain it to anyone, only ever had Tommy and her mother explain it to her. "I don't get scared," Loup said slowly. "So it kinda is like being stupid, but only in this one way. It means I have to think extra hard and be careful, but sometimes I forget. And sometimes I don't understand what other people are feeling or what I'm supposed to be feeling because I just don't know. See? So what you said, it helped me understand. That's why I said thanks."

"You're bullshitting me." T.Y. sounded uncertain.

"No."

"Okay, prove it!" he challenged her.

"You want me to do something dumb on purpose?" Loup shook her head. "No way. I promised."

"I think you're lying."

"T.Y." Loup sighed, feeling more tired and sad than she ever had in her short life. "Think what you like, okay? Just promise me you won't say anything. I guess I shouldn't have told you. But I always had Tommy to tell me when I needed to think and be careful, and I won't for a while. I screwed up right away, huh? I just thought it would be nice to have a friend."

He flushed guiltily. "Tommy's your brother?"

"Yeah."

"That's my real name, too." T.Y. fiddled with the comic. "Thomas Yorke. No one remembered what my parents called me, so Sister Martha named me after her grandfather, but then she said it felt too weird to call me by his name." He looked up. "Do they know?"

"Sister Martha and Father Ramon?" Loup nodded. "Yeah."

He blew out his breath. "Shit." A bell clanged somewhere. "We better go; that means dinner." T.Y. stood and put out his hand. "I'm sorry. Friends?"

Loup smiled. "Yeah."

T.Y. tugged her to her feet, grunting at the unexpected effort it took. "Okay. Wow." He paused. "On the roof . . . that's what you meant, isn't it? About not thinking. Because that was pretty stupid, standing up there like that. One slip, and sploosh."

"I wouldn't have slipped," Loup said. "But yeah."

He eyed her. "You *do* need a friend."

TWELVE

The first days were strange.

It was a different world with its own rules. Loup was used to a simpler world. At home there was the diner, which was Grady's domain, and there was the apartment with her mother and Tommy. There was the gym and its hierarchy, but it didn't really matter because she wasn't a part of it. It was Tommy's world, and she was his little sister. As long as she stayed quiet and out of the way, no one noticed her. Even Miguel had gotten good at ignoring her.

Not here.

There was Father Ramon and Sister Martha and Anna, and all of them were very concerned about her well-being.

And there were the other kids.

Once, there had been more—dozens. Some had succumbed to the last wave of sickness; others had grown up and moved out. Now there were only eight. That was a good thing, she learned. It meant that fewer people were dying. In Sister Martha's words, it meant that the *mortality rate* had tapered off, and that people were developing *immune systems* to cope with the sickness.

It still seemed like a lot of kids to Loup.

There were more boys than girls. In addition to T.Y., there was Mack and Diego—the boys who'd served as pallbearers and grave diggers at her mother's funeral. There was impetuous C.C. Rider, named for an old song that he'd liked when he was little, bouncing up and down on those nights after the generator was shut down and Sister Martha brought out the ancient hand-cranked machine that played scratchy old recordings. There was scholarly Jaime in his glasses, and little Dondi, the youngest at seven.

Dondi's name wasn't really Dondi, either. That came from some incomprehensible, boring old comic strip about a boy with big, dark eyes and protruding ears.

For the girls, there was sharp-witted, sharp-tongued Jane— Crazy Jane, the nickname shared as a dour jest Loup didn't get. There was sweet, dim Maria, who was in love with Diego. And there was Kotch, imperious Katya, already promising to turn into a tall, blond beauty.

"Kotch is a bitch," T.Y. confided at the first dinner. "Don't let her bother you."

Katya rapped his knuckles with a serving spoon. "Shut up, bug!"

"Ow!"

"Children." Father Ramon's deep voice silenced them.

Loup learned that Mack's name was a nickname, too. Mack the Knife.

"It's an old song, too," T.Y. whispered to her. "But that's not how he got the name. He stabbed his father to death."

"Why?" she whispered back.

"His old man beat his mother." His whisper dropped an octave. "Killed her."

They accepted her with wary curiosity. Her loss made her one of them. Some, especially Maria, offered genuine sympathy. But Loup was *different*, and in the company of her peers, she learned for the first time that children have a keen ability to recognize that which is *other*.

The routine was easy enough. In the morning, they had lessons with Anna from eight until noon. At noon, they helped serve a free lunch of rice and beans to needy parishioners. Once that was over and they'd helped clean up, they were mostly free until dinner.

Some of the kids did other things to help out. Mack was good at fixing things. Clever, organized Jane helped keep the dispensary in order. Jaime was fascinated by computers, of which the church had several in various states of disuse. They weren't good for much, but Jaime tinkered with them and would talk about them at length to anyone who would listen.

"They used to be able to *talk* to one another," he explained to Loup, stroking the hard plastic case. "They used to be able to do all kinds of things." His eyes flashed behind his glasses. "I've read about it. Old manuals and newspapers. You could type on the computer and talk to someone in China, just like they were right there in the room with you."

Loup eyed the dun-colored box doubtfully. "How?"

"Fiber-optic cables," Jaime said in a reverent tone, as hushed as T.Y. talking about comics. "Broadband *wireless*."

The words meant nothing to Loup, but she liked hearing him talk. In her experience, all that computers were good for was playing the program of *educational software* that was supposed to teach her to read better. Usually it stopped working within minutes.

"The system's degraded," Jaime said. "Hardware, software. All of it."

"Okay," Loup agreed.

"But I bet it's not everywhere." He gazed into the distance. "I bet it's still out there."

She liked Jaime because he didn't talk down to her and he wondered about things beyond Outpost. "I'll find out for you," Loup said. "When Tommy wins a prizefight."

Jaime's narrow shoulders stooped. "No one's ever going to win one of those fights, Loup. They're rigged."

"Tommy will," she said. "He'll take me with him."

"Yeah?" Jaime regarded her without hope. "Come back and tell me."

"I will."

He laughed, a short bark. "While you're at it, tell the rest of the world we're out here rotting in the desert. Because from what I understand, I think they've pretty fucking well forgotten we ever existed."

"Okay," Loup said steadily.

Jaime shook his head. "Weird kid."

On Saturday, Tommy came to see her. He got permission from Sister Martha to take her to the fight. Already, in a week, Tommy looked taller and older than Loup remembered. Sorrow had made a man of him.

He stooped in the courtyard. "You doing okay, *loup-garou*?"

She shrugged. "It's okay here. But I miss Mom."

"I miss her, too." Tommy hugged her in a warm, strong embrace, one she could return without having to be careful. It felt good. He straightened and smiled at her. "Come on. Coach gave Kevin his first prize match. He beat Miguel for it. Mig's pissed as hell, he's been waiting so long. But he lost fair and square, and I say Kevin's got a shot. He's a junior heavyweight, same as I'll probably be."

This time, they had a good spot in the square, near the challenger's corner. Floyd greeted Loup with a cordial nod. Kevin McArdle, bouncing on his toes, rolled his head on his neck, loosening his muscles. He leaned over the ropes to touch glove to fist with Tommy, smiled at Loup. She smiled back at him, happy to see him.

The arc lights shone.

This year's army champion shed his robe, baring a muscle-ribbed torso. He shrugged his shoulders a few times, stamped his feet, and shook out his gloved hands. Threw a quick flurry of punches into the air, then settled onto the balls of his feet, waiting. His blond hair was shaved bristle short. In the harsh glare of the lights, he looked nearly bald, patient and unhurried.

Tommy glanced at Loup. She shook her head. "You're sure?"

"Yeah," she said softly. "Four rounds. Maybe five."

"No."

"Yeah."

"Well, I'm not betting against him."

The first three rounds were good ones. Skipping on agile feet, Kevin ran rings around the champion. He landed solid body shots. His freckled skin gleamed. He feinted and jabbed, scoring point after point. The army champion waited for an opening.

In the fourth round, he connected with a high right cross off his rear foot. It rocked Kevin's head back and split the skin above his left eyebrow, opening a deep gash. The soldiers roared. The referee paused the fight and Floyd managed to get the bleeding under control. He squeezed the cut closed and kept pressure on it, then iced it and applied a heavy-duty coagulant.

They finished out the round, Kevin's eye swelling.

It didn't last. In the fifth round, Kevin was visibly slower, while the army champion was just warming up. He worked the cut mercilessly, getting Kevin to lower his guard with a flurry of body shots, then snapping quick jabs at his head. The gash opened wide, bleeding profusely. A sheet of blood crept down the left side of Kevin's face. He shook his head, swiping at it with one gloved fist. The champion clouted him hard on the ear with a right hook, and Kevin went down. He got up before the count, but the referee called the fight.

"TKO," Tommy murmured.

The general made his way down to the ring. Loup watched him out of the corner of her eye. He seemed genuinely pleased with both men's performances. Kevin McArdle grinned through the bloody mask streaking his face.

"That'll want stitches, young man," the general said. "But you've got balls." He nodded at the coach. "Floyd."

"Bill," Floyd replied.

And that was that. Tommy led Loup away from the ring and bought them both ice creams. They sat on the low wall surrounding the square and watched soldiers and Outposters collect their winnings. The Outposters slipped away into the night, or at least the men did. The soldiers crowded into Salamanca's to spend their winnings or drink away their sorrow at losing. A lot of them had women with them. Somewhere inside the nightclub, which had grown to encompass almost an entire block lining the square, a band was playing.

"My father took Mom there the night they met," Tommy said.

Loup licked her dripping ice cream bar. "You ever go?"

"Nah." He shook his head. "It's for soldiers and women. Even Garza's boys only show up there as muscle." Tommy glanced down at her. "How'd you know this time? I really thought Kevin had a shot."

She considered, finishing her ice cream. "I could tell that guy hit really hard."

"Before he even threw a punch?" Tommy asked.

"He threw some warming up."

"Yeah, but . . ." Tommy's voice trailed off. Loup tried, but she couldn't always explain how she knew what she knew, like how hard a fighter hit without seeing a single blow land. "I don't think he hits any harder than Miguel. And Kevin beat Miguel."

"Miguel's lazy. And he's impatient." Loup sucked the last sweetness from the ice cream bar's wooden stick. "This guy wasn't. I bet Kevin will do better next time, if he doesn't get punch shy."

"You think Kevin can beat him?"

She tossed the wooden stick unerringly into a trash can. "On points, maybe. If he got lucky and went the distance. But probably not."

"What about me?" Tommy asked.

Loup cocked her head at him. "Not yet, no."

"Aw, c'mon!"

"Tommy, you're only seventeen!" She lowered her voice. "I know Floyd thinks you're a year older, but you're not, okay? And you know what he says about bringing fighters along too fast. You're gonna be the best one there. But if you try too soon, you're only gonna lose. And maybe get hurt, bad."

"That wouldn't scare *you*," Tommy observed.

"No." Loup smiled. "But it should. You taught me that much, huh?" She hopped lightly down from the low wall. "We should go. They'll be calling curfew."

He steered her through the crowd, one hand on her shoulder. When they reached the church, the gate was already locked. Tommy rang the bell hanging there, and Diego came out to admit them.

"Hey, kid," Diego said to Loup. "Better hurry. I won't tell."

"Thanks."

"I'll see you soon. We'll go get burgers at Grady's." Tommy knelt to hug his sister. "You're okay here? Really?"

"Yeah." She nodded. "It's not so bad. I'm learning to read again, and a bunch of other stuff. I think maybe Mommy was worried about that."

"Yeah." Tommy flushed. "Guess the gym wasn't the best place for you, huh?"

Loup shrugged. "I learned stuff."

"Stuff you can't use," he said. "Not like here."

"True," Loup said thoughtfully. "This week, I learned what *fucking* is. I mean, I kind of knew. I've heard the guys talk about it, but not exactly, you know?"

Tommy's voice cracked. *"What?"*

"Pssst!" Diego whistled, swinging the gate closed. "Curfew, curfew!"

"Shit," Tommy muttered, watching them leave. "Maybe the gym was better than the church."

THIRTEEN

T.Y. managed to keep Loup's secret for a little over a week.

She found out he'd spilled it when C.C. Rider walked up to her in the rec room and asked, "What would you do if I said I was going to beat the crap out of you?"

Loup stared at him. "What?"

"What would you do if I said I was going to beat the crap out of you?" he repeated, his tone cheerful and curious. Mack the Knife lifted his head out of a comic book. Katya and Maria stopped playing Ping-Pong and stared at C.C. He was a good-looking boy of twelve or so with thick blond hair and green eyes, and he'd never been anything but friendly toward her. Even now, he sounded perfectly nice.

"You're crazy," Loup said flatly.

"Here goes!" C.C. feinted a punch at her. She blinked at him, unmoving. "You warned her!" he accused T.Y., who entered the room at a run.

"C.C. . . . ," he panted.

"For real, now," C.C. warned Loup. His next punch wasn't a feint. She angled her upper body a few inches to the right and let his fist sail past her head, then drove a quick right jab into his stomach. The air left his lungs with an audible huff. C.C. landed hard on his butt and sprawled, mouth agape, his chest heaving as he struggled in vain to breathe. He made choking sounds.

"Jesus!" Katya dropped her Ping-Pong paddle and raced to his side. "What did you do, you freak? Maria, get Sister Martha!"

"Wait!" T.Y. pleaded.

"He's okay," Mack said calmly. "Relax," he said to C.C. "You had the wind knocked out of you. Just give it a second."

C.C. nodded in breathless understanding.

Loup turned to T.Y. "You told him."

He hung his head. "Sorry."

Mack walked over to Loup. "Told him what?"

Everyone was listening. On the floor, C.C. pushed himself to sit upright, taking deep, racking breaths as his locked muscles unfroze. Loup considered Mack with his plain, scarred face and his too-adult voice. There was something steady in his gray eyes, something she recognized. Mack the Knife had been to a place beyond fear.

"I'm *sorry!*" T.Y. repeated.

" 'S'okay." Loup shrugged. "I guess it probably would of come out anyway."

She went to fetch the brittle tabloid, the artifact of her father. By the time she returned to the rec room, all the church's kids were there, watching and waiting. Whatever T.Y. had told C.C., he'd obviously repeated it to them.

Mack read the story without comment, then passed it on. Almost everyone read it in silence. Jane made a scornful sound. Dondi sounded out the big words. Loup waited, perched on an arm of the rec room's worn, stained couch.

"Jaime?" Mack asked when everyone had read it.

"Well, it's mostly bullshit, of course." Jaime adjusted his glasses. "Sensationalized bullshit. This isn't a real newspaper, nothing like what you find in the archives. But that doesn't mean there's not some kernel of truth there. Jesus, look what the government's done to *us!*" He peered at Loup. "Did you know your father?"

"No." She shook her head. "Tommy did."

Jaime's glasses gleamed. "And your father left him instructions, you say?"

"Yeah," she said softly. "Him and my mother."

"Oh, puh-leeze!" Crazy Jane folded the tabloid carelessly, slapping it against her palm. "You're not gonna ask me to believe—"

"Don't do that." Mack's low voice silenced Jane. He took the paper away from her and gave it back to Loup. "I don't know how much of this is true. But if any of it is, the army would want her, right?" he asked Jaime. "To run tests and shit?"

"Count on it," Jaime agreed.

"That's why you were keeping it a secret?" Mack asked Loup. She nodded. "Yeah."

"Then we will, too." Mack looked around at the others with his hard gray eyes. "We've gotta be loyal to each other. We're all we've got, right? If anyone talks . . ." He paused. "Don't."

His last word hung in the air.

Loup decided she liked Mack the Knife.

"We'll help keep an eye on you," Mack added. "Like T.Y. *said* he was gonna do, right?" He looked around again to make sure everyone nodded. T.Y. looked shamefaced.

"I'll go along, but I'm not buying it." Jane folded her arms over her chest. "I think you all made this up to make Loup feel better about not knowing how to read and write. Or maybe you and T.Y. just wanted to seem cool."

"Yeah, right," C.C. wheezed. "I volunteered to take a punch in the gut."

"*You* might!" she retorted.

"No, but he might as well have," Mack said laconically. "Even if it wasn't true, it's pretty stupid to go throwing punches at someone who grew up in the boxing gym."

"She's just a kid!"

"So are you." Mack eyed Loup. "How strong are you, anyway?"

"Like lifting weights?" She shrugged. "I dunno. Tommy never let me try at the gym. He was afraid someone would see."

"Let's try something." Mack rolled up his right sleeve, baring a thin, wiry arm. He held out his hand, planting his feet like a boxer. "Indian-wrestle me."

"Huh?"

Mack beckoned. "Give me your hand and put your right foot on the outside of mine. Yeah, like that." He gave a quick, fierce grin, his hand tightening on hers. "On the count of three, we both try to pull each other off balance. Got it?"

Loup smiled back at him. "Yeah."

"One . . . two . . ."

Loup felt the series of minute shifts in Mack's stance and grip and knew he wasn't going to wait for the three count. She braced herself, her body swaying only a little as he yanked on her arm with all his might. "Three," she commented. Mack grunted, hauling at her. She let him, not yet pulling in the opposite direction. His wiry muscles stood out beneath his pale skin.

"She's got a lower center of gravity," Jaime observed.

"Fuck that!" Mack's face was turning red. "You're not even trying, are you?"

"Not yet," Loup agreed.

His grip tightened harder. "C'mon!"

She exerted a little bit of pressure, shifting Mack's weight to his forward leg, slowly and steadily, then gave one strong, fluid yank. Mack stumbled past her, his arms flailing, threatening to fall headlong. Loup pivoted and caught his arm, steadying him before he planted himself face-first in the carpet.

"Cheater," she said without malice.

"Didn't matter, did it?" Mack laughed unexpectedly, his eyes sparkling. It transformed his face. "Shit, you're fast, too! That was fun, wasn't it?"

Loup grinned. "Yeah."

"Oh, great," Jane muttered. "Our resident sociopath has found a kindred spirit."

The light went out of Mack's face, turning it hard and old beyond his years again. "If you want to put that big brain to good use, Jane, why don't you look into what kind of genetic research was going on thirty, forty years ago? Aren't there old medical books in the clinic's dispensary?"

"Journals," Jaime murmured. "It would be in journals."

"Whatever," Mack said. "Maybe you could find something that would help us figure this out."

"Figure out what?" Katya waved a dismissive hand in Loup's direction. "Wolf-girl's a freak. You already figured that out."

"Hey," Diego said mildly. "Pax Olivia, guys." It was the phrase Father Ramon used to invoke the rule against fighting in the church's orphanage, and it quieted them. Diego wasn't a natural leader—that was Mack—but at fourteen, he was the oldest and it carried a certain authority.

"I'm sorry, Mack," Jane said in a small voice. "I didn't mean it."

He nodded stiffly. " 'S'okay."

"Guys?" Maria said, wondering. "What if this *means* something?"

"Like what?" Diego asked.

Maria looked around shyly. "You were born on Santa Olivia's day, weren't you?" she asked Loup, who nodded. "I heard Sister and Anna talking about it. Right in the middle of the town square with the effigy of Santa Olivia looking on and everything."

"Yuck," T.Y. said.

"Yeah, but . . ." Maria crossed herself. She'd been raised a believer and nothing she'd learned about the dubious credentials of the clergy in Outpost had shaken her considerable faith. "What if it's a sign? A sign from Santa Olivia herself? She was just a kid, right? I mean, look at her." She pointed at Loup. "Doesn't she look a little like Santa Olivia?"

Everyone looked at Loup.

"Yeah," C.C. admitted. "A little bit, anyway."

"So!" Maria clasped her hands together. "As a child, Santa Olivia came to bring peace to fighting armies." Her eyes shone. "Maybe she's come back!"

Katya snorted.

"Peace, my ass," Mack muttered.

"Jesus himself said he came to bring not peace, but a sword." Jaime lifted his head, the light reflecting off his glasses. "To set men against their fathers and daughters against their mothers. Maybe that's what Outpost needs to reclaim its place in the world. Maybe our time has come, time to take back the birthright that our fathers and mothers gave away. Maybe Loup's arrival isn't meant to evoke Santa Olivia's basket of peace, but her sword of war."

"You don't believe that," Jane scoffed.

Jaime bent his head toward her. "I believe in the power of symbols."

"You would!"

"Pax Olivia," Diego murmured.

After her exertions, Loup's stomach was beginning to grumble and the conversation was sailing over her head. She wished they would all shut up. "Guys?" she asked plaintively. "Isn't it almost time for dinner?"

FOURTEEN

In the year that followed, war did break out in Outpost, but it was a war that owed nothing to either the fabled El Segundo or Loup Garron's presence.

It happened because shrewd, greedy Hector Salamanca finally died, expiring in bed with a smile on his face and a hysterical nineteen-year-old mistress beside him. Hector Salamanca died well.

Danny Garza, acting on his own ailing father's behalf, moved swiftly and smoothly, extending an offer to Hector's eldest daughter Rosa on behalf of the Garza clan to assume operational control of her hereditary properties in exchange for a percentage of the proceeds they generated. He discovered too late that Rosa had long been anticipating her grizzled father's death, and had used her father's ill-gotten gains to hire away a good percentage of Clan Garza's muscle right under his nose.

Thus began the turf wars.

At first the army turned a blind eye. If a single military serviceman was threatened, the MPs would appear, riding in armored vehicles, truncheons or pistols in hand. When that happened, people disappeared. But so long as it was only Outposters fighting Outposters, they left the locals to sort it out.

Factions formed.

From time out of mind, the church had been neutral territory. It stayed so, but just barely. Though Father Ramon swore a blue streak, he couldn't get assurance of safety save behind the church's gates. The streets on which the church's orphans had been wont to play stickball became fair game. Only on Fridays when the military doctor came to the free clinic was a security detail provided.

For the better part of a year, the fighting went unchecked. Any semblance of rough justice the Garzas used to administer was gone. Danny and Rosa's men waited in alleys to ambush one another, scouted out each other's secret meeting establishments, and staged raids, abused each other's women.

At the church, it meant long lines at the clinic to stitch wounds and set broken bones. The clinic stayed open long hours seven days a week, manned six out of seven by an exhausted Sister Martha. Every other day, there was a burial. Lessons were held on a catch-as-catch-can basis. All of the kids lent a hand in any way they could.

If nothing else, Loup was good at digging graves.

The shared work drew them all closer together. Then, too, there was an odd backlash of resentment from the townsfolk of Outpost, forced to choose sides in the endless turf war. They resented the fact the church remained neutral, that everyone there was safe within its walls and no one was forced to choose sides in the endless, pointless turf war. The town's school closed its doors and bands of aimless teens cruised the street outside the church, yelling taunts.

"Hey, *santitos!* Hey, little saints! You wetting your pants in there?"

It was mostly boys, but some girls, too—sharp-tongued and cutting. The Garzas' supporters sported dun camouflage handkerchiefs from some stash bartered from the PX, either as do-rags or tied around an ankle or arm. Rosa Salamanca's followers wore vests, mostly shirts with the arms torn off, with a crude salamander painted on the back. Sometimes they'd get into fights with one another or hassle the parishioners waiting nervously for a free lunch or a visit to the clinic, but for the most part there seemed to be a tacit agreement that the street was a neutral zone designated for the purpose of taunting the little saints of Santa Olivia.

It bothered Loup more than anything since her mother's death, because she couldn't understand it.

"Why do they do it?" she asked Sister Martha. "All we do is help you and Father Ramon, and all you do is help people."

"Sweetheart, that's a tough one." Sister Martha sighed. "There's a little piece of goodness in most people, enough so that when they're doing bad things, somewhere deep inside, they know it and feel guilty. It's like a thorn in their heart. When they see people doing good things, it drives the thorn a little deeper. That makes them hurt and angry."

"But it's not our fault!" Loup protested.

"No, of course not." Sister Martha laid a hand on Loup's cheek. "But it's a lot easier to blame someone else than accept blame for your own failings. Don't be too hard on them. They're young and it's pretty bad out there right now. They see you kids as having the one thing they can't have. Safety, security. They resent you for it. Does that make sense?"

"I guess." Loup paused. "Is it true about you and Father Ramon?"

Sister Martha smiled wryly. "Which part?"

"That you're not what you pretend to be."

"Yes." Sister Martha didn't hesitate. "It's never been a real secret. We pretended to be what Outpost needed us to be."

"Why?" Loup asked.

"Because there was no one else," the nun-who-wasn't-a-nun said simply. She unbuttoned the plain gray jacket she wore over her clothing and loosened the white collar at her throat, blue eyes gazing into the past. "I was fourteen when everything fell apart. When the first epidemic hit, I was here with my parents on vacation. My father liked to golf. They both died in the first wave."

"And you ended up here?"

"Yes." Sister Martha's gaze returned. "Along with hundreds of others. I was one of the survivors. As I grew older, I felt it was my duty to help. That's how I met Ramon. It was bad, Loup. Worse than you could imagine. So many people died. Then the army came and some things were better, but it was worse in a different way."

"It went away so fast," Loup murmured, remembering her mother's words. "And people just let it happen."

"Most did," Sister Martha agreed. "Others, like the Garzas and Salamancas, grabbed for the biggest piece of what was left. And some, like poor old Father Gabriel, lost their wits." She flexed her fingers, regarded her worn, cramped hands. "People need hope, symbols. After Father Gabriel died, Ramon and I tried to give that to them."

"You do," Loup said. "But why doesn't everyone?"

"Oh, honey!" Her face softened. "That's one of God's biggest goddamned mysteries, isn't it? And if I ever meet the motherfucker, I'll be sure to ask." She patted Loup's cheek again, then rose. "I've got to get a letter off to the chaplain begging for more splints and dressings. You okay?"

Loup thought about it. "Yeah."

If there was one other place in Outpost that was a haven from the fighting, it was the gym. Even with Miguel Garza's presence, the invisible mantle of the general's sponsorship kept Rosa Salamanca's men at bay.

That changed nine months into the turf war, when a half dozen of them armed with pipes and chains jumped Miguel as he was leaving with a couple of his boys.

"You should of seen it, Loup!" Tommy told her, his voice awed. "A bunch of us, me and Kevin and Javier, were gonna go help . . . I know Mig's a pig, but he's kind of our pig, you know? But Coach says, 'Step aside, boys.' And he comes out of the back with this gun . . ." He held his hands apart. "This big. Walks outside, cool as can be, and fires one shot into the air, then aims it at the guy beating on Mig and tells him he's got three seconds to disappear."

Loup's eyes widened. "No!"

"Oh, yeah!" Tommy nodded, grinning. "Should of guessed Coach would be the one guy in Outpost allowed to carry a gun."

She whistled. "They run?"

"Better believe it."

It heralded a tipping point in the turf wars. The rumor in Outpost, which not even Tommy could confirm, was that Floyd Roberts went to General Argyle and told him that if he didn't do something about the situation, there would be no more monthly boxing matches. It was true that the fights were canceled for three months running, and it was true that the general chose that time to crack down on security in town. Suddenly, there was a stricter new curfew. Suddenly, there was a brand-new office where Outposters could apply for permits to be out after curfew. Suddenly, there were armed soldiers patrolling the streets at all hours, enforcing a new ban against brawling in public.

It worked, mostly.

A large number of the worst violators were detained in the army brig. A handful of them never came back. At the end of three months of steady attrition, Danny Garza and Rosa Salamanca met under the supervisory gaze of a bored lieutenant and hashed out terms of a stalemate that very much resembled the arrangement their fathers had established twenty-some years ago. The violence and antagonism didn't disappear, but it went deeper underground.

The monthly prize matches resumed.

The curfew and the ban and the soldiers stayed.

FIFTEEN

"They keep tightening the screws!" Jaime said bitterly, his shoulders hunching. "Jesus! The fucking army owns us. Don't you *feel* it?"

"Yeah," Mack said in a reasonable tone. "But what do you expect us to do, man? We're just kids."

Jaime glared at him. "I don't know!"

"Hey, c'mon, c'mon!" C.C. bounced lightly on the balls of his feet. "Pax Olivia, huh? We're kids, so let's be kids." He waggled a broomstick. "Chores are done and the street's empty," he said invitingly. "And dinner's not for an hour."

"I'll play," Loup offered.

"No batting," C.C. warned her. They had a fairly good supply of old tennis balls that some enterprising soul had stolen from the country club before the army had occupied it, but long before the turf war, they'd found out that letting Loup bat was a sure way of causing their supply to dwindle alarmingly.

"I'll play outfield and keep lookout," she agreed.

"Cool."

The gangs of taunting teens were less frequent since the army patrols had begun, but they still came sometimes. Father Ramon had uttered a strict injunction against engaging them, which meant they had to abandon the street if a gang was spotted. But today the street was clear. Loup took a post at the north end of the street, on the corner between a bodega and the long-abandoned post office. Any ball that got past her would be judged a home run. Any ball that landed on a roof to either side was also a homer. T.Y., Jaime, and Jane took up positions between her and C.C., marking first, second, and third bases.

Everyone had come out, whether to play or not. It was still a luxury to be out on the street. Diego and María sat on the curb, holding hands and whispering. Katya sat beside them, looking bored. Mack was tinkering with an old skateboard while Dondi waited impatiently.

"Play ball!" C.C. shouted, tossing a tennis ball in the air. He swung solidly and connected. Jane, positioned at second base, jumped for it and missed. T.Y. scooped up the ball on the bounce and lobbed it back. "Second base!" C.C. called. "I'm bringing it home!"

This time he hit a solid line drive at Jaime, who caught it with a surprised grunt, then yelled, "You're out!"

They all shifted places except for Loup. Jaime whiffed and missed the ball completely to the accompaniment of derision and catcalls. Jane got a first base hit, then went out on a pop-up that C.C. caught easily. On the curb, Mack put away his screwdriver and handed the skateboard to Dondi, who rolled happily away. And then T.Y. scored a mighty hit that ricocheted off the cement wall beside the bodega and veered away at a sharp angle.

It was the kind of shot Loup loved. The instant the stick connected with the ball, she could tell how hard a hit it was; and the instant the ball left the stick, she knew where it was going. Unless they went way over her head, fly balls were easy. Ricochets were fun, because she had to guess the ball's next trajectory and get in motion before it hit. She guessed right more often than not, but not always.

This time she guessed right, racing past the bodega and snatching the ball out of the air on the fly. Back at home base, T.Y. groaned. Loup laughed and hurled it back. Out of the corner of her eye, she saw a skinny figure duck out of sight down the cross street.

"Shit." She gave a sharp whistle. "Lookout posted!"

"Alone?" T.Y. called.

"Yeah!"

A lone lookout at one end of the street was probably watching for patrols. It meant the gang would approach from the other end. T.Y. trotted toward the south corner, then pivoted and came back at a run. "Salamanders!"

They gathered their balls and retreated, grumbling, behind the wrought-iron gate. The Salamanders converged and thronged the gate, hooting and yammering, rattling it on its hinges.

"Hey, *santitos!* Whattsa matter? Scared to play?"

There were only six of them, none older than sixteen. Loup stared at the nearest one through the bars without blinking. He had a shaved head and a crooked nose. He grinned at her and made kissing sounds. "You like what you see, *mija*? Come see me in a few years!"

"Don't talk to them," Diego said in a low tone.

"Whattsa matter, big boy?" Shaved Head laughed. "You look too old to be babysitting the kiddies! You a faggot, huh? You wanna suck my dick?"

"C'mon." Diego turned his back on the Salamanders and made a shepherding motion in the direction of the church. "Let's get out of here."

"Diego!" Maria clutched his arm and pointed.

At the far end of the street stood Dondi, skateboard under his arm, looking small and lost, still the baby of the lot at almost nine years old. The Salamanders whooped and raced after him, running him down in seconds. "Okay!" Shaved Head said cheerfully. "We gonna party now, *santitos!*"

"Maria!" Diego said. "Get Father Ramon!"

The Salamanders dragged Dondi into the middle of the street. One snatched the skateboard from him, hopped aboard it, and went weaving away. A pair of them yanked Dondi's pants down, then, to double the indignity, hoisted him by his ankles and held him upside down. Dangling above the concrete, Dondi squirmed and hollered. Shaved Head began unfastening his belt. "Hey, *santitos!*" he shouted. "We're gonna give your little buddy a whupping! Ain't any of you got anything to say about it? Are you all pussies or what?"

A rare fury washed over Loup, rising like flames. She reached for the gate's latch without thinking.

"No." Mack caught her wrist.

In the street, the first smack of the belt sounded. Dondi cried out with genuine fear and pain. The Salamanders laughed. The one who'd stolen Dondi's skateboard attempted to pop an ollie along the curb.

"Mack." Loup forced his name out past the odd sense of weightlessness in her chest. The belt smacked. Dondi hollered.

Mack met her eyes and nodded. "Watch my back. Try not to show off." Without waiting for a reply, he grabbed the broomstick from T.Y. and slipped the latch, then ran into the street with Loup at his heels. He swung the broomstick like a bat, cracking it across the back of Shaved Head's skull.

Shaved Head went down like a sack of potatoes. The Salamanders dropped Dondi and circled Mack, who lashed out in all directions with the broomstick. Loup picked the nearest one with his back to her, lowered her head, and drove her right shoulder into the small of his back. He pitched forward, sprawling face-first on the pavement. She knelt astride him, grabbed his hair, and banged his forehead on the concrete.

There was more whooping and shouting as more orphans piled into the street. A Salamander kicked Loup in the ribs, trying to dislodge her from her victim. Pain blossomed, fueling the fire in her veins. She narrowed her eyes, watching the sneakered foot return on its vicious arc, then rolled out of the way, catching the foot at its apex and shoving hard. The boy toppled over backward, arms windmilling. C.C. Rider leaped atop him and began to pummel him, laughing.

Loup bounced to her feet.

Three Salamanders were down. Mack was holding off two. The kid on Dondi's skateboard was hurtling toward him, looking pissed. Loup moved to intercept him. He didn't even bother to look at her. She stomped hard on the upturned nose of his skateboard and sent him sailing.

"Asshole!" Crazy Jane kicked the kid in the side of the head when he landed, then sat on him.

Diego waded into the fray to retrieve a dazed Dondi. One of Mack's attackers peeled away and went after him, but Jaime jumped on his back and got him in a relentless choke hold. The Salamander staggered, trying to pry his arms loose.

"Hey!" T.Y. nudged Loup. The Salamanca lookout posted at the north end was pelting toward them at a dead run. "Wanna double-team him?" He puffed out his thin chest. "You gotta be careful. I'll step up."

Loup glanced at Mack. His last opponent was down. Mack had one foot on his chest and the butt of the broomstick planted on his throat. "Do it," she agreed, sidling to one side.

The lookout flailed, stopping. "Outta my way, bug!"

T.Y. punched him in the belly.

"Fuck!" The lookout punched T.Y. in the nose, then yelped as Loup circled behind him and kicked him in the butt. "Shit!" He whirled on her. Loup skipped backward, beckoning to him. Over his shoulder, she saw Mack coming, raising his broomstick and preparing to swing. She blew the Salamander a kiss.

The broomstick connected.

One more down.

"Hey! *Hey!* Patrol!" The Salamanca lookout left to keep watch on the south corner raced down the street, sneakered feet slapping the pavement. He skidded to a halt, looking dumbfounded. "Guys! We gotta beat it."

Mack cocked his broomstick over one shoulder. His gray eyes were as cool as cool could be. "Take 'em."

The Salamanders were efficient. They'd lost fights before, though never with the little saints of Santa Olivia. They gathered their wounded, and in the case of Shaved Head, their unconscious, and hurried with alacrity toward the north end of the street, rounding the corner and disappearing. By the time the two soldiers appeared, the Salamanders were gone.

When the orphans of Santa Olivia turned to make a retreat

of their own, they found Father Ramon standing in front of the gate, arms folded, shaking his head at them.

"Oh, shit," T.Y. muttered.

The soldiers strolled down the street, then stopped and planted their hands on their belts, gazing at the motley collection. Blood was dripping from T.Y.'s nose onto his shirt. Jaime's glasses were askew. Mack had a knot on one cheekbone and was doing his best to hide the broomstick behind his back.

"Uh-oh." One of the soldiers took out his baton, tapping it against his palm. "You kiddies been brawling?"

He looked official and menacing in his desert fatigues, but his face was young. Katya sidled over to him, tossing her hair. "It was just a silly fight over a game they were playing, Officer. Kid stuff, you know?"

"Oh, yeah?" The soldier smiled at her. "Sure they weren't fighting over you, sweetheart?"

Katya sniffed. "They're just boys."

"Little boys grow up fast." He fished a pack of gum out of his shirt pocket. "Spearmint?"

She took a piece. "Thanks."

"Hey there, Padre." The second soldier caught sight of Father Ramon behind the gate. "These your kids?"

"In a manner of speaking." Father Ramon's voice was as dry as dust.

The soldier eyed Mack. "What're you hiding there, son?"

"Nothing." Mack showed him the broomstick. "We were playing stickball."

"Stickball, huh?" His expression lightened briefly, then hardened. "How come I don't see any balls?"

"That's why we were fighting," C.C. explained, bouncing up and down.

Both soldiers eyed him. "Why's he doing that?" the first asked.

"He just does," Katya said.

"It was my fault," Jaime said in a mournful tone. He took

off his glasses, trying to twist them back into shape. "I lost our last ball. Hit it onto the roof of the bodega. Now everyone hates me."

Loup, doing her best to remain unobtrusive, snuck a glance toward the gate. Father Ramon took a smooth step sideways, the skirts of his cassock hiding the dirty tennis balls they'd piled there when the Salamanders had arrived.

"Yeah?" The second soldier smiled unexpectedly. "Tough luck, kid. I been there. We used to play stickball in the Bronx. Sucks to be the one to ruin everyone's fun."

"Yes, it does," Jaime agreed.

"Okay." The soldier tousled his hair with an older brother's rough affection. "Play nice, huh? Stay out of trouble." He regarded his companion. "You about done making time with the jailbait, Jeff?"

"Just about," Soldier Jeff said amiably, winking at Katya.

The other nodded to Father Ramon. "See you, Padre."

With that, they continued on down the street. T.Y. breathed a sigh of relief, snuffling through his bloody nose. "That was close."

Father Ramon opened the gate. "Oh, believe me, children, it's not over."

Dinner was late that evening. All of them but Dondi, who had been taken to the dispensary, waited in the rec room, rehashing the details of the fight with a mixture of covert pride and creeping anxiety. When the bell finally rang, there was no food on the table and Dondi was still missing.

"Sit," Father Ramon said.

They sat.

He stood at the head of the table and surveyed them, his face unreadable. Sister Martha and Anna flanked him, and even Anna's sweet, pretty face was a cipher.

"I've spoken to Dondi and I understand why you disobeyed," Father Ramon said. "That's not why I'm still angry. It's not because you endangered yourselves, or even the church. Do you know why?" His dark gaze swept over them as they shook their heads, confused. "Children!" He raised his voice. "Because of the way in which you rushed to Dondi's defense, those unruly boys *dropped* him on his *head* in the middle of the street. Do you know what could have happened?"

"He could have broken his neck, Father," Jane murmured. "Could have ended up paralyzed."

"Yes." Father Ramon nodded. "That's exactly right."

"Is Dondi okay?" Mack asked in a gruff tone.

"Yes." He didn't mince words. "He'll be fine. But the point is that noble impulses can lead to disastrous results if you don't *think*." His fist crashed on the table, making everyone but Loup jump. "Understand?"

They nodded.

"Good." Father Ramon pulled out his chair and sat. Sister Martha and Anna sat on either side of him. He made a shooing gesture to Katya and Maria, who were on kitchen duty, and they hurried to retrieve dinner. "Let us give thanks," Father Ramon said, folding his hands. "Thanks for the food that we eat, and thanks that our young friend will survive unharmed. Thanks that due to Katya's flirting and a homesick soldier's indulgence, our covenant here remains whole."

C.C. snickered.

"I'm not finished." Father Ramon pointed at him. "As penance, all of you who fought will serve guard duty for the next month, because I'm sick and tired of hearing Garza's and Salamanca's punks harass us and our parishioners." He hoisted his water glass. "Despite the fact that you all had the ill grace to defy my edict, at least you had the good grace to *win*. And against my better judgment, I must confess that this pleases me. Any questions?"

They shook their heads.

"No, sir!" Mack added crisply.

"Good." Father Ramon drank. "Amen."

SIXTEEN

Things changed in the way that things do.

Word that the orphans of Santa Olivia had defeated a gang of young Salamanders leaked. The Salamanders sought revenge. The youngsters of the Garza Gang tried their hand. There were a handful of short, sharp scuffles in which the Santitos, the Little Saints of Santa Olivia, fought to a win or draw.

It won them respect.

Word came from on high that the church wasn't to be bothered. The marauding, taunting gangs vanished.

Loup missed them.

Puberty descended on the Santitos, dividing them. Diego and Maria were already a lost cause, as was Katya, fond of flirting with soldiers. C.C. and Mack were the next to shoot up in height, shoulders broadening and voices deepening. Even Jaime and Jane embarked on a cautious, prickly courtship that involved a good deal of bickering and breaking up.

Miguel Garza finally convinced Floyd Roberts to give him his first prize match. He didn't win, but he went the distance. True to form, instead of pushing himself harder, he rested on his laurels and slacked off on his training. When he fought in his second match six months later, he was caught flat-footed and knocked out in the sixth round.

"My turn comes next," Tommy told Loup with surety.

He wasn't the only one who thought so. Rumors were beginning to circulate in Outpost that Tom Garron was an up-and-coming contender. He worked tirelessly as Floyd Roberts' right-hand man at the gym, and he trained relentlessly. Tommy had succeeded in winning the admiration and respect of most everyone he encountered. Still, Floyd held off granting him a prize match.

The year that Loup was thirteen, Tommy finally got his first prizefight and the church got a new orphan.

The latter happened first. Loup was in the bell tower with T.Y. the day that Pilar Ecchevarria arrived. Technically, the bell tower was off limits and had been ever since Father Gabriel had plunged to his death from it over two decades ago, but the Santitos had long used it as a trysting place and it was one of the many things to which a blind eye was turned.

On that day, T.Y. was teaching Loup to kiss.

"Close your eyes," he complained. "I can't do it with you staring at me."

"Okay." She closed her eyes.

T.Y. kissed her with slightly dry lips, then stuck his tongue in her mouth, wiggling it against hers. He pulled away. "It feels weird."

Loup opened her eyes. "Yeah, no kidding!"

"No." He flushed. "I mean *you* do."

"Maybe you're doing it wrong," she suggested.

T.Y. shook his head. "I'm doing it exactly how Jane showed me. You feel weird, that's all." His flush deepened. "Sorry!"

"Maybe Jane was messing with you," Loup murmured.

"I don't think so." T.Y. sounded miserable. "She was trying to make Jaime jealous."

A commotion in the outer courtyard broke the awkward silence that followed. They peered over the edge of the bell tower to see a solidly built woman of middle years marching toward the church's front door, dragging a much younger woman behind her by the hand and haranguing her all the while.

"Wanna see what's up?" T.Y. asked in a brighter tone, grateful for the distraction.

Loup sighed. "Sure."

By the time they'd descended from the tower, the young woman was waiting alone in the vestibule, looking bored and sulky. Despite her expression, she was a pretty girl with brown hair shot through with a streak of blond and an abundance of nubile charm.

"Hey," T.Y. greeted her.

"Hey," she said without interest.

Beyond a closed door onto a chamber where Father Ramon met with parishioners, voices were raised.

". . . prefer that children be fostered by family members whenever possible," Father Ramon's deep voice was saying.

"That child's body is the Devil's playground!" the haranguing woman's voice shouted over his. "If you don't take her—"

Loup looked at the newcomer. "They talking about you?"

"Yeah." The girl shifted in her seat. "My aunt. She caught my uncle messing with me."

T.Y. whistled.

"It was no big deal." The girl shrugged. "He'd pay me five bucks to sit on his lap and bounce around a little."

"And you did it?" T.Y. asked, aghast.

Her hazel eyes flashed. "Hell yes, I did! They wouldn't let me get a job, wouldn't pay me a dime, expected me to wait on them and their brats hand and foot and be grateful I had a roof over my head. How else was I ever gonna get out of there? So yeah, I did it."

T.Y. put up his hands. "Okay, okay!"

"He offered me ten if I'd let him play with my tits," the girl said, mollified. "I told him to go fuck himself."

The door to the conference chamber opened. Father Ramon stood there with a weary look on his face. The woman behind him was smirking.

"Pilar Ecchevarria," he said to the newcomer. "Welcome to the Church of Santa Olivia."

She stood, full breasts moving in an interesting fashion behind her worn men's overshirt, and smiled sweetly at him. "Thank you, Father."

He averted his eyes and addressed the older woman. "How old did you say she was again?"

"Thirteen," she said sourly.

The Father sighed and crossed himself.

For better or worse, Pilar's arrival changed the dynamic once again. Once she'd settled into the routine of the place and realized she was well and truly free of her unpleasant relatives, she turned out to be fairly good-natured and a little lazy. But even at thirteen, Pilar drew boys like honey draws flies—including the attention of the soldiers who lingered outside the gates to flirt with Katya and give her little gifts.

"Can't you keep her out of my way?" Kotch snapped at C.C. and Mack.

They exchanged glances.

C.C. grinned broadly. "We can try."

The Santitos paired off, broke up, and reunited in new configurations, endlessly bickering over the ramifications. Even T.Y. grew three inches taller and sprouted a few sparse hairs on his upper lip. With no Salamanders or Garzas to trouble them, flirting had replaced fighting and stickball as the activity of choice. The only ones left out were Loup, to whom puberty was slow in coming, and Dondi, too young for it yet.

"I miss the old days," Dondi said forlornly to Loup.

She ruffled his hair. "So do I."

It was near the end of the year when Tommy finally got the nod from Floyd Roberts. After a certain amount of negotiation, Father Ramon agreed that all the Santitos would be allowed to attend the fight, albeit with himself and Sister Martha and Anna as chaperones. They got a prime spot, massed behind the challenger's corner with Floyd's grudging blessing.

The arc lights were blazing.

They shone on Tommy as he entered the ring. He shrugged off his robe to reveal a sculpted physique resembling a young god's, his fair hair haloed by the lights. The Outposters roared. Pilar Ecchevarria caught her breath.

"*That's* your brother?" she asked Loup.

"Yeah," Loup said absently.

She was watching the army's current contender, all business. He was a big man with an Italian-sounding name and calm, watchful eyes. He and Tommy were well matched in height and reach, but she guessed he had five years and twenty pounds on her brother, all of it solid muscle.

"Hey, sweetheart!" Tommy leaned over the ropes, blue eyes twinkling. "So?"

"You're not in the same weight class," Loup said softly. "That guy's gotta be a heavyweight."

"Yeah, I know." He banged his gloves together, bounced on his toes. "It's close, but we waived it. You wanna fight, you gotta accommodate. Happens all the time here; you know that. And Coach doesn't have any heavyweights. So? Whaddya think?"

Loup looked into her brother's open, earnest face and saw what he needed. "Knock him dead, *mijo*."

It was a good fight, but for the first time, she watched with a strange sense of emptiness. The first time Tommy took a jab to the face, Pilar let out a shriek and clutched Loup's arm.

"Aren't you *scared*?" she breathed.

"Yeah." Loup smiled wryly. Pilar didn't quite understand about her, but she'd put her finger on the matter nonetheless. "Yeah, I think I am."

The fight went the distance. Tommy's training held him in good stead, but his inexperience showed. Loup listened to her fellow Outposters cheer at every blow Tommy landed and wince every time he took a shot. She watched Tommy's left eye swell and turn an angry hue of red. He flashed her a grin when the referee okayed him to continue, so that she'd know he was fine. She smiled back at him, wishing she could feel the way other people did when a loved one was in danger. And throughout it all, Pilar kept a tight grip on her arm, which made her feel even odder.

Then it was over.

The decision was unanimous for the champion. He gave a brief victory salute, then knocked gloves with Tommy.

"Good fight, kid."

Swollen eye and all, Tommy was beaming through the sheen of sweat and Vaseline on his face. The empty feeling inside Loup went away, replaced with pride. The other odd feeling lingered.

"Will you introduce me?" Pilar whispered in her ear.

Loup shrugged. "Sure. But I'm gonna tell him how old you are."

Pilar rolled her eyes. "You could at least let him guess."

"He'd guess wrong," Loup said.

"That's the idea."

All the Santitos thronged around when Tommy sat on the edge of the ring, his legs dangling, his robe draped over his shoulders. Loup gazed up at him. He grinned down at her and touched her cheek with his gloved fist.

"How'd I do?" he asked.

"Good." She smiled at him. "Really good, Tommy."

SEVENTEEN

In the next year, Tommy fought in two more prizefights, both against the same guy, whose name was Celino Rossi. He lost both, but with each fight, his performance improved. The first was another unanimous decision, but the margin was narrower. The third was a split decision, with one of the three judges scoring in Tommy's favor.

It was the closest any Outposter had ever come to winning, and the town loved him for it.

"My brother, the hero," Loup commented.

He laughed. "Do you hate it?"

"Nah." She smiled back at him. "People need symbols."

That was one thing that happened that year. Another was that Loup turned fourteen and slid through puberty as quickly and unexpectedly as she'd slid from Carmen Garron's womb.

In the space of six months, her bones lengthened and her body reknit itself into a series of sleek, compact curves and deceptively dense muscle, filled with impatient energy. The mirror showed her a face with high, rounded cheekbones, dark, lustrous eyes, and a set of full lips.

Some things it changed.

Some it didn't.

"I'm sorry!" C.C. whispered, lifting his head. "It just feels . . ."

"Weird?" Loup suggested.

"Yeah." He propped himself on one arm above her. "Not bad-weird, not exactly. It's kind of like kissing a guy, only *more*." He traced the curve of her lower lip. "More intense, you know? Like, *too* intense."

"Since when do you kiss guys?" Loup asked.

C.C. smiled serenely. "Oh, whenever. You know Forrest Street? There are army guys who'll pay to let you do stuff to them. I go there sometimes."

Two other things happened in the year Loup was fourteen.

The first was that Pilar Ecchevarria's aunt died and her uncle tried to abduct her.

It happened after the funeral, brazen as could be. They gave Pilar's aunt a nice burial and Father Ramon gave the eulogy. When it was over, Pilar's uncle simply grabbed her wrist and hauled her toward the door, ignoring her protests, while Father Ramon was mingling with the other guests.

"Hey." T.Y. nudged Loup.

She angled her way deftly through the crowd and intercepted them on the steps. "Let her go."

Pilar's uncle squinted at her. "Out of my way, brat."

Loup kicked him in the shins and skipped backward onto a lower step. He growled and lunged at her, one hand extended. She caught his arm and tugged, planting her feet. Pilar's uncle fell, sprawling. His chin struck the stairs and he bit his tongue.

"What the *hell* is going on here?" Father Ramon roared onto the scene, the skirts of his cassock swirling, eyes ablaze.

"You okay?" Loup asked Pilar.

"Yeah." Pilar hugged her. "Thanks, sweetie." Hugged her, kissed her face. Too many times, too long and lingering. Heat rose between them. Pilar pulled away, her color rising unexpectedly. "Thanks," she repeated.

Loup felt dizzy. "Sure."

Father Ramon prodded Pilar's uncle's ribs with one foot. "Get out."

"Pervert!" Pilar's uncle spat, spraying blood.

The Father folded his arms. "Get out."

He left and didn't come back. That was the first thing. The second was worse, much worse. Because the second big thing that happened the year that Loup Garron was fourteen was that Katya was raped.

It might not have happened if Mack hadn't found a spare key to the gate in a utility closet, but he had. And once the word got around, Katya begged him to let her use it to sneak out after curfew. It was the sound of her sneaking back in the small hours of the night, bumping and clattering, that woke the girls' room.

"Jesus!" Crazy Jane said in the dark, sleepy and irritable. "Turn on the damn light and find your damn bed."

"The generator's off for the night," Maria offered. "I'll light a candle."

"No!" Kotch didn't sound like herself.

Too late; Maria had already struck a match. The candle flared to life, the warm glow revealing Katya disheveled, her blouse torn and untucked. Her lips were swollen and there was a reddening mark on the left side of her face.

"Jesus!" Jane repeated in a different tone. "What the hell happened?"

"What the hell do you think?" Katya said dully.

"Aw, baby!" Pilar clambered out of bed and led Katya to her own bunk. "Here, sit down. Was it one of those soldier-boys?"

"Yeah."

"Bastard." She smoothed Katya's hair. "Maria, go fetch Sister Martha, will you?"

"No!" Katya protested. "I don't want them to know!"

"Baby, you've got to tell them," Pilar said gently. "There's a line and that boy crossed it. Father Ramon won't let him get away with it any more than he let my uncle take me back, okay?"

In the end, Maria went despite Katya's protests. Sister Martha came quickly and without offering reproach, her face grim. She led Katya to the infirmary.

The next day, the whole story got out. Kotch had snuck out after hours to meet one of the soldiers she'd been flirting with over the past year—not Jeff with the gum, but a good-looking young guy named Ken Braddock. He bought her drinks at Salamanca's and danced with her, offered to walk her home. On the way back, he stopped in an alley and demanded a blow job. When Kotch refused, he hit her in the face, shoved her up against the side wall of an abandoned restaurant, and raped her.

The mood in the church was tense. Father Ramon was in a fury, waiting to hear from the army's legal counsel. Katya was silent and withdrawn. The Santitos were on edge, unsure how best to help her.

"I say we go after the bastard," Mack muttered.

Jaime shook his head. "He'll be court-martialed. I've read about these things. The army has standards, even here."

Jaime was right, but he was wrong, too.

The army took a month to conclude its investigation. A tall, lean man with a colonel's stripes came to take statements from Katya and the others. He promised to get to the bottom of the affair.

He didn't.

When Colonel Stillwell came back, it was with a mouthful of diplomatic apologies. He delivered it in the vestibule, only slightly disconcerted by Father Ramon's glower and the watchful presence of the Santitos arrayed behind him. "I'm very sorry, but it seems that no one can corroborate the young lady's story," he said, sounding quite sincere. "Private Braddock's companions that evening have testified under oath that he never left the nightclub." He spread his hands. "There's simply no evidence."

"I *saw* the evidence!" Sister Mary said sharply.

The colonel bent his head toward her. "It may well be that the young lady was assaulted. However, there is no evidence whatsoever that Private Braddock was responsible."

"His friends are lying," Katya said in a lifeless tone.

Something in the colonel's gaze hardened. "Perhaps, young lady, you should think twice before placing yourself in compromising situations."

Kotch looked away.

Loup's blood sang with rare, cold anger.

"So you mean to let him get away with it," Father Ramon said grimly.

"The evidence is what it is." Colonel Stillwell made another graceful, apologetic gesture. "I'm sorry. Perhaps they are lying; perhaps not. I can only base my judgment on the testimony given, and as it stands, it exonerates Private Braddock." He paused. "I suggest you keep a better watch over your flock, Father."

Father Ramon gritted his teeth. "I'll keep that in mind."

There was another consultation, one meant to be kept secret. Danny Garza came to the church to meet with Father Ramon. Loup, whose ears were sharper than most if not quite super, was posted to listen at the door of his chambers. When it was over, she reported to the Santitos in the rec room.

"The Garzas aren't gonna be any help," Loup said simply. She shot a sympathetic look at Kotch. "Not unless you want to sign on with them. Then they'd provide some protection so it wouldn't happen again."

"Sign on?" Katya asked in a low voice.

Loup nodded. "You know."

"As a whore." Now Katya's voice shook. "Jesus fucking Christ! I thought he *liked* me, that's all!"

"You should of just given him the blow job," Pilar murmured.

Kotch glared at her. "*You* would have!"

"Probably," Pilar admitted.

"Pax Olivia," Mack interjected absently. He ran his hand over his hair. "Okay, so it's us, then." He looked around at the Santitos. "Everyone in?"

"We can't get caught, Mack," Jaime said. "That's a line *we* can't cross. We'll get disappeared if we do. And if we fuck him up too badly, they'll turn this town upside down. Someone will pay for it, even if it's not us."

"Humiliate him," Jane suggested.

"Yeah." Mack nodded. "That's good."

"You guys are crazy," Pilar said. "C'mon! He's a grown-ass soldier with all his buddies around him."

"Yeah, but we've got a secret weapon. One that'll leave him with a story no one will believe. One he might not even have the balls to tell." Mack looked at Loup. "You in, kiddo? It's a risk."

Loup grinned. "Hell, yeah."

T.Y. elbowed her. "Told you you were a superhero!"

"We'll still have to get him alone," Jaime said pragmatically. "If there are witnesses, Loup's toast."

"True," Mack acknowledged. "We'll need bait." He glanced at Pilar. "Bait he can't resist."

"Jailbait," C.C. added.

"Aw, *fuck!*" Pilar said in disgust.

"He doesn't have to know you're in on it," Mack said mildly. "All you'd have to do is get him alone in a dark alley and run like hell when Loup shows up. Whaddya say? Does he know your face?"

"No." Pilar chewed on her thumbnail. "Oh, fine! Fuck. I'll do it."

"Thanks," Katya said softly.

EIGHTEEN

Yeah, sure! It's a *real* private place, soldier!"

Pilar's voice, breathless and giggling. She led Ken Braddock by the hand into the deep shadows beneath the bleachers in the square. All the arc lights were off. The perimeter was lit by light spilling from the nightclub, but the square itself was dark.

"You gonna give me some sugar now?" The soldier's voice was deep and confident.

"You bet, baby." Pilar wriggled against him.

"Sweet." He kneaded her buttocks.

"Hey." Loup stepped out of the shadows, her voice somewhat muffled by the bandana tied over the lower half of her face. She cocked her head at Pilar. "Get lost. We've got business."

Pilar shrank back against a support and let out a squeak.

"What the *hell*?" Private Braddock sounded profoundly amused. He rested his fists on his belt and looked down at Loup. "Whaddya want, kid? I'm busy."

"Go, child," Loup intoned. She sketched an arcane gesture Jaime had devised in Pilar's direction, spoke the words he'd given her. "This man intends no good. The spirit of Santa Olivia bids you flee. Flee!"

Pilar fled.

"Aw, shit." Braddock gazed after her, then back at Loup. "What the fuck? What is this, Halloween?"

Loup beckoned. "I come bearing a message from Santa Olivia. Will you hear it?"

"Hell, no!" Braddock turned to go. Loup punched him in the kidneys, eliciting a grunt. He turned, stooping with pain. "Mother*fucker!*"

She landed a left cross to his jaw, a few inches off center. Careful, not hard enough to break his jaw. His eyes rolled up in his head and he sagged in a satisfying manner. Loup caught him as he fell, whistling softly.

Shadowy figures converged.

"Nice work." Mack's gray eyes glinted.

"Thanks," Loup whispered back.

The Santitos worked quickly. They stripped Private Braddock's pants to his ankles. They bound his arms and legs with twine. They smudged his brow with a dusty cross and pinned a note to his chest.

RAPIST.
SANTA OLIVIA DOES NOT FORGET.

"Good?" Mack asked Katya.

She stared at the soldier, then kicked him in the ribs. "Yeah. Good."

They scattered, racing through the town and dodging patrols, exhilarated by their success. Pilar was waiting inside the gate. Father Ramon had confiscated the spare key, but handy Mack had figured out how to pick the lock.

"Hallelujah, Santa-fucking-Olivia!" T.Y. whispered as they crept back into the darkened church.

The next day brought rumors and the return of Colonel Stillwell, who held a lengthy private conference with Father Ramon and Sister Martha. Loup tried to eavesdrop, but Anna chased her away.

"I don't think you want to be anywhere near the colonel today, Loup," she said in a meaningful tone. "Any of you."

Loup sighed. "Okay."

The colonel left after an hour. Father Ramon and Sister Martha emerged without addressing the incident. Once again, the Santitos were forced to wait and wonder until dinner. Once again, when the bell rang, they trooped in to find the table empty and their patrons waiting in silence. The silence stretched, unbroken.

"Are we in trouble, sir?" Mack asked.

Father Ramon folded his arms. "Any reason you should be?"

"No."

More silence.

"It seems the young man who committed a sin of violence against Katya had a strange encounter last night," Father Ramon said at length. "A visitation, as it were. It seems Santa Olivia and her basket of plenitude has turned into an ass-kicking masked avenger." His gaze went around the table, settling on Loup. "I don't suppose any of you know anything about it?"

"No," they chorused.

He heaved a sigh. "God have mercy on me, I don't know whether to laugh or cry."

"Both," Sister Martha said wryly. "Fortunately, the story is so very unlikely that we were able to convince the colonel that the young man is obviously covering for comrades who played a prank on him, and one that he well deserved. Since he is in fact guilty as hell and his friends know it, it seems the likeliest truth."

Katya gave a tight smile.

"Which is not the same as *being* the truth," Father Ramon added. His gaze bored into Loup's. "I sincerely hope Santa Olivia doesn't plan on taking up a career of administering vigilante justice."

"What's a vigilante?" Loup asked.

The Father pointed at her. "You, I suspect. Are we clear?"

The Santitos exchanged glances.

"Clear, sir," Mack muttered.

"Good." Father Ramon pulled out his chair and sat. Diego and C.C. went to the kitchen to bring out dinner. When it was served, the Father folded his hands. "Let us give thanks," he said. "Thanks for the food we are about to eat, and thanks that none of you got caught. Because messing with the U.S. Army is a whole different can of worms than brawling with the Salamanders, children."

"A-fucking-men," Sister Martha added with heartfelt fervor.

Still, the rumors persisted and spread.

It was a pair of MPs that had found PFC Ken Braddock under the bleachers in the early-dawn hours, trussed and furious and raving. But the garbage collectors of Outpost were already out and about, hauling their carts, and they heard and witnessed the encounter.

"Was it you?" Tommy asked his sister in a low voice. "Tell me the truth, Loup. You wouldn't do anything that stupid, would you?"

She looked at him and lied. "Nah. The guy made it up."

"Thanks." Tommy hugged her, smelling of clean sweat. "You doing okay, sweetheart?"

Loup shrugged. "I guess."

"What's wrong?"

She eyed him sidelong. "I feel weird. I mean, other people say it. For kissing and stuff. I feel weird to them." She shrugged. "No big deal. It kind of sucks, that's all."

Tommy turned several shades of red. "Who says?"

"T.Y.," Loup said. "C.C. Crazy Jane."

"Jane?" he repeated.

Loup shrugged again. "She taught T.Y. how to kiss, so I asked her to show me. I thought maybe he was doing it wrong, but I guess it's me."

"Shit." Tommy walked away. Loup sat on the edge of the inner sparring ring, legs dangling. When Tommy came back, his face was still red. "Okay," he muttered. "Mommy . . . before she died, she told me a couple of things that I might need to tell you someday. But I felt weird about it, you know?"

"Okay," Loup agreed. "So?"

He cleared his throat. "Well, one was kind of about sex."

"Yeah?"

"Yeah." Tommy's flush deepened. "I guess for your father it

was kind of like you're saying with everyone but Mom. She was different. Most girls kind of freaked out. Our mom was the first girl who didn't. So maybe there aren't a whole lot of people in the world for you. Does that make sense?"

"Yeah," Loup said softly. "Do *you* think I feel weird?"

He shot her a horrified look. "I'm *not* kissing you!"

She laughed. "No, just . . . you know. Like when you hug me?"

Tommy thought about it. "I guess. I don't know, Loup. You're just you, you know?"

"What if I wasn't your sister?"

He looked away. "God, I don't know! There are some things you can't ask guys to think about, okay?"

"Okay," Loup said mildly.

"So there's no one?" Tommy looked back at her. "No one who doesn't feel that way?"

"Pilar, maybe." She shrugged. "But she has a crush on *you*."

Tommy smiled a little. "Yeah, well, she's too young. Even if she is a walking sex bomb." His smile faded, his expression turning uncomfortable. "Do you, um, like girls? Is that part of it?"

"I like Pilar," Loup said honestly. "Does it matter?"

"No." He was quiet a moment, then leaned down to kiss her cheek. "No. You know what, *loup-garou*? It really, really doesn't. That's just one more thing you're not afraid of, right?"

"I guess." She cocked her head. "What else?"

"What *what else*?" Tommy laughed. "You're not afraid of anything."

"What else did Mom say that you haven't told me?" Loup asked. He didn't answer. "Tommy?"

"I don't want to say." He looked at his feet.

"Tommy."

He dragged his head up. "That you might not live real long."

"Why?"

Tommy rubbed his eyes with the heel of one hand. "That's what Martin told her, okay? Your father. The scientists who studied him and the other guys thought they'd have a . . . a . . ." He pronounced the words carefully. "A *shortened lifespan*."

"Oh," Loup said. "How short?"

"Thirty-five years," he said. "Maybe forty."

She laughed. "Oh, hell! That's a long time."

"No." Tommy grasped her shoulders and tried to shake her. "It's not, Loup. And I'm sorry I never told you, but that's one reason I'm trying so hard to win us a ticket out of here, okay? I don't want to grow old without you. Out there, there are probably people who could help, people who aren't part of the army. Scientists and guys like that. I know I'm not smart, but we could find people who are, you know?"

"Aw, Tommy." Loup sobered. "Just quit worrying about me, okay?"

He eased his grip. "I do, though."

"Yeah," she said. "I know." She fell silent, frowning and counting on her fingers.

"What is it?"

"It might not be true," Loup said. "Those scientist guys, they said my father couldn't have kids, right?"

Tommy nodded. "Yeah."

"So maybe they were wrong about this." She shrugged one shoulder. "But I was just thinking that if they weren't, it means he's already dead, doesn't it?"

"Probably," Tommy said gently. "I'm sorry."

"You think he got to Mexico?" Loup asked. "To that place with the funny name and the fish that he told you about?"

"You bet I do."

"I always thought maybe I'd go look for him someday when I was grown up," Loup mused. "After you won a prize match and we got out of here and found out what the real world was like. I promised Jaime I'd come back and tell him; then I thought I'd try to get across the wall. I bet I could make it. Find my father, find out about other stuff, too. Like what he said about El Segundo being made up."

"I'm sorry, honey," Tommy said again. "I didn't know you thought about looking for him."

" 'S'okay." She summoned a faint smile. "I been thinking about it more lately, I guess. Just thinking it would be nice to know him, to know other people like me."

"There still might be, you know," he said. "What if Martin wasn't the only one to have a kid? They were all trying to get to the same place, all the Lost Boys. I bet Martin wasn't the only one to make it. There might be a bunch of little *loup-garous* running around Mexico."

Loup's eyes brightened. "You think?"

"Yeah, sure." Tommy ruffled her hair. "You've gotta tell me what goes on in that hard head of yours, Loup. I don't want to shove *my* dreams down your throat, okay?"

"You're not." She shook her head. "I wanna see you win a match more than anything. That comes first."

He smiled. "You sure?"

"Yeah," she said. "I'm sure."

NINETEEN

Outpost simmered with the tale of Santa Olivia's vengeance. The army released a statement claiming it had been a prank played by soldiers on one of their own, but the story continued to circulate.

"Fucking liars," Mack muttered the day the statement was released.

"They're nervous," Jaime said. "Folk heroes are the sort of things that start insurrections. Anyway, we should be glad they're lying. Takes the heat off us."

"*I'm* not," Katya said with unexpected bitterness. "They got away with it in the first place by lying. Those guys, Braddock's friends, they're just as guilty as he is. I wish Santa Olivia could pay *them* a visit."

"I'll do it," Loup offered.

The Santitos exchanged speculative glances.

"No," Mack said firmly after a moment. "It's too dangerous. We can't take the risk. No more vigilante justice, remember?"

Loup sighed. "Okay."

"What if Santa Olivia did a good deed instead?" Maria suggested. She flushed as the others glanced at her. "You know, performed a miracle?"

"Um, hello?" Jane pointed at Loup. "She's not actually a saint, dummy!"

Maria turned a deeper shade of pink. "I'm just saying!"

"Sister Martha says God helps those that help themselves," Jaime mused. "Maybe we could make our own miracle." He nudged T.Y. with one sneakered toe. "You're the one survived the bomb, miracle boy. Any ideas?"

T.Y. didn't look up from his comic book. "Nope."

Jane rolled her eyes. "This is ridiculous."

"It doesn't have to be a miracle," Maria said stubbornly. "It would just be a good deed, like Santa Olivia feeding the soldiers."

"Hello?" Jane repeated. "Have you noticed that's what we *do* here? Tend the sick and feed the poor?"

"Not the O'Brien kids," Pilar said absently, leafing through a decades-old fashion magazine.

"Who?"

She glanced up. "Celia O'Brien's kids. They lived on my street. She won't take charity from the church on account of, um, all the godless fornication, so her kids are half-starved all the time. I used to give 'em handouts out the back door after I fed my uncle's brats."

"So we sneak them a basket of food?" Jaime frowned. "It's a nice gesture, but not much of a miracle."

"Money," C.C. suggested, bouncing a tennis ball off the wall. "*Big* money."

Jane gave him a scathing look. "And where are we going to get big money?"

He tossed the ball again. "Steal it from the Salamancas."

Diego shook his head. "Bad idea."

"No, see, here's the thing," C.C. explained. "Not the club; they've always got Garza muscle there. But Rosa Salamanca, she ran their gambling racket for ages. She still counts all the money herself every night and puts it in an old safe in her office. Doesn't trust anyone else. I know this guy whose brother works for her. He told me all about it. He read about how to crack a safe in some old detective novel, even showed it to me. He wanted me to steal a stethoscope from the infirmary."

"Did you?" Maria looked horrified.

"Nah." He grinned. "I'm not *that* stupid. If the take was short the next day, the Salamanders would be hard on the lookout for anyone flashing cash. But if a thousand bucks went missing and turned up as a miracle . . . that'd be different, huh? I bet Rosa Salamanca would keep her mouth shut about it."

They digested that in silence.

"You actually think you could crack a safe?" Mack asked.

C.C. nodded confidently. "An old-timey one? Yeah."

Mack glanced at Loup. "Think you could force a locked door open?"

She nodded happily. "Uh-huh."

"And *I* could repair the damage so it looked like we'd never been there." Mack gave a slow, hard smile. "I like it. Let's do it."

Three days later, they put their plan into action.

Pilar and Maria went on a scouting mission, bringing a basket of canned goods to the O'Brien household in the church's name. They returned to report that Celia O'Brien chased them off her doorstep with a broom, disparaging the church and calling them names.

"I don't think she remembers me real fondly," Pilar commented.

The children, they reported, hovered behind their mother and watched the proceedings with wide, hopeless eyes set in gaunt faces.

"Definitely hungry." Maria crossed herself. *"Pobrecitos."*

Mack snuck out to spend a night watching Rosa Salamanca's office, which had once been the Citizens National Bank. He returned to report that the bank was locked and unattended between the hours of two a.m. and eight a.m.

C.C. cracked his knuckles. "So it's a go?"

"It's a go," Mack confirmed.

They stole out of the darkened church and crept through the streets in time to watch Rosa Salamanca and her goons lock the office and leave. Once, the Citizens National Bank would have been protected by alarms and surveillance cameras, but the equipment hadn't functioned for decades. There was only a locked door and the threat of Salamanca vengeance. Loup put her shoulder to the door, testing the lock's resistance.

"Keep it quiet," Mack whispered.

Loup nodded. She planted her feet and pushed hard—harder, steady, and deliberate. Something gave way with a low screech and pop, and rattled onto the floor inside. She eased the door open.

"Hold on." Mack caught her arm. "I think you shoved the plate clean out of the frame. Let me find the pieces. I gotta put this thing back together."

They waited while he groped on the dark floor, watching the empty streets for patrols or headlights. C.C. bounced on the balls of his feet. "The doctor is in the house," he crooned, stroking the stethoscope hanging around his neck.

"You'd better know what you're doing," Loup commented.

C.C. grinned at her. "Watch and see!"

"Okay," Mack called curtly. "Let's move."

Inside, they lit a pair of candles stuck in lanterns made of old tin cans with a few holes poked in them to let out just enough light. They found the safe sitting in the empty modern vault. The vault had been looted long ago, its door sagging open, but the old-fashioned safe looked sturdy and intact.

"Ohh-kay." C.C. sank reverently to his knees before it, plugging the stethoscope into his ears. "Let the doctor work."

Mack beckoned to Loup. "C'mon. I need you to block the door while I fix the lock. Can't do it without light."

She stood in front of the glass door, listening to Mack rustle and curse as he attempted to repair the lock by the faint illumination of his makeshift lantern. The stars overhead were bright and distant. Outpost was quiet, all the clubs closed, all the soldiers except a few MPs back on base or shacked up with women they'd never marry.

"Got it," Mack said softly. He blew out his candle as Loup ducked back inside.

"C.C.?" she asked.

Mack shook his head. "I don't know what I was thinking believing that fucking lunatic could actually crack a safe."

There was a stifled whoop from farther inside the bank.

"Shit!" Loup breathed.

They found C.C. sitting on his heels with an awed look on his face. The stethoscope hung forgotten from his ears. The safe door was open and inside was an enormous stack of bundled cash and receipts. C.C. looked up, his eyes shining. "Mack, man . . . we could clean them *out*."

Mack hesitated.

"No," Loup said in an adamant tone. "C.C. was right the first time. You want to start the turf wars all over again with the church in the middle of it? This is a miracle, not a robbery. We take a thousand bucks for Santa Olivia to give to the O'Brien kids, and not a penny more."

"Okay, okay!" C.C. heaved a sigh, snatched two bundles of cash, and handed them to Loup. She tucked them into the envelope Jane had procured and shoved the envelope into the back pocket of her jeans. He gave the safe one last longing look, then closed the door and spun the lock. "We're out of here."

The O'Brien house was small and run-down, sitting on a scrubby lot on a street the MPs didn't bother to patrol. They circled to the east side. The window of the bedroom where Pilar swore the kids slept was ajar. Loup hung from the windowsill by fingertips, peering into the darkened room.

"See anything?" Mack whispered.

"Nah, too dark."

"If it's the mom, she'll scream bloody murder."

"Shhh." She listened hard. "It's okay. It's kids. I can hear them breathing."

"How can you tell it's *kids* breathing?" C.C. asked.

"Kids breathe different from adults. Hold my legs." She worked the screen loose while Mack and C.C. braced her below, then eased it down. "Here."

"Careful," Mack murmured.

"Uh-huh." Loup hauled herself up on one forearm, raising the window with her free hand. The wood creaked. She tugged her neckerchief up to cover her lower face. "Okay, miracle time."

It was dark and frowsty inside the bedroom. As her eyes adjusted to the lack of starlight, she made out small figures sleeping two and three to a bed. In the nearest, a boy of some ten or eleven years was awake and staring at her with wide eyes, clutching the sheets to his chest.

"Hi," Loup said softly, crouching at his bedside. "It's okay. Don't be scared. Do you know who I am?"

He shook his head.

"I'm the spirit of Santa Olivia." She fished the bulging envelope out of her jeans pocket and handed it to him. He squinted at the message written on it.

PRIDE IS A SIN.
SANTA OLIVIA DOES NOT FORGET.

Loup struggled to remember the speech Jaime had written for her in the event that one or more of the kids had awakened. "Give this unto your mother and tell her behold, Santa Olivia bids her take this gift and feed her children. Let her accept it with grace and, um, be reminded that it is sinful to cause others to suffer for her self-righteous pride. Especially kids. And when the money runs out, she should accept the church's charity. Okay?"

"Okay," the boy whispered. A glimmer of awe dawned in his stricken gaze.

"Good kid." Loup straightened and patted him on the head. "Okay, amen and good night."

"Okay," he repeated, thin fingers clutching the thick envelope.

The other kids were beginning to stir. Loup made a quick exit out the window, dangling from one hand long enough to prop the screen back in place when Mack handed it to her. They beat a careful retreat to the church before the sky began to lighten.

C.C. yawned. "Good miracle, guys."

Mack thumped his shoulder. "Nice work on the safe, Doc. Don't forget to put the stethoscope back before Sister Martha misses it." He smiled at Loup. " 'Night, Santa Olivia."

" 'Night."

There were low, excited murmurs emanating from the boys' dormitory after Mack and C.C. entered it, but everyone in the girls' room was asleep. Loup sat on her cot and yawned, wriggling agilely out of her jeans.

"Hey." In the next bunk, Pilar lifted her head sleepily. "Everything go okay?"

"Yeah. Yeah, it did."

"Good." For a moment, it seemed like Pilar was going to say something else. Loup sat and watched her in the dim light, waiting. Her blood beat steadily in her veins. But Pilar only sighed and said, "Good," a second time and settled back into her dreams, hugging her pillow, her breathing turning slow and deep.

The room smelled like clean linen and sleep.

Loup crawled into bed and slept.

TWENTY

The following day, Loup went to the gym to help Tommy with his chores.

She kept her head down and listened to the idle chatter of the men training there. By midafternoon, the story of Santa Olivia's latest miracle had broken.

"A thousand bucks!" Bob Reyes said in awe. "Just like that, out of nowhere. A goddamn fuckin' miracle. You know what I could do with a thousand bucks?"

Miguel Garza snorted. "Not as much as you think. A thousand bucks is chicken feed."

"To you, maybe." Kevin McArdle worked a speed bag. "Not to me, not to Bob. Not to someone like Celia O'Brien."

"Stiff-necked cunt," Miguel said without any particular malice. "Cousin of yours, isn't she?"

Kevin McArdle stalked away without answering.

Tommy watched him go. Loup watched Tommy. "Is it true?" she asked innocently. "She's his cousin?"

"Yeah." Tommy watched Floyd Roberts intercept McArdle. "Stiff-necked, too."

"Coach has that kind of money, doesn't he?" Loup asked.

"Yeah," he said slowly. "That would be just like him, wouldn't it? Not to let anyone know."

She shrugged. "I guess, sure."

Tommy eyed her. "But the kid said he saw a girl. Santa Olivia. You don't know anything about it?"

Loup widened her eyes. "Where would I get a thousand bucks, Tommy?"

It was the question no one could answer. As C.C. had predicted, Rosa Salamanca kept her mouth shut about the thousand-dollar shortfall, unwilling to acknowledge the possibility of an error in her bookkeeping, unwilling to admit to a breach in her security at the cost of debunking a miracle. Who had a thousand dollars to spare? There were only a few people in Outpost who could have done such a thing. None of them stepped forward to claim it.

None of them denied it, either.

At dinner, Father Ramon fixed the Santitos with a hard gaze. "Children?"

C.C. Rider batted his lashes. "Father?"

Father Ramon's mouth twitched. "I confess, if this is your doing, I cannot fathom the *how* of it. If it has inspired others to take up the banner of Santa Olivia, let us pray that for the sake of her children, Celia O'Brien will take the lesson to heart and cease to begrudge our charity."

"Hear, hear." Sister Martha hoisted her water glass. "Let the rigid stick of self-righteousness be dislodged from her very uptight ass."

Father Ramon coughed.

"A-fucking-men," Loup supplied helpfully.

She was on KP duty with Mack that night. While they washed dishes together, Loup told him about an idea that had come to her at the gym.

"Snakes," Mack mused.

Loup nodded. "I listen to the guys, you know? Bob Reyes, he works at the golf course. Said he found a nest of snakes in the rough just past the fourth hole. Just green snakes, nothing poisonous. He left them there. And someone who lies, you call them a snake, right?"

"You're thinking about the assholes who lied to cover for Braddock?"

"Uh-huh." She nodded again. "We could put them in their jeep, maybe. Just to let them know they didn't get away with it, not really."

Mack's gray eyes glinted. "So it's not really vigilante justice, huh? Just a message to let them know Santa Olivia is always watching."

"Yeah."

"Let's see what Jaime and the others think."

Jaime wasn't impressed.

"It's really nothing more than a prank, isn't it?" he observed. "I mean, you could pull it off without witnesses, which is good, but after the thousand-dollar miracle, it's kind of a letdown."

"Oh." Loup was disappointed. "Even if you wrote one of your great messages?"

"Still a prank," Jane agreed dismissively.

"The snakes are a nice idea, though," Jaime assured Loup. "Very nice use of symbolism."

She sighed. "Thanks."

Maria cleared her throat softly. "What about a plague of snakes? If they like, you know, fell from the sky?"

"Yuck," Pilar commented.

"But rather impressively biblical and miraculous." Jaime steepled his fingers. "Maybe we could build some sort of catapult?"

"Oh, please!" Jane scoffed. "Wouldn't it be a hell of a lot easier to drop them from the roof?"

"*What* roof?"

"The nightclub." Katya's voice was fierce and taut. "I know the exact spot. The veranda on the back; that's where they go to smoke dope. The MPs, they don't patrol around there unless there's a fight. Ken and his buddies bragged about it. It's got an overhanging roof."

Mack glanced at Loup. "Scouting expedition?"

She was already on her feet. "Yep."

They surveyed Salamancas' nightclub in the light of the setting sun. It was a ramshackle affair that had spread to encompass a number of buildings. The buildings were close together. Apart from the flat extension overhanging the veranda, the rooftop on the original building had a slight pitch. Most of the other buildings had flat roofs. Mack watched Loup gauging the distance between them.

"Think you could do it?"

"Yeah."

His voice hardened. "You'd better be *damn* sure, Loup."

She gave him a surprised look. "I wouldn't say it if I wasn't."

Toward the end of the block was an old apartment building with a fire escape, its rooftop almost touching the adjoining building, an abandoned café not yet annexed by the sprawling Salamanca complex.

Loup nodded at the fire escape. "That'll work. Mack, I can get up and over and back and down, no problem. But how am I gonna know I've got the right guys? I know Braddock, but not the others. Even if I knew what they looked like, it's gonna be hard to recognize them from overhead."

Mack scratched his chin. "Yeah. We need Kotch on lookout. Think she'll do it?"

"To get back at them? Hell, yeah."

They staked out a place for the lookout in a narrow alley across from the veranda with a rusting Dumpster bin providing handy concealment. Loup snatched a pair of binoculars from an unattended jeep with casual ease.

"Might need these," she said. "It's not gonna be easy to pick out faces at that distance."

"Loup!" Mack looked slightly alarmed.

"What?" She shrugged. "I don't wanna rain snakes on the wrong guys."

They made it back before curfew. In the early gray hours of dawn, C.C. and T.Y. snuck out to go snake hunting on the golf course. They returned triumphant with a heavy, squirming pillowcase that the Santitos examined that afternoon with varying degrees of disgust and fascination.

"Kinda cute, huh?" C.C. offered, extracting a long, wriggling green snake. "You wanna pet him?"

"Ohmigod." Pilar sounded faint. "Get that thing away from me."

"They're harmless, I swear." Loup peered into the pillowcase at the mass of twining coils. "Poor snakes. I feel bad for them."

"They're serving the greater good," Jane said laconically. She swung a rustic wicker basket from one hand. "Look what I found in the storeroom. There's a stack of spares."

Jaime adjusted his glasses. "Santa Olivia's basket?"

Jane nodded. "Since Santa Olivia won't be making an appearance this time, it'll be the perfect vehicle for her message, don't you think?"

He smiled at her in total accord. "Perfect."

They wrote out a message and tied it to the handle of the basket.

FORK-TONGUED LIARS.
SANTA OLIVIA DOES NOT FORGET.

Eight hours later, Loup lay plastered flat on the roof overhanging the veranda of the nightclub, peering at the heads of the soldiers below as they came and went. A haze of pungent smoke drifted upward. Santa Olivia's basket was beside her, overflowing with a knotted pillowcase that writhed in a series of peculiar bulges. She waited and waited, periodically glancing toward the alley where Mack and Katya were concealed.

Waited.

And waited.

She thought about Tommy's father taking their mother to Salamanca's for a drink the night they met. About him promising to marry her. It sounded like he'd been one of the good guys, like his son. She felt bad lying to Tommy about playing Santa Olivia, but he'd be scared and mad if he knew. He'd yell at her for not being *careful*. And he would be right, of course. Tommy was usually right.

But Tommy hadn't seen Kotch the night of the rape, all of her careless confidence in shreds. He hadn't had to stand by a helpless witness while Colonel Stillwell chose to blame the victim.

And the O'Brien kids . . .

Loup thought about the glimmer of awe and hope in the boy's eyes and smiled. Sometimes it was worth being a little careless. Maybe God had forgotten about Outpost, but it didn't hurt to let people believe Santa Olivia remembered them.

An owl hooted.

"Shit," she muttered, recognizing Mack's signal. She peeked over the edge of the roof. Three new guys had sauntered onto the veranda. She memorized the tops of their heads. One had a little nonregulation ducktail of hair curling over the collar of his BDUs. "Okay," she whispered to the snakes, unknotting the pillowcase. "Sorry about this, really."

The soldiers leaned on the railing, sharing a joint and chuckling in low tones. Somewhere out there in the darkness, Mack and Katya were making their furtive way back to the church.

Loup waited.

People came and went. PFC Braddock's companions lingered to enjoy a leisurely high. If they'd picked up girls that night, they weren't offering to share their stash. Lying flat on her belly, Loup maneuvered the pillowcase into position, holding the opening shut. A lone green snake found its way out and slithered around her wrists, its forked tongue tickling her skin as if to ask a question.

"Cut that out," she whispered to it.

The ducktailed soldier pinched out their joint and flicked the roach into the darkness. He and his comrades sauntered back toward the club and passed beneath the overhanging roof.

Loup upended the pillowcase.

Snakes fell like rain, twisting in midair.

The ensuing shouting was surprisingly gratifying. "Mother-*FUCK!*" someone yelled, his voice rising above the din. "Mother-fucking *snakes!*" She grabbed the basket and let it dangle, taking a split second to appreciate the scene. Soldiers batting furiously at their cropped hair, yanking at the collars of their BDUs, trying to shed their shirts. On the veranda, snakes wriggling everywhere, just trying to get away.

She let the basket fall.

"The hell?" One of the soldiers looked up, fumbling for his flashlight.

But Loup was already in motion, already on her way. She crossed the flat expanse of the overhang and scrambled up the shallow pitch of Salamanca's roof on all fours. She vaulted over the peak and found her feet. By the time the flashlight's beam sought to tag her, she was already on the downslope and running.

It felt good.

So good.

There was starlight; enough to see by, just barely. At the edge of the roof, Loup leaped. Air and the abyss. She launched herself and crossed it, landing solidly on the roof of the next building. Behind her there was a commotion. She kept running, dodged a defunct ventilation duct.

Leaped again.

Solid.

It was easier without carrying a basketful of snakes.

The fire escape almost came too soon. Loup scrambled down it. By the time her feet found purchase on the street, the commotion was well behind her, half a block away.

She melted into the darkness.

Gone.

TWENTY-ONE

Petitions to Santa Olivia began appearing at the church.

It had been a long time since there was anything resembling real religious devotion in most of Outpost. Father Ramon celebrated the mass on Sundays and people still came, but for the comfort and familiarity of ritual. Everyone more or less knew he wasn't a real priest, and there was the matter of his relationships with Sister Martha and Anna. The church had retained its standing because of the services it provided—the clinic, the free lunches. Caring for the dying and the dead, taking in the orphans of Outpost. Whatever else was true, everyone knew that Father Ramon and Sister Martha had worked tirelessly for many years to keep the community alive.

Faith wasn't much of an issue.

But now it was different. People weren't dying of the plague. The church hadn't taken in an orphan since Pilar Ecchevarria, and she didn't exactly count. Even the rumors about El Segundo had been muted.

And Santa Olivia had been seen in Outpost.

Santa Olivia had performed miracles.

Outposters trickled into the church at all hours to light votive candles to the child-saint's effigy, until the church ran out of candles. They left petitions written on folded scraps of paper in Santa Olivia's basket. The statue of Our Lady of the Sorrows looked on in seeming approval, the rusty tearstains on her face fading.

"Listen to this." Crazy Jane read aloud. " 'Santa Olivia, my husband is cheating on me with that whore Linda Flores. Please make his dick go limp.' "

"You shouldn't steal those!" Maria protested. "It's sacrilegious."

"Why the hell not? Father Ramon just throws 'em away. He's afraid we'll get ideas." Jane read another. "'Blessed Saint Olivia, my father buried my mother's jewels in a sand trap on the golf course twenty-five years ago. They died in the plague. Now I work tending the greens. I been digging and digging, but I cannot find them. I beg you to come to me in a dream and show me where.'" She laughed. "Greedy fucker!"

There were pleas to heal injuries and cure sicknesses, pleas for wealth and love. But mostly, there were pleas for vengeance.

The Santitos read them with morbid fascination.

"'Old Salamanca ruint my family.'" T.Y. squinted at a scrap. "'I beg you to make his daughter poor. Fair is fair.'"

"'Danny Garza's men killed my father,'" Mack read. "'Santa Olivia, please strike him dead.'" He cocked an eyebrow at Loup. "Tempted?"

She shook her head. "No vigilante justice. We promised."

"We're lucky we got away with the snakes," Jaime agreed. "I think Santa Olivia had better lie low for a while."

"Aw!" Pilar, sitting on C.C.'s lap, sighed. "This one's so sad!"

C.C. snatched it from her. "Lemme see."

"No!" She glared at him and took it back. "I don't want you to laugh at it."

"I won't laugh!" he protested.

Loup stirred. "Read it."

"'Santa Olivia, I am an old man and I have lived through many things,'" Pilar read slowly. "'I have lost everything I loved, one piece at a time. My wife. My daughter. My grandchildren. All I had left . . .' It's pretty long, you guys."

"That's okay," Mack said. "Keep reading."

"'All I had left in these last years of my life was my dog Badger,'" Pilar continued. "'He was a good dog and a good companion. Sometimes he leaves the yard, but only a little. There is a police patrol that passes every morning in a jeep. They used to be friendly, but lately, it is a bad pair. The soldier who drives always swerves and pretends he's going to hit Badger. Yesterday he did. He killed my dog.'" She looked up, eyes bright with tears. "Isn't that terrible?"

"Fucking soldiers," Katya muttered.

"They're bored," Jaime said in an objective tone. "And they're not being held accountable by the military. The bad ones are acting out."

Kotch shrugged. "Whatever."

"There's more." Pilar turned the letter over. "'The patrol is the one that passes my house on Tenth Street at six or seven in the morning. I do not know the soldier's name, but he has a deep dimple in his chin and thick eyebrows. I do not wish him harm, but I pray that one day he repents of having killed an old man's last happiness.'"

Loup's skin prickled. "Mack."

"Yeah." He met her eyes. "It's almost like he knows. You know, we didn't exactly *promise*. We just said we understood, that's all. You wanna check it out?"

She nodded. "Uh-huh."

"Could be a setup," Jaime warned them. "I'm telling you, we're pushing our luck. The general is *not* happy about this business."

"What if it's not?" Mack countered. "You willing to put that big brain to work figuring out a plan?"

"Let me see the petition." Jaime read it silently to himself, then sighed. "Oh, shit. That's too damn pathetic for words. Fine, if it checks out, I'm in."

It checked out.

Jane and Dondi went on the first scouting expedition, claiming that Father Ramon had sent them to canvas the neighborhood asking for donations for the votive candle fund.

"The old guy's for real," Jane said when they reported back, sounding uncommonly subdued. "Looks about a hundred years old. He goes shuffling across the kitchen to get a dollar out of a cookie jar. I notice this empty dog dish on the floor and ask if he's got a dog . . ." She stopped.

"His mouth started shaking and he got all shaky," Dondi finished for her. "He said 'I used to,' like he was gonna cry."

Mack looked at Jaime. "Any ideas?"

"One." Jaime looked at Loup. "Let's go into the courtyard."

There was a rock garden along the east wall of the inner courtyard with several good-sized boulders and a few sickly cacti set amid a sea of pebbles.

"How big a rock could you lift and throw?" Jaime asked.

Loup cocked her head. "Dunno."

"Let's find out."

The biggest one was about three feet tall, the centerpiece of the rock garden. Loup shifted it experimentally and knew right away it was too heavy, too awkward. She surveyed the others and chose a boulder that was roughly two feet in diameter. She squatted and grabbed it, lifting with her legs.

"Jesus," Pilar murmured.

Loup took a couple of steps back and heaved the boulder. It fell with a resounding crash, pebbles grinding beneath it. "That's about it," she said, slightly breathless. "I could *lift* a heavier one, but not throw it."

"Jesus," Mack echoed. He went over and managed to lift the boulder a few inches, his face red with the strain. "That thing must weigh two hundred pounds." He straightened. "So what are you thinking?"

Anna poked her head into the courtyard. "What in God's name are you doing out here? What was that sound?"

"Nothing!" T.Y. called.

"I was messing with the rock garden," Loup added. "Sorry! Nothing broke."

Anna shook her head and withdrew.

They trooped back to the rec room where Jaime revealed his plan. "Okay, here's the thing. They've got extra patrols on the nightclub, so that's out. And we can't risk luring them again," he said. "They're not stupid. They'd figure it out and start looking for whoever served as bait. So. If we want to convince them it's a *real* miracle, Santa Olivia's got to make an appearance and do something impossible, then vanish."

"Throw a rock?" Mack frowned.

"A rock most grown men couldn't lift," Jaime said. "A rock with a message on it. Right through the windshield of their jeep."

Loup nodded. "Not bad. How do I vanish?"

"We'll have to identify the soldiers and study their route." Jaime leaned forward, elbows on his knees. "Pick a spot where you can run like hell, because you're not gonna be hidden this time. How fast is your fastest?"

"Pretty fast, I guess." She shrugged. "I don't know how fast for how long. Tommy never let me try."

Jane sniffed. "I like your rock idea, Jaime, but you need a better getaway."

"Hey." Jaime spread his hands. "I don't have a lot to work with."

"Let's get the route worked out first," Mack said pragmatically.

It took a week of covert surveillance. Identifying the patrol was easy enough. Mack and Diego waited on the street outside the old man's house. The jeep passed in the early morning. The driver slowed down to yell at them for loitering, slowly enough that they were able to note his dimpled chin and thick eyebrows. After that, it was a matter of working backward and forward, posting different Santitos at different corners, making notes of which way the patrol vehicle went. They also noted that the driver did in fact make a habit of swerving toward dogs on the street.

Jaime found an old map of the town in the church's archives and traced the route. Once that was done, they staked out the patrol a few more times to confirm that the route didn't vary.

"Okay," he said when they reconvened. "I've been thinking about the getaway." He pointed to a spot on the map. "Corner of

Fisher and Juarez. There's an apartment building on the west side of Fisher with a side alley that ends in a wooden fence about eight feet tall. Think you could clear it, Loup?"

She shook her head. "I can't jump that high. I'm better at jumping distances than height."

"Oh." Jaime looked crestfallen.

"What if you had a rope?" T.Y. asked. He glanced at Jaime. "Is it a flat-top fence or pointy?"

"Pointy."

"So we could loop a rope over one of the points. Loup could use it to climb the fence and take it with her." T.Y. grinned. "Poof! Santa Olivia vanishes."

"That would work," Loup agreed.

"She still has to get back to the church," Jane warned them. "It'll be daylight and those soldiers have radios. They're already on edge. They'll be swarming all over the place in minutes."

"All she has to do is cut through the swap market at Flores . . ." Jaime studied the map. "Hmm. Lot of people would see her. The swap market starts early."

"Loup needs a disguise. One that she can take off and blend in with the crowd." T.Y. whacked one of his beloved comics against his hand. "Hello? Superman? Clark Kent?"

"Santa Olivia," Pilar said. She pointed upward. "She wears a pretty blue dress and a white kerchief over her hair."

"Superheroes don't wear pretty blue dresses!" T.Y. protested.

Katya snorted. "Does anyone here *have* a pretty blue dress?"

"We could sew one," Pilar offered. The Santitos stared at her. "Okay, *I* could sew one!" She shrugged. "What? My fucking aunt made me sew for her brats all the time. Sew and clean and cook. I've got domestic skills up the butt, okay?"

C.C. rolled his eyes. "This is just silly."

"Yeah," Mack said slowly. "It is. But that's the point, right? This has to be too crazy to be true." He grinned. "A pretty little girl in a pretty blue dress hurls a boulder grown men can't lift, then disappears. What else could it be but Santa Olivia herself?"

"I'm not that little," Loup commented.

"You're not that big, either," he told her.

"Yeah, well, we'd need fabric." Jane glanced at Pilar. "There's a bunch of hospital scrubs from the plague days in the clinic. They're light blue. I think the color's pretty close to Santa Olivia's dress. Would that work?"

Pilar nodded. "Sure."

Mack clapped his hands once, briskly. "Let's do it!"

TWENTY-TWO

H old still," Pilar murmured, her mouth full of pins. "Okay."
Loup looked at herself in the mirror.

Her reflection looked back, wide-eyed and caramel-skinned, wearing a pretty blue dress patched together almost seamlessly, trimmed with white lace purloined from a curtain. A white kerchief cut from a pillowcase tamed her thick black hair.

"Santa fucking Olivia," Pilar said with satisfaction, putting down her pins.

Loup took a deep breath. "Yep."

"Is it too tight?" Pilar's hands skimmed her waist, lighted, and lingered. "Remember, you're gonna have to wear it over other clothes and strip it off quick after you clear the wall."

Loup looked over her shoulder.

"Sorry!" Pilar's color rose, but she didn't pull away, not exactly. "It's just so weird, you know? You don't *look* like you oughta be able to lift that rock, baby." One hand slid upward, palm tracing the projection of Loup's right shoulder blade, fingers brushing the bare nape of her neck beneath the kerchief. Exploring; hungrily, half-unwittingly. "But you *feel* like it."

"I know," Loup said softly.

"Yeah." Pilar snatched her hands back as though Loup's skin had scorched them. "So whaddya think? Too tight?"

Loup sighed. "Can you give me another inch?"

"Sure." Pilar busied herself with the pins.

She shouldn't do it. Loup *knew* she shouldn't do it. It was a bigger risk than they'd taken before. It was stupid and careless and everything Tommy had taught her not to do. But it was so appealing in so many ways. There was the lure of the righteous fury that had run in her veins the night they'd taken down Private Braddock—the clean, crisp deliverance of justice administered in two punches. That same anger sang on behalf of the old man, George Figueroa, whose dog had been killed.

Alive.

It was a way to feel alive.

And there was the camaraderie of the Santitos—a clan, a pack. Jaime and Jane lending their wits, Mack his leadership. Everyone pitching in, everyone doing their part. Giving people hope, giving people something to believe in. It felt good. It felt like the way things were supposed to feel.

And Pilar . . .

"Fuck," Loup muttered to herself, standing at the crossroads of Fisher and Juarez, the white kerchief tied neatly over her unruly hair, a dark kerchief masking the lower half of her face. Below, a pretty blue dress, beneath which Loup was sweating through a second set of clothes. She rolled the boulder into the center of the road from where Mack and Diego had left it, hauling it in a garbage cart under cover of darkness. Across from the apartment building was an abandoned gas station. An elderly woman sold tomatoes in front of the empty pumps. She looked curiously at Loup as she set up her wares.

The jeep came, kicking up a trail of dust.

Everything else went away.

The driver saw her and the boulder and braked. The jeep didn't have a top. The driver stood up, shading his eyes. Beneath the rim of his helmet, he had dense eyebrows. The dimple in his chin was so deep it was in shadow.

"The fuck, bitch?" he called. "Move!"

"I bear a message from Santa Olivia," Loup called, speaking from the script Jaime and Jane had written for her. "You destroyed an old man's last happiness. Santa Olivia bids you repent of your thoughtless cruelty!"

The driver leaned on the horn. "Move your ass, you freakshow!"

Loup hoisted the boulder, positioning it on her right shoulder. There were words written on it in white paint Mack had found in a shed.

DOG KILLER.
SANTA OLIVIA DOES NOT FORGET.

The soldiers in the jeep gaped. She summoned a surge of strength and threw it hard. There was about a yard of space separating the two men. Loup threw it between them. She didn't wait to hear the crash, the tinkle of glass splintering in a spiderweb, the soldiers' surprised curses. She just fled.

Past the tenement, down the alley.

God, it felt good. Tommy had never let her *go*. Loup ran faster than she'd ever run in her life, faster than she'd run on the rooftops, faster than anyone had ever run. The walls of the tenement rushed past. Her vision narrowed, focusing. She saw the fence looming before her, saw the dangling rope. Leaped without slowing, catching the rope halfway up the fence. She swung her body outward and her feet found purchase on the vertical surface. Loup scrambled up and over, pausing at the top to unhook the rope.

She dropped and ran, coiling the rope as she went.

Across the street was a building that had been a place where people took their cars to get their brakes and mufflers fixed. It was empty, long since stripped of anything useful. The garage bay door was dented and battered, the front door to the office unlocked, glass panes shattered. Loup ducked quickly through the latter, then made her way into the garage.

There was the woven plastic shopping satchel Jaime had left for her, half full of worn kids' clothes too small for even Dondi, stolen from the church's stores. Loup upturned the bag, dumping out the clothing onto a cement floor dark with ancient grease stains. She stuffed the coiled rope into the bottom of the bag, then yanked off the dark kerchief knotted around her face, stripped off the blue dress, and unpinned the white kerchief atop her hair, cramming them atop the rope. She piled the kids' clothing back into the bag.

Done.

Her pulse slowed, steady and calm. She slipped out the back door and walked casually down Flores Street toward the town's other long-defunct bank, the National Bank of Commerce, where the swap market was held. Behind her, a commotion was beginning to spread.

"Loup!" On the outskirts of the bank's parking lot, Maria was waiting for her with an identical plastic satchel over one arm and Dondi beside her. She looked pale and terrified, but she did her best to play the role. They'd been chosen as the most innocuous, least threatening members of the Santitos. "What's going on back there?"

Loup shook her head. "No idea." She could hear soldiers shouting and the sound of racing feet coming around the corner. It quickened her blood again, but when she smiled, it came from a calm, happy place inside. "Come on," she said to Dondi. "Let's see if we can't find you some new clothes."

He grinned back at her. "Thanks, sis."

The parking lot was already half full, the regular traders spreading their wares on blankets and sitting beside them on plastic chairs. All the good spots under the shelter of the drive-through lanes were already taken. A dozen of the irregular shoppers, mostly women with children in tow, were picking over goods and haggling, hoping to make a good trade. By the time the soldiers arrived, Loup and the others had already blended into the mix.

The soldiers worked their way through the market, questioning people. More soldiers arrived, spreading out block by block. A buzz of excitement and rumor arose.

"Hey!" The dimpled soldier blocked their way. "We're looking for a girl in a blue dress. Seen one?"

"No, sir." Loup risked a quick glance at his face, reckoning he'd seen no more of her than her eyes. "No dresses. We're hoping to trade boys' clothes for my brother." She opened the bag. "See?"

He gave a cursory glance. "You?" he asked Maria and Dondi.

"No, sir!" Maria squeaked nervously.

It made him suspicious enough to rummage in her bag. "All right." He jerked his cleft chin. "Move along; go home. Market's gonna be closed today." He gave Dondi a tight smile. "Sorry, kid."

"What did she do?" Dondi asked with wide-eyed innocence. "The girl in the blue dress?"

The soldier's eyes narrowed. "Nothing you need to worry about."

Two more patrols stopped them on the way home, but they were questioning everyone. Both times, they let them go. Maria looked ready to faint. Once they were inside the church gate, her knees gave way. "I can't do this again," she whispered. "Don't ask me again, please."

"Okay." Loup caught her by the elbows. "You were great. You did great."

"Crybaby!" Dondi scoffed. "Did not. You almost gave us away."

"Shut up!" There were tears in Maria's voice.

An armored car rumbled down the street, bristling with soldiers. Loup glanced over her shoulder. Risk. Tommy's voice echoed in her head, telling her to be *careful*. "Um . . . maybe we'd better go inside."

The Santitos were waiting in a fever of expectation. They fell on Loup, Dondi, and Maria, hustling them down to the rec room.

"Well?" Mack demanded. "Did it work?"

"Yeah." Loup overturned her bag. "It worked." She picked out the coiled rope, the blue dress, and kerchiefs. "But Jane was right. The army's fucking swarming. I think we better hide this shit." She glanced around the room at the grimy petitions scattered about. "And those. Those oughta go back in Santa Olivia's basket. Except for the one."

"Aw, c'mon!" C.C. bounced on his toes, eyes bright. "What are you scared of? You *did* it! We're celebrating! Tell us about it!"

Loup gazed at him.

C.C. stopped bouncing.

"Loup's right," Mack said. "I'll put the rope back in the cemetery toolshed where I found it. T.Y." He gestured. "Pick up this shit and put it back in Santa Olivia's basket." He met Loup's eyes. "Okay if we burn the dress?"

Loup looked at Pilar.

Pilar shrugged. "I can always make another."

"No traces." Jaime sat on the butt-sprung couch, clenching his fists in his hair. "Mack's right. Loup's right. Let's get rid of the evidence, Santitos. This was an insanely stupid thing we did. I don't know what the hell any of us were thinking." His head came up, glasses reflecting the light. "It actually *worked*?"

"Yeah." Loup smiled slowly. "It did."

TWENTY-THREE

Outpost was ablaze with rumor.

It ran rampant on the streets. It worked its way through the military echelons. Colonel Stillwell came back to speak to Father Ramon. His men searched the church. They found nothing, but they confiscated all the petitions in Santa Olivia's basket.

"No more," the colonel warned the Father. "I don't know if you had anything to do with it, Padre, but you're the guy who speaks for Santa Olivia in this town, so I'm holding you accountable for her. Either you put an end to it, or I'll have a man stationed here to keep watch over you and your flock every hour of the day. If anything else happens, I'm holding you to answer for it. I'll shut down the church if I have to. I don't believe in miracles. And I don't know what the fuck is going on here, but no more petitions."

Father Ramon inclined his head. "Of course."

He sent for Loup, alone.

She waited, sitting opposite his desk in his study. Father Ramon smoked meditatively, regarding her, stubbing out cigarettes in a cut-glass ashtray. He finished two and was working on a third before he spoke.

"Why?"

Loup passed him the petition they had withheld.

Father Ramon read it in silence. "I see." He put out his third cigarette and lit a fourth. "Foul habit," he said, gesturing. A trail of smoke followed his hand. "Do you know it was almost eradicated in the United States when I was a boy?"

Loup shook her head.

"Of course not." Father Ramon inhaled, exhaled a long plume.

"How could you know? When the flu came and took so many, many of the survivors decided foolish vices were one of the few things worth living for. So." He gestured again. "We indulge." His wide mouth twisted. "Now we do so at the sufferance of the U.S. Army, who are willing to supply us with that which we require in return for our cooperation in the process of our own disenfranchisement."

"Like everything," Loup said.

"Yes." He stubbed out his fourth cigarette with a vicious twist, then held up the half-smoked butt. "But when all is said and done, *this* does not sustain me. What sustains me is the knowledge that despite everything, I am doing good work in the world. Do you understand?"

"No."

"It can be taken away, Loup." The Father leaned forward. "All of it. Every vice supplied and virtue sustained. The good colonel threatened me today. If Santa Olivia makes another appearance"—he waved one hand, setting eddies of smoke to roiling—"I will be held accountable for it and the church will be closed."

"Why?" she asked.

"Because Colonel Stillwell does not believe in miracles," he said wryly. "And he needs to punish someone." Father Ramon smoothed the remnants of his fourth cigarette and relit it, squinting at her through the rising coils of smoke. "I know you didn't act alone. You're not a follower, but you're not a leader, either. All I know with certainty is that you *did* act, Santa Olivia, and I cannot say that of the others. That's why you're here and they're not."

Loup didn't reply.

Father Ramon sighed. "Ah, Loup! I had my suspicions about the snake incident, but I was willing to give it a pass, hoping it would be the last. Did I not make myself clear when we spoke before? After Santa Olivia's first appearance?"

She nodded. "Yeah, pretty much. I'm sorry, Father. We just thought—"

He pushed the scrap of paper with one nicotine-stained finger. "An old man and his dog. Jesus have mercy, I understand, I do. But it's not worth the risk. Clearly, I didn't express myself forcefully enough." He set down his smoldering butt and steepled his fingers. "Tell me, Loup. Are you jealous of your brother? Do you envy him?"

"Tommy?" She thought about it. "I guess I do."

"Because people see him as a hero in waiting," Father Ramon said gently. "The hope of Outpost—"

"It's not *that!*" Loup interrupted in a surprised tone. "Tommy's a good fighter, Father. He's really good. And he's worked really hard for a long time. People ought to think what they do about Tommy."

"So?" he prompted her.

She frowned. "He gets to do what he's good at and I don't. I'm happy for him, but I wish I could. Wish I could run as fast as I wanted, jump as far, hit as hard. Wish I didn't have to be careful all the time. It's what I'm good at. Tommy can and I can't. That's envy, right?"

"So you don't begrudge him?" Father Ramon asked.

"Why would I begrudge him?" Loup echoed in perplexity. "It's not his fault."

He eyed her. "Sometimes, Loup Garron, I don't think we speak the same language. I find myself at a loss. What becomes of this emotion we call *envy* when it is uncoupled from fear and malice? Does it remain a sin? Or is it simply an honest assessment of the human condition?"

"Sir?"

Father Ramon waved away his comments. "Never mind. I've grown old enough to return to the theological musings of my youth. Let me speak plainly." His face hardened, graven lines bracketing his mouth. "If Santa Olivia makes another appearance, I'll banish you from her church. *All* of you."

Loup's eyes widened.

"Yes." He nodded. "Go tell the others."

The news made them despondent. Santa Olivia had been such

a tremendous success, it seemed a shame to abandon her. But Father Ramon had laid down the law, and the Santitos agreed it wasn't worth the cost.

"I'd be okay," Mack said in his steady way. "Some of us would. Not all. Where's Dondi gonna go?"

"I'd manage!" Dondi protested.

"What, begging? Or you gonna be a runner for the Garzas?" Mack shook his head. "What about the girls?"

Katya scowled. "What about us?"

"You'd be turning tricks inside three months," he said in an implacable tone. "Pilar, too."

Pilar lifted her head. "Hey!"

"Well, you would. Unless your uncle got to you first," Mack said, unperturbed. "We gotta let it go."

They did.

Outpost didn't. The rumors about Santa Olivia persisted. When the petitions were banned at the church, they began appearing in the village. They were scrawled on walls in charcoal and pencil and chalk—anything that could write, anything that had survived. The army hired local men to go about with buckets of whitewash, covering over the petitions with broad, sloppy strokes. Still, ghostly images of old pleas bled through the whitewash and new ones continued to appear atop it.

Tommy knew it had been her; after the miracle of the boulder, he had to know. Loup didn't admit to it when he questioned her, only told him that Father Ramon had promised that Santa Olivia wouldn't be making any more appearances. Tommy nodded grimly, satisfied.

Graffiti petitions continued to appear on the walls.

Loup read them wistfully, remembering.

What it had felt like . . .

Alive.

But time passed and things changed. Diego turned eighteen and got a job working at the reservoir. He moved out on his own, and four months later, Maria joined him. They began planning a small wedding. Mack and Katya started dating, somewhat to their own surprise, and settled into a new role as the senior couple among the Santitos. Jaime and Jane broke up and reunited on a weekly basis. Pilar began dating a kid named Joe Torres who tended bar at a club owned by Rosa Salamanca's youngest son. She had plans to upgrade to Rory Salamanca when the opportunity presented itself. C.C. spent a good deal of time getting into trouble on his own. Loup and T.Y. had a handful of awkward trysts that left them both unhappy.

"I really like you!" T.Y. said in frustration. "It's just—"

Loup sighed. "I know."

And elsewhere in Outpost, Celino Rossi, the army's junior heavyweight champion, was rotated out of service. For a few months, there wasn't anyone in that weight class to fight a prize match.

Then there was a new one.

"McArdle's up," Tommy informed Loup. "He gets the first shot."

She cocked her head. "Who's next?"

"Me or Mig." He grinned. "If McArdle loses, it's Coach's call."

She went to the match with Tommy.

Kevin McArdle lost the decision by a narrow margin. McArdle had grown into a solid, mature fighter, and the new champion wasn't as good as the last. He wasn't bad, but he wasn't great. He was tall and lean, barely making weight at a hundred and seventy-seven pounds. His name was Ron Johnson and he was twenty-four years old. Mixed heritage, with milk-chocolate skin, green eyes, and rufous hair. He shifted his feet too much, wasting energy. When his arm was lifted in victory, he beamed, sweating.

"You'll take him," Loup murmured to her brother.

"You're sure?" Tommy asked.

She nodded. "Yeah."

Two weeks later, Floyd Roberts made his decision. The announcement was posted all over town. In three months' time,

Ron Johnson and Tom Garron would face each other in a prize match.

Outpost went wild.

Over half the town had seen Johnson's match against McArdle. Boxing was the only game in town. They knew their fighters, and they knew Tom Garron was their hero in waiting. They saw what Loup saw. This one, Tommy could take.

It put Miguel Garza in a fury.

He rounded up a group of his brother's henchmen. They descended on the gym, armed with lead pipes and lengths of chain, aiming to change the coach's mind. Floyd Roberts faced them down with his shotgun. After a five-minute standoff, an armored car filled with soldiers rolled to a stop in front of the former Unique Fitness building. Miguel and his boys ran. The next day, Danny Garza and Floyd Roberts had a private meeting in which the elder Garza sought to change the coach's mind by power of persuasion.

"No deal," Tommy reported to Loup. "Coach says Mig might have worked longer for this, but I've worked harder. He won't budge."

Loup thought. "You think Miguel might come after you?"

"Nah." Tommy shook his head. "Coach told Danny if anything happens to me, Mig will never get another shot at a prize match. Danny promised to keep him in line." His irrepressible grin bloomed. "This is *it*, Loup! The ticket, our ticket!"

She frowned. "Do you really believe the general will let us go?"

"Yeah. Yeah, I do." He laid his hands on her shoulders. "Look, I wondered, too. But I asked Coach. He knows General Argyle better than anyone. He said Bill Argyle's a man of his word. If he said it, he meant it. There might be conditions. We might have to sign some stuff, promise we won't talk about Outpost. They might have people watching us, so we'll have to be careful. But if I beat this guy, they *will* let us go." He hesitated and searched her face. "You do want to come with me, don't you?"

"Yeah." Loup thought about the unanswered prayers to Santa Olivia scrawled on the town's walls, about T.Y.'s apologies, Mack and Katya together, and Pilar angling to land one of the wealthy Salamanca boys. She thought about a new future opening before her. "More than anything, Tommy."

He kissed her cheek. "That's my girl."

TWENTY-FOUR

In the three months between the announcement and the match, excitement reached a fever pitch in Outpost.

Santa Olivia's name day came, and Loup turned fifteen. The remaining Santitos helped carry the saint's effigy into the town square. Under the watchful eyes of armed MPs, the townsfolk picnicked and celebrated. They didn't put petitions in Santa Olivia's basket—Father Ramon had effectively halted that practice—but they prayed openly for Tom Garron's success, beseeching the child-saint's aid. Fresh graffiti prayers appeared on the walls, outstripping the efforts to whitewash them.

And everywhere that Tommy went, he was mobbed by well-wishers.

Loup watched her brother move around the square, his bright blond head bobbing above the crowd.

"Damn!" Pilar murmured at her ear, near enough that her breast brushed against Loup's arm. "Are you *sure* he's not interested?"

Loup looked at her. "Jesus, Pilar!"

She flushed, drawing back. "*What?*"

Loup smiled wryly. "Nothing. I'll miss you."

"Yeah?" Pilar gave her a quizzical look. "Me, too. You're lucky." She was quiet a moment, then nodded at Tommy. "He's such a good guy, your brother. He looks out for you. I never had anyone in my family like that."

"He's the best," Loup agreed.

The Festival of Santa Olivia came and went. Tommy ignored the adulation and trained like hell. He trained in the gym, sparring with anyone who'd give him a bout. He lifted weights until his muscles burned, pushed through the pain and lifted more. He wrapped his hands and worked the bags. He ran endless laps through the town, bare-chested beneath the burning sun, the arid air burning off his sweat. He grilled Kevin McArdle on his match with Ron Johnson. He listened avidly to Coach Roberts and followed every piece of advice he gave. Still, the mantle of the town's adoration settled over his broad shoulders and clung to him, whether he willed it or not.

By the time the night of the match arrived, Tom Garron glowed.

It was the same scene it had always been, and yet, somehow different. General Argyle and the other ranking officers sat in the VIP seats. A throng of uniformed soldiers filled the rest of the bleachers. Outposters crammed every corner of the square, standing and craning to see.

The arc lights flared to life.

Tom Garron entered the ring, a frayed satin robe resting over his shoulders. The crowd roared when the announcer introduced him. Tommy raised one gloved fist in acknowledgment. The crowd roared some more. Men and women, young and a few old, children—the ragtag remnants of the town once known as Santa Olivia. All their hopes and dreams were pinned on him. He bore the burden with grace.

Loup cheered louder than anyone.

"And in this cor—" The announcer's voice cut out briefly as the lights dimmed, then returned as the generator hiccupped, and growled back into life. *"Weighing in at a hundred and seventy-eight pounds, the defending champion, Ron Johnson!"*

Hundreds of uniformed servicemen cheered, trying to rival the roar that had greeted Tommy. They didn't come close.

It didn't faze Ron Johnson. He entered the ring without fanfare, shrugging out of his robe to reveal the army's standard red-and-white trunks. The Outposters booed him.

Loup cocked her head.

Ron Johnson didn't throw any warm-up punches. He

stretched, cocking his head from side to side. Rolled his shoulders, bounced twice on his toes. Then he stood still, waiting.

Loup's skin prickled. "Tommy!" She called his name until he came over. "It's not the same guy."

"What?" He glanced over his shoulder. "Sure it is."

"No." She shook her head. "It looks like him, but it's not. He's wider through the shoulders and his hair's shorter."

"So he trained hard and got a haircut."

"*Look*." She pointed. "Look at the way he stands; look at the way the canvas sinks. Tommy, it's not the same guy." She lowered her voice. "I think he's like me."

Tommy looked again, then back at her. "You're seeing things," he said. "I know you're lonely and you don't want to be the only one. We'll talk about it later, okay?"

"*. . . touching moment as the young fighter's baby sister wishes him luck!*" the announcer improvised.

"What if I'm right?" Loup asked. "You'll get hurt. Bad."

"You're not," he said. "Even if you were, I've got ten pounds and two inches on him."

"Tommy, that's nothing! If I'm right, you don't have *any* pounds on him, and two inches is nothing! Even I—" The expression on his face stopped her.

"Garron!" Coach Roberts shouted. "We've got a fight here, boy!"

"You think you could take me," Tommy said incredulously. "I've spent my whole life training for this, and you actually think you could step into this ring, half my size, and take me down, don't you?"

Loup met his gaze without blinking. "Yeah, I do."

He turned away. "I've got a fight."

Once the boxers touched gloves, the bell rang and the fight started. All around Loup, people cheered wildly. She watched the first round feeling hollow inside, an emptiness where fear should be.

It wasn't obvious at first. Tommy was the better boxer. His

footwork was precise, his upper-body movement honed to the point of instinctiveness. His jabs were clean and crisp. But the wasted effort Ron Johnson had evinced in his fight against Kevin McArdle had disappeared. Although he didn't seem to move that quickly, somehow, he managed to move just enough that Tommy's punches didn't connect solidly, managed to sidestep out of every attempt to clinch. He didn't go on the offensive, making the crowd boo.

"He's slippery," Tommy said to Floyd Roberts when the first round ended. "McArdle didn't say he was so slippery."

"He's holding back!" Loup called in frustration, clutching the ropes.

Floyd squirted water into Tommy's mouth, ignoring her. "Let him come to you. He's a young fighter. The crowd'll get to him."

Loup glanced across the ring. Ron Johnson sat quietly in his corner, his expression unreadable. "No, it won't!"

"Loup." Floyd looked down at her. "Go away."

She watched Ron Johnson rise, watched the canvas dip under his weight. "Sir, there's no way he's fighting at a hundred seventy-eight. Ask for a new weigh-in. A public one. You didn't actually see it, did you?"

The coach blinked at her with colorless eyes, a slow scowl spreading across his face. "You're out of your mind, and even if you weren't, it wouldn't be the first time we've given a few pounds of leeway. Child, if you don't leave him be, I'll have you thrown out. Your brother doesn't need this nonsense."

Tommy wouldn't even look at her.

The second round dragged like the first. The crowd booed louder. Johnson didn't rise to the bait, remaining evasive on defense.

"Tommy's ahead on points though, right?" T.Y. offered, squeezing through the crowd to join Loup. "That's good, right?"

She shook her head. "This fight hasn't started."

It started in the third.

It started when Ron Johnson made a misstep and Tommy landed a solid punch, a punch he'd inherited from the Minnesota farmboy who had been his father, a lazing, looping left hook that seemed to begin slowly and landed with deceptive speed, clobbering Johnson's right ear. Johnson paused, dazed.

"*Oooh*," the announcer cried. "*Johnson got his bell rung!*"

Tommy skipped backward, shaking out his arm as though it stung. He knew, Loup thought. In that instant, when the first solid punch landed, he had to know.

"Move in, Garron! Move in on him!" Floyd Roberts shouted.

Ron Johnson glanced into the stands. Loup followed his gaze and saw the general nod.

The tide turned.

This time, when Tommy moved in on him, Johnson stood his ground. They exchanged a flurry of blows.

Loup winced.

"That guy's better than I remembered," T.Y. said.

"It's not the same guy," she said dully.

It didn't last long, and Johnson held back the whole time. He was being *careful*. She knew; she could tell. But he stepped it up, slowly, slowly. Tommy pressed him; Tommy was good. He kept his feet moving, kept dodging, threw combinations Johnson didn't expect. He kept scoring points, kept boxing well. It didn't matter. Johnson turned the heat on, degree by degree. He moved a little quicker, hit a little harder. He landed shots to the body that blossomed into bruises. Quick jabs that rocked Tommy's head back.

"Fuck him," Tommy said thickly at the end of the fourth. A silent Floyd smeared coagulant on a cut under one eye. "He's going down."

"Tommy." Loup clung to the ropes. "Take a dive."

He slewed his gaze around to her, still hurt and angry. "Fuck you!"

Tommy went down in the seventh. He took a right cross to the temple, then a left uppercut to the chin. His eyes rolled up in his head, showing the whites. His knees sagged. He hit the canvas hard.

The Outpost crowd wailed. Soldiers cheered.

As soon as the referee finished the count, army medics swarmed the ring. Within a minute, Tom Garron was on his feet, his face averted. The referee raised Ron Johnson's hand in victory.

"*Fucker!*" Loup stooped and found a pebble, threw it.

"Hey!" T.Y. said in alarm.

The rock grazed Ron Johnson's cheek. He looked at Loup with his calm green eyes. And then T.Y. wrestled her backward into the crowd and Father Ramon and Sister Martha and all the remaining Santitos were there, offering condolences. Depressed Outposters streamed past them. Loup shrugged them off, seeing her brother leave the ring, hooded beneath his robe, head bowed.

"Tommy," she breathed.

"Sorry." His shoulders twitched. "You were right. I tried. I had to try."

"It wasn't fair! We've got to tell someone."

He met her eyes. Beneath the shadow of his hood, the hurt and anger was gone, replaced by defeat. "It's not worth it. Go home, Loup. Go back with your friends. I'll talk to you later." He turned away.

"Tommy!" she protested.

"Let him be, now." Floyd Roberts interposed herself between them. He wasn't angry either, just sad. "Times like this, a man needs to be alone. He'll send for you when he's ready."

"That guy, Johnson, he's not normal," Loup said stubbornly.

The coach shook his head. "Let it go, child."

They left her, walking slowly away. The milling crowd made way for them. MPs began announcing that since the match had ended, curfew would begin for anyone without a permit. Soldiers began heading to bars to celebrate, though the mood in the square had even them somewhat subdued. Loup stood and watched Tommy and Floyd and others from the gym walk away, wondering why she still felt empty inside.

"Loup." Mack appeared, his voice gentle. "Come on. Everyone's waiting. We've got to go."

It was over.

TWENTY-FIVE

B ack at the church, the Santitos discussed the fight.
"You're sure?" Jaime asked Loup.

"Yeah." She nodded. "From the minute he walked out. He looked like him, but he didn't move anything like him."

"Twins?" Mack suggested. "But how could one be normal and the other . . ." He gestured. "Like Loup."

"Genetic experimentation," Jane said in a dark tone.

"Exactly," Jaime agreed. "Loup, you said your father and the others were taken into custody by the U.S. when they were boys, right? And they started to do experiments before the pandemic hit?"

"That's what he told my mother."

"Well, they sure as hell kept that DNA on file," Jaime said. "And whatever results they got." He glanced at the northern wall of the rec room, toward the distant border of the cordon where no-man's-land turned into a place called America. "They would have gone back to it when things calmed down. Started doing new experiments. Maybe trying to make their own breed of supermen." He looked back at them, glasses flashing. "Identical twins could be an important part of the experiment. It provides a built-in control group for any genetic alteration."

Pilar made a face. "Say it in English, Jaime."

He started explaining.

"Fuck that." C.C., lying on the floor, began bouncing a worn tennis ball off the opposite wall. "They *cheated*."

"So what do we do?" Katya asked. "Complain?"

Loup shook her head. "Tommy said it wasn't worth it."

"They'd probably bury it anyway," Jaime said. "All they have to do is bring out the original guy. We don't have any proof he's got a genetically modified twin. We'd sound like lunatics."

C.C. tossed the ball rhythmically. "So we're screwed?"

"Would you cut that out for ten seconds?" T.Y. leaned over from the couch and batted the ball out of his hands. "We're not screwed. It was one fight. Tommy has to demand a rematch, that's all."

"And have them pull the same shit?" Katya asked in a cynical tone.

"No." The idea kindled a spark of hope in Loup. "Coach Roberts has to make 'em do the weigh-in in public, that's all. Right in the ring, right before the fight, so there's no time to make a switch. Then they'd have to use the real guy."

"Who Tommy can beat," T.Y. concluded.

"Think your brother will go for it?" Mack asked Loup.

"I don't know." She thought about the way he'd looked afterward—depressed and defeated—then about how he'd looked before the fight—glowing. How he'd looked the day they'd snuck into the gym into the first place, how he'd lied about his age and begged the coach to train him. How hard he'd worked. "Yeah. Yeah, I do. Tommy's not a quitter."

Mack nodded sagely. "He just needs time to get over having his ass kicked." He yawned. "Okay. Tomorrow's another day. One way or another, we'll fight the good fight. 'Night, Santitos."

They dispersed to their bunks, feeling better for having discussed it. Tommy's stunning defeat had hit everyone hard. It felt good to have an explanation; better to have a plan.

Loup fell asleep picturing the rematch. She pictured Tommy fighting the real Ron Johnson and outboxing him at every turn. She imagined the general himself coming from the stands to raise Tommy's hand in victory and pictured Tommy's beaming grin, a grin wide enough to erase even the memory of the broken, beaten look he'd worn after the fight; that, and the hurt, betrayed look he'd turned on her earlier.

You didn't have to feel fear to hurt for someone you loved when they were in pain. But it could all be made better.

She fell asleep smiling.

She woke to lamplight and Sister Martha's face bending over her pillow.

"Loup." There was a world of sorrow in the Sister's voice.

The empty feeling came crashing back. "What is it?"

"There are men downstairs," Sister Martha murmured. "Soldiers. Mr. Roberts sent them to fetch you." She laid a hand on Loup's shoulder. "Tommy collapsed an hour ago. Mr. Roberts convinced them to take him to the medical facilities at the base. He thinks you should go."

Loup scrambled out of bed and reached for her clothes, moving without thinking.

"Jesus!" Katya grumbled, waking. "Is there a tornado in here?"

"What?" Pilar asked sleepily from an adjacent bunk.

"It's Tommy." Loup headed for the door. "I have to go."

"Loup." Sister Martha caught her arm, her voice urgent. "These are soldiers. Slow down. Be *careful*."

Loup shook her off. "I have to go."

At the sight of the soldiers in the antechamber, she caught herself out of habit. Careful. It wouldn't help Tommy if she was exposed. The soldiers stood at attention, waiting. Father Ramon was with them, looking old and tired.

"Are you Loup?" one of the soldiers asked. He had a kind face.

"Yes."

"I'm Sergeant Buckland and this is Private Simons." He reached out one hand. "We're here to take you to your brother."

She put her hands behind her back. "Okay."

He hesitated, then withdrew his hand. "Okay. This way, honey."

There was a jeep waiting in the street, its motor idling. Sergeant Buckland opened the door for Loup. She climbed into the backseat. She could feel the vibrations of the engine. The soldiers got into the front seats, Sergeant Buckland driving. The engine rumbled as he put the jeep into gear and accelerated, the vibrations growing stronger. Somewhere in the back of her mind, Loup thought that Mack would be jealous. He'd always admired cars. There was an old one in the garage he liked to tinker with, wondering what it would be like to make it run. None of them had ever ridden in one.

It felt strange.

So strange.

They drove through the town square. The center was dark, but the bars were still open. Soldiers were drinking, laughing, and flirting. Outposters with permits were pouring drinks, serving soldiers. There was a line at the torta vendor's cart.

They drove to the outskirts of town and kept going. Ahead, the base loomed. It wasn't lit up as much at night as Loup had imagined, only at the checkpoints. The first one was at the gate where the chain-link fence that surrounded the entire complex began. A soldier with a rifle over his shoulder approached the car when Sergeant Buckland stopped. Buckland and Simons showed him their ID cards and a piece of paper with their orders written on it. The soldier on guard duty leaned over, squinting at Loup.

"Okay." He waved them on.

Darkness, then another checkpoint. The same procedure, another guard waving them on to a different section of the base.

The base was huge, filled with enormous cinder-block buildings and anonymous streets. It was no wonder the soldiers tried to get out of there and spend time in Outpost whenever they could.

They parked in front of one of the big buildings. Loup shook her head when Sergeant Buckland tried to help her out of the jeep.

"It's gonna be okay, honey," he said kindly. "The army's got good docs. They'll fix your brother up."

The other soldier didn't say anything.

They showed their cards and papers to another guard at the door, then ushered Loup inside. It was bright inside, a harsh white light flooding everywhere. Everything seemed hard and polished and clean. Aside from the guard at the door and the soldiers escorting her, the men wore blue hospital scrubs like the ones that Pilar had sewn into a dress for Santa Olivia. Some had white coats over them, some didn't.

"This way."

They led her down a hallway. Even the floors seemed shiny. They passed rooms with beds. There was more machinery here than Loup had ever seen in her life. Despite the wealth of electricity they must have used, she couldn't even hear the omnipresent sound of a generator.

Another hallway, this one blank and featureless. And then through a set of doors and into a room with a few chairs. Floyd Roberts was there, talking to a tall man with blood spattered over his white doctor's coat. The coach turned his head and gazed at Loup. His colorless eyes were bloodshot.

The emptiness inside her expanded and swallowed everything.

"I'm sorry." Floyd Roberts came over and put his hands on her shoulders. "Tommy's gone."

She shook her head. "No."

He squeezed her shoulders, blinked his bloodshot eyes. "They did everything they could for him, Loup. *I* did everything I could."

It didn't make sense. "But he was okay!"

"Your brother suffered a subdural hematoma," the doctor said gently. "It means he was bleeding inside his brain. Sometimes it doesn't show up right away. We attempted to perform an emergency craniotomy, but we couldn't stop the hemorrhaging in time. I'm sorry."

The two soldiers who had escorted her removed their caps in a gesture of respect.

"No," Loup said again. "Tommy got up. He was *fine*."

"It only seemed that way," the doctor said even more gently. "I'm very, very sorry."

"Loup." Floyd squeezed her shoulders a second time. "Let the soldiers take you home. I'll take care of everything here."

She pulled away from him. "I want to see him."

"I don't think that's a good idea," he said.

"*Now.*"

The doctor drew Floyd away. They conferred in low tones. Then the doctor went away through another set of doors.

"Give him a minute," Floyd said wearily.

Loup waited without moving, staring fixedly at the doors. A few minutes later the doctor came back and beckoned to her. "Come with me."

He led her to a white room with a table in the middle of it. Tommy lay on the table with a sheet drawn up to his chest. His eyes were closed and his face was slack. A blue cap covered his head. The cut under his left eye had begun to close. Loup walked over to the table and touched his face. Only skin, only flesh. His body was empty.

"Tommy," she whispered. Her eyes burned with tears that wouldn't fall.

Empty.

She stood there for a long time, one hand on Tommy's cheek. When Floyd came to ease her away, she didn't budge.

"You have to go, Loup." When she didn't answer, he turned to the doctor. "I think she's in shock. She's rigid."

"Here." The doctor took her other hand. "Give me your arm, sweetheart."

She let him roll up her sleeve without protesting, gazing at Tommy's face. There was a prick when the needle went in, then a sensation of warmth spreading. She turned her head and stared at the doctor.

"It's just a sedative," he said softly. "It will help."

The shot made the emptiness recede. It took her will with it. It took her voice, too; or at least the will to speak. Nothing seemed real and there weren't any words left to say. This time when Floyd told her to go with the soldiers, Loup went.

They drove her back to the church in silence. It was late enough that Outpost had grown quiet. Father Ramon heard the jeep approaching and met them outside the gate, hollow-eyed with worry.

"Your brother?" he asked Loup.

She couldn't get the words out.

"I'm afraid he didn't make it," Sergeant Buckland answered for her. "The girl's in shock. The doc said he gave her a shot to help her through the worst of it. She hasn't said a word since." He touched the brim of his cap. "I sure am sorry, honey."

Loup nodded.

"God have mercy," Father Ramon murmured.

TWENTY-SIX

They buried Tom Garron the following afternoon.

It seemed like half the town came to the funeral. Everyone wept when Father Ramon gave the eulogy. People who had known Tommy spoke. Floyd Roberts. Kevin McArdle. Even Danny Garza gave a speech about Outpost's lost hope and the death of dreams. Loup heard it in a daze, dry-eyed. The Santitos surrounded her, offering comfort. She shook them off.

"Let her be," Mack said briefly.

At the grave site she watched Mack and C.C. shovel dirt. Miguel Garza approached her.

"I just want to tell you I'm real sorry, kid." He sounded genuine. "Your brother and me, we had our differences, but it wasn't nothing personal. I never wanted to see him go down like that." He hesitated. "And yeah, it could of been me. You ever need anything, tell me. I owe Garron one."

Loup nodded, wordless.

And then it was done. Father Ramon planted a makeshift cross that Mack had built at the head of the grave. Floyd Roberts hung Tommy's boxing gloves from the cross. After a moment of silence, the mourning crowd began to disperse.

Loup lay down on the sparse dusty grass, curled on her side.

This time there was no doctor to give her a shot and make her compliant. There was only a shell of emptiness encompassing a vast knot of pain. She wrapped herself around it. It had hurt when her mother had died, but this was worse, so much worse. It should have been Tommy's moment of triumph, the fulfillment of all his hopes and dreams. Instead, he was just *gone*.

No warning.

No time to say goodbye.

People talked to her, pulled at her. Sister Martha, Anna. The Santitos. Father Ramon. Their voices were distant and buzzing. She ignored them. All she wanted to do was lie still and hold the hurt in one place, because it felt like it would explode into a million pieces if she didn't.

"... can't just *leave* her!" Pilar protested.

"Ever see a dog get hurt?" Mack asked. "That's what they do. Hole up and wait to live or die. We all treat Loup like she's one of us. She's *not*."

"We'll give her time." Father Ramon's deep voice. "But I want someone to stay with her. I don't want our Santa Olivia doing anything foolish."

"I'll stay," T.Y. volunteered.

"We'll take shifts," Mack agreed.

As the sun crawled across the sky and sank in the west, they came and went. Loup was aware of them in a vague way, some more than others. T.Y. talked to her and tried to lift her spirits. Jane tried to reason with her, alternately coaxing and scolding. C.C. chattered incessantly, driving her deeper into herself. Dondi pleaded.

Day turned to night.

Jaime sat cross-legged, reading a book by the light of a kerosene lantern; and then Mack came, also blessedly silent. Hours passed. He didn't speak at all until Pilar came to relieve him, wrapped in a woolen blanket.

"Hey."

"Hey. She okay?"

Mack shrugged. "Dunno."

Everyone else had left her alone, had only talked at her. Pilar plopped down beside her, felt at her. "Jesus! You're stiff as a board. Are you cold?" She tugged insistently at Loup's shoulders, shifting her head onto her lap. "C'mere, baby."

The shell of emptiness cracked, letting in a ray of exasperation.

"Pilar." Loup opened her eyes onto darkness and spoke for the first time since seeing Tommy's body. Her voice came out low and hoarse. "Don't fuck with me. Not tonight."

"Shhh." Pilar stroked her. "Be quiet."

That was all. Over and over, as though she was soothing a child or petting a cat, and yet not. It was warm, rhythmic, and comforting. And as much as Loup wanted to resist it, her locked muscles loosened bit by bit, and the tight knot of pain inside her began to unravel and unknit. It didn't explode. It just hurt.

"That's better," Pilar whispered, cupping her cheek. "You can't cry like regular people, can you?"

"No," Loup murmured. "Tommy said I cried when I was a baby, but even then there were never any tears."

"You can have my tears." Pilar traced the curve of her lashes with one finger. "I cried all afternoon."

"It's not that."

"Tell me."

Loup gazed at darkness. "I should've stopped the fight. Tommy knew. The first time he hit the guy, he *knew* I was right. I told him to take a dive, but he was mad. Because I told him, yeah, I could take him. I shouldn't have said it. I should've just stopped the fight."

"You tried, didn't you?" Pilar asked softly.

"I shouldn't have *tried*. I should've just done it." She moved her head. "All I had to do was climb into the ring. I could've made that Johnson guy show what he really was. And I didn't."

Pilar's hands went still, then resumed, warm and soothing. "Yeah, and they would've taken you away if you had. Baby, Tommy would have hated that more than anything. Swear to God, your brother would *rather* have fucking died than lose you that way."

"He did," Loup whispered.

"I told you, that boy loved the hell out of you." Pilar stroked her hair. "You know, it's funny. The two of you didn't look a thing alike. But the way his face would light up whenever he came to fetch you, I don't think anyone in the world ever doubted he was your big brother."

"Yeah?"

"Yeah."

The ache of loss shifted, settling into her bones. Loup sighed. "Aw, Jesus! It's not *fair*."

"No," Pilar said with sorrow. "It's not."

"I listened to Tommy all my life! Why couldn't he listen to me just once when I told *him* to be careful?"

"I don't know, baby." Her hands moved steadily. "I wish he had."

Loup closed her burning eyes. "So do I."

For a while, that was all. It was enough. They were quiet. The stars moved across the big desert sky. The lantern burned low, guttering.

"Honey?" Pilar shifted, her voice apologetic. "You think maybe you're ready to go inside? My legs are falling asleep, and if you stay out here any longer, Katya's up next. We all agreed to take turns."

"Yeah." Loup levered herself upright, extending one hand. "Okay."

"Okay." Pilar rose with her aid, her body stiff, the blanket still draped over her shoulders. They stood, hands loosely clasped. "It's okay to be sad, baby. It is. It's okay. We're all sad."

"Yeah?" Loup asked.

"Yeah." Pilar kissed her. First her cheek, then on the mouth. Her tongue slid past Loup's lips, quick and darting at first, then lingering. It felt very good and very surreal. "Umm." She pressed two fingers against Loup's lips. "Let's say we just dreamed that part, okay?"

"Jesus, Pilar," Loup murmured against her fingers.

"Come on."

She let Pilar lead her back to the church without arguing. She didn't have the heart for it. Whatever was between them would wait.

There were a handful of people waiting up, sitting around the table in the dining hall. Father Ramon, Sister Martha. Anna, all the older Santitos. They gazed at Loup with questions in their eyes.

"I'm okay," she said. "I just want to sleep."

Their expressions eased. They let her be, let her climb the stairs in peace. In the darkened room the girls shared, Loup crawled into bed without bothering to remove her clothes. She closed her eyes and fell asleep, taking her grief with her.

TWENTY-SEVEN

L oup slept for twelve hours.

When she awoke, it was afternoon and Tommy was still dead. She sat on her bed for a while, feeling the deep ache of loss and watching dust motes sparkle in the slanting sunlight.

She made a decision.

Downstairs, the church had returned to its normal routine. Katya and T.Y. were washing dishes after serving lunch to a few dozen parishioners. They gave Loup tentative smiles when she entered the kitchen.

"I was supposed to be on KP duty," she said, remembering.

Katya shook her head. "Not today."

Anna came in carrying a half-empty pot of soup. "Are you hungry, honey?" she asked hopefully. "Soup's still warm."

"Thanks." She felt them watch her eating and finished quickly. "I'm gonna go over to the gym. I was pretty rude to Mr. Roberts, and he really did try to save Tommy. I need to thank him."

They exchanged doubtful glances. "I'll be back by dinner," Loup added. "I promise."

"I'll go with you," T.Y. said, drying his hands.

She shook her head. "I'd rather go alone."

"Do you swear that's all you're doing?" Anna knit her brows. "Really and truly?"

"Really and truly," Loup agreed. "I'm going to talk to Mr. Roberts and I'll be back by dinner."

Anna sighed. "I guess it's okay."

The town felt different as she walked along the streets. Smaller, emptier. More drab. Tommy's death had crushed one more spark of Outpost's spirit. When she reached Unique Fitness, she found it locked up tight. The big windows through which Tommy had gazed so avidly long years ago had been painted black on the inside. Someone had written on the outside of the glass with a wax candle.

SANTA OLIVIA, WHY HAVE YOU FORSAKEN US?

Loup began pounding on the door.

It took a long time for Floyd Roberts to answer, but she was patient and didn't tire easily. She set up a steady, rhythmic banging and kept it up until Floyd came and yanked the door open. His eyes were still bloodshot and his expression was furious. He had a bottle of whiskey in one hand and his shotgun cradled in his arm. When he saw her, his expression changed.

"Loup."

"Can I talk to you, sir?"

He hesitated, then gestured with the bottle. "Might as well. You're about the only person I can stand to see right now."

She followed him into the gym. It felt dark and cavernous with the windows painted over, but underneath the paint fumes, it smelled the same, like sweat and mildew.

Floyd took a long pull on his whiskey bottle. "You do know how goddamned sorry I am about your brother, right?"

"Yes, sir." Loup nodded. "Thank you."

"I loved that boy like a son." He sloshed the bottle. "Never told him, of course. Not my way. But he was good-natured as the day was long. Worked like a horse, never complained. And my God, he loved to box!" He took another pull. "It was a fluke. A goddamned fluke."

"What's a fluke?"

The coach squinted at her. "An unlikely accident."

"Oh." Loup took a deep breath. "I want you to train me. I want to beat the guy that killed Tommy."

A series of emotions crossed his face, settling on sadness. He set the whiskey bottle down on the edge of the nearest boxing ring. "I understand, child. I truly do. But that's not the way. I can't teach a little girl to fight."

"I'm a year older than Tommy was when you started teaching him," she said. "Two years. He lied about his age."

"Sonofabitch," Floyd murmured. "That doesn't—"

"And I'm almost five foot six. Tim Roscovich's the same height and you train him."

"He fights as a welterweight," he replied without thinking, then caught himself. "Loup, for God's sake—"

"Weigh me." She met his eyes. "Weigh me like I begged you to weigh the guy who killed Tommy. I weigh enough to fight in his class. He's the one that doesn't. It wasn't a *fluke*. It wasn't the same guy. And I'm like him. I know he's bigger and taller and heavier, but he's not a very good boxer. He never had to be. Make me one, and I'll beat him."

"Loup." Floyd retrieved his bottle and drank. "Grief does strange things to people, child. Go home."

"Remember the jump rope?" she pressed him. "A long time ago? I didn't lie. I'd never used one before. You wondered. You've wondered."

He closed his eyes. "Go home."

"And I wasn't in *shock* the other night. That's just the way I am."

"Loup—"

"Watch." She waited until he opened his eyes, then walked over to the nearest heavy bag. It hung inert from its chain. She cocked her head, studying it, then hit it hard, putting all her weight behind the punch. The bag jumped, the chain rattling. A seam split open, sand trickling out.

Floyd Roberts stared at her. "You overreached," he said at length. "In a fight, you'd have left yourself overextended and off balance if that hadn't landed."

"I was trying to make a point," Loup said mildly.

"So I see." He watched the sand trickle. "What are you?"

She fished her most treasured relic from the back pocket and handed the brittle, yellowing page to him. "I don't know. My father was one of these guys."

He scanned the article. "This is tripe."

Loup shrugged and took it back, folding it carefully. "Maybe. I dunno. Anyway, he was different and so am I. And so was the guy who killed Tommy. Jaime says if any of it's true, the army would have kept samples of their DNA. That they would have done experiments. Maybe with twins. So will you train me?"

"Twins," he murmured.

She nodded.

"I am too goddamned drunk to be having this conversation." Floyd looked at the bottle in his hand, then at Loup. "Santa Olivia. That was you, wasn't it? You threw a two-hundred-pound rock through a jeep's windshield?"

"Yeah."

"Christ have mercy." He raised his gaze to the ceiling. "I should turn you in. You know I should. I'm not on your side, Loup Garron. I've done my best to train fighters in Outpost, but I'm not one of you. I'm an American citizen. I'm doing a job, a favor to an old friend. While I'm here, I answer to Bill Argyle. I answer to the U.S. Army."

"They tricked you and Tommy's dead. Will you train me?"

For a long time, he didn't answer, only stared at the ceiling. She didn't know what he'd say, what he'd decide. Only that she had to ask. Loup waited, patient and motionless, while her fate hung in the balance. And after a long, long time, his gaze returned, colorless and bloodshot, but resolute.

"Yes."

TWENTY-EIGHT

Loup kept her word and made it back in time for dinner, where she ate her way steadily through three plates of food.

"Holy shit," C.C. observed. "You gonna start on the table next?"

"C.C.," Sister Martha murmured in reproach.

"I didn't eat anything yesterday," Loup said. It was true; grief had eradicated her appetite. It wasn't why she was ravenous, though. She was ravenous because Floyd had begun testing the limits of her abilities. He wouldn't let her hit the bags or lift the heaviest weights, but he'd let her run on one of the treadmills as fast and long as she wanted. Or at least he had until the motor began to smell hot.

"Are you feeling a little better today?" Pilar asked.

"Yeah." Loup glanced at her. Her voice softened involuntarily. "Thanks."

Pilar turned pink and looked away. "Sure."

No one would let Loup clean and clear when dinner was over, so she asked Father Ramon and Sister Martha if she could talk to them in private.

"Of course, child," Father Ramon said kindly. "Whatever you need."

He didn't look so beneficent when she told them her plan.

Sister Martha looked appalled. "Coach Roberts *agreed* to this?" she asked incredulously. "Was the man drunk?"

"Yeah, kinda," Loup said. "But I think he meant it."

"Loup." Father Ramon shook his head. "I can't let you throw your life away like this."

"What life?" She shrugged. "What have I got left with Tommy

gone? You made me promise to stop pretending to be Santa Olivia. The Santitos are all growing up in ways I'm not a part of." That wasn't *entirely* true, but it might as well be if Pilar was going to kiss her, then tell her to pretend it never happened. "There's nothing I can do to help you guys that someone else doesn't do better except dig graves. But this, this I can do. And I want to do it."

"Of course you do," Sister Martha said gently. "Honey, you're upset and grieving, and yes, you have very . . . unusual . . . gifts. Give yourself time to heal. Vengeance is never the answer."

"It's not vengeance." Loup struggled to find the right words. "I don't want to kill the guy. I don't think he meant to kill Tommy. It was a, a *fluke*. I just want to beat him. I want to make it happen the way it was supposed to happen."

"He'll have rotated out of service by the time you're ready," Father Ramon observed.

"Ramon!" Sister Martha exclaimed.

"Well, he will."

"Yeah." Loup nodded. "Coach Roberts thought of that. He said it'll take at least three years to make me good enough if I'm right about the guy, and even then it's a long shot. But he's pretty sure if General Bill doesn't die or retire before then, he can get him to bring the guy back. And if he can't . . ." She shrugged again. "Maybe they've got others like him. I dunno. I'll fight whoever they give me. It wouldn't be as good, but the point is to win. To make Tommy's dream come true. It's what everyone wanted."

Father Ramon eyed her.

"You cannot possibly be considering this," Sister Martha said to him.

He ignored her. "You do know that win or lose, they'll take you into custody?" he asked Loup. "There's not going to be any magic ticket north for you."

"I know. But maybe it'll be better than spending my life digging graves, pretending to be something I'm not, and dying young." She held Father Ramon's gaze. "And there *might* be one for someone else if the general keeps his word. Maybe even two. That's what he's always promised, one for the winner and whoever they pick. The coach thinks it's possible."

"Jesus," Sister Martha murmured.

Loup looked at her. "Sister, I'm gonna do this one way or another. I need a place to train in secret. If you're willing to help, it'll be a lot easier. Coach'll donate some equipment, say it's in Tommy's memory. We can push Father Gabriel's old car out of the garage and set it up in there. But it probably means that they'd figure out that you helped when it comes to the fight, so if you don't want to, I understand."

"Loup's father might have been a deserter, but she was born here in Outpost, after all," Father Ramon said. "It's not a crime to help her. There's no statute about harboring the illegitimate offspring of genetically altered soldiers."

"There would be if it had occurred to them!" Sister Martha said tartly. "It's only common sense." She was silent a moment. No one else spoke. "They'll know one thing for sure," she said at length. "They'll know we sheltered Santa Olivia."

Her words hung in the air.

"Yes," Father Ramon said in a wondering tone. "They will indeed."

Sister Martha sighed.

Loup looked from one to the other. "Does that mean yes or no?"

"Maybe God does move in mysterious fucking ways." Sister Martha rose. "I think it means yes."

When Loup told Floyd Roberts the next day, he gave a grunt of approval. "Good. Let me make a couple of calls. I'll have it delivered."

"Yeah?" Loup said in surprise.

He smiled sourly. "What were you going to do, hump it across town on foot? There are folks in the army feel pretty bad about your brother's death. Let me put 'em to work for you. Just keep your head down."

"Yes, sir."

"Good girl." Floyd patted her head. "I want you to start slow while I have time to think about this. We're going to need a plan. No boxing, no fostering bad habits until I have the chance to teach you myself. You remember how I started Tommy?"

"Jumping rope," she said.

"Right. And that I know you can do." He hefted her right arm, felt at her muscle tone. "You want to press weights, I guess that's okay. Don't think we have to worry about these bones turning brittle." He nodded at the nearest bench. "Show me your technique."

Loup trotted over obediently. The barbell in the cradle held two hundred and twenty-five pounds. She positioned herself and did a set of fifteen reps, slow and steady, then eased the bar back into the cradle.

"Wrong!" Floyd poked her hard in the belly. "Warm up and stretch first. Always. Understand?"

"Yes, sir."

He looked sideways at the barbell. "Jesus lord God. All right. It was fine otherwise. Keep it light, whatever that means for you. Don't . . ." He sucked meditatively on the inside of his cheek. "Don't try to press more than three hundred for now. You're still a kid. Lots of sets. Wide grip, close grip. Alternate. Use a spotter. Got it?"

Loup sat up. "Yeah."

"Conditioning," Floyd mused. "That's going to be a big part. You're right; our man's not going to work as hard because he doesn't have to. But it's sure as hell not going to be enough. Still, it's a starting place." He scratched his stubbled chin. "All right. You'll get your gear tomorrow. Do what I told you. Treadmill. Jump rope. Bench. Nothing more. Come back in a week, and we'll talk. Okay?"

"Okay."

The next morning, Loup recruited Mack and T.Y. to help her clear the church's garage and told them why. There wasn't much in the garage except the old maroon Mercedes that had belonged to Father Gabriel, dead before any of them were born. Mack, who knew about cars even though he'd never driven one, climbed behind the wheel and put it in neutral. Loup and T.Y. pushed it out of the garage and onto the cobbled drive.

"Sweet." Mack got out of the car and patted its chassis. "Bet this baby could go back in the day." His hard gray gaze settled on Loup. "So you're really gonna do it, huh? No matter what?"

"Yeah." She nodded. "Will you help?"

T.Y. rumpled his sweat-damp hair. "Fuck yeah, we'll help!"

The coach was as good as his word. Ten minutes later, a military supply truck pulled up outside the gates and honked its horn.

"Hey!" Sergeant Buckland leaned out of the passenger-side window. "Got a delivery here for the Little Saints of Santa Olivia! Any takers?"

His men unloaded the equipment with deft efficiency, uniformed soldiers hauling a bench press and innumerable weights and dumbbells, a motorless treadmill, a heavy bag and a speed bag and countless other pieces of flotsam and jetsam into the garage.

"Guess you boys will have fun with this, huh?" the sergeant asked Mack.

Mack smiled thinly. "Guess we will."

"Hey." He spotted Loup, who was trying to keep her head down, and came over to sling an arm around her shoulders. "How you doing, honey?"

She pulled away. "Okay."

Sergeant Buckland repeated the words he'd spoken the night Tommy died, his voice soft and sincere. "I sure am awfully sorry about your brother."

"Thanks," Loup murmured.

"Okay." He patted her awkwardly. "You take care, now."

The soldiers left and the Santitos set about installing the equipment. Loup was holding the heavy bag up while Mack stood on a ladder and secured the chain around a beam when Pilar wandered into the garage.

"Hey, wow," Pilar said to T.Y., who was arranging weights on a rack. "What's going on?"

"Loup's gonna train to fight the guy who killed Tommy," he informed her.

There was a brief silence. "Are you *serious*?"

"Hell, yeah!"

"Okay," Mack called down. "See if it holds."

Loup let go of the bag. It swayed gently. The beam creaked, but it held. She turned around. "Where'd Pilar go?"

T.Y. shrugged. "Dunno. Why?"

She sighed and contemplated the equipment. "No reason, I guess."

TWENTY-NINE

It helped.

It helped to have something to do. All the grief, all the sorrow, all the emptiness and anger—Loup channeled it into physical activity.

She skipped rope.

She lifted weights.

She ran on the treadmill until it broke and Mack had to fix it, and then she ran some more.

When a week had passed, she went back to the gym and met with Floyd Roberts. This time, his eyes weren't bloodshot. He showed her different exercises with barbells and dumbbells and gave her a chart with a weekly regimen.

"Understand?" he asked.

Loup nodded. "Yes, sir."

It was mindless work, but it felt good. Good to push until her muscles burned and ached with fatigue. Sets and sets of reps and reps. Loup resumed her chores around the church. Every free moment, she spent in the garage. She worked relentlessly, mindlessly, fixed on a single goal.

"You have officially become the most boring person on the planet," T.Y. informed her.

"Read to me."

He cracked open the yellowing pages of an old novel. " 'It was the best of times, it was the worst of times; it was the age of wisdom, it was the age of foolishness . . .' Are you sure?"

Loup ran, going nowhere. "Just keep reading."

T.Y. read.

They helped; they all helped, the Santitos. Except Pilar, who had set about ignoring her in a determined fashion. The others read stories to her. Jaime and Jane read articles from old science magazines. They took turns spotting her while she lifted weights, steady and patient.

Pilar continued to ignore her.

"Show me." Floyd held up his hands, covered in defensive punch mitts. "I want to see a jab, a straight jab. Nothing else."

She punched.

Left.

Right.

Left.

He grunted. "Don't *lean*, child!"

"Sorry," Loup murmured.

"You hit like a goddamned truck." He repositioned her with impersonal hands. "But in a real fight, the goddamned truck's going to hit back. Again."

Footwork and shadowboxing. Sometimes she thought about Tommy while she trained. Sometimes as a goad, remembering the hurt on his face when she'd told him she could take him. Remembering the way he'd snapped at her when she told him to take a dive. Remembering his face, slack and lifeless, on the operating room table. But mostly about the good times. How he was always trying to protect her from herself. How his face lit up when he saw her, just as Pilar had said.

All the memories of Tommy made her heart ache.

She thought about Pilar, too.

Floyd reopened the gym. He scrubbed the black paint from the windows, replacing it with blinds. He procured a permit for Loup so she could be out during curfew. In the early mornings and late evenings, he closed the blinds and taught her. Different punches, then combinations. He let her start working the bags. Days and weeks passed, marked by the steady rhythm of punching.

The Santitos continued to grow and change. Mack turned eighteen and Father Ramon offered him a job as the church's handyman and a private room above the garage. Mack accepted.

Katya broke up with him and started dating Sergeant Buckland.

For the space of a month, the church acquired two new orphans after a house fire killed their parents—a brother and sister with shocked, traumatized faces. They spent a lot of time clinging to Pilar. For as much as she'd complained about taking care of her aunt's children, she was good with kids. But then an uncle surfaced from a monthlong bout of grief-stricken drunkenness and came to claim them.

Loup kept working.

Pilar kept ignoring her.

It wasn't until Diego and Maria's wedding, four months after Tommy's death, that Loup found a chance to talk to her. The wedding was small; aside from the Santitos and church staff, only a couple of friends that Diego and Maria had made since they left were in attendance. But it was a warm affair, the first joyous occasion since before Tommy had died. The reception was held in a seldom-used hall and Father Ramon had managed to procure a case of champagne for it.

"I'll serve," Pilar offered. "Joe's teaching me to bartend."

Loup waited until everyone else's glass was full before she approached the table. Pilar poured a glass deftly and handed it to her without meeting her eyes.

"Wow." Loup sipped. "Bubbly."

"Yeah, well, it's champagne."

"Pilar." She set down the glass. "Why are you mad at me?"

Pilar looked past her. "You can't guess?"

"No." Loup reached across the table and touched her wrist. "Look, I didn't tell anyone. But—"

"It's not that." Pilar did look at her then. She shook her head. "Jesus, Loup! Never mind. If you can't figure it out, it's not worth talking about. Leave me alone, okay?"

"*I'm* not the one—"

"Hey!" C.C. bounded up behind her, extending his empty glass. "This stuff rocks! One of us should get married every day!"

"Gimme that." Pilar grabbed his glass and refilled it. "There you go, loverboy."

He grinned at her. "Wanna get back together? Just for the night?"

"Maybe," she replied in a teasing tone. "Ask me later after I've had a few."

"Deal!" C.C. said cheerfully, bounding away.

"Here." Pilar's voice changed. She picked up Loup's glass and thrust it at her. "Just forget about it, okay? Forget it ever happened."

"*Why*?" Loup asked in frustration.

Pilar folded her arms. "Because."

That was all. Loup watched Pilar pour and flirt. She watched Diego and Maria dance when the hired guitarist began to play, gazing into each other's eyes. She watched Father Ramon and Sister Martha dance together, and watched Anna watch them, calm and contented. Jaime and Jane—still bickering, still together. Dondi, grown unexpectedly tall, squiring one of Diego and Maria's newfound friends with newfound gallantry. Katya agreeing to dance with TY, since her sergeant wasn't in attendance. Pilar abandoning her station to dance with C.C. They started making out on the dance floor with considerable abandon.

"Hey, *loup-garou*." Mack touched her shoulder.

She shivered. "Tommy used to call me that."

"Yeah, I know." His calloused fingertips brushed the nape of her neck, hesitated, pulled away. "I'm sorry. You wanna dance?"

"Sure."

Mack held her with resolve.

"You don't have to fake it," Loup said, resigned.

"I don't mean to." He touched her lips, his gray eyes unwontedly gentle. "It's just—"

"Weird?"

"Yeah." He kissed her softly. "Weird."

THIRTY

L oup dated Mack for the rest of the year. It wasn't good, but it wasn't bad, either. In an odd way, it was comfortable. It was one more thing to help keep the grief at bay. Mack understood her better than the rest of the Santitos. He was patient and gentle, and he kept trying long after the others had given up.

Not long after they started dating, there was a rematch scheduled between Ron Johnson and Kevin McArdle. The news sifted slowly through Outpost, received with apprehension.

"What happened to Mig?" Loup asked Floyd Roberts. "I thought it was his turn."

"Superstitious," he said laconically. "He won't do it. Will you come? I want you to take a look at the guy."

She didn't hesitate. "Yeah."

The night of the fight, she studied Ron Johnson as he entered the ring. Watched the way he moved, the way he stood, the way the canvas dipped under his weight. Floyd raised his white eyebrows in inquiry.

Loup shook her head. "That's the original guy. The one Kevin fought before. It's not the guy who killed Tommy."

The coach nodded. "I told McArdle something was hinky with Tom's fight. I'll let him know this one ought to be clean."

The fight was pretty awful. The crowd was sparse, subdued, and anxious. Even the military spectators weren't rooting hard for the guy who'd accidentally killed a local hero. Kevin McArdle was pale and sweating, nervous and off his game. When he got knocked down in the ninth by a glancing blow that caught him off balance, he almost stayed down for the count.

The Outpost crowd rallied and cheered when McArdle rose in

time. He managed to finish the fight, and although he lost by an overwhelming margin, they cheered him for surviving.

"I'm finished," he told Floyd calmly when he left the ring.

The coach nodded. "I understand. But you did a good thing, son."

It helped leaven the town's despair. The Festival of Santa Olivia came and Loup turned sixteen. The town square was filled with picnics and music, kids chasing one another with hollow eggs filled with confetti.

A year ago, everyone had been praying for Tom Garron's success. She found herself looking for him, trying to spot that bright blond head that stood out above the crowd.

Instead, she saw Pilar, laughing and flirting with some guy Loup didn't know. One of Salamanca's gang, probably. Pilar had gotten bored with Joe the Bartender. When she broke up with him, he promptly offered her a job. She was good for business. Now she worked an afternoon shift at the bar almost every day, and came home almost every week with some love token from a besotted patron.

"Told you you'd start hooking," Mack had said cynically.

Pilar had shrugged, complacent. "I get paid for pouring drinks. The rest is just shopping around."

Now she caught Loup's eye and for once didn't look away. Instead she came over, suitor in tow. "Hey, this is Eric. He said you guys used to kick each other's asses back in the day."

"Thought you looked familiar," Mack said.

Eric shook his hand. "You're the guy with the broomstick."

Mack gave his hard smile. "Yeah."

"You doing okay?" Pilar asked Loup, her voice soft. "I was thinking about your brother earlier. All of this kinda reminded me."

"Me, too." Loup swallowed. "Thanks."

"Sure." Her gaze lingered. "Be extra nice today, Mackie."

"You bet."

They both watched Pilar's ass as she walked away.

That night, Loup lost her virginity in Mack's room above the garage. "I want to do it," he said adamantly. "I *want* to want it."

It wasn't bad, but it wasn't good, either.

He shuddered inside her, coming into a rubber. "Jesus! Ow!"

"Did I hurt you?"

Mack rolled off her. "That's what I'm supposed to ask."

"You didn't." Loup regarded him. "But I did, didn't I?"

"Honestly?" He took a deep breath. "Yeah, you might say it's too much of a good thing. It's a little like having your dick stuck in a vice grip." He cupped her cheek. "Loup, it's no good for you, either. And I don't know how to make it good for us. I wish I did."

"I know." She sat up, wrapped her arms around her knees. "It's not your fault. Maybe it's just like what Tommy said. Or maybe I'm just not into guys."

"Girls?"

"Maybe." Loup shook her head. "I dunno. I got Jane to give me a kissing lesson once, and it wasn't any different than it was with you or T.Y. or anyone else. But . . ."

"But what?" Mack prompted.

She smiled sideways at him. "Pilar kissed me once, too. She doesn't want anyone to know."

He snorted. "Yeah, that would fuck with her plans to marry a Salamanca." He hesitated. "It was different?"

"Yeah." Loup rested her cheek on her knees. "It was."

"Poor you." Mack pushed himself upright and stroked her hair. "Do you want to keep trying to make this work? Or do you want to say we tried and go back to being friends?"

She lifted her head. "We'd still be friends?"

"Always."

"Yeah?" Loup drew a line down the thin white scar that creased Mack's face. "I guess maybe that would be best. But thanks for trying. And thanks for tonight."

Mack smiled. "That's what I'm supposed to say."

"I know." She smiled back at him, leaned forward, and kissed him. She wished she didn't feel his tiny shudder of involuntary withdrawal. It was subtle, but it was there. "I better go."

After Mack, there was only training.

Two weeks after her sixteenth birthday, Floyd Roberts took a step he'd never taken before. On one of the evenings when they were meant to train, he invited Loup into his inner sanctum. He had a roof garden atop the Unique Fitness building, a burgeoning wealth of potted plants, thriving despite the desert air. A patio table and a pair of comfortable chairs.

"Wow." Loup gazed around. "Did Tommy know about this?"

"Yes." Floyd set down a bottle of whiskey. "He did."

"You met with him up here?"

"I did." He poured two measures of whiskey. "Sit. I missed your birthday. You're allowed one drink to celebrate." Floyd passed her a heavy package. "Here."

She opened them to find four weighted straps.

"Wrist and ankle weights." He picked up his glass and gestured. "Use them while you train. That way, you'll fight lighter and stronger without them."

"Thanks," Loup said.

"You're welcome." Floyd drained his glass and set it down with a bang. "So I talked to Bill last week. General Argyle. I told him I was training a young fighter who was better than anyone I'd ever seen, better than Tom Garron. A young fighter who has sworn to beat the man who killed Tom Garron."

"Yeah?"

"Yes." He refilled his glass. "Suffice it to say that he's intrigued."

"Good," Loup said simply.

"Good, yes. I've been thinking. All this while, I've been thinking." Floyd exhaled whiskey fumes. "We have one—*one!*—advantage in this fight. And that's that we know what we're up against and they don't." He nodded. "Hence the weights. But it's not enough. It's not nearly enough." He leaned forward. "Loup, you've got to train for one very specific fight, one against a bigger, stronger opponent. We can't do stronger, but we can do bigger. You need a sparring partner. And you need a good one."

She sipped her whiskey, feeling it burn on her tongue. "Mack would do it."

"Your boyfriend?" The coach shook his head. "No, no, no! I mean *good*. I was thinking of asking McArdle. How do you feel about trusting him?"

Loup tilted her head. The sun was setting, the sky streaked with orange and purple. From the rooftop vantage point, she could see the tops of the high cliffs that flanked Outpost. "What about Miguel?"

"Miguel Garza?"

She nodded. "At Tommy's funeral, he told me to ask if I ever needed anything. He said he reckoned he owned Tommy one on account of Tommy dying in a fight Mig wanted for himself. That's why he's superstitious now. But he's good, isn't he?"

"Garza?" Floyd sighed. "When he wants to be, yes. Do you trust him?"

Loup rolled another sip of whiskey over her tongue. She remembered Mig threatening that he had his eye on her. "Not exactly."

"So why not McArdle?"

She drank the rest of the whiskey at one gulp, savoring the rush of heat down her throat, the sense of her head lightening. "Because I do trust Miguel Garza to do one thing, sir, and that's hit me as hard as he fucking well can. And that's what it's gonna take to get me ready, isn't it?"

He nodded grimly. "You have a point."

THIRTY-ONE

A few days later, they met in the gym after hours.

Coach Roberts had asked Miguel to stay after his workout, and Miguel had agreed with a mix of irritation and curiosity. No one thought Loup's presence there was odd. She'd nearly grown up there as a child. After Tommy's death, she'd taken on a few of the odd jobs he did around the place, keeping the equipment clean and working. This evening, she made herself more unobtrusive than usual.

"Whaddya want, Coach?" Miguel asked when the last fighter had left.

Floyd Roberts locked the door and pulled the blinds. He beckoned Loup over. "I'm looking for a sparring partner for Loup."

Miguel's nostrils flared. He didn't laugh. "She's a girl."

"I know."

"A *kid*."

"Sixteen," Floyd acknowledged.

Miguel folded his arms over his bare chest, muscles swelling. He'd stripped off his training gloves, but he hadn't showered yet and his skin gleamed with sweat. He was thicker than Tommy, built like a bull. He eyed Loup. "Is this a joke?"

She held his gaze. "No."

"You." Miguel shook his head. "There's always been something off about you, kid. Something not quite right. Loopy Lou." He traced circles in the air beside his head. "Think she's gotten to you, Coach. Better have your head examined."

"Tom Garron didn't fight the same man Kevin McArdle did," Floyd said. "They looked alike, but they weren't. Loup's sure of it and I believe her. The man who killed Tom Garron was . . . different. So is Loup."

Something shifted in Miguel's expression. "Prove it."

The coach brandished a pair of punch mitts. "Do you want to pitch or catch?"

Miguel cracked his knuckles. "Whaddya think?"

"You got it." Floyd tossed the punch mitts to Loup. She slid her hands into them, tightening the straps, then took up a defensive pose. "Ready?"

"Yeah." She nodded at Miguel.

He threw two punches at her padded hands—straight jabs, nothing fancy. But he hit hard, harder than Loup expected. Lazy and superstitious or not, he had explosive punching power and he didn't hold back. She stood her ground and caught both his punches without yielding an inch. She felt the impact of it all the way to her bones. It made her body reverberate, made her grin with unexpected delight.

"Jesus!" Miguel blew out his breath.

"Convinced?" Floyd asked him.

He shook his head. "Gimme the mitts."

Loup waited for him to adjust the straps, waited for him to set himself. Miguel nodded, grim-faced. She threw a pair of lightning-fast straight crosses and watched his strong arms fly outward under the impact, leaving him wildly exposed. She stepped inside his guard and tapped him lightly on his chin.

"You fucking little freak!" Miguel lunged at her.

She skipped backward. "You promised!"

"Promised *what*?" He glared.

"To help," she reminded him. "At Tommy's funeral, you promised to help if I asked. I'm asking you for help, Miguel. Please?"

The word slowed him, softened him. "Aw, kid."

"Please?" Loup begged.

"Fuck." Miguel swore softly, almost cordially. He flexed his padded hands, still stinging from landing bare-knuckled punches.

Slewed his gaze around at Floyd Roberts. "You're training her to go up against him."

"I am."

"What a fucking freakshow." He shook off the training mitts and folded his arms over his chest, taking a stance. "I want a goddamn shower and a goddamn drink. Then we'll talk. I'm a goddamned Garza, and we don't give away something for nothing."

They adjourned to the rooftop after Miguel had showered and dressed in clean clothes. Floyd plied him with a generous glass of whiskey and a cigar.

"Nice." Miguel lounged at ease, puffing contemplatively. "You've got access to goodies even that bitch Rosa Salamanca can't get her hands on, don'tcha, old man?"

"Yep," Floyd said.

Miguel blew a smoke ring. "What're you offering?"

"What are you asking for?"

"Good question." He stretched out his legs and regarded Loup. "Loopy Lou. Kept your secret pretty well, kiddo. Whatever you're offering, I bet the army would offer a whole lot more to know about you." A realization struck him. "Aw, shit! Santa Olivia. Santa fuckin' Olivia. That was you, wasn't it?"

She couldn't see any point in lying. "Yeah."

"Huh. Nice work." One corner of his mouth quirked, then straightened. "You know there's no way you can pull this off without getting caught, right?"

"I know."

"So what's to stop me from walking away and turning you in?" Miguel asked, genuinely perplexed.

"Honor." Floyd answered the question. "Pride."

"Shit!" Miguel looked at him. "You serious?"

"I am," the coach replied.

"Shit." Miguel rose and walked some distance away, cigar in one hand, whiskey glass in the other. He stood, smoking, his back to them. "Yeah, that and the fact that I'd get lynched in town for being the guy who ratted out Santa fuckin' Olivia, who turns out to be the beloved kid sister of the sainted Tom Garron."

Floyd smiled. "Never thought you were stupid, Mig."

"The hell you didn't, Coach." He turned around, drank down half his glass. "I got a brother, too. I answer to Danny. The Garzas have it made in this town. We get a cut of everything Salamanca touches. Booze?" He sloshed his glass. "I can get booze. Booze, pussy, weed, nice clothes. Whatever I want. This?" He jabbed the cigar at them. "Sure, it's a good smoke, but I'm not going behind Danny's back and putting *my* ass on the line for a ten-dollar cigar."

"Wouldn't expect you to," Floyd agreed. "I'll take the fall. I'm pretty sure I can protect everyone who had anything to do with this. Everyone but Loup."

Miguel scowled. "Pretty sure."

"Pretty sure," Floyd said steadily. "As you say, I'm an old man. I've known Bill Argyle a long time."

"It's not enough."

"What do you want?"

"Out." Miguel jabbed his cigar at the horizon. "I want a ticket out of this dust patch. I wanna walk down a city street. I wanna see a forest. I wanna see the ocean. I wanna drive a car. I wanna fuck beautiful women I haven't known since I was five years old. I wanna walk into stores filled with shiny new things and spend my fuckin' money on anything I want, including ten-dollar cigars. I want out."

Floyd shook his head. "I can't make you that offer, son."

Loup stirred. "You said you thought the general would honor his word if I won. One ticket, maybe two."

"Yes," he said slowly.

"So if Loup wins there's a ticket?" Miguel asked. "Are you *pretty sure* about that?"

"Pretty sure, yes."

Miguel looked at Loup. "I want it. If there's two, I want 'em both."

"One." She held his gaze without blinking. "If there's one, it's yours. If there's two, I want Father Ramon to decide who gets the other one."

A muscle jumped in his jaw. After a moment, he nodded and shifted his gaze to Floyd Roberts. "How long you think to get her ready?"

"Two years."

"Johnson'll be gone by then. Or whoever the fuck he is."

"I can get him back," the coach said.

Miguel downed the rest of his whiskey and licked his lips. "Yeah, well, once he's gone, I want my pick. I'll have at least a year, right? If I think I've got a shot at the new guy in my weight class, I wanna take it. No more playing favorites, no more dicking me around. I'm not getting any younger, Coach. My window's getting mighty fuckin' narrow, if you know what I mean. I wanna pick my shot. Deal?"

Floyd hesitated, then nodded. "You've got my word, son."

"And if I win, all bets are off." Miguel sucked on the cigar, blew out a plume of smoke. "I'm taking my two tickets, and me and Danny are out of here. I'll keep my mouth shut, but you and the freakshow are on your own. Understood?"

"Understood."

"Good." Miguel returned and dropped heavily into the chair, holding out his glass for a refill. He contemplated the smoldering cigar in his hand. "Y'know, this is a pretty goddamned good cigar, Coach."

"Uh-huh." Floyd nodded. "Don't make a habit of it. Bad for your wind."

Miguel laughed humorlessly. "Some coach. Thanks for the advice, old man." He reached out with one long arm, stubbed out the cigar in a potted marigold. His gaze settled onto Loup, filled with a complicated mixture of sympathy and antagonism. "I meant what I said, kid. I *am* sorry about your brother. And if they fucked him over and slipped in a ringer, it sucks even more. I get it. But you do know I'm gonna do my best to beat the living shit out of you before you get anywhere near a prizefight, right?"

"Yeah." Loup smiled at him with surpassing sweetness. "Thanks, Miguel. I'm counting on it."

He shook his head. "Freakshow."

THIRTY-TWO

Are you out of your mind?" Mack held the heavy bag braced while Loup pounded on it, gloved fists a blur. "Miguel Garza?"

"Yeah, I know." She concentrated. "But he's good."

"I don't trust him."

"Me neither." Loup worked the bag for another ten minutes, hitting at full strength and full speed. Mack grunted and struggled to keep his feet. "Okay, break." She stepped back and wiped sweat from her brow with one forearm. "He's still one of us, though. I think he'll keep his word."

"He'd better." Mack picked up a roll of duct tape and began wrapping another layer around the bag to keep the seams from splitting. "Because if he turns you in, I will fucking kill him, Loup." His gray eyes were calm and focused. "I will."

She picked up a recycled bottle between her gloves and drank a long swig of water. "I don't think he will. You should of heard him. He's got everything anyone could want here and it's not enough. He wants a ticket out, bad. Cars and oceans and forests." She drank again, then lowered the bottle. "You ever think about it?"

"Getting out?" Mack kept wrapping. "I dunno. Not that much. It's home. It's what I know. You?"

"Some." Loup shrugged. "Tommy used to talk about it. All the stuff we'd do and see. I don't care about that so much. Now that he's gone, if I went anywhere, I'd want to go south. Over the wall."

"It's a fucking war zone, Loup."

"Maybe." She pointed with her chin. "Put some more there;

the old stuff's coming loose. I dunno. Jaime's been reading all these old magazines and newspapers. He thinks my father was right. That the government made up all that stuff about El Segundo so people would go along with it."

"With what?"

"The walls. The cordon. The bases." She took another drink, then set the bottle down carefully. "He says there's nothing in it about us. No one knows we're here. Isn't that weird?"

"I guess." Mack finished with the tape. "So why south?"

" 'Cause that's where my father went. Him, and the other guys like him. Someplace with a funny name and lots of fish. I have it written down. He's probably gone now, but maybe there are other kids, you know? Like me." She cocked her head and regarded the bag. "Guess it doesn't matter now, does it?"

"Loup." Mack came over and put his hands on her shoulders. "You *don't* have to do this."

She gazed at his familiar face. "Yeah, I do."

"Okay." After a moment, he nodded. "Let's get back to work."

Miguel Garza kept his word. Three days after they struck their deal, Floyd ordered Loup to report to the gym on the following Sunday morning.

"Ten a.m.," he said. "I don't open until noon on Sundays. That'll give you time to warm up, time to spar a few rounds, clean up before the boys arrive. I want you in proper gear. You can change in your brother's old room, wash up afterward. There's no shower, but there's a sink."

"Okay," Loup agreed.

"Have you been training with the weights I gave you?" Floyd asked. "Full speed?" She nodded. "Good girl. Leave them off for this. Find your measure in the ring. We can put them on later." He hesitated. "Speed's a problem. That's my biggest worry. You're going to have to dial it down in the ring and match Miguel's pace. Otherwise, you'll just run rings around him."

"I can do that," Loup said. "It's pretty much what I've had to do all my life."

"I know." He rubbed his chin. "That's what worries me. If our man's been training against opponents as fast as he is . . ." His voice trailed off.

"I don't think he has," she said. "I really don't. He wasn't a good enough boxer. No one's ever pushed him. Not in the ring."

Floyd sighed. "I hope to hell you're right, child. All right, let's go ransack the storeroom and see what we can find to fit you."

He found sparring gloves and headgear that fit without much difficulty and there were unused mouth guards sized for younger fighters or lightweights. Clothing wasn't a problem. The women's locker room had been taken over by the fighters Floyd trained years ago, but he'd salvaged dozens of abandoned gym bags and Loup had rummaged through them at the outset, laying claim to a handful of garments that fit.

Boxing shoes and a groin protector were another matter.

"I can requisition a pair of shoes in your size," Floyd said. "Boys' shoes will be fine and you can use your regular gym shoes for now. But this." He held out the smallest groin protector at arm's length, squinting at the bulging cup. "They do make them for women. But I can't see how I can requisition one without raising a red flag."

"I don't need it."

"Oh, no!" He shot her a dour look. "Loup Garron, I'm setting a sixteen-year-old girl to sparring with a grown man. There's no way on God's green earth that you're getting into that ring without proper gear." He shoved it at her. "See if it fits well enough otherwise."

Aside from the cup being too big, it fit.

"Live with it," Floyd said.

Loup shrugged. "Okay."

"You don't get embarrassed easily, do you?" He looked quizzically at her. "Do you even *understand* embarrassment?"

"Not really," Loup admitted.

Floyd shook his head. "Sometimes I truly wonder what it's like being you."

"That's okay," she said. "I wonder what it's like being everyone else."

When Sunday morning arrived, she returned to the gym. After stretching and warming up, she put on her gear in the upstairs office room that had served as Tommy's bedroom. It felt strange and empty. Floyd hadn't changed anything because there wasn't much to change. Tommy's clothes had been donated to the church. He hadn't really had anything else, just a lonely cot sitting in the middle of the room.

Downstairs, Miguel had arrived, hungover and surly. He didn't bother to warm up, only grunted at her as he wrapped his hands. "You ready to do this?"

She put in her mouth guard. "Yeah."

Floyd wrapped her hands, laced her gloves. The sparring gloves were different from the ones she was used to for working the bags—bigger, thick and dense with padding. She banged them together experimentally.

"Jesus," Miguel muttered, shoving his mouth guard in place.

Floyd checked her headgear, smeared Vaseline on her cheeks, chin, and brow. "Okay. You're wearing the groin protector?"

Loup nodded.

Miguel gave a muffled laugh. "You wearing a codpiece, Garron?"

She ignored him.

"I'm surprised as hell that you know that term, son." Floyd checked Miguel's headgear, then picked up his gloves. "Hands."

He thrust them out. "I'm full of surprises, Coach."

"We'll see." Floyd finished lacing the gloves, smeared his face with Vaseline. "Into the ring."

They climbed into the ring and faced off.

Miguel glowered.

Loup stared back at him, a sense of heady exhilaration filling her.

"Okay." Floyd raised one hand, holding a stopwatch. "We'll figure out what we want to work on later. Right now, I just want to see what you do together. On my go, the first of three two-minute rounds. Have at it, but keep it clean. You start on my word, you stop on my word, or I'll throw you both out on your asses." He counted. "One, two, three . . . go!"

Miguel came at her fast and hard, trying to pummel her. Loup evaded him without thinking, her feet skipping lightly over the canvas.

"Slow the hell down, Loup!" the coach shouted. "Stand and fight!"

She slowed, matching her pace to Miguel's. He threw a low right straight and she let it past her guard, let him land it.

It hurt more than she expected, pain blossoming in the center of her chest. Loup blinked. Miguel grinned around his mouth guard and hit her again, a crisp jab that caught her on the cheekbone and rocked her head back. Bright sparkles filled her vision. She shook her head, trying to clear it. He landed a glancing blow to her padded left temple.

"Chin down! Hands up!"

Hours of training deserted her, swept away on a tide of pain and instinct. It was a *hell* of a lot different fighting someone who hit back. This wasn't a street brawl; it was a sparring match, and Miguel had years of experience on her. She lashed out wildly, but Miguel was still in motion and evaded the blow. He moved in on her and began pounding her upper torso with right and left hooks.

"Loup! Elbows in! Block him, for Christ's sake!"

She broke away and scrambled backward, breathing hard. Her nerves were jangling with pure adrenaline, her head was ringing, and dull pain was spreading throughout her body.

It was still exhilarating.

"Had enough?" Miguel called.

Loup smiled, eyes sparkling. "Hell, no!"

His wide mouth quirked. He beckoned with his gloved hands. "Okay, little girl. You give me an inch, and I'll take a mile. Now put your chin down and your hands up, and let's teach you to box."

THIRTY-THREE

L ife settled into a new rhythm.

Loup continued to train in the garage. The Santitos continued to assist her, especially Mack, who even figured out a way to heat the material of her groin guard and reshape it to fit better.

On Wednesday evenings and Sunday mornings, she sparred with Miguel.

After their first bout, the coach had her concentrate on defense. All the long hours spent shadowboxing gradually began to pay off as she learned to put the moves into practice in the ring, catching or slipping Miguel's punches, ducking or twisting enough to let them roll harmlessly off her shoulder. Miguel was good enough that sometimes they still landed, but Loup was learning.

"When're you gonna let her fight back, Coach?" Miguel complained. "Feels like I'm doing all the work."

"When I'm confident that Loup has sufficient discipline in the ring to control her actions," Floyd said absently, jotting notes on a clipboard. He glanced up. "You do realize she's only fighting at half her capacity?"

"So you say. Y'know, I'd kind of like to see it. Seems like maybe that first encounter was a goddamn fluke. I'm starting to wonder if this is all worthwhile."

Floyd set down his clipboard. "You want a *real* demonstration? You want me to turn her loose in the ring?"

Miguel folded his arms. "Yeah."

"All right." The coach walked away and came back with a body protector. "Come here."

Miguel laughed. "Are you fucking kidding me?"

Floyd shook his head. "Nope." He buckled the protector in place. "All right. Shake hands and have at it. Loup, if you hit him anywhere but on the shield, I'll throw you out. Try not to break his ribs."

"Okay," she agreed.

They touched gloves. Loup let Miguel flick a couple of quick jabs at her head. She caught them, then blurred into motion, hitting him with the same shot she'd let him land on her the first time. A low right straight, powering past Miguel's too-slow effort to deflect it, driving hard into the thick foam of the protector.

It knocked him off his feet, knocked him to the canvas, knocked the wind out of him even through the shield. His mouth gaped and his chest heaved just like C.C.'s had years ago when she'd hit him, except that Miguel was a lot bigger and she'd hit him a lot harder.

"Relax, son," Floyd said calmly. "Shallow breaths." He climbed into the ring and helped Miguel sit upright, unbuckled the protector and prodded at Miguel's ribs. "No bones broken. You didn't bust a gut, did you?"

Miguel shook his head, gulping for air.

"Good." The coach's eyes crinkled in a smile. "Now you know for sure."

It marked the beginning of a strange friendship between them. After the incident, Miguel didn't complain about the slow pace of Loup's training. He treated her with rough affection. Sometimes on Wednesday evenings, he'd invite her to join him on the gym roof while he smoked one of the coach's cigars.

"So why'd you do it?" Miguel asked on one such occasion. "The Santa Olivia thing?"

Loup told him about Katya, and the O'Brien kids, and the old man with his dog.

"The thousand-dollar miracle?" He was surprised. "That

was you, too? I always figured Coach had a hand in it on account of the bitch was McArdle's cousin. Where the fuck did you little urchins find a thousand bucks?"

Loup smiled. "Stole it from Rosa Salamanca's safe."

He laughed soundlessly. "Why'd you quit?"

She told him about Colonel Stillwell's threats.

"Fuckers act like they own us." Miguel blew a smoke ring. "And I guess they goddamn well do."

"I thought you Garzas were tight with the army brass," Loup commented.

"Yeah." He gazed at the horizon. "We keep things under control. Make sure the system runs nice and smooth for them, make sure their boys get all the booze and pussy they want and no one gets hurt. My father always wanted to be a big man. When the army took over, he saw his chance." He blew another smoke ring. "My father was an asshole."

"So are you, Mig."

He gave her an amused sidelong glance. "Yeah, but I'm not stupid. Like to think if I'd been around when the army came, I'd have had the sense to get my family the fuck out of town, not make a shitty deal to serve as head overseer for life on Plantation Dust Patch."

"Is that why you started boxing?" Loup asked him. "To get out?"

"Yeah, that and I hit hard." Miguel regarded his cigar. "Might of been better off if I wasn't a Garza. Maybe I would of wanted it more, worked harder."

"Like Tommy," Loup said softly.

"Like Tommy," he agreed. "But then . . ."

"Yeah."

They sat in companionable silence for a while. A memory struck Loup.

"You said you saw my father once," she said. "Punched him."

"You remember that, huh? Yeah."

Her voice turned wistful. "What was he like?"

Miguel didn't answer right away. He sat and smoked, the tip of his cigar flaring and fading. "Steady," he said at length. "Same way you are. He didn't even flinch when I hit him, like it wasn't even worth his while to notice. I know I was just a kid, but I hit hard. Same eyes as you, same weird way of looking at people without blinking."

"Do I look like him?"

"I only ever saw him once," Miguel said. "Didn't your mama or your brother ever tell you?"

"Yeah," she said. "But they're gone."

"Aw, kid." He studied her face. "Yeah, some. The eyes. And he looked . . . he didn't look American, you know what I mean? Or maybe he just didn't sound American. I dunno." He shook his head. "Sorry."

"Thanks."

"You take after your mama, too." Miguel pulled on his cigar. "I remember her better. She was a pretty lady."

Loup smiled. "Thanks."

He eyed her. "You got a boyfriend?"

"No, but—"

Miguel cut her off. "Hey, don't get any ideas. No offense, but the idea of messing around with anyone who can knock me on my ass doesn't exactly do it for me. But there's all kinds of perverts out there. Guys who get off on the idea of getting knocked around by a nice-looking girl. You wouldn't even have to fuck 'em. And nobody keeps a secret like a pervert, especially an army pervert. You could make good money. I could hook you up with Dolores Salamanca; that's one of her specialties."

"No, thanks," Loup said.

"It's good money," he repeated. "Hell, you'd be doing 'em a favor! Nothing worse than being stuck on a two-year tour of the dust patch with an itch you can't scratch."

"Yeah, maybe." She shrugged. "But we're already taking enough risks. I don't want to get busted because I was scratching some pervert's itch." She was silent a moment. "Anyway, I don't want to be wanted that way. I just want to be wanted in the normal way."

"Good luck with that." There was sympathy in Miguel's tone.

Loup smiled wryly. "Yeah, thanks."

"Hey. Whatever happened to your father, anyway?" He tapped ash from his cigar. "One thing I *do* remember, they all looked happy as hell together. I remember 'cause it pissed Danny off. But he split, right?"

"Yeah," she murmured. "South. He and the other guys like him. They were all trying to get over the wall and into Mexico. But he was gonna stay after my mother got pregnant."

Miguel whistled. "So why'd he go?"

Loup glanced at him. "You don't know?" He shook his head. "Your brother Danny threatened to turn him in to the army as a deserter."

"Oh." Miguel was quiet. "Shit, I'm sorry, kid."

"It's not your fault."

"Yeah, I know." He ground out his cigar and leaned forward, elbows braced on his knees. "Our father really *was* an asshole. He was tough on us, too. Sometimes it got pretty bad. Danny was the oldest. He had to be a hard guy. To protect himself. To protect me, until I got big enough to beat the shit out of pretty much anyone in town."

"Yeah?"

"Yeah." Miguel blew out his breath. "Yeah."

"I'm sorry, Mig," Loup said steadily.

He shot her another sideways glance, quick and flickering. "Yeah, well." He rubbed the heel of one beefy hand over his eyes. "Cry me a fuckin' river, right? Whatever. Everyone here's got a sob story."

"Santa Olivia," Loup agreed.

"Santa fuckin' Olivia." Miguel stood, extended one hand. "C'mon, kid. You're a bad influence on me."

It startled her. "I am?"

He tugged her to her feet. "It's a joke, freakshow. I've got this weird feeling you're making me less of an asshole."

"Good luck with that," Loup said.

Miguel laughed.

THIRTY-FOUR

Once Floyd Roberts was satisfied that Loup's defense was becoming ingrained instinct, he added the wrist and ankle weights to her sparring regimen and insisted on another three months of the same.

"I'm dying here!" Miguel complained.

The coach's colorless gaze fixed on him mercilessly. "You're also working harder and becoming a better boxer, son."

"Me?"

Floyd's mouth wrinkled. "You hadn't noticed?"

Training.

Sparring.

At the end of three months, on a stormy Sunday morning, the coach allowed Loup to begin practicing offense in the ring. After so long, at first she was tentative.

"Hit him!" Floyd said in disgust.

Miguel spread his arms. "Hit me, little girl!"

She threw a fast, blurred jab at the center of his chest, pulling it at the last second.

"Oof." Miguel bent, then straightened, realizing the blow had never landed. He grinned at her and began flicking jabs at her head, light on his feet, pressing and insistent. "C'mon. C'mon, bitch. I can take it."

Loup breathed slowly, deeply.

She matched her pace to his. Slow, dreamlike. Traded blows; catching his, deflecting his. Throwing her own, careful and hesitant. Miguel caught them, turned them aside, scowling at her.

"Faster!" Floyd barked. "Loup, step it up."

She went faster.

A simple jab combination: right, left, right. Right, right. Knocking, knocking. The last shot tagged the edge of Miguel's padded chin. His head went sideways, the mouth guard flying out.

"Break!" the coach shouted. "Someone's at the door."

Loup winced. "You okay, Mig?"

"Yeah, yeah." He made a shooing gesture. "Make yourself scarce, kid."

She retreated to Floyd's office until he came to tell her it was safe. "It's just one of your young friends from the church. Said she was in some kind of a jam and knew you'd be here."

She returned to the gym to find Pilar Ecchevarria looking nervous and apologetic. Miguel was hanging over the ropes, trying unsuccessfully to banter with her.

"Hey." Pilar shivered. "I'm really sorry to bug you, but this sewer line broke at the bar this morning, so Joe sent everyone home. And I thought it would be fine because it's so early, but then this creepy guy who used to hang around and stare at me until Joe banned him started following me and saying gross things, and I got freaked out. When I saw the gym, I remembered you'd be here. Is it okay if I stay until you're done and walk home with you?"

"It's okay by me, sweetheart," Miguel offered. "But you can't blame a guy for staring."

Loup glanced at the coach, who nodded. "Yeah, sure."

"Thanks."

The next two rounds went badly. It was distracting to have Pilar there, watching. Loup couldn't find her rhythm, couldn't match Miguel's pace. She went too slow and the coach yelled at her; then she went too fast and Miguel yelled at her. Too slow again and even her defensive rhythm was thrown off, letting Miguel land a couple of unexpected low jabs to her rib cage.

"Break!" Floyd called. "Go wash up and call it a day."

Miguel spat out his mouth guard and leaned over the ropes,

eyeing Pilar. "How about I stay here and keep you company while Loup scrubs down?"

She shivered again and turned to Loup. "Can I go with you?"

"Sure, if you want."

In the room that had been Tommy's, Loup stripped off her sparring gear, stowing everything carefully. Dirty clothes went in the gym bag. She washed at the sink with a washcloth, scrubbing her skin with deft, practiced motions. Pilar sat and waited on Tommy's old cot.

"Does it hurt? Getting hit like that?"

"Yeah, it hurts." Loup turned to reach for a towel, quickly enough to catch Pilar watching her.

Pilar flushed. "Stupid question, I guess." She was quiet a moment, trying not to watch Loup drying off. "So, hey. Whatever happened with you and Mack? I thought you guys were so good together."

"In a lot of ways." She stepped into clean underpants, grabbed a clean tank top. "But after we slept together, we figured out that was never gonna be one of them."

"How come?"

"Because Mack wished I was normal." Loup pulled the tank top over her head, tugged it in place. She looked directly at Pilar and told her the truth. "And I wished he was you."

This time, Pilar turned bright red. She opened and closed her mouth a couple of times before getting any words out. "I'm not queer, okay?"

"Jesus, Pilar." She sighed. "I don't care what you call it. But if you don't like me, why do you look at me the way you do? Why did you kiss me that night in the cemetery?"

"Your brother had just died!" Her voice rose, indignant. "I was *comforting* you!"

Loup laughed. "With your tongue?"

"Fuck you!" Pilar shook her head and stood, looking away. "I'll wait downstairs and take my chances with Miguel fucking Garza."

"Fine."

She finished dressing and returned to the gym to find Pilar waiting alone, a mutinous look on her face. When they left the gym, the sky was low and glowering, clouds roiling overhead. For the space of several blocks, they walked quickly and intently, neither saying a word.

"Any sign of your creep?" Loup finally asked.

"No." Her voice was stony.

"Pilar." Loup caught her arm, forced her to halt in the middle of the street. "Look, I'm sorry! I wasn't making fun of you. I *do* like you. I like you a lot. And I think you like me, too. But I think you're scared, and I don't understand why. I'm not good at that kind of thing. Is it because I'm a girl? Or because I'm different? Or just because of what people would think?"

"Jesus!" Pilar's eyes flashed. "I'm not *that* fucking shallow!"

Thunder rumbled. Loup let go of her arm and waited.

"Oh, God." Pilar covered her face. "Okay, maybe a little. It's just . . ." She exhaled hard, lowered her hands. "I don't know why I have this thing for you. It doesn't fit. It's not part of the plan. And I know you all think I'm shallow and vain because I've got a pretty face and great tits and I want to marry a rich guy, but you know what? I don't care. It's what I've got to work with. I like guys. Guys like me. All I want to do is find one who's reasonably nice and reasonably cute, with enough money that I don't have to work my ass off for the rest of my life. Is that so wrong?"

"No," Loup murmured.

Rain spattered down, spotting the dusty street.

"Yeah, so *why*?" Pilar demanded in frustration. "Why do I have to feel this way? Why *me*? T.Y.'s had a crush on you forever! Mack gets you better than anyone else! Hell, C.C.'s crazy enough for anything, and even fucking Jane would at least find it *interesting*! Why do I have to be the freak who gets insanely turned on by the mutant girl?"

Loup smiled.

"It's not funny!" Pilar yelled at her. "Jesus! And it's not the only reason! It's not even the main reason! Jesus! How can you still not get it? You're not dumb, Loup. You oughta be able to figure this out. I know you can't get scared, but you can hurt, baby. I've *seen* you hurt."

The rain began to fall harder.

"I'm sorry," Loup said softly. "Will you please just tell me?"

"Two days." Pilar looked up at the sky, then back at her. Tears and raindrops mingled on her cheeks. "*Two days*. That's all the time you waited before you decided you were gonna fight the guy who killed Tommy. And if he doesn't kill *you*, it doesn't even matter if you win or lose. They're gonna take you away." She dashed the tears from her eyes with an impatient gesture. "It's gonna hurt a whole lot less to lose you if I never had you."

"Oh."

Veils of rain beat down on them. Headlights sliced through it, the sound of a military vehicle's horn cutting through the thunder and downpour.

"C'mon." Loup grabbed Pilar's hand. They ran for cover, steps splashing, taking shelter in the overhang of a boarded-up office building. The armored truck roared past them, throwing up sheets of water.

And then they were alone, water pouring from the eaves.

Pilar glanced at her, breathing hard from their dash.

Loup returned her gaze, steady and unblinking

"Oh, fuck it," Pilar whispered. She took Loup's face in her hands and kissed her, hard and deep. The rainwater was cool, but her skin was warm beneath it; and there was no pulling away, only pushing closer. Closer and closer. She pressed Loup against the door, kissed her hungrily, her tongue agile and expert. Pilar's breasts pressing against hers, nipples erect with cool rain and desire. One leg pressed between her thighs. Her hands slid down to Loup's waist, under her tank top, craving skin. Loup wound her arms around Pilar's neck, kissing her back.

It was exhilarating.

Better than fighting, better than anything.

"Oh, my God," Pilar murmured, breaking the kiss. Her open mouth slid over Loup's throat, tasting her skin. Her hands slid upward. "You feel so fucking good I think I might lose my mind."

Another military vehicle passed in the driving rain. Someone in uniform whistled and hollered.

Pilar pulled back with an effort, eyes glazed. "We should—"

"Yeah." Loup glanced behind her at the boarded-up door. She drove one elbow backward, splintering plywood, then wrenched the door open. "C'mon."

"Jesus!" Pilar said fervently.

They scampered up the stairs. The first unlocked door opened onto an abandoned insurance office with a big leather couch in the waiting room.

"C'mere." Pilar fell backward onto it, pulling Loup atop her. "Oh, fuck yes!" She peeled off Loup's tank top, sank one hand deep into her hair and grabbed her ass with the other, reclaiming her mouth and wriggling urgently beneath her. "More. I want more of you."

"More," Loup agreed, dizzy with wanting.

There was more; there was an abundance of more. And it was good, all good. Once they got the rest of their clothes off, it was even better. Naked, skin against skin, slick with rain and desire. "Mmm." Pilar thrust against her, beneath her, hands urging her. "Oh, baby. Right there. Like that."

It was like riding a wave, or like Loup imagined it would be. A wave of sheer pleasure, powerful and overwhelming. For the first time in her life, she didn't feel wholly in control of her body. She moved, couldn't stop moving, driven and relentless. Didn't ever want to stop moving.

"Jesus!" Pilar shuddered, clutching her hard.

When it burst, it burst like a wave, too. Waves of pleasure, crashing and breaking.

Stillness was a long time in coming.

"Whoa." Pilar opened her eyes. "Wow."

Loup caught her breath. "So is that what it's like for everyone else all the time?"

"Are you kidding?" Pilar laughed. "No, honey. I think that's what they call fireworks. Shit, I didn't even know you could get off like that. You're just . . ." She ran her hands over Loup's back, then cupped her face and kissed her. "Mmm."

It started things all over again.

Loup moved downward, exploring. It was different, so different: soft skin, full curves instead of hard angles. But mostly it was different to have that subtle withdrawal replaced by urgent encouragement, to have someone want to touch her as much or more as she wanted to touch them.

"Jesus Christ!" Pilar gasped when Loup swirled her tongue around one nipple.

She lifted her head. "What?"

"Nothing." Pilar's hands tightened in Loup's hair. "Baby, I think you were wasted on guys." She paused. "And you don't get tired easily, do you?"

Loup shook her head and smiled. "Uh-uh."

Pilar sighed happily. "I think I'm in fucking heaven."

Outside, the storm passed. The skies cleared, then darkened again. Another storm rolled into town. Pilar rolled Loup onto her back, kissed her and smiled at her, eyes heavy-lidded with pleasure.

"My turn."

It wasn't until the aftermath of the second storm that they lay quiet and calm, still entwined. Pilar ran one hand over Loup's skin, caressing her from shoulder to hip, her touch soothing and drowsy.

"Ever since that night, I've thought about touching you," she murmured. "Other things, too. But just *touching* you. God! I've dreamed about it."

Loup propped herself on one elbow. "So I don't feel weird to you?"

"Different, yeah. Weird's not the word I'd use." Pilar hesitated. "Don't laugh?"

"I won't."

"Expensive." She flattened her palm against Loup's waist, stroked her. "You feel expensive. You ever have tequila? It's a good buzz, but you know how there's something nasty about the taste?" Loup nodded. "Well, that's the cheap shit. You can't get the really good stuff anymore. It's all made in Mexico. But Hector Salamanca bought a shitload of it before the wall went up. There's not a lot left, but we keep a bottle in the bar for Rosa. We're not even allowed to sell it." She watched her hand glide over Loup's skin. "Joe poured me a taste once, and holy shit, it was good. Smooth, no bite. You wanted to sip it to make it last. I could of drunk the whole bottle. It tasted like liquid gold." Her hand went still. "You feel like it tasted."

"Oh," Loup said in a soft voice.

"Yeah, oh." Pilar smiled wryly. "Expensive. Does that make me shallow?"

"No." Loup smiled back at her. "Maybe it makes you a . . . oh, fuck. What's the word? Floyd taught it to me. A *connoisseur*."

"I like that." She traced the curve of Loup's cheek. "Though I've gotta tell you, the whole cute and deadly thing gets me, too."

"Yeah?"

"Yeah. Maybe there's something wrong with me."

"No." Loup shook her head. "And I don't think you're shallow, either. You're good with people, all kinds of people. And you *are* good at comforting them. Those kids whose house burned down. Me. And Kotch . . . the night Kotch was raped, you were the first person to go to her. You didn't have to agree to be the bait when we went after the guy, but you did, even though it was dangerous. And you're the one who thought of helping out those poor O'Brien kids. So quit saying it, okay?"

"I'll try." Pilar kissed her, lingering. "Thanks."

"Yeah." She ran a lock of Pilar's hair through her fingers,

finer and silkier than her own. "I really *do* like you. A lot. It's not just . . ."

"Epic sex?"

"Epic sex," Loup agreed.

"So can I talk you out of it?" Pilar didn't say what. She didn't need to.

Loup tensed. "No."

"Are you sure?"

"No," Loup said honestly. "I think you could talk me into or out of a lot of things. But I think . . . I think this is something I need to do. Something I was meant to do. But right this second, I'm not sure of anything."

"So you'll let me try?" Pilar persisted.

"Does that mean you won't ask me to pretend today never happened?"

Pilar made a face. "Yeah." She wrapped her arms around Loup, pulled her closer. "Yeah, I guess it does."

THIRTY-FIVE

The sky was clear and the sun was setting by the time they left the office building.

"Wow." Pilar blinked. "We missed dinner."

"I know. I'm starving."

"I've got money. You want to get a bite? You've got a curfew permit, right?"

"Yeah." Loup nodded. "Thanks."

"No problem." Pilar glanced sideways at her. "I'm not exactly in a hurry to get back, you know? It's gonna be weird."

"Are you gonna be okay with it?"

"Maybe."

They went to the diner where Loup had grown up. Grady had died some five years ago, but the new owner, a distant cousin named Rudy, had always been good to her when she'd come in with Tommy. The diner was mostly full with soldiers and a few Outposters, but they found an empty booth in the corner.

"I feel like everyone's staring at us." Pilar ducked her head, studying the menu. "Like they know."

Loup laughed. "Pilar, they wouldn't stare so much if you'd do up another button on your shirt."

She glanced down at her cleavage. "That button's worth a thirty percent increase in tips."

"I bet."

Their eyes met. Pilar flushed, but she didn't look away. "I'm sorry. I'm trying to get used to it. It's just really sudden, you know?"

"Like a flash flood," Loup agreed.

"Or fireworks."

"Yeah." Loup's stomach growled. She'd missed lunch, too. And between sparring with Miguel and the afternoon with Pilar, she'd expended a lot of energy. "Hey, do me a favor? Order a side of fries. Or a double, if you want fries. I don't get tired easily, but I have to eat a lot afterward. Tommy always used to—" She realized Pilar was staring at her with a dreamy look. "Are you listening to me?"

"What?" Pilar shook herself. "Um, no."

"Order extra fries," Loup said gently. "It won't look as weird if we both do. I need food. A lot of food."

"Okay."

They got two burgers, two double orders of fries. Loup ate steadily, feeling the edge of fatigue and weakness recede as her body's reserves were replenished. She finished her fries, surreptitiously took half of Pilar's. She finished those and watched Pilar toy with a half-eaten burger. "Are you going to eat that?"

"No." Pilar shook her head and switched their plates. "You're worse than a guy, baby."

"I can't help it."

"I know." A wicked smile flickered across Pilar's face. "So I gave you a pretty good workout, huh, Supergirl?"

"Yeah." Restored by food, Loup was aware of a sense of profound, blissful lassitude permeating her entire body. Every time she moved, it sent aftershocks of pleasure through her. "Yeah, you did."

"You should see your hair."

"My hair?"

Pilar nodded. "You've got a bad case of sex hair, baby."

Loup tried to untangle it with her fingers. "It's kind of got a life of its own."

"Leave it. It's kinda cute. Sexy." A funny expression crossed Pilar's face. "I can't believe I'm sitting here saying that to you. I have to admit, I'm a little freaked out. And I'm really, really not looking forward to facing the Santitos."

"We don't have to say anything."

"I'm not *ashamed*, okay? I'm just freaking out."

"I know. I know!" Loup raised her hands in a peaceable gesture. "Take your time; freak out. Tell them; don't tell them. It's up to you. But we should head back. It's late. I've got a key to the gate, but they're gonna be wondering what the hell happened to both of us."

Pilar sighed. "Okay."

Outpost was fairly quiet in the aftermath of the storms. A few soldiers called out to them when they crossed the square and an MP made them show their permits to be out after curfew, but they made it back to the church without any trouble.

"Did Mackie give you that key now that he's the handyman?" Pilar asked, watching Loup unlock the gate.

"Yeah." She opened the gate. "Sometimes I run late on Wednesdays when Miguel feels like talking."

"Miguel *Garza*?"

"He's not as big of a jerk as he acts." Loup locked the gate behind them.

"You think he's gonna be upset?"

"Miguel?"

Pilar shook her head. "Mack."

"I dunno. Maybe a little." She looked at Pilar, shadowy in the faint moonlight. "He knew how I felt."

"About *me*?" Pilar sounded startled.

Loup smiled. "Yeah, about you."

"Jesus." Pilar slid her arms around Loup's neck, slid her hands into her tangled hair. Kissed her, pressing her against the bars of the wrought-iron fence until renewed desire pulsed between them, hot and urgent. "I swear to God, I could eat you up with a spoon," she murmured. "Do we have to go inside?"

"Ummm . . . no?"

"No, we do. We really kinda do." Pilar stepped back, blew out her breath. "Okay. I can do this."

Inside the church, Anna met them in the antechamber with a worried look that turned to one of relief. "Oh, good! We expected you both back in time for dinner today, and you were out so late. Is everything all right?"

Pilar flushed. "Fine."

"Fine," Loup echoed.

"Are you hungry?"

"We ate at the diner," Loup said.

"Oh, good." Anna gestured. "I think the others are watching a movie downstairs in the rec room."

"Maybe we can just slip in without them noticing," Pilar said hopefully.

"Maybe."

They descended the stairs to find Mack patiently untangling a length of videotape from the ancient VHS machine, while everyone else lounged around reading or looking bored.

"Hey!" T.Y. glanced up. "What the hell happened to you guys? Loup, I waited half an hour for you. I thought it was my turn to read to you."

"Sorry. I forgot."

"You forgot? You forgot training?"

"Yeah." She nodded. "I forgot."

"So where were you guys?"

"Well, I went in to work and there was this sewer pipe that burst," Pilar began explaining. "So Joe sent everyone home, but then this creepy guy who used to hang around started following me and saying shit, so I got freaked out. Then I saw the gym and remembered Loup was there, then we got caught in the rain, and . . . Oh, fuck it." She rolled her eyes. "We hooked up, okay?"

C.C. lifted his head out of a comic book. "*Whaaaat?*"

"It's a joke, C.C.," Jane said without bothering to look up.

"I'm not laughing," he said.

"I didn't say it was a good one."

Mack glanced at Loup. She returned his gaze steadily. He gave her a rueful smile. "So, was it different?"

"Yeah," she said softly. "It was."

"Good." He nodded. "I'm happy for you."

"You're serious." T.Y. looked from Pilar to Loup and back. "You're fucking serious? You two?"

"Yes!" Pilar raised her voice. "Get over it, okay?"

"God, Pilar." Jane put her book down. "Was one gender not enough to contain your sluttiness?"

"Fuck you. It's not like that."

"What's it like?" Dondi asked. He patted the seat of the couch. "I think you should come over here and tell me *all* about it."

"Me, too," C.C. agreed.

"Look." Pilar took a deep breath. "Kotch has a thing for guys in uniform. I have this . . ."

"Mutant fetish?" Loup suggested.

She turned pink. "*You* fetish, anyway."

"Interesting," Jaime observed. "You know, it probably is some sort of genetic mutation. Natural selection responding to an artificial strain introduced into the gene pool. Fascinating that it would arise spontaneously in different geographic areas . . . How long have you felt this way, Pilar?"

"A while," she muttered. "Can we please stop talking about it?"

"And cross gender barriers, too," he continued, musing. "That must be one powerful predilection." He glanced at Loup. "And you feel the same way about Pilar?"

She smiled. "Uh-huh."

"They just spent . . ." Mack glanced at the clock on the wall. "About seven hours fooling around, Jaime. I think it's a fair bet that Loup feels the same way." He eased the last tangle of tape out of the VCR and began rewinding it. "Shall we try this again? We've got a little while before I have to shut down the generator."

Loup stretched out on one of the big pillows strewn around the floor. After a moment, Pilar came and sat cross-legged beside her. "What are we watching?"

Mack eased the tape back into the VCR. "*The Sound of Music.*"

"Again?"

"It's one of the only ones that still works."

They watched the camera pan over the Swiss Alps and zoom in on a twirling, singing Julie Andrews.

"Fast-forward!" T.Y. called. "We were at the part where Liesl kisses the Nazi."

Mack obliged. The tape squeaked, but it kept running. Unwitting Liesl danced with her suitor in the gazebo while the rain streamed down around them. Loup turned her head and caught Pilar smiling at her. She smiled back. "Hey."

"Hey, yourself." Pilar stroked her arm, let her hand rest on Loup's back.

Katya offered her only comment of the evening. "I don't care what else you do, but just so you know, you two are *so* not having sex in the dorm room."

THIRTY-SIX

The first months were the best.

To Loup, it *felt* like rain in the desert. She knew it had gotten worse since Tommy's death, but she hadn't truly known how much she longed for the simple human contact that everyone else enjoyed as a matter of course.

And sex.

Lots and lots of sex.

The church had its share of trysting spots agreed upon by the Santitos and their predecessors. The bell tower. The choir room. The cot room in the dispensary after hours. The rec room was supposed to be off limits, but people used it anyway.

"Anyone could walk in," Loup reminded Pilar, conditioned by years of thinking about being careful.

"I don't care." Pilar's tongue circled her navel. "Jesus! I could bounce a quarter off your belly."

"Wanna try?"

Pilar glanced at Loup under her lashes, yanked at the button of her jeans. "Nope."

It was good—better than good. After a year and more of honing her body into a fighting weapon, Loup relearned it as an instrument of pleasure, giving and receiving alike.

A lot.

It affected her training. For the first month, Loup walked around in a state of erotic stupor. She moved automatically through her private regimen, maintaining her mindless discipline. In the ring, she sparred mechanically against Miguel, deflecting his blows without effort, finding no trouble going on a slow-motion offense, careful not to hurt him.

"Good," Floyd said. "Good."

"It's *not* good!" Miguel spat out his mouth guard and glared at Loup. "You're not trying. You're not pushing yourself. You think I can't tell? I can feel it. I know you, kid. I know you better than you think."

"She's doing well, son," the coach said.

Miguel shook his head. "Not well enough." He studied her. "You don't want it the way you did."

"I do!" Loup protested.

"Prove it."

She tried, but it was hard. Miguel couldn't push her as hard as she needed to push herself. They sparred. He got better; she stayed the same. Still, she tried.

After the initial revelation, most of the Santitos accepted their relationship with mild bemusement, surprised, more than anything, that Pilar had committed to it so wholeheartedly. She still flirted with her patrons at the bar, but she stopped accepting dates. On every evening but Wednesday, Loup fell into the habit of going to pick up Pilar when her day shift ended to walk her home.

The bar was a rustic little place called the Gin Blossom, mostly frequented by members of Rosa Salamanca's crew. Loup liked to enter unnoticed and watch Pilar serve drinks and flirt, wearing her bartending outfit of low-slung jeans and a man's white shirt knotted around her midriff and unbuttoned low. Pilar always looked cheerful at work, but when she saw Loup, her hazel eyes would brighten, and she'd greet her with a "Hey, baby!" that made Loup's heart do a flip-flop.

Pilar's bevy of casual suitors figured it out the first time she followed up her greeting with a kiss, leaning across the bar to grab Loup by the back of the neck and plant one on her lips. A collective groan went around the bar. But they liked Pilar too much to give her a hard time, and Outposters remembered that Loup was Tom Garron's little sister.

"I didn't think you'd be that open about it," Loup said frankly when they walked home that evening. "Us, I mean."

"Yeah, me neither." Pilar squeezed her hand. "But I meant what I said that day, Loup." She stopped and gave her a serious look. "I don't want you to go through with it. I don't want to lose you."

"I know," Loup murmured. Over Pilar's shoulder, she could see a faded petition to Santa Olivia on the wall of a bodega, words bleeding through the whitewash. Outpost hadn't quite forgotten Santa Olivia.

"Yeah, well, I figure I can't ask you to give up something like that if I'm not even willing to be honest about us." She shrugged. "You were right. There was a part of me that was just scared of what people would think. Turns out it's not that bad."

"I'm glad."

Pilar searched her face. "*Are* you thinking about it?"

"I don't know. I'm having a hard time thinking about anything but you."

"It's a start." Pilar smiled. "Let me give you more to think about." She kissed her again, there on the sidewalk, one of those deep, ardent kisses that made Loup's head spin. Pilar Ecchevarria was a very, very good kisser. A jeep full of soldiers came alongside them and slowed, cheering and honking their horn. This time, Pilar ignored them and just kept kissing her. Something struck the sidewalk near their feet.

"Cigarettes." Loup glanced down in wonderment when Pilar released her. "They threw a pack of cigarettes at us."

"I'd of rather had money." Pilar picked it up. "Thanks, guys!"

They honked and hollered, then sped onward.

Loup shook her head.

"Fringe benefits," Pilar said. "Who knew? Bet we could make a lot of money putting on a sex show, you and me. Dolores Salamanca's got a place. We'd be the hottest thing on the ticket." She laughed at Loup's expression. "I'm kidding! C'mon, walk me home, Cute and Deadly. I gotta get you alone someplace, fast."

It wasn't all good.

Their relationship created a measure of distance between Loup and Mack. He was a true friend and genuinely glad for her, but she knew it hurt him somewhere deep inside to see her find so effortlessly with Pilar what he'd tried so hard and wanted so badly to give her.

And then there was T.Y.

T.Y. was jealous. Deeply, morbidly jealous. He continued to help Loup train, but he did it with a profound and annoying sullenness.

"Why are you so pissed?" Loup asked him when she figured it out. "Jesus, T.Y.! You weren't jealous when I was with Mack."

He spotted her through a set of fifteen reps. "Because he's *Mack*."

She eased the barbell into the cradle. "What's wrong with Pilar?"

"You don't get it." T.Y. shook his head. "It's a guy thing."

"So it's because Pilar's a girl?"

"No. I dunno. Not exactly." He fiddled with the barbell, adding weights for her next set. "Remember when you came here? I was the first person to make friends with you. I was the first person you told your secret."

"Yeah, I know." Loup's voice softened. "You thought I was a superhero."

"Yeah." T.Y. gave a faint smile, head averted. "I thought it was some kind of sign. You had superpowers, and I was the miracle baby."

"The bomb baby," she said, remembering.

"Yeah." He looked up. "When we were kids, I thought we were meant to be together. When it didn't work out . . ." He shrugged. "Mack, I could deal with. He's cool. He's Mack the Knife. You don't get jealous of Mack the Knife. But . . . shit, Loup! You really *are* special. Don't get me wrong, I like Pilar okay, but you're not supposed to end up with a lazy, gold-digging waitress. And yeah, it pisses me off and makes me jealous."

"She's a bartender."

"You know what I mean."

"She's good at it, too."

"That's not the point!" T.Y. yelled.

"Yeah, I know." Loup sat upright, rubbed her brow with one forearm. "Look, we've all done KP duty with Pilar; everyone knows she's got a lazy streak. Not when it's something she likes. She likes tending bar. She likes to flirt. *I'm* the last thing in the world she wanted to want. And aside from everything else, I'm not exactly gold-digger material, you know? This isn't easy for her, but she's doing it anyway."

"For now," T.Y. muttered.

"I don't *have* a whole lot of time, T.Y. And this is nice. It's the first truly nice thing in my life since . . . ever, I guess. I might be different, but I still feel a lot of the same things normal people do. I get lonely. I like being liked. I like being wanted. I like the way I feel when Pilar smiles at me. I like that I make her feel the same way. So if you can't be happy for me, can you please just get over it?"

"Are you *trying* to make me feel like shit?"

"No."

He heaved a sigh. "Okay, okay. I'll try."

Afterward, it was better. T.Y. made an effort not to sulk. Loup kept trying to push herself.

And trying not to think about Pilar's request.

Pilar didn't press her. She had good instincts. But it was there. It was there in her touch, there in the serious look she got sometimes.

I don't want to lose you.

In the end, it was Miguel who got her to talk about it. He invited her up to the coach's rooftop garden after one of their Wednesday-night sessions, savoring a scotch and a cigar while Loup drank a bottle of water.

"So." Miguel puffed. "You know, if you take away the soldiers, this is a damn small town, kid. Not a lot to talk about. People get bored. Sooner or later, everything gets around."

"Yeah, so?"

"So I think I know what's got you so distracted." He held out one hand. "If memory serves, she stands about so tall and has a nice rack. What's her name?"

Loup sighed. "Pilar."

"Pilar." Miguel nodded. "Right. Sam Ecchevarria's kid. I remember when her father passed some seven, eight years ago. Loup, you can't fool me. Coach thinks you're doing okay, but he's not in the ring mixing it up with you. He's usually right, but it's different with you. I can feel things he can't see. So is that it? You start diddling the hot babe and suddenly your heart's not in the game?"

"Sort of."

"Sort of or yes?"

"Sort of," Loup repeated. "Pilar doesn't want me to do it. She doesn't want to lose me. Most of me *does* want to. It's the only thing in my life that makes sense. But when I started, I didn't have anything to lose. Now I do."

"Yeah, I get that." Miguel eyed her. "From the dopey look you've been wearing for the past month or so, I'm guessing she's been sexing you up real good. And I'm guessing that's kind of a new thing for you, huh?"

Loup smiled. "Yeah."

"Cut yourself some slack. You're a kid. A freaky-ass kid, but a kid. You've got a bad case of puppy love and all kinds of crazy hormones running around inside you." He sipped his scotch and smacked his lips. "Doesn't mean it's gonna last. But right now's not a good time to make big decisions. Look, you're a year, year and a half away from being ready. You decide to back out then, fine. No one's gonna hold you to it. Even I'm not that big of an asshole."

"Thanks."

"Don't thank me yet." Miguel pointed at her with his cigar.

"I still want my end of this deal. I wanna call the shots, pick my matches. Coach says you're making me a better boxer. So we're gonna keep this up. You're gonna get your head back in the game for *my* sake. Push yourself, push me. Your little sweetie-pie complains, you tell her you're doing it for me. Deal?"

"Yeah. Thanks, Mig."

"I'm not doing it for you."

"Yeah, right." She smiled at him. "But, Mig . . . if you're anywhere near serious, you've gotta work harder outside the ring. Hit the treadmill, work the bags harder. Lay off the cigars and booze. You're not in shape to go twelve rounds."

He puffed on his cigar. "One good one's all I need."

"Miguel."

"Lay off, freakshow."

THIRTY-SEVEN

After her talk with Miguel, Loup found it easier to concentrate in the ring. Thinking about it in terms of helping him to train was like flipping a switch. Suddenly, she was able to push herself again.

Even if it was sort of a lie.

She told Pilar she'd promised to keep training with Miguel and that she'd promised not to make any decisions right away. Pilar accepted it, more or less.

"I bet Coach Roberts would pay you decent money to train a few of his best guys in secret," she said. "That could be a real job for you, baby. One you'd like." She licked Loup's earlobe. "We could get an apartment."

Loup squirmed. "It's still living in slow motion."

"Living with me?"

"Not you." She shook her head. "Sparring with normal people."

"Oh." Pilar blew in her ear, smiled when Loup wriggled again. "It'd be nice, though. Nice big bed. No more getting carpet burn from fooling around on the floor of the choir room."

"Yeah."

"It sucks for you, doesn't it? The slow-motion thing?" Pilar propped herself on one elbow. "Does it feel like that when you're with me?"

"You? No." Loup slid her hand around Pilar's neck, pulled her down to kiss her. "Aside from the times I was Santa Olivia and training in the garage, you're about the only thing that doesn't."

Pilar traced the full curve of her lower lip, gazing into Loup's eyes. "Do you ever wonder what it would be like to be with someone like you?"

"I used to."

"It might be amazing. Super intense."

"I dunno," Loup said. "*You're* pretty amazing."

Pilar smiled. "I'd wonder, though, if I were you."

Loup folded her arms behind her head. "I guess I do. Not so much the sex, not anymore. But just what it would be like to be around people like me. To not have to work all the time to figure out what everyone's thinking and feeling because it's so different. To understand them. I think that would be nice."

"That place in Mexico?"

"Uh-huh."

"I'd send you there if I could, baby." Pilar leaned over and kissed her, her hair falling around Loup's face. "Swear to God, I would." Her expression was grave. "I could stand losing you if it meant you were happy."

"Let's not talk about it."

"Okay, okay."

Elsewhere in Outpost, Ron Johnson finished his tour of duty and was rotated out. Coach Roberts got the scoop on his replacement in the army boxing circuit.

"Big Irish kid named Terry Flynn," he reported. "Southpaw. He's got a couple inches on you, Mig. Struggles to make weight." He eyed Miguel. "When's the last time you weighed in, son?"

"We've given *them* a few pounds plenty of times!" Miguel protested.

"Doesn't mean they'll do the same," Floyd said laconically. "So do you want the first shot at him?"

"Nah." He shook his head. "I wanna see him in action."

"Okay." The coach nodded. "I'll put in Bob Reyes, then."

Miguel hesitated. "You think Bob's got a shot?"

"Nope." Floyd wrinkled his mouth. "But he'll take it anyway, for the loser's purse."

"Good." Miguel pointed at Loup. "I want you to watch the match with me, and I want to know exactly what you think."

"I can tell you what I think right now, Mig," she said. "I told you already. You need to hit the treadmill."

He ignored her. "Can you fight left-handed?"

"Sure."

"Good. That's the way we'll do it from now on."

"It'll throw off her training," Floyd commented.

"I don't care. I'm making it part of the deal." Miguel shrugged. "Hell, maybe it'll be good for her. She can mix it up when the day comes, keep her guy off balance and guessing."

Floyd looked thoughtful. "You may actually have a point, son."

"I keep tellin' you, I'm not stupid."

The date for the prize match was set. It would take place in six weeks. Loup began sparring left-handed with Miguel. When she went about her chores at the gym, she watched Bob Reyes preparing for his bout and felt bad for him. He was a nice guy—a greenskeeper and a family man, one of the ones Tommy had called the Real Men. He could have used a left-hander to spar against, but there wasn't anyone in Floyd's stable. She thought about Pilar's suggestion, tried to imagine a life in which they shared an apartment with a nice big bed and Loup worked with Coach Roberts to make his boxers better.

The part about Pilar and the bed was nice.

Everything else felt hollow.

"It's not fair," she said to Miguel during one of their talks.

"What's that, kid?"

"Life."

He laughed. "You just figuring that out?"

"No." Loup shook her head. "It's bugging me, that's all. Bob's had his ass kicked a dozen times and he's gonna get it kicked again because he's got four kids and the army pays him shit wages to keep the golf course nice."

"Bob should of kept his dick in his pants after two," Miguel said. "Or worn a goddamn rubber."

"He shouldn't have to. He *likes* having a big family."

Miguel shrugged. "That's life."

"Here, yeah." Loup waved one hand. "All the jobs are shit jobs. Work for the Garzas, work for the Salamancas. Bouncers, waitresses, garbage haulers. Work for the army. Caddy, cut grass on the golf course, clean bathrooms at the base, work on the reservoir."

"It's a living."

"It sucks," she said. "And no one knows we're here."

He shrugged again. "Yeah, it does. But whaddya gonna do about it?"

"Me? Nothing, I guess. I'm fucked no matter what happens. But you could, Mig. If you win a ticket out, you could do something about it. Tell someone." Loup cocked her head, considering. "You *are* smart, a lot smarter than anyone thinks. You could figure out a way."

"Oh, *hell* no!" Miguel said in disgust. "If I win my own ticket out, me and Danny are pulling up stakes on the Garza empire and heading north to see forests and oceans and cities, and wallow neck-deep in fast cars and pussy. And if you win a ticket for me, I'll do it alone. I'll sign any fucking thing the army asks and keep my mouth shut."

Loup gazed at him. "You sure about that?"

He looked away. "Yeah, I'm sure."

"No, you're not."

"Keep me out of your crusade, Santa Olivia," Miguel muttered. "I'm nobody's goddamn hero."

"You could be."

"I'm not."

The night of Bob Reyes' prize match the weather was cool and crisp. Autumn in the desert, a big sky full of stars. Free beer and a fight; Outpost was happy. Soldiers filled the stands; Outposters thronged the square. Loup went with Pilar, who kept a tight grip on her arm. The announcer introduced Bob Reyes.

"Hey!" Ringside, Miguel gave a sharp whistle. "Over here."

An aisle cleared, closed behind them.

"Nice," Miguel said absently, gazing at Pilar's breasts. "You're Sam Ecchevarria's kid, right?"

"Um, hello?" She pointed at her eyes. "Up here, loverboy."

He grinned. "Honey, you flaunt it, a man's gonna look. Hey." He cuffed Loup on the shoulder. "Here he comes. Pay attention."

Loup tuned out the announcer, concentrating on Terry Flynn's entrance. For some reason, she'd imagined him as a redhead like Kevin McArdle, but he wasn't. He had fair skin, close-cropped black hair, and pale blue eyes, and he moved with easy grace. He was a big strong guy, confident in his skill. Everything about him said he wasn't taking this match seriously.

Everything about him said he didn't have to.

"Hey, he's kinda cute," Pilar offered.

Miguel peered down at her. "I didn't think you swung that way."

Pilar sidled closer to Loup. "Not lately, no."

"Fuckin' waste," he observed without malice. "So? Tell me, kid."

"It isn't gonna be pretty," Loup murmured. "This guy's good and he knows it."

The bell rang for the first round.

They watched Terry Flynn pound the hell out of Bob Reyes. Up and down the ring, working him systematically. Bob pretty much just covered up and took it, essaying a feeble offense, waiting to collect his paycheck. Pilar clutched Loup's arm hard, wincing at every blow that landed. When the bell rang, she relaxed her grip slightly.

"Sorry."

"It's okay." Loup smiled at her. "You did that the night Tommy had his first big match, remember?"

"Yeah." Pilar smiled back at her. "I remember."

Miguel's hand descended on Loup's head, turning her gaze back toward the ring. "No canoodling."

"What's *canoodling*?" Pilar whispered into Loup's ear.

Loup shivered.

"Ecchevarria!" Miguel raised his voice. "Get your goddamn tongue out of her ear. This is serious business."

"We're not gonna see anything new for the rest of this fight, Mig," Loup said mildly. "Not unless Bob grows an extra set of arms."

"Shut up and watch."

She was right. After the first round, Terry Flynn backed off a little, content to treat the match as though it were a workout, not a prizefight, and he was sparring with a mismatched partner. They could see the relief on Bob Reyes' face, and Loup was glad for him. He lost on points by a huge margin, but he was still standing when the bell signaled the end of the final round. A big grin split his face and Outpost cheered. In the spirit of good sportsmanship, Flynn gave him a one-armed hug.

"Aw, fuck!" Miguel said in disgust. "C'mon. I'll buy you both a beer. Loup, I wanna know what you think."

They went to a bar called the Jericho—another small, local place, this one favored by the Garzas and their crew. Miguel picked a secluded corner table that was already occupied.

"Out."

The occupants deserted it. A bartender hurried over with three bottles of beer.

"Okay." Miguel sat across from Loup, leaning forward. "Coach said you could predict fights. He said all you had to do was *see* the fighters to get it right most every time. If you'd seen 'em fight, always."

"Not always, not exactly."

"Damn close, though."

"Yeah."

"Hey." A young guy with a pool cue in his hand approached the table. "Wanna play?" he asked Pilar.

Miguel scowled. "Beat it!"

"Sure, I'll play," Pilar said in a good-natured tone. She got up, ruffled Loup's hair. "I don't need to listen to boxing talk, baby."

"Okay."

"So let me have it," Miguel said when she was gone. "You know me. You've seen the new guy. How's it gonna play out?"

"Right now?" Loup took a swig of beer. "Outside of conditioning, you're pretty evenly matched. He doesn't hit as hard as you do, but he's a little faster and he's slippery. You're a good boxer. So's he, and he's fucking fit as hell. If you don't take him down in the first three or four rounds, he wins. Right now, that's what I see happening."

He leaned closer. "So how do I beat him?"

"Jesus, Miguel!" She shook her head. "You want strategy, ask the coach. I'm not a coach."

"Yeah, but you *see* things," he persisted.

Loup sighed. "You want me to say something like, he drops his guard when he throws a left uppercut, right?"

Miguel's eyes lit up. "Yeah, exactly!"

"He does, but only a little. It's so quick most people wouldn't see it. *I* could tag him, sure. You couldn't. Mig, I'm sorry. I mean, I can guess what the coach's gonna say, but so can you."

He grunted. "Treadmill and bag work."

"Uh-huh."

"Yeah, well, thanks for trying." Miguel leaned back, drained half his beer. He gave the bottle a rueful look. "Guess I'm just looking for a shortcut, same as always." He glanced across the bar. Pilar was leaning over the pool table, lining up a shot. Two guys were jostling each other in an effort to assist her. "Looks like you've got some competition there, kid."

"Nah." Loup smiled. "She's just having fun."

Across the bar, Pilar sank her shot. She straightened, caught

Loup's eye, and blew her a kiss. One of the guys staggered, pretending to clutch at his heart in dismay.

"No wonder you're all goo-goo eyed," Miguel said wryly. "You two are about as cute as a box of fuckin' kittens."

She laughed.

"You doing okay with it?" His voice softened. "Figuring shit out?"

"Not exactly," Loup said honestly.

Miguel nodded. "I get that."

THIRTY-EIGHT

C oach Roberts gave Miguel six months to get in shape.
"Six months!" Miguel puffed out his chest in indignation. "Oh, c'mon. I'm not that bad off. I get to call my shot, that's the deal. Three."

"You want to call the shots or you want to win, son?"

He acquiesced with ill grace. "Fine. Six months."

Inside the ring, Miguel pushed himself. He had Loup to help him and he liked fighting. Outside the ring, he struggled.

Loup struggled, too.

Her world was in flux. The Santitos were dwindling, changing. Mr. Ketterling, the bitter teacher who'd hit Tommy with a yardstick, had long since drunk himself to death, replaced by a piecemeal series of volunteers. Father Ramon talked Danny Garza into providing funding to let Jaime teach a special program for some of the brightest kids in Outpost.

"Hey, that's perfect for you!" T.Y. said enthusiastically when Jaime told them the news. "That's great!"

"God, you're an idiot," Jane muttered.

"He's just trying to be nice." Jaime smiled wistfully. "Yeah, T.Y. It's great."

"So what would *perfect* be?" Mack asked.

"College." Jane answered for him, throwing a textbook across the room with unexpected force. "Graduate school. Jaime ought to be studying biological engineering, not playing teacher. I want to go to medical school."

"I thought Sister Martha offered you an official position in the dispensary," C.C. commented.

Jane shot him a withering glance. "And that's as good as it

gets. I'll be an assistant to an unlicensed, self-taught nurse pretending to be a nun. Someday, God willing, I'll even inherit the job."

"At least you're doing something *good* with your lives," Loup offered.

Pilar gave her a troubled look.

"Yeah," Jaime agreed. "That helps. It really does."

It wasn't a lot of money, but together it would be enough to allow them to move out and rent an apartment a block away. There was plenty of *space* available in Outpost, but precious little that offered electricity and running water.

For that, you had to pay.

Katya found a way, too. In the Outpost tradition that had begun a generation earlier, her Sergeant Buckland had made the offer to keep her in style. She made her announcement the same night, inspired by Jaime and Jane's.

"And you all called *me* a gold-digger!" Pilar said with asperity.

T.Y. flushed. "You heard about that?"

She shook her head. "Lucky guess."

"Yeah, well, that was before you decided to switch teams and run for Dyke of the Year," Jane said. Genuine concern tempered her usual sharp edge. "Kotch, are you sure?"

Katya defended her choice. "He's not like the others."

"Not a dog-killing rapist, you mean?" C.C. drawled.

"Fuck you!"

"Pax Olivia, guys." Mack silenced them. "Katya, *are* you sure? I've talked to Mike Buckland; he seems like a decent guy. But he's a soldier. In a year's time, he's out of here."

"Not if he gets promoted to staff sergeant." Her cheeks were pink—half anger, half nervous defiance. "He says he'll stay. Extend his tour, get a bonus. He says in another two, three years, they'll lighten up on the restrictions. And maybe we can get married."

"Honey, they all say that," Pilar murmured.

Katya set her jaw. "Michael means it."

"I hope to hell you're right," Mack said quietly.

The church never felt *empty*; it was the center of too much activity, especially during the day. Even the Santitos who left drifted back for dinner half the time, and sometimes it felt like old times. C.C. and T.Y. stayed, doing their part to keep the church running. Casting nets, trying to figure out what to do with their lives. There was Dondi, still the baby of the family at fifteen, not ready to leave the nest. Mack, living above the garage—a steady presence and a pair of steady hands.

And as always, there was Father Ramon and Sister Martha and Anna, the collective beating heart of Santa Olivia.

But at night it felt emptier.

Which wasn't all bad.

"Wow," Pilar said the first night that Jane and Katya were gone. She held the oil lamp aloft, surveying the rows of empty cots, casting angular shadows the length of the narrow room. "Weird. I guess it's just us now, baby." She looked sidelong at Loup. "Do you think we oughta—"

"Are you kidding?" Loup was already shoving their cots together and rearranging the sheets. "Hell, yeah."

"Stupid question," Pilar agreed. "C'mere."

They made love for hours that first night, trading positions, experimenting, reveling in the luxury of the time and plenitude of a shared bed and a night to spend in it. Bare skin against skin, a tangle of tongues and desire, bodies sliding together. The lamp burned low, guttered, went out. The sky lightened in the east, pale gray dawn showing in the high-arched windows.

"Loup." Pilar whispered her name, fingers tangled in her hair. "I love you."

Loup lifted her head, eyes soft. "I love you, too."

"I wanted to say it first." Pilar's fingers tightened. "Because I'm scared and you're not."

"Pilar . . ."

"Hush." Pilar kissed her. "Just hush, baby."

It lay between them, unspoken. At night it almost didn't matter. There was the bed and solitude and unbroken stretches of time. The novelty showed no signs of wearing off. There was the tenderness of those whispered confessions, the hectic giddiness of those first months growing into something deeper and more solid.

But during the day it was different.

With the Santitos dwindling, those who remained spent more time assisting with the day-to-day operations of the church. Loup spent more time training alone. She kept her promise to Coach Roberts and didn't lift weights without a spotter, but she spent hours working the bags and running on the treadmill by herself.

Like the treadmill, her thoughts ran in an endless loop, going nowhere.

There was the crushing moment of Tommy's defeat and the worse horror of his death, the bleak despair that had settled over the town. The blackened-over windows of the gym, the scrawled petitions to Santa Olivia. There was the pervasive sense that she could undo it. That she could change the ending, make the dream come true after all. Not for herself, but for Tommy.

For all of Santa Olivia.

And then there was Pilar, who loved her and didn't want to lose her. Who made her happy in a way no one else ever had. Who had altered her life without hesitation for her, setting all her earlier hopes and dreams aside. Pilar, whom she loved.

She had to choose between them, and she didn't want to.

Loup ran and ran and went nowhere.

THIRTY-NINE

As winter gave way to spring, Loup tried praying to Santa Olivia.

She'd seen it done, mostly by older members of Outpost, but she had only a vague notion of how to go about it. Religious instruction was something largely neglected among the Santitos. Father Ramon and Sister Martha had too much else to do, and Anna had worked hard enough just to get the rudiments of a secular education into them. The clever ones like Jaime and Jane had eventually taken their studies into their own hands. The rest of them merely abandoned their lessons and drifted toward adulthood.

Loup sat on her heels, gazing at the child-saint's effigy.

Santa Olivia stood in her niche, wearing her blue dress and her white kerchief, clutching her basket of plenty. Her wide dark eyes stared back, unblinking. To her right, Our Lady of the Sorrows bent a sympathetic gaze downward, pale rust stains on her cheeks.

"Santa Olivia," Loup whispered. "Tell me what to do."

She waited.

There was no answer, only the sound of footsteps behind her.

"I'm sorry." It was Anna's voice. She hesitated, then continued. "Are you all right, Loup?"

"Yeah. Just thinking."

Anna came alongside her and studied the effigy. "Such a sweet face. You know, *she* was there when you were born, too. Santa Olivia. You were practically born under her shadow, right there in the town square."

"Do you think it means something?" Loup asked.

"I think everything in life means whatever we make of it," she said gently. "Do you want to talk about what's bothering you?"

"I have to choose."

"Yes." Anna didn't ask what. It hadn't been discussed aloud, but she knew. On some level or another, they all did. "Are you seeking guidance?"

"Yeah."

"I hope you find it."

"Yeah." Loup took a deep breath. "I had this thought that maybe if Miguel wins, that would be a sign. That maybe he was the one meant to do it after all, and I was meant to help him. Do you think it might be true?"

Anna was silent a moment. "I can't answer that for you, Loup," she said at last. "You have to look inside your own heart for the answer."

"Why did you choose what you did?" Loup rose in a quick, fluid motion. She gestured around. "This. Them. Father Ramon and Sister Martha. How did you know?"

Anna smiled. "I looked inside *my* heart. It may seem strange, but it was a strange time. I love them both very much. And I believed very strongly in the good work they were doing. I still do."

"So you didn't have to *choose*."

"Between love and doing what I believed in?" she asked. Loup nodded. "No. But no one else understood, and in the end, I lost all my friends. All hard choices require a sacrifice. That's what makes them hard, Loup."

"That sucks."

"Yes," Anna said. "It does."

Santa Olivia's name day came. Loup was seventeen. Tommy had been dead for almost two years. She'd been training for almost two years. While everyone else was picnicking in the town square, Pilar let them into the Gin Blossom and poured them both a surreptitious inch from the expensive tequila that the bar kept on hand for Rosa Salamanca.

"Happy birthday, baby."

It was good, better than good. So smooth. It warmed without burning, a mellow warmth that spread and glowed.

You feel like it tasted.

"Thanks," Loup whispered.

"You bet." Pilar smiled, but there was a shadow of sorrow behind it. She twined her fingers with Loup's, lifted her hand, and kissed her knuckles. "C'mon. We better get out of here before I get in trouble."

And then it was past and the date of Miguel's match was hurtling down on them. He was ready, as ready as he'd ever been. Sparring with Loup in private, learning to fight a southpaw. Sparring with a couple of the other fighters in public, fighters closer to Terry Flynn's height and reach. Working on a strategy with the coach, practicing his combinations. Running, jumping rope, working the bags, and hitting the weights. He'd dropped ten pounds. Miguel was still built like a bull, but he was a leaner, fitter bull.

"Whaddya think *now*?" he demanded two nights before the fight. "I got a shot? Huh? Huh?"

"Yeah, Mig." She nodded. "You've got a shot. A real good one."

When the night came, he was cheered, long and loud. Miguel Garza might have been feared more than he was loved and resented more than admired, but he was one of Outpost's own, born and bred. In the ring, he turned around slowly, raising his arms. His robe was fancy and new. It had a blue bar with a single star across the shoulders and two broad vertical stripes, one red, one white.

Half the crowd roared louder.

"I don't get it," Pilar said.

They were near Miguel's corner. Coach Roberts glanced down,

a fierce light in his usually watery eyes. "That's the Texas flag, child. Used to be *your* flag."

"Oh."

Miguel shrugged out of his robe with a flourish. The flag motif was repeated on his trunks. He raised his arms again, reveling in the adulation.

"Don't show off, Mig," Loup murmured under her breath. "Save your energy."

Pilar took her customary grip on Loup's arm. "You really think he has a chance?"

"Yeah, I do."

"Would it change anything if he won?"

Loup turned her head, looked into Pilar's worried eyes. "Yeah," she said softly. "I guess it would."

"Okay." Pilar swallowed. "I'm gonna cheer my fucking head off for Miguel fucking Garza, then, okay?"

"Okay." Loup squeezed her arm. "So am I."

It was a good fight, the best Outpost had seen in years. The two men were evenly matched. Miguel was a brawler by nature, but he had the experience, training, and wits to harness his strength and fight a good inside game. Terry Flynn relied on his reach and speed to keep Miguel at range.

During the first few rounds, it was Flynn who struggled. He hadn't expected Miguel to be so prepared to fight a left-handed opponent. Miguel took advantage and pressed him, trying to close at every opportunity, softening him up with flurries of body blows. He landed a few solid jabs to the head, and in the third round, a combination ending with an uppercut that sent Terry Flynn staggering against the ropes.

The crowd roared.

Pilar's nails dug into Loup's arm.

Loup caught her breath at the simultaneous darts of hope and regret that lanced through her.

But then the referee stepped in between the two men. Miguel skipped back, bouncing a little. Flynn dragged himself off the ropes. He shook off the blow, tapped his forehead a couple of times, reminding himself to keep his guard up.

The match continued.

Tasting victory, Miguel pressed harder, going for the knock-out. He had Flynn on the defensive and he knew it. But the near miss had sharpened Flynn's focus. He found his rhythm and his defense improved.

"Slow *down!*" the coach shouted at Miguel between rounds. "You've got a lot of fight ahead of you, son! Pace yourself!"

"Aw, c'mon! I'm *killing* him out there!"

"No, you're not! Slow the fuck down, Mig!" Loup called.

His gaze slewed around, and he gave her a curt nod.

It was close. It was so very, very close. At the end of six rounds, Miguel was way ahead on points. Despite trying to pace himself, in the seventh, he began to flag. He held his ground, but Flynn began to score points on him. They weren't hard blows—nothing dramatic, nothing Miguel couldn't shake off in disgust.

But they counted.

By the eleventh and twelfth rounds, Miguel was spent. He plodded after Terry Flynn, swinging, but the snap was gone from his punch. Flynn was tired, too. Still, he kept moving, kept circling, kept landing outside jabs and straights.

The bell rang, ending the match.

"So?" Pilar shivered. "Who won?"

"I don't know," Loup said soberly. "I truly don't. It all depends on how the judges score it."

The judges took forever to deliberate, tallying and retallying the points. The crowd on both sides grew restless, booing and shouting catcalls.

At last the decision was announced. It was a split decision and it was close, very, very close.

Miguel lost.

FORTY

A pall settled over Outpost.

It wasn't as bad as Tommy's death, when hope had been raised so high then dashed so low, but it was bad. Miguel Garza went on a weeklong bender, drunk and belligerent. He got in a number of fights and broke one guy's jaw. When a couple of soldiers heckled him at Salamanca's nightclub, he went after them. It took four bouncers to hold him back, and if he hadn't been a Garza, he would have been detained and charged with assault.

He didn't show up to keep his sparring date with Loup that week, which didn't surprise her. What *did* surprise her was that Miguel showed up the following Sunday morning, still drunk and bleary-eyed.

"Okay, little girl," he slurred. "It's all on you, now. Let's fight."

"Miguel, you're in no condition to get in the ring," Floyd said.

"Shut up, old man."

"Mig, we can ask for a rematch," Loup said. "You damn near had him. That match could have gone either way."

"No." Miguel shook his heavy head. "No. I tried. I don't wanna work that fuckin' hard anymore. They're never gonna give it to any of us on points. System's rigged."

"You damn near KO'd him in the third!"

"Yeah, but I didn't." He wavered on his feet. "Whaddya want? This was always your fight, kid. Don't put it on me. You wanna change your fuckin' mind, change your fuckin' mind. Do you?"

"I don't know," Loup murmured.

"Well, you're goddamn well gonna have to decide!" Miguel

pointed. "Either get out or get in the ring. Right now, I need to hit someone and either it's gonna be you or I'll go find someone else."

She got in the ring.

Miguel went after her with drunken ferocity, ignoring Floyd's protests. Loup let him come after her and keep coming, catching or deflecting his blows with ease. She hit him back a few times, good, solid shots that sent shudders rippling through his thick, muscled body.

When it was over, he was panting and sweating, booze reeking from every pore, but he was calmer and clear-eyed. "Thanks, kid."

Loup nodded. "Sure."

"I mean it. You gotta decide."

"I know."

Still, she put it off. The choice hung over her, heavy as a stone. Another week passed, then another and another. Miguel kept their sparring dates, though more often than not he was drunk and sluggish in the ring.

Her uncertainty deepened.

In the small hours of the night, she dreamed of Tommy. His face fixed in concentration as he trained. His face glowing with pride in the ring. His face slack and lifeless on the operating table, a blue cotton cap hiding the damage to his skull.

But then she would awaken and see Pilar's face looking soft and sweet with sleep, sunlight picking out the highlights in her hair where it fanned across the pillow, brown silk streaked with blond.

"Don't look at me that way," Pilar murmured, catching her at it. "I can feel it."

"What way?"

She opened her eyes. "Like you're memorizing me."

It was a month after Miguel's loss that things changed. He showed up for their Sunday-morning session sober and steady. He listened to Floyd's injunctions and obeyed them scrupulously.

For the first time in weeks, they had a good session, and Loup felt Miguel was pushing her to the best of his ability.

"Good work," the coach allowed. "Hit the showers."

"Hey." Miguel caught Loup's arm. His brown eyes were somber. "Wait for me after you scrub down. I wanna talk to you, okay?"

"Yeah, sure," she agreed.

She washed and changed, taking her time. Miguel took notoriously long showers, heedless of whether it used up the limited supply of hot water. Today he was quicker than usual, and she didn't have to wait long before he emerged, black curls damp, smelling of soap.

"C'mere." He led her over to the weight benches. They sat facing each other on adjacent benches. Miguel breathed a heavy sigh. "Look, I don't like to meddle in other people's shit, okay? And I don't know how things are with you. This might be nothing. But you're facing a big choice, and God help me, I kinda care about you. I thought you oughta know what's going on."

"What?"

"You know how I told you everything gets around in this town?" he asked. Loup nodded. "Well, your girl's been seeing Rory Salamanca."

Loup stared blankly at him. "Pilar?"

"Um, yeah." Miguel ran a hand over his damp hair, awkward. "Last couple of Wednesday nights, anyway."

"Are you sure?"

"Yeah." His voice was unwontedly gentle. "I'm sure."

She stood up so fast her head spun.

"Whoa." Miguel rose, put his hands on her shoulders. "Slow down, kid. People are coming. You don't want 'em to see you breaking the sound barrier." He tightened his grip. "You gonna be okay?"

Loup blinked. "I dunno."

"Take it easy." He tried to shake her rigid shoulders, but they wouldn't budge. "See, this is why I don't do relationships. This shit happens. Happens to everyone. You're not the first, won't be the last. Don't do anything crazy. Go for a walk, clear your head. Okay?"

"Okay."

Outside, the sun was blazing high overhead. Spring, and it was already hot as hell in Outpost. Loup walked aimlessly, scuffing the dusty streets, her gym bag slung over one shoulder. She felt dizzy and disoriented, and there was a bone-deep ache in her chest like Miguel had landed a good one on her.

You can hurt, baby. I've seen *you hurt.*

She found herself at the public school. On a Sunday, it was locked and abandoned. She sat on the front steps where she and Tommy had sat side by side so long ago. There was a flagpole outside the entrance. She hadn't noticed it before. It still held the remnants of a flag, faded and tattered. A colorless rag snapping against the hard blue sky. If she squinted, she could still make out the lone star in the faded field, the two stripes.

It reminded her of Miguel's loss.

Santa Olivia's loss.

Loup rose—too quick, again. Dizzy. Anyone watching would have seen only a blur between sitting and standing. Tommy's voice in her memory. *Be careful!*

Careful.

She took slow, deep breaths until the dizziness passed, then made her way to the Gin Blossom.

This time Pilar saw her enter. There was no brightening of her eyes, no quick, glad smile on her lips. It faltered and died the second she saw the expression on Loup's face. "Hey," she said quietly.

"We need to talk."

Pilar nodded and turned to Joe Torres, who was counting bottles and making notes on a clipboard. "Joey honey, can you cover my shift today? Please?"

He agreed, grumbling.

They walked out side by side, not touching, not talking. Not until they reached an abandoned stretch of street. Office buildings, boarded and abandoned. Not so very long ago, they'd taken shelter from the rain here.

Loup halted and faced Pilar. "Rory Salamanca."

"Yeah." Pilar shivered, covered her face with her hands. Dropped them. "I wondered how long it would take you to find out."

"How long did it?"

"Not long. It's only been a couple of weeks."

Her heart ached. "Yeah, well, I know he's rich. And he's reasonably cute. Is he nice, Pilar? I hope at least he's nice."

"Yeah," Pilar said softly. "Yeah, actually, he is. Turns out he wanted to ask me out a while ago, but he thought it would be creepy, thought I was too young. He waited a couple of years. He's old-fashioned, you know?"

"Does he even know about me?"

"He knows," she murmured. "He asked. I told him . . . I told him it was nothing. Kid stuff. Just a way to screw with the guys' minds, keep them off my back." She swallowed. "I told him you were the one took it too serious. I told him I was gonna break it off with you."

"*Why?*" Loup whispered, eyes burning.

"Don't look at me like that." Pilar shuddered. "Jesus! Get mad. Yell at me."

"Pilar, *why?*"

"Because I'm tearing you apart!" Her raised voice echoed off the empty street. "Do you think I don't know it? See it? Goddamnit, Loup! I know what you have to choose; *you* know what you have to choose. And if you don't, what the fuck happens to us? Five years from now, ten years from now. You'll be trapped here. Stuck living in slow motion and hating me for it."

"No." Loup shook her head. "I'd never blame you."

"Oh, hell! You know what?" Pilar laughed in despair, gave a hiccup that was half sob. "You're right, you wouldn't. Baby, you don't even know *how* to be petty and spiteful and cruel. But *I* would. I'd see you being miserable every goddamn waking hour, and I'd blame myself for it. And one day, I'd start resenting you for making me feel like shit about myself . . ." Her shoulders shook.

Loup was silent.

Pilar got her breathing under control, wiped her eyes. "I love you." Her voice broke again. She took another minute. "And if I were a better person, I'd . . . I'd do what I oughta do. Quit asking you to let go of your dream. Stand by you, support you. Be glad I had you as long as I did, then give you a kiss and send you off like some goddamn war bride getting ready to be a widow." She shook her head, sunlight glittering on her tear-stained cheeks. "I'm not that brave, Loup. I'm not that strong."

"Why couldn't you just tell me?"

"Because I'm *not* that strong!" She drew a long, shaking breath. "I'm not strong enough to let you go, either. I need you to push me away."

"Toward Rory Salamanca?" Loup asked.

"Whoever, whatever. Rory was there." Pilar gave a slight, weary shrug. "I don't care. After you, it's all cheap tequila."

Loup lifted her gaze, letting the sun dazzle her burning eyes. She looked back at Pilar. "Is this really what you want?"

"No," Pilar whispered, tears making slow, steady tracks down her face. "But it's what I can live with."

Loup closed her eyes, letting the world go black. "Okay."

FORTY-ONE

It ended as abruptly and completely as it had begun.

Pilar moved out that afternoon.

"What the fuck?" T.Y. said in bewilderment, entering the garage where Loup was training with Mack. "Did you hear? Pilar just packed her shit and fucking *left*. Did you guys have a fight?"

Loup, working the speed bag, didn't answer.

"She told C.C. that Rory Salamanca was gonna let her have a room over the bar. Loup?"

She concentrated on the bag.

"What's going on?"

Mack glanced at Loup's face. "Shut up, T.Y."

"I just wanna know!" he protested.

Mack pointed at the door. "Not now. Go away."

He left, complaining.

Loup picked up her tempo, increased her force. A bolt in the swivel gave way and the bag went flying. "Shit."

"'S'okay." Mack hunted for the bolt, unperturbed. "I can fix it."

"Thanks."

He nodded.

Without Mack, it would have been unbearable. He'd always been the one who understood her best. He gave her the time and space to endure the hurt, made sure that others did the same.

And it *did* hurt.

Loup understood why Pilar had done it. She understood that her inability to choose had driven Pilar to it, and she understood that it was the only way Pilar could let her go. It didn't make it hurt any less. She moved through the days in a waking daze of loss and loneliness, her chest hollow and aching.

But in the ring, her focus sharpened.

It was all she had left. She felt it the first time she entered the gym, permeated with the smell of sweat and mildew and memories of Tommy. The ring stood empty, waiting. Beside it, Floyd was consulting a chart and Miguel was wrapping his hands.

"Hi, kid." Miguel met her eyes. When you took away the soldiers, Outpost was a small town. He knew. "You ready to do this?"

"Yeah." Loup took a deep breath. "I am."

And for a space of time, the world narrowed down and the hurt went away. There was only the steady dance of traded blows and sliding steps. Too slow, too stately; but it was training. Practice. It was the beginning of a long trajectory that would end in another ring, another dance. One that took place under blazing lights, with cheering crowds and an opponent who moved like lightning and hit like thunder.

One that would make a difference.

"Good work," Floyd said. "Good work."

Afterward the hurt came back. She washed and dressed slowly in Tommy's room. He'd never spent much time there and his presence had faded. The memory of Pilar was stronger. Pilar, pretending not to watch her. Storming out in anger when Loup called her on it.

Relenting.

Kissing her, rain-soaked.

Loup shook her head, trying to shake off the memory like a fighter shaking off a shot to the head.

She went downstairs to find Miguel already finished and waiting for her. "Hey, kid." He jerked his chin at her. "You ever gotten *really* good and drunk? Falling down, puking in the gutter drunk?"

"No," she said.

He clapped her shoulder. "Tonight's the night."

She thought he'd meant the rooftop, but Miguel took her to the Jericho.

"You need to be around people." He plunked a bottle of whiskey on the table between them. "Life goes on. For you, not so long. You're gonna do this thing, you gotta make the most of what's left." He poured a couple of shots. "Drink."

It was good whiskey.

You feel like it tasted.

I don't care. After you, it's all cheap tequila.

Her eyes burned.

"Jesus!" Miguel said in disgust. "Quit lookin' like a goddamn martyred saint on the cross." He refilled her glass. "Get pissed off, bitch and moan. Pick a fight. Or cry in your cups. I don't care."

You can't cry like regular people, can you?

"I can't," Loup said. "And I'm not."

"Can't and not what?"

"I can't cry like normal people. And I'm not pissed off." She drank the second shot, regarded the empty glass. "Not sure I can get drunk, either. I feel it at first, but it always burns off quick."

"'Cause you have a freaky-ass metabolism." Miguel poured again for both of them. "Drink faster. So how come you're not angry? She dumped your cute little ass for the rich boy."

It's all cheap tequila . . .

"Yeah." The third shot made her head swim. She watched Miguel drink his second, refill their glasses. "I know."

"So get mad."

"Can't." Loup shook her head. "Not at Pilar."

Miguel sighed, clinked his glass to hers. "Okay, kid. Just get drunk, then. Trust me, it helps."

He kept pouring and Loup kept drinking, two drinks to every one of his. And there came a point in the night when the whiskey swamped her metabolism, when the room wavered around her and there was only the tenuous now and the promise of oblivion.

No hurt.

Only this.

She was vaguely aware of Miguel walking her back to the church, her steps unsteady. A couple of MP patrols stopped them, but he made them go away. He was a Garza. It meant something in Outpost.

At the gate, Loup fumbled for her key.

"Hey, sweetheart." Miguel was drunk, too. He turned her around and pushed her against the closed gate, pinning her there with the weight of his body. "What about a payback fuck? C'mon, think about it. You could see her Salamanca, raise her a Garza."

She lifted her head with an effort. "Thought I didn't do it for you, Mig."

He stroked her cheek. "I like you like this."

The wrought-iron bars pressed into her back. Memories. *I swear to God, I could eat you up with a spoon.*

"Drunk?"

"Vulnerable."

"I don't want this, Miguel," Loup said softly. "Don't be this way. This isn't who you are. You're better than this."

He gazed at her, his face close to hers. "Maybe you think too much of me."

"No." A jolt of adrenaline ran through her, clearing the worst of the cobwebs from her head. She pushed him away—not hard, but hard enough to make him stagger. "Maybe you don't think enough."

"Fuck!" Miguel caught himself. "I'm only trying to help."

"Yeah, well, maybe, in your own weird way. Mig, I'm not as messed up inside as you think I am." Loup eyed him, but he kept his distance. "Or maybe I am, but not in the way you think. Pilar didn't leave me because she'd been waiting for Rory Salamanca."

"No shit," he said sourly.

"It was the only way she could think of to set me free to do this."

Miguel pulled a flask from his pocket and took a long drink. "Pretty goddamn shitty way."

"Yeah," Loup agreed sadly. "It was."

He held out the flask, drank again when she declined it. "Why didn't you tell me before?"

"At the Jericho?" She shrugged. "Like you say, it's a small town. I don't want it getting back to Rory. I don't wanna screw this up for Pilar. I screwed up her life bad enough already, and it's not her fault I couldn't make myself choose."

"Santa fuckin' Olivia." Miguel shook his head. "Fine. Enjoy your martyrdom."

She watched him stagger away, then let herself through the gate and made her way to a lonely cot in the dark, empty dormitory room.

FORTY-TWO

Miguel missed their next two sessions.

"I thought that boy had turned a corner," Coach Roberts mused after Miguel failed to appear a second time. "Did the two of you have some kind of falling-out?"

Loup sighed. "I guess."

"Hmm." He studied her. "Made a pass, did he? And you turned him down?"

"How'd you know?"

Floyd's mouth wrinkled. "Let's just say I've known Miguel Garza a long time. He takes opportunities where he sees them, and he doesn't like people saying no to him. If that's all it is, I imagine he'll come around." He rubbed his stubbled chin. "You're a good influence on him, Loup. It troubles him."

"So what do we do?" she asked. "Just wait?"

"No," he said slowly. "No, I think this is a good time for you and me to have a serious talk, child." He put aside his charts. "I'm given to understand you've been experiencing some hesitation. Something to do with a . . . young lady."

A pang of loss lanced her. "Mig told you?"

"He voiced some concerns, yes."

"Yeah." Loup ran one taped hand through her hair. "Well, I'm not experiencing hesitation anymore, sir."

"It's all right if you are." Floyd's voice was gentle. "For whatever reason. Nothing's been set in motion yet, nothing's official. We can call this off today and I promise I'll bear you no ill will. It's been a privilege and an adventure to train you."

"No." She shook her head. "I'm ready."

"Well, *ready*—"

"Ready to make it official." Loup met his eyes, her gaze steady. "To set things in motion, set a date. I'd like that. I'd like to have something to work toward."

He pursed his lips. "You're sure?"

She nodded. "I'm sure."

"All right." Floyd rubbed his chin again, taking on a sly look. "What would you think about Santa Olivia's name day?"

Loup's eyes lit up. "Seriously?"

"Seriously." He allowed himself a smile. "It falls on the third Saturday of the month next year. Your eighteenth birthday, if I'm not mistaken. If we're going to do this, we might as well do it with style and panache, Loup Garron."

"And you think I'll be ready? *Ready* ready?"

"*Ready* ready?" Floyd's smile deepened. "Well, it's nine months away. I can't guarantee anything except that in nine months, you'll be as ready as *I* can make you. This is uncharted territory, child."

"What about Mig?"

"Ah, Miguel." His smile faded. "I suspect he'll return in his own good time. But with your permission, I'd like to bring Kevin McArdle into this. It will be good for you to have a different sparring partner. He's out of practice, but I think he'll be willing and I think he's trustworthy. He was close to your brother."

"Okay."

The coach fixed her one more time with his pale, watery gaze. "And you're sure? One hundred percent sure?"

"Yes," Loup said simply.

He nodded. "I'll talk to McArdle. And I'll talk to Bill Argyle. Set the wheels in motion."

"Thanks, sir." She hesitated. "What's gonna happen to you when this all comes out?"

Floyd waved one hand. "You let me worry about that, child."

On the following Sunday, Loup arrived at the gym to find Kevin McArdle already there, warming up with a jump rope.

He'd always been diligent. His pale, freckled body had lost a bit of muscle tone, but he still moved the rope in a steady blur, feet skipping effortlessly.

"Hey, Loup!" Kevin greeted her with a smile, folded the rope over one arm. "What're you doing here, kiddo?"

"You didn't tell him?" she asked Floyd.

He shook his head. "Easier to show than tell."

"Huh?" Kevin glanced between them. "You asked me to help out with a special training project."

"A top-secret project," the coach agreed.

"Loup?" His voice was incredulous.

"Change and warm up," Floyd said to her, then to Kevin McArdle, "You'll see."

There was something exciting about the prospect of sparring with someone new, even if it was in slow motion. At least it was something. She knew Kevin; she'd watched him train since she was a kid. She'd seen him fight half a dozen times. Still, it would be different to step into the ring with him, because it was another step toward a fixed destination.

Motion.

Progress.

Loup warmed up slowly, skipping rope just quickly enough to get the blood flowing. She tapped the bags gently, watching Kevin watch her out of the corner of one eye, bemused and uncertain.

"Good enough," the coach said. "Gloves and gear."

He checked their headgear, made sure their mouth guards were in place, laced their sparring gloves. They climbed into the ring together.

"This is crazy." Kevin smiled at her around a mouthful of molded plastic, his coppery hair disheveled by the headgear. "But hell, okay. I don't mind. Think I still remember how this works." He smacked his gloves together. "Whaddya want, Coach?"

Floyd didn't look up from his charts. "From you? Oh, just go at her with everything you've got."

"Huh?"

"You heard me. We'll work out a program later." He glanced up. "Loup, I want you on defense only today. McArdle's faster than Miguel, but he's out of practice."

"Okay!" she called cheerfully.

"On my say-so, *go!*"

Kevin McArdle blinked at Loup, then took a gliding step forward and essayed a slow, careful jab at her head.

She batted his hand away. "Aw, c'mon."

The coach raised his voice. "I said *everything*, McArdle! For God's sake, the girl's able to handle anything Miguel Garza's thrown at her."

He stared at Loup. "He's serious."

"Uh-huh."

He blinked again. "*You're* serious."

"Yeah." Loup raised her gloved fists. "Listen, just try it, okay?"

"Okay." Kevin sounded dubious, but he came at her with a combination, a little faster than before. When she caught his blows with ease, his eyes widened. He picked up the pace and began to press her in earnest. Loup breathed slowly, trying to match his pace. He was a little clumsy, a little out of practice, but he was good. Faster than Miguel, though he didn't hit as hard. He didn't have the same killer instinct, either. Still, she admired his deft footwork as she caught and deflected, slipped and ducked.

"Holy shit!" When the coach called an end to the first round, Kevin was grinning. "Holy *shit!*"

"Yep," Floyd said laconically. "It's a goddamned miracle, son."

"What *are* you?"

"I dunno exactly," Loup admitted. "It's some kind of genetic-engineering thing. My dad was an experiment who ran away, so no one knows for sure. But the guy who killed Tommy, he was like me. Different. Remember Coach said there was something off about that fight? It wasn't the same guy you fought, Kevin. It was his twin or something."

Kevin exhaled hard, looked from one to the other of them. "You're going after him, aren't you?"

"Yep," Floyd repeated. "You in, son?"

His grin widened. "You're goddamn right I am, sir!"

FORTY-THREE

Days turned to weeks.

Weeks turned to months.

There wasn't much difference between them. Training and chores; training, training, and more training. Evenings spent with the remaining Santitos. There was Mack the handyman, Dondi—and T.Y, who stayed for Loup's sake. C.C. Rider came and went, peripatetic. He'd taken to hanging out with some of the Salamanders who were their old adversaries. Sometimes he crashed at one of their places, sometimes he returned to the church.

If there was gossip about Pilar, C.C. brought it.

"Rory Salamanca's moved her into his place," he announced at dinner one night. "His mom's pissed."

Everyone went quiet and looked at Loup.

"Is she doing okay?" she asked.

"Rosa?"

She shook her head. "Pilar."

"I guess." C.C. shrugged. "Not working as many hours at the bar."

"Well, that's what she always wanted, isn't it?" T.Y. observed. Loup looked sideways at him. "Well, *isn't it*?"

Father Ramon coughed into his hand. "The meat loaf is particularly savory tonight. Did you do something different, Anna?"

"Me?" Anna smiled. "No."

"I put chipotles in it," Dondi said helpfully. "Got 'em from Mrs. Escobar. Do you like it?"

"Very nice."

It hurt; it still hurt. Loup hadn't seen Pilar since the day she found out, the day Pilar left. Not since they returned to the church together and parted ways without speaking. The break had been clean and absolute.

In some ways, that was good.

It let her focus, wholly and absolutely, on a single fixed goal. A single path, a single course. One fight, one moment in time. The faceless crowd wouldn't matter. Nothing would matter but what happened in the ring. Nothing would matter but facing off against the man who'd killed Tommy.

Thunder and lightning.

"I think we've got him!" Floyd Roberts said to her some six weeks after she'd made the commitment. His face was flushed, exultant. "Bill's been mighty curious about this young mystery fighter with a bone to pick. I told him I thought you'd be ready come spring. I asked for the match, for the date. Told him if he gave us Ron Johnson, you'd take him apart. He agreed to everything."

"That's great." Loup cocked her head. "Coach? When you were setting up Tommy's match, did you tell him you thought Tommy could take his guy?"

"I did." His color faded. "God help me, I did. We had a side bet."

"So that's why he put in a ringer."

His mouth wrinkled. "I suspect."

"Is that why you're helping me?"

"Guilt?" He laid a hand on her shoulder. "It always has been, child. You knew that. I told you, I loved your brother like a son."

Loup nodded.

"But *you*." Floyd's grip tightened on her. "I confess, I want to see what happens. After all these years, I still believe in the science of boxing. I want to *see* it play out at that level."

At the end of three months, Miguel Garza staged an unexpected return. Loup arrived at the gym on a Sunday morning to find him warming up alongside Kevin McArdle.

"Hey, kid." Miguel greeted her with a jerk of his chin.

"Hey, Mig!" She was glad to see him. "You back?"

"Maybe." He left off the heavy bag and leaned against the wall, folding his arms over his chest. "Kinda figured you must of recruited McArdle. He was tight with your brother. Like to see how you match up against him. You mind, Coach?"

Floyd shook his head. "Nope."

Miguel watched them spar, offering a number of jeering comments about Kevin's abilities. It drove him to be more aggressive than usual, which Loup appreciated. He actually caught her by surprise when she tried to move inside on him, landing a right hook to the side of her padded head.

"You hit like a girl, McArdle!" Miguel called.

Kevin grunted. "Is that supposed to be ironic, Garza?"

Miguel laughed.

"So I been thinking," he said when they finished their session. "Loup could probably use more time in the ring, huh?"

"Probably," the coach allowed.

"The little girl wears you out, doesn't she?" Miguel said to Kevin, who was breathing hard and sweating. "You're quick on your feet, that's good. But you don't hit hard enough to give her a taste of what it's gonna be like."

Kevin wiped his forehead. "You think you do?"

"Not if that fucker's got anything near Loup's firepower. But I got an idea." Miguel tossed a pair of sparring gloves at Floyd, who caught them reflexively. "Whaddya think, Coach?"

He hefted the gloves. "Weighted?"

"Uh-huh." Miguel nodded. "Buckshot." He gave a lazy grin. "Can't use it for anything else, might as well put it to good use."

"Jesus, Garza!" Kevin sounded appalled.

"What?" He shrugged. "You're a decent guy, but you're a bit of a pansy, McArdle. Good as she is, Loup's green. She's gonna step in that ring without ever having had a real match. That can't be helped. I can't give her one, and neither can you. This might help level things."

"It's worth a try," Floyd said. "But you'll wear yourself out right quick trying to box in those things, son."

"Yeah, well, you'll still have McArdle." Miguel shrugged again and took the gloves back. "If you ask me, we oughta take Loup outta the headgear a few times." He hoisted the gloves. "Let me work her over with these, get in some good, solid shots. She needs to know what it's like to get hit and hit hard."

"Jesus, Garza!"

"What do you think?" the coach asked Loup.

She thought about the first time she'd sparred with Miguel and how it had thrown her off her game once she'd let him land a solid shot on her. It didn't bother her anymore—she'd grown far too disciplined—but Ron Johnson would hit a hell of a lot harder than Kevin or Miguel. "It can't hurt."

"Sure it can." Miguel grinned. "That's the point."

Floyd nodded. "We'll try it."

They put the plan into action the following Wednesday. After Loup went a brisk three rounds with Kevin McArdle concentrating on strategy, Floyd unfastened her headgear and laced Miguel into the weighted gloves.

"God have mercy," he muttered, glancing at Loup. "I'm going so far out on a limb here, you might as well call me a squirrel." He took a deep breath. "Okay. Let's have one clean round."

It was different, but not all that different. She could feel the extra weight when she caught Miguel's punches, that was all.

"Break!" The coach sighed. "All right, if we're going to do it, let's do it. Loup, on my say-so, pretend Miguel catches you off guard. Miguel, hit her with a combination. Go!"

They circled warily, trading blows.

"Now!"

Miguel went straight for her head, throwing two right jabs and a left cross. The pain was explosive. Loup held her ground and kept her guard up. Through the bloodred tide of pain and the dazzling brightness bursting in her head, she sensed Miguel moving in on her. She bobbed instinctively, feeling a breeze as his right hand soared past her left ear. Miguel grunted. She ducked her chin and began pounding his torso with hooks.

"Break!"

Loup squinted at the coach, realizing her left eye was already swelling. He looked back at her, mildly horrified. "Was that okay?"

"Yes." Floyd cleared his throat. "Um . . . yes. Let's call it a day. Loup, I'll get you an ice pack."

"Okay. Can we try it again next time?"

He looked at her and sighed. "God have mercy."

Afterward, Miguel invited her to join him on the rooftop, acting as though he'd never been away. They sat in companionable silence, Miguel smoking a cigar, Loup holding an ice pack to her face.

"So," he said eventually. "Sorry about that, kid."

"Hitting me? You were supposed to."

"Bailing on you." He puffed on his cigar. "I kinda took myself by surprise that night. Guess I got some weird feelings about you."

Loup lowered the ice pack. "Yeah, well, that *vulnerable* thing's a little pervy, Mig."

"I know." He pointed at the ice pack. "Put it back. Twenty minutes on, twenty minutes off."

She pressed it to her face.

Miguel smoked. "So is our deal still good?"

"You gonna keep your end of it?"

He grinned. "You want me to hit you some more, huh?"

"Yeah, I do." Loup looked curiously at him over the edge of the ice pack. "Do you get off on it, Mig?"

"Nah." He shifted, leaning his elbows on his knees. "Not exactly. I mean, I do get off on fighting in a way. You know?"

She nodded. "I know."

"So in that way, yeah." Miguel flexed his hands. "I like hitting. It feels good. And you're so goddamned hard to hit, it feels *really* good. But I know it's bullshit, too. Like my father wanting to be a big man. He couldn't of done fuck-all in this town if the army didn't let him. I couldn't lay a fucking glove on you in the ring if you didn't let me. I'm not my father. I know the difference."

"Okay."

He glanced at her. "Would it matter?"

"If you got off on it?" Loup shrugged. "Might make me feel like I needed a shower."

Miguel laughed. "God, you're a weird kid!"

"Yeah, I know."

"I heard your girl's moved in with Rory Salamanca," he said. "You talk to her?"

Loup shook her head. "No."

"Too bad." He smoked in silence for a while. "I been thinking about what you said before."

"About Pilar?"

"About winning a ticket out of here, you little freak." Miguel met her eyes. "Look . . . I can't promise anything. I don't even know what the hell's out there or if anyone gives a flying fuck about us. But if it happens, I'll try, okay?"

She lowered the ice pack, eyes shining. "Seriously? Seriously, Mig?"

"Yeah, seriously." His tone was gruff. "Back with the ice, Loup."

"Thanks, Miguel."

"Shut up."

"Okay."

FORTY-FOUR

Loup got used to getting hit hard.

The coach didn't like it, but he allowed it—at least enough times that the pain and the effects of the impact no longer came as a shock. If it happened in the ring, she'd be ready for it. Once Floyd was satisfied of that fact, he insisted that they cut back on using the weighted gloves.

"I'm worried about long-term damage, child," he said.

Loup shrugged. "I'm not exactly planning on a long-term life, sir."

"You don't know that." Floyd pointed at her. "I understand why you're doing this, and you understand why I'm helping you. But you're too young to give up hope. You've no idea where your life might lead you."

"What do you think they'll do to me?" she asked.

He was silent for a long moment. "I can't say for sure. I wish I knew. No doubt they'll study you, run tests on you. In time, I imagine they'd like to recruit you. But . . ." His voice trailed off.

"But what?"

"It's the Santa Olivia business that troubles me. She may be gone, but believe me, she's not forgotten." Floyd frowned. "As the day draws nearer, I wonder if we might not be wise to rethink the date."

"Reschedule? Why?"

"You got under their skin when you pulled those stunts, child. I'll tell you the one thing Bill Argyle fears more than anything else, and that's having a full-fledged insurrection in this town. He'd have to put it down and put it down hard. It would be ugly."

"So that's the one thing the general fears more than anything else, huh?" Loup said softly. "More than El Segundo?"

The coach didn't answer.

"There isn't any El Segundo, is there?" She studied him. "How come we're here? How come they put up the walls and built the bases?"

"It was a time of terrible fear and rampant death," Floyd said in a gentle tone. "When the pandemic began to spread, Mexico was hit hard. People fled over the border, carrying sickness. Sometimes there was violence."

"So they built the walls to keep them out? Why not just say so?"

"I suppose it sounded . . . callous." He glanced at Loup's uncertain face. "Cruel, heartless. And there were raids, though not on the scale they claimed. But it was easier to convince people to go along with it if they believed there was a vast plot against the nation." His mouth twisted. "Hordes of desperate brown people clamoring to invade the Southwest and take over our hospitals by force."

"Oh." Loup thought about it. "So are we at war with Mexico, or not?"

Floyd didn't answer for a moment. "Not officially, no. Let us say that the legend of El Segundo began as a useful fiction with some faint basis in fact. But that was a long time ago, and it has long since become a charade used to justify radical actions that should have been rectified years ago."

Loup blinked. "What does that have to do with me pretending to be Santa Olivia?"

"It does and it doesn't." Floyd sighed. "Child, Bill Argyle's not a bad man, but he's part of a very bad enterprise. I do believe he's torn. There's a part of him would like to see this edifice cracked open. That's why he offered a ticket north to any fighter who could win a prize match. And there's a part of him that's scared to see it happen, because some very bad things have been done in the name of protecting this country, and it's going to be an unholy scandal if and when the truth comes out. That's why he sabotaged the one fighter I told him could do it."

"Okay." She wasn't entirely sure what he meant.

"What he doesn't want is to have it happen here." He pointed at the floor. "Not in Outpost, not on his watch. When you pulled that Santa Olivia business, he was terrified that the town would rally behind whoever was responsible for it, and he'd be forced to put down a full-scale insurrection. Against a bunch of unarmed civilians, it would have been a goddamned bloodbath, and it would have been mighty hard to keep a lid on that kind of atrocity. It's always galled him that he couldn't get to the bottom of it. So when you ask me what they'll do to you, I don't know. The revelation of your existence is going to open up the proverbial can of worms. They're going to want to know if it was part of a widespread conspiracy. They're going to want to know who else was involved. They're going to question you. Hard."

"Okay."

Floyd looked ruefully at her. "Okay, says the girl who doesn't mind getting punched in the face with a fistful of buckshot. Loup, is there any evidence after all these years that anyone helped you? Any proof?"

She shook her head. "No. I mean, they'll figure out people like Father Ramon guessed it afterward, but there's no way they can prove anyone helped me."

"Good." He nodded. "Insist that you acted alone. Whatever they do, stick to your story. And no matter what they say, no matter what they promise you, don't trust them. I suspect in time they'll have to accept it as nothing more than childish pranks played by a very . . . unusual . . . child. One, perhaps, with a delusion of destiny."

"Santa Olivia."

"Precisely."

"So why do you wanna change the date?" Loup asked.

"I'm not sure it's wise to foster the semblance."

She puzzled out the meaning. "I don't think it matters, sir.

They're gonna know anyway. And I don't think people are gonna rise up over this, try to make them give me back or anything. It'll just give them . . . I dunno. Hope, maybe. That things can change, that we're not always gonna be all alone here."

"Delusions of destiny," Floyd murmured.

Loup shrugged. "Well, it's a pretty crappy destiny, but yeah."

"All right. We'll keep the date." He fell silent again, regarding her with his watery gaze. "Loup, there *is* a chance that Miguel Garza will come out of this with a ticket to the outside world. If he does, he'll be very closely monitored. If someone like Miguel were to get in touch with the better angels of his nature and take it upon himself to become Outpost's least likely hero and, say, contact the media in an attempt to bring the edifice crashing down, I very much hope that he would be circumspect."

"Circumspect?"

"Careful."

She gave him a look of wide-eyed innocence. "Okay. But I don't see Mig being that guy, sir."

He returned a dry smile. "Neither did he."

The old year gave way to the new. Loup's training intensified. She maintained a base level of conditioning, running endless miles to nowhere on the treadmill in the garage. Working the bags, hitting the weights. She began sparring four times a week, Kevin and Miguel working a staggered schedule. She honed her skills, all of them dedicated to fighting a taller, stronger opponent.

Defense: slipping and ducking and crouching, making herself an impossibly small target.

Offense: getting inside, working the body. Scoring points.

"It's not enough!" Miguel, sweating, scowled at her. "You gotta go for the knockout, Loup. You *gotta*."

"Okay." She threw an uppercut, connecting with the side of his padded chin.

Miguel's eyes rolled up in his head, showing the whites. His knees gave way, his body sagging to the canvas.

"Break!" Floyd called.

"You okay, Mig?" Loup stood over him, peering at him.

"Yeah." His eyes opened. He moved his jaw experimentally, lying flat on his back on the stained canvas. "Yeah. Like that. Trust me, you can't count on the judges, sweetheart. That game's rigged. You gotta give the people something they can *see*. Something they can believe in, something no judge can ignore."

"I'll try."

"Good."

Days that had crawled began to pass more quickly. With a month to go, word leaked out from the army that the fighter who'd killed Tom Garron was returning to fight a mystery opponent on Santa Olivia's day. The town began to buzz with speculation. Bets were made, hoards of money changing hands. The popular money was on Miguel Garza, amid complaints that it was all a publicity stunt.

"Sure wish I could place a bet on *you*," T.Y. said. "I'd make a pile."

"Don't you dare."

"I won't. I won't! Even C.C.'s not that dumb." He watched Loup ease a barbell back into its cradle. "We all kept your secret pretty good, huh?"

She laughed. "You blabbed to C.C. a week after I told you!"

T.Y. flushed. "Yeah, well, after that."

"Yeah, you did."

He handed her a water bottle. "I'm gonna miss the hell out of you, Loup."

She drank. "I thought I was the most boring person on the planet."

"Don't tease. I mean it. Don't worry, I'm not gonna pull a Pilar and try to talk you out of it. I get why you've gotta do this. Haven't I been here every day, helping you? I'm gonna miss you, that's all." T.Y. shrugged. "Nothing's gonna be the same without you."

Loup smiled. "Thanks. I'm gonna miss the hell out of you, too." She drank again, lowered the bottle. "And Pilar *did* get it."

"I wondered if you were gonna let that slide." He added weight to the barbell. "You seen her?"

"No." She laid back down on the bench.

It wasn't entirely true. Once, when her heart was especially restless and aching, Loup had walked past Rory Salamanca's house on her way home from the gym. It was late enough that almost all the residential areas were dark, generators shut down for the night. Not the street where the Salamanca family lived. All Rory's lights were ablaze. Inside, Rory and Pilar were sitting at a dining table while an older woman served dishes. Rory was talking, gesturing animatedly, while Pilar listened to him with her chin in one hand.

She didn't look enthralled, but she didn't look unhappy.

Loup had watched for a long time, then walked home.

"Are you *gonna* see her?" T.Y. asked.

"Why do you care?" Loup hoisted the barbell and did a set. "You're the one never thought she was good enough for me."

"Yeah, but you did."

FORTY-FIVE

The last month fled.

It seemed impossible after all the endless hours of training, but it did. Day after day slipped away until there were almost none left.

"I want you to come in tomorrow for a last session with Miguel," Floyd said on the second-to-last day. "Mig, can you make seven a.m.?"

He grunted. "If I have to."

Floyd consulted his chart. "You do. Okay, Loup. Miguel in the morning, then a light workout on your own. Don't overdo it. You're primed and ready. We don't want to overtrain and take the edge off."

"Okay."

He looked up. "How are you feeling?"

"Good," she said simply. "I'm glad it's almost here."

The coach nodded. "Good girl."

Back at the church, Sister Martha pulled Loup aside and asked about her regimen for the last day.

"Why?" Loup asked after telling her.

The nun-who-wasn't-a-nun smiled. "Anna and Ramon wanted it to be a surprise, but I wanted to make sure we weren't interfering with Mr. Roberts' orders. We're planning a supper in your honor." A shadow of sorrow colored her smile. "A last supper, I suppose. A reunion. All the Santitos will be there."

She caught her breath. "All?"

Sister Martha amended her words. "Almost all."

"But not Pilar." Loup cocked her head. "Did you invite her?"

"No." She hesitated. "I didn't think you'd want . . . No. I

didn't think, to be perfectly honest. After so many years, I ought to know you better. Of course you'd want her there." She gave a brisk nod. "I'll send Dondi over with an invitation right away."

"No, don't. I'll do it."

"You're sure?"

"Yeah." Loup smiled wryly. "I was gonna go over there tomorrow anyway."

"Of course you were." Sister Martha touched Loup's cheek, her blue-gray eyes soft. "Our fearless child. I wish to fucking Christ I was sure letting you do this was the right choice."

"I didn't exactly give you a choice," Loup admitted.

"True."

On the eve of Santa Olivia's day, she awoke filled with a sense of brightness. At the gym, Miguel eyed her, yawning.

"What are you so fuckin' happy about?"

"I just am."

After they warmed up, Miguel pulled himself together and gave her a good final sparring match, crisp and forceful. The coach nodded his approval, setting his charts and notes aside for the last time.

"You're ready, child," he said when they finished. "You're as ready as God and man can make you."

"So that's it?" Miguel spat out his mouthpiece. "We're done?"

"*You* are."

He hesitated. "What about you, kid? Whaddya gonna do with yourself today? You want company?"

"Nah." Loup shook her head. "I've got some stuff to do and they're having a special dinner for me at the church tonight."

Miguel shrugged. "Okay, then."

"Thanks, Mig." She touched her gloved fist to his shoulder. "For everything. I never thought I would of said this to anyone after Tommy died, especially you, but you've been kind of like a brother to me." She grinned. "A big grouchy, pervy brother."

He laughed. "Yeah, well . . . I'll see you tomorrow, huh? Me and McArdle will be in your corner."

"We'll meet here at five," Floyd confirmed. "They've agreed to postpone the weigh-in until tomorrow. I've arranged for an escort to the town hall."

"Fancy, fancy," Miguel said.

"It's a big day." His gaze rested on Loup. "You know what to do?"

She nodded. "A light workout today. Lots of carbs, early to bed. Tomorrow, nothing but warm-up and stretching."

"Good girl." Unexpectedly, Floyd pressed his lips to the padded brow of her headgear. His watery eyes swam. "Godspeed, child."

"Thanks, sir," Loup whispered. "To you, too. For everything."

He flapped a hand at her. "Go."

She washed and changed, ventured out into the sunlight. It was late morning. The spring sky was hard and blue overhead. Loup breathed the arid air, filling her lungs. The streets of Outpost looked dusty and squalid. For some reason, the sight filled her with tenderness.

She slung her gym bag over her shoulder for the last time and walked to Rory Salamanca's house.

Knocked on the door.

Pilar answered it.

"Hey," Loup said softly.

"Hey." Pilar gave her a tearful, dazzling smile that made Loup's heart roll over in her chest. "Hey, yourself."

"Is it okay that I'm here?"

"Are you serious?" Pilar wiped her eyes. "I've been trying to work up the nerve to go see you all morning."

"Yeah?"

"Yeah." She sniffled. "I was scared you wouldn't want to see me. Scared it would screw with your head."

"It won't."

"Okay." Another dazzling smile. "Will you come in? Please?"

"Yeah." Inside, Loup dropped her gym bag in the living room

and looked around. Everything was clean and expensive, polished surfaces gleaming. Nothing was new, but it had all been maintained with exquisite care. "Nice."

"I guess." Pilar shrugged. "Rory's mom chose everything. He pays someone to keep it up."

Loup gazed at her. "You look good."

Pilar flushed. "*You* do."

"Thanks."

"Sure." Pilar's blush deepened. "Do you, umm, want something? Soda or juice? A glass of water?"

"Water, yeah."

Pilar led her into the big, fancy kitchen, poured a glass of water with ice. She handed it to Loup, their fingers brushing.

"Thanks," Loup whispered.

"Uh-huh." Pilar swallowed. "He's not here, if that's what you're wondering. Rory."

"No?"

"No." She raked a hand through her hair. "He won't be back until five or six."

"Okay." Loup drank. "I guess . . . I just wanna know, Pilar. Are you okay? Are you happy?"

She leaned against the gleaming kitchen sink, folding her arms under her breasts. "I'm okay. *Happy's* a pretty big word, you know? I like . . ." She glanced around. "Being pampered, I guess. Being taken care of. Most of the time, anyway. Rory can be sweet. Sometimes he makes me laugh. His mother hates my guts. She doesn't trust me." She shrugged again. "She's got pretty good instincts, Rosa Salamanca."

"Why?"

"I spend way too much time thinking about you." Pilar met her gaze without flinching.

"Me, too."

"Yeah?" Pilar's eyes brightened.

"Yeah." Loup smiled. "I still have to do what I have to do. But I think about you every day, Pilar. I miss you."

Her color rose again. "So . . . there hasn't been anyone else?"

"No." Loup shook her head. "Mig got drunk and hit on me, but no."

"Miguel *Garza*?"

"Yeah." She laughed. "He's okay in his own jerky way, though. More than okay. He's been a real good friend to me." She drank more water. "So C.C. said you weren't working as many hours at the bar."

"Yeah," Pilar said slowly. "Rory's got a jealous streak. Typical guy, you know? He likes knowing other guys want what he's got, but then he gets suspicious."

"He doesn't—"

"No." Her voice was adamant. "No, he just sulks. I wouldn't put up with any bad shit from him. I got that much out of living at the church. From knowing you and the Santitos. I wouldn't."

"Okay." Loup finished her water, set down the glass, and looked around. "So what do you do all day? Play housewife?"

Pilar made a face. "Not even. I told you, Rory's got someone who comes to clean. His mom doesn't trust me to do a good enough job. I mean, not that I *want* to, but . . . shit! I'm not even allowed to cook because I can't make his favorite meals just right."

"You hate cooking."

"I hate cleaning," she said. "I don't mind cooking."

Loup smiled. "You used to."

"Yeah, I guess." Pilar smiled back at her. "Now I kind of miss it. Be careful what you wish for and all that, you know?"

"Is it? Everything you wished for?"

She blew out her breath and didn't answer. "You wanna know what I do all day lately? It's stupid. I made something for you. Probably a dumb idea."

"What?"

"It's dumb. I shouldn't even show you."

"Pilar!" The sense of exasperation was so familiar, it made her laugh. "C'mon."

"Okay, okay." Pilar led her through the house to a sunny room overlooking the backyard. It held a daybed and a sewing table. "I spend a lot of time here. It's the one room that's kind of mine."

"Sewing?"

"Sometimes, yeah. Sometimes just daydreaming." She picked up a gleaming mass of satin, smoothed it. "Here."

It was a boxing robe. The robe was blue, as blue as a summer sky. The hood, trim, and sash were white.

"Santa Olivia's colors," Loup murmured.

"Yeah." Pilar nodded. "I got the idea from Mig's robe. Stupid, huh?"

"No." Her eyes burned. "Jesus, Pilar! It's wonderful."

"Try it on."

It fit perfectly and felt incredibly luxurious. "Where'd you get the fabric?"

"Oh, I made Rory get it." Pilar adjusted the hood. "Salamancas can get their hands on anything. It took three tries to get the right color." She smiled wryly. "He thinks I'm making myself a fancy dress. Won't he be surprised. But then, I guess a lot of people are gonna be pretty goddamn surprised tomorrow, huh?"

"Yeah, they are."

"Loup." Her name, breathed softly. There was an ache in it. Pilar pushed back her hood, cupped her face. She feathered kisses all over her face—her cheeks, eyelids. The corners of her mouth, the tip of her nose. Over and over, unable to stop. Kissed her lips, tenderly at first, then with rising passion. She shuddered, lifted her head. "I shouldn't do this."

"Rory?" Loup asked.

"No. God, no. You. The fight."

"It's okay."

"It's just . . ." Pilar took a sharp breath, tears in her eyes. "I love you so fucking much. And I promise, I promise I won't get hysterical or ask you not to go through with it—"

"Pilar."

"I won't! I can do it. I can be brave; I can be a war bride. I won't even cry. I promise. I just want this, I want this to remember—"

"Pilar." Loup wound her arms around her neck. "Shut up."

She smiled through tears. "Seriously?"

Loup smiled back. "Very seriously."

It should have been bittersweet, but it wasn't. It was sweet, achingly sweet. A year's worth of hurt melted away. They fell onto the daybed. Loup kissed away the tears Pilar had promised not to cry, held her down and kissed her hard and deep until Pilar made an inarticulate sound of pleasure and yanked on the sash of her robe.

Sweet.

So sweet.

Sunlight spilled through the window, spilled warmth over their bare skin. It was even better than her memories—better, deeper, more. Soft and slick and tender, hard and urgent. They made love for hours, pouring a lifetime's worth of love and desire into a single afternoon.

It was only afterward that it was bittersweet.

They were quiet in the aftermath, lying entwined in a tangle of shed clothing, the gleaming satin robe spread beneath them. Pilar lay with her head pillowed on one arm, gazing at Loup, tracing the curve of her cheek over and over.

"Memorizing me?" Loup asked softly.

"Yeah." Her smile didn't reach her eyes. "I am."

"I wish—"

"I know." Pilar kissed her. "Hush, baby."

Her stomach growled. "Pilar?"

"Hmm?"

"I'm starving."

Pilar laughed; sat up and ran her hands over her face. "Yeah. Yeah, of course you are. C'mon, baby. I'll cook for you."

She rummaged through the refrigerator and scrambled eggs and chorizo in the shiny kitchen, looking impossibly sexy in nothing but a half-buttoned shirt. Loup perched on a stool, watching.

"Here." Pilar slid a heaping plate across the counter.

"You don't want any?"

She shook her head. "No."

Loup ate quickly and methodically. "Did you know that's how my parents met?"

"In a kitchen?"

"Over eggs and chorizo." She forked another mouthful, swallowed. "In the diner. Oh, shit, I forgot."

"What?" Pilar looked alarmed.

"Will you come to dinner tonight?" Loup glanced up at her. "At the church? Everyone's going to be there. All the old Santitos."

She shivered. "They must hate me."

"No one hates you." Loup finished and pushed her plate away. "Will you come? Please?"

"Do *you* want me there?"

"Yeah. Yeah, I do."

Pilar took a deep breath. "Okay."

FORTY-SIX

It was late in the afternoon when they left Rory Salamanca's house. Pilar locked the door, then turned and kissed Loup ardently. Next door, drapes twitched in the nearest window.

"Um." Loup nodded in that direction.

"Fuck it." Pilar kissed her again, sinking both hands deep into her hair. "That old witch Rosa's got spies everywhere. I don't care."

"No?"

"No." Another kiss. "I'm gonna tell Rory the truth after tomorrow."

"Yeah?"

"Yeah, well . . . yeah." She smiled ruefully. "I guess I owe him. And no matter what happens, I'm gonna be a fucking wreck. I'm not gonna be able to hide it. And he's gonna have questions, a lot of questions. Starting with, gee, honey, how come you never told me that cute little girlfriend you *said* you weren't serious about isn't entirely human?"

"What do you think he'll do?"

Pilar shrugged. "I haven't the faintest fucking idea. You're gonna turn this town upside down, baby. All bets are off." She was quiet a moment. "Just so you know, I'm not gonna be there tomorrow."

Loup searched her face. "Why?"

"I don't think I could stand it," she said honestly. "I have a hard time watching the fights as it is. You . . ." She shook her head. "I'm being as brave as I can, Loup. I can't watch you get hurt. And I *can't* watch them take you away. I'd fall apart."

"Okay."

"Are you sure?"

"Yeah." Loup nodded. "I understand. I do."

"Thanks." Pilar gave her another dazzling smile and took her hand. "Okay, I won't say another thing about it, I promise."

It felt strange and familiar, wonderful and terrible to approach the church for the last time, Pilar's hand in hers, holding on for dear life. It was to be an early dinner and most of the Santitos were already there, milling around the dining room, falling back into old patterns.

"Shit, Loup!" T.Y. glanced up. "We were starting to . . . oh."

A few heartbeats of silence passed.

Sister Martha crossed over without hesitation, kissed Pilar's cheek with genuine warmth. "Welcome back, dear. I'm so glad you could join us."

Without letting go, Pilar eased her death grip on Loup's hand and smiled with relief. "Thanks, Sister. Me, too."

And then it was okay—or as okay as it could be. The Santitos shook their heads, still bemused by it, but strangely unsurprised that the relationship no one had ever imagined had reemerged in full force on this night of nights.

Accompanied by Pilar, Loup went upstairs to drop off her gym bag. She unpacked the boxing robe and hung it on the front of the wardrobe, the blue silk shimmering in the fading light.

"I should of ironed it for you." Pilar examined it. "Guess it got a little wrinkled, huh?"

Loup smiled. "I guess."

"Some saint." She gave her a sparkling sidelong glance. "It's not too bad. I think the worst of it will come out overnight." She looked around the room. "Jesus! It's so empty in here."

"Yeah, I know."

"Has it been lonely?" Pilar's voice was wistful.

"Yeah."

"I'm sorry, Loup." She shivered. "So sorry."

"I know, I know." Loup stroked her hair. "Don't talk about it, okay?"

"Okay." Pilar pulled her close, kissed her with lingering desire. "I guess we have to go downstairs, huh?" she whispered against her lips.

"Yeah." Loup kissed her back. "We really do."

Downstairs, Katya had arrived, making the Santitos complete. She looked good—happy and content despite the odds. It seemed her Sergeant Buckland was one of the good ones after all, at least so far.

The mood should have been somber and strained, but it wasn't. They talked, reminiscing, reliving old quarrels and old affairs. The fights with the Salamanders during the turf wars. The exploits of Santa Olivia.

"Don't ever admit any of you were involved in it," Loup warned them. "I gotta tell them it was all me."

"How many of you *were* involved?" Father Ramon asked in curiosity.

They glanced around at one another. Jaime cleared his throat. "Pretty much all of us, Father."

He shook his head. "I should have known."

A little before sunset, they sat down to eat. It was a simple meal. Loup worked her way steadily through a small mountain of pasta, mindful of the coach's injunction to eat a lot of carbs. In between bites she gazed around the table, fixing all their faces in her mind. T.Y., her oldest friend. Mack, steady as a rock. Diego and Maria, so good-hearted, taking turns holding their year-old baby. Katya, loyal despite herself, her hauteur mellowed. Sharp-tongued Jane and brilliant Jaime, who deserved so much more opportunity than Outpost gave them. C.C. with his madcap energy, and Dondi the baby all grown up.

And the heart of the church.

Anna, a calm, gentle presence. Sister Martha, acerbic and tireless. Father Ramon, who had done more to provide for Outpost than anyone.

And then there was Pilar, sitting beside her, stealing glances at her. Doing her best to be brave, and doing it well.

They made her heart ache, all of them.

Especially Pilar.

But it wasn't a bad pain, not exactly. It felt right. Hard, but right.

They finished eating and fell to squabbling over KP duty. Loup volunteered and was shot down; Pilar's offer to assist was met with disbelieving jeers.

"Oh, let them," Sister Martha said with asperity. "Jesus, children! Loup and Pilar wash, C.C. and Katya dry."

"And afterward we will adjourn for a toast," Father Ramon added.

It was strange and familiar all over again. All the Santitos had spent long hours in the kitchen scrubbing dishes. Breakfast dishes, dinner dishes, the massive vats of food they provided for the daily free lunch. Loup and Pilar shared the sink, heads leaning together, hands brushing beneath the soapy water.

"I asked Mack to walk me home," Pilar murmured. "I don't think I can say goodbye to you on Rory's doorstep, baby."

Loup nodded. "Yeah, me either."

"Damn, Pilar!" C.C. held up a platter she'd passed him. "This actually doesn't need to be washed again. You've changed, girl."

She flushed. "I'm trying."

"We're *all* trying, honey," Katya said without irony.

When the last dish was washed, dried, and stowed, they returned to the dining room. Father Ramon had a bottle of wine and an array of glasses before him. Once they'd taken their seats, he opened the wine. The cork squeaked. He poured an inch into every glass, passing them around the table.

"My predecessor was something of a connoisseur," he said. "This is a bottle he was saving for a special occasion. I reckon this is it. Lift your glasses."

They did.

"Profundity fails me." Father Ramon's gaze rested on Loup. "And perhaps that is fitting, since words have never been your strong suit, Loup Garron. I said once that you were neither a leader nor a follower. I think perhaps you're something more rare. A catalyst. A catalyst for change, hope, faith. This group of you, God willing the last of you, have been different. What does it mean to live without fear? What lessons are we to take from your presence among us?" He shook his head. "I don't know. I know only that in your own way, you inspire us."

"Hell, yeah," Mack muttered.

"Umm . . . thanks?" Loup offered.

The Father smiled wryly, hoisting his glass to Sister Martha. "I defer to your particular brand of eloquence, my dear."

She nodded. "Loup? Kick his ass."

The Santitos cheered and drank. Maria and Diego's baby squalled. Loup sipped her inch of wine, savoring it. It tasted like chocolate and cherries and leather and things there weren't names for.

"Thanks." Her eyes burned. "Just . . . thanks."

And then it was over—the last supper, ended. There were only goodbyes to be said. Some of them she would see tomorrow, but for others, this was the last time. Loup said them all, lingering.

Sure, but hurting.

Pilar was the last and hardest.

Loup walked her to the gate. Mack went on ahead a discreet distance, a shadowy figure waiting in the dark street.

"So . . . ," Pilar whispered, fighting tears.

"Yeah." Loup hugged her hard. "I love you," she whispered against Pilar's hair. "And if I can find a way to make it back to you, I will. I promise. No matter how long it takes."

"Just be safe, baby." Pilar kissed her softly, then pulled away with a shiver. She wiped her eyes. "But if you can, I'll be waiting. I'll always be waiting."

She nodded.

Pilar walked away without looking back. Loup watched her join Mack, watched him slide a sympathetic arm over her shoulders. Pilar leaned against him briefly. And then they moved on down the street until darkness swallowed them.

Inside, Sister Martha gave her a compassionate look. "Are you all right, sweetheart?"

"Yeah." Loup took a deep breath. Her chest ached, but it was a bittersweet pain. There was still that inexplicable sense of rightness. "I can't explain it, but yeah, I am. Thank you."

"You should get some sleep," Sister Martha said gently. "Tomorrow's a big day."

"Yeah." Despite everything, Loup smiled. "It is."

FORTY-SEVEN

Loup slept soundly and late, awaking to a room filled with sunlight. The boxing robe Pilar had made for her hung from the wardrobe, gleaming like a swath of sky. The sight made her smile.

Yesterday's sense of brightness lingered, tempered with sorrow and honed with purpose.

Ready.

She felt ready.

The church was mostly empty. Of course—it was Santa Olivia's day. They'd already taken the effigy to the square. People would be celebrating, indulging in a last fevered round of speculation about the night's coming fight.

Mack wandered into the kitchen and found her plowing through a bowl of reheated pasta. "Morning." His gray eyes crinkled. "Loup, is there a point where you should *stop* eating so much?"

"Yeah." She swallowed. "Probably around two o'clock. Is everyone at the square?"

"Uh-huh." He sat opposite her at the kitchen table. "They'll be back around four for the final goodbye. T.Y., maybe earlier. He really wants to walk over to the gym with you."

"Yeah, he would. That's nice. But I'm glad you're here now." She smiled at him. "Thanks for walking Pilar home last night."

"Sure."

"No, really."

"Yeah, well." Mack smiled wryly. "Who'd of thought, huh? She's still crazy about you." He picked at a flaw in the tabletop.

"I'll keep an eye on her when you're gone. I don't trust Rory Salamanca."

"Thanks, Mack." Loup's voice softened. "You're a really, really good guy."

He shrugged. "I care about you."

"I know. I love you, too."

He kept her company while she worked out in the garage. A light warm-up and stretching, Floyd had said. She ran a few miles on the treadmill, skipped rope, did a few light reps on the weights. Worked the bags for just long enough to make sure her rhythm was crisp and sure, to dispel the lingering sense of languor in her body.

The hours passed slowly, but they passed.

T.Y. came at three, nervous and jittery. "God, it's a fucking madhouse down there! The Salamancas set up betting tables practically before the sun was up, and there's still lines around the square. They're crowding out the picnic."

"They still betting on Mig?" Loup asked.

"Yeah, he's still the favorite. But now the big action's on whether the mystery contender's gonna win, lose by KO, or go the distance."

She smiled. "You make a bet?"

"Hell, yes. Win, all the way." T.Y. rumpled his hair. "But, Loup . . . what happens if you lose?"

"T.Y.," Mack said in a warning tone.

"No, it's okay." Loup shrugged. "It'll suck. There's no guarantee, T.Y. The guy's bigger and stronger, and for all I know, he's been training as hard as I have the past three years. Maybe even with guys like him, like me. If he has, I'll lose. And if I do, after working so hard and giving up . . ." She didn't finish the thought. "It'll suck worse than almost anything in my life. But at least I will have tried. And no matter how much it hurts, it'll never hurt as much as losing Tommy."

"You won't lose," Mack said steadily. "Will she, T.Y.?"

"No." He said it again, more forcefully. "*Hell*, no! You're Santa fuckin' Olivia, Loup. You won't lose."

She laughed. "It's okay, seriously! I'm not scared of losing."

"Yeah, well . . . you're not scared of anything," T.Y. observed.

"True."

"But you know when you oughta be, don't you? Your brother taught you to figure that shit out." Mack's voice had gone gentle. "Sorry, I'm kind of slow today, *loup-garou*. It's not the fight. It's what comes after, isn't it?"

"Yeah." She nodded. "And you. All of you."

"Don't you worry about us." He put one hand on her shoulder. "We made our choices same as you did, okay? All of us. We'll keep our mouths shut like you said. But don't doubt for an instant that we're not there behind you, because that's where we fucking well *chose* to be. Me, T.Y., all the Santitos. Father and Sis and Anna." He grinned, hard and fierce. "Even that washed-up coach and Miguel fucking *Garza*. Our choice. Got it?"

"Got it."

"Good." Mack settled back into his chair.

"Floyd's not washed up," Loup said mildly. "He's a good coach."

Mack eyed her. "He'd better be."

"He is."

The last hour slipped away. The others returned from the celebration in the square: Father Ramon, Sister Martha, and Anna, and Dondi assisting them. Loup packed her gym bag, folding Pilar's robe with care. She'd been right; the worst of the wrinkles had come out.

More goodbyes. In a way, they'd been said last night. Today was just a formality.

"Godspeed."

"Hey, happy birthday!"

"Godspeed you, child."

"Kick his ass."

"Take care of yourself, *loup-garou*."

It was almost too much, stifling. All the love, all the compassion. The scent of cigarette smoke clinging to Father Ramon's cassock, his face lined with craggy old age, suddenly shocking. Out of the church, in the open, arid air, Loup shook herself.

"Is it okay that I'm here?" T.Y. asked.

"Yeah." She looked at his worried brown eyes and took his arm. "C'mon, miracle boy. Walk me to the gym."

Outside the shuttered windows of the Unique Fitness center, T.Y. halted. "I don't belong in there, do I?"

"No," Loup said thoughtfully. "Probably not."

"Loup." He put his arms around her waist and kissed her cheek with only the slightest, slightest hesitation. "I don't care what happens tonight. I don't. Win or lose, I still think you're a superhero. I always did."

"Yeah, and you were always wrong." She smiled. "Thanks, T.Y."

The bells on the door jingled as she entered the gym for the last time. Floyd, Miguel, and Kevin were all there waiting.

"Are you ready, child?"

"I'm ready."

FORTY-EIGHT

T hey arrived at the town hall in a pair of armored vehicles. The military escorts Floyd had arranged barely glanced twice at Loup. Instead, they gave speculative looks at Miguel and Kevin, wondering which of them was the mystery contender, assuming Loup was merely the girlfriend of one or the other.

That was okay. Floyd didn't want anyone to know until the last possible minute. The worst thing that could happen would be that the general would cancel the fight and take Loup into custody without anyone ever knowing.

Ever since the fights had begun, the town hall had been used as a staging ground for the fighters to get ready. Floyd whisked them into the room used by the challengers. It had been a conference room, once. Now it was outfitted with an examining table, cupboards for storage, and a privacy screen.

The coach nodded at the privacy screen. "Go ahead and change."

She put on her gear and attire. The groin protector Mack had altered to almost fit. Royal blue boy's trunks that the coach had requisitioned, a sports bra and a white tank top that he'd approved from the items salvaged from the women's lockers. A pair of boy's boxing shoes, another requisitioned item. She shook out the robe and hung it over the screen.

"Nice," Miguel said. "Where'd that come from?"

"It was a present."

They could hear the muted roar of the crowd gathered in the square and the strains of a band playing. Inside, it was quiet. Someone knocked on the door.

"That'll be someone about the weigh-in. Loup, duck behind

there." Floyd pointed at the privacy screen. "I'll tell them we want to wait until the last possible minute."

Kevin eyed Miguel. "They'll believe it if they think it's Mig, all right. You'd struggle to make weight again, Garza."

"Fuck you," Miguel said without heat.

"Element of surprise," Floyd said calmly. "We need to keep them guessing. Don't want to taint the betting pool."

They went for it.

Loup reemerged. She perched on the table while Floyd wrapped her hands, making sure it was done perfectly, then laced her gloves. Miguel donned a pair of punch mitts to help her warm up while the coach and Kevin went over a checklist of items for the corner. It was the first time in over a year that she'd trained without wrist and ankle weights and it made her feel light and quick.

"Moving good," Miguel said approvingly. "Good. You look good, kid. Loose, relaxed." He peered at her, then frowned. "Actually, you look a little dopey. Jesus Christ! Did you get *laid*?"

She smiled, ignoring a startled glance from Kevin McArdle.

"Ecchevarria, right?" He shook off the mitts. "Goddamnit, Loup! You don't get laid the night before a fight. If this costs you your edge—"

"It won't."

"—that better have been one goddamn good piece of—"

"It won't, Mig!" Loup raised her voice. "This isn't just a fight." She nodded at the door. "In fifteen minutes, I walk out there, and no matter what happens, my life changes forever. I gotta be able to do it with no regrets, okay? Pilar and I didn't have an ending. Now we do."

He folded his arms. "It was stupid."

"Miguel." Floyd looked up, his expression unreadable. "Done is done. Let her be."

"Fuck," Miguel muttered. "Lemme see your hair. You got it braided nice and neat?"

"It's fine."

He examined her. "No, it's not. You wanna French braid so it lies nice and tight, doesn't swing around. Turn around. I'll do it."

Loup gave him a disbelieving look.

"*What?*" Miguel shrugged. "I used to braid my mama's hair, okay? She taught me how. Get over it."

"I'm so gonna blackmail you with this, Garza," Kevin called.

Miguel scowled in his direction. "Not if you don't want your face rearranged, you're not."

He finished. Loup shook her head experimentally. "Yeah, that's better. Thanks, Mig."

He shrugged. "Hey, I want my ticket out."

"Yeah, right."

"Oh, shut up." Miguel wrapped one arm around her in a rough embrace, his lips grazing her forehead. "Just beat the fucker, okay?"

She took a deep breath. "Okay."

There was another knock at the door.

Time.

Loup slid into the boxing robe Miguel held for her, easing her gloved fists through the wide sleeves. He settled it over her shoulders, knotted the sash loosely, and settled the hood atop her head.

"The fuck?" The MP who'd come to fetch them glanced from Kevin to Miguel, still clad in street clothes, at Loup, and finally the coach. "Sir?"

"Mystery contestant," Floyd said laconically.

"Is this a joke?"

"No joke." He pointed. "Let us weigh in."

The MP turned to a companion. "Send someone to tell—"

"There'll be no sending someone!" the coach interrupted him. "All the terms have been agreed to. I promised Bill Argyle the match of a lifetime, and I mean to deliver. Don't get in the way of this, son. Don't dash his dreams unless you're prepared to bear the cost. Just stand back and marvel."

He hesitated.

"Do it, boy!" Floyd barked.

"Okay, okay!"

The scales were in the spacious foyer. The uniformed official took one look at Loup and glanced up in surprise. "You can't—"

Floyd nudged Loup. "Just do the weigh-in."

She stepped onto the scales.

The weight marker dipped. The official slid it, then slid it again. He licked his lips. "Ah . . . I think it's off."

"Oh?" Miguel leaned over him. "Was it off when *Ron Johnson* weighed in?"

"No. No, but that was yesterday."

"Must of been his twin, then. Doesn't matter." Loup stepped off the scale. "Are we good? You wanna test it?"

"Ahhh . . ."

Kevin McArdle gave a short, sharp whistle. "Loup! They're announcing you!"

"We're doing this." Miguel steered her toward the door. "You do know they're gonna laugh, kid? Right?"

"She doesn't care," Floyd said.

"I don't care," Loup agreed.

"Go." The coach put his wrinkled lips to her ear. "Afterward, don't trust, don't believe. Whatever they promise, whatever they threaten, don't believe it. Remember that they'll say anything. But don't fight them, either. It will only give them reason to continue. You'll be all right sooner or later." He shoved her. "Go! We'll be right behind you."

She went.

The crowd was massive, roaring. They didn't laugh, not right away. The announcement of the mystery contender's name hadn't quite sunk in among the Outposters and it meant nothing to the soldiers. Most of them hadn't even begun their rotation when Tom Garron had been alive. Lines of guards cordoned off the path to the ring, blocking onlookers' views.

Then Loup climbed into the ring.

The crowd quieted, uncertain, seeing only a smaller-than-expected figure in a vivid blue robe. She pushed back her hood. It could have been a loose white kerchief slipping from her hair.

The soldiers in the bleachers erupted in howls of laughter, hoots of derision, and catcalls of disappointment. But among the Outposters in the square, there was a hush as her name went around, its meaning dawning on them.

They remembered Tom Garron.

And on the heels of that revelation, a second significance dawned. A girl in a blue dress; a girl in a blue robe.

"Santa Olivia!" someone shouted.

Others took up the cry. "Santa Olivia! Santa Olivia!"

On a platform ringside, the commentator was announcing Ron Johnson, but the cries drowned out his voice. In the VIP section of the stands, the general had risen, his face red and furious beneath his white hair. He made his way toward the ring even as Floyd entered behind Loup, while Kevin and Miguel went to take their places in her corner.

Loup glanced back the way she'd come and saw Ron Johnson paused in the cordon. He looked exactly as she remembered him, only a little older. He met her gaze, green eyes calm and unsurprised.

The general climbed into the ring. "What the *fuck* is the meaning of this, Floyd?"

"Match of a lifetime, Bill," the coach said evenly. "Just like I promised."

"Are you out of your mind? This isn't a match, it's manslaughter." The general raised his voice. "People, go home! There's not going to be a fight!"

"Hold on." Floyd cleared his throat. "Army had some deserters a while back, didn't it? Nineteen, twenty years? Real special folk. One of them was here long enough to leave a kid behind."

General Argyle drew a sharp breath, understanding. "You can't do this."

"You want a riot on your hands?" He pointed at the crowd. "Tell them."

Loup watched Ron Johnson climb into the ring while the old men argued. The arc lights brought out the reddish tint to his close-cropped hair, at odds with his brown skin. He moved with economic grace, not trying to hide what he was this time. Their eyes met again in silent understanding.

"You're his sister," he said to her.

"Yeah."

"I'm so very sorry. It was a terrible accident."

"I know."

The Outpost crowd was chanting. *"Santa Olivia. Santa Olivia!"*

Ron Johnson gazed out at the throng. "You know you're fucked, right?" he said calmly. "Santa Olivia or not, they won't let someone with your DNA run around loose."

"I know." Loup's skin prickled. "You knew about me."

His gaze returned to her. "I knew." His voice dropped to an almost inaudible level. "Once this is over, I'll try to help you if I can."

". . . violated every trust I placed in you!" the general was shouting.

"Damn straight I did!" Floyd shouted back. "You wanted to have it both ways, Bill, but when push came to shove, you stacked the deck! You put in a ringer against my boy! Her goddamned *brother!* When this is over, I'm willing to pay the price and so is Loup. But right here, right now, are you going to be a man and keep your word, or throw away whatever's left of your integrity?"

General Argyle opened his mouth to reply.

"Sir?" Ron Johnson interrupted. "You did give your word."

It deflated him. He looked at the chanting, weeping Outpost crowd; the soldiers clamoring for something, anything. He looked at Loup with tired, rheumy eyes. "You understand you'll be taken into custody no matter what the outcome."

"Yes, sir."

"And you'll make it clear you're coming voluntarily?"

"Yes, sir." She nodded. "If you keep your word about the two tickets north."

His mouth flattened into a grim line. "Dear God, you can't possibly expect to win."

"But if I do?"

He shook his head. "Santa Olivia, is it? I'm afraid you forfeited that right when you took up arms against the U.S. Army."

Floyd snorted. "Arms? She threw a rock."

"There were supposed to be two tickets," Loup said. "You promised. I should be able to give one away."

"To one of your *conspirators*?"

"I don't know what that means. But I promised it to Miguel Garza if he'd help train me to fight."

The Garza name gave the general pause; then he compressed his lips again and shook his head. "He protected a known felon."

"Mig didn't know."

"Of course he fucking well knew!" he shouted at her.

The crowd noise grew louder

"Not for sure. No one did. I never admitted it to anyone but the coach," Loup lied steadily. "Anyway, I'm here, aren't I?"

Louder.

General Argyle cast his gaze heavenward.

"You always knew this day was coming, Bill," Floyd said softly. "Somewhere, somehow. Here or there. And a part of you has always wanted it. Do the right thing."

He lowered his gaze, his face grim. "Don't presume on our friendship. I'll allow the fight, but I'll not tolerate blackmail. If this town threatens to riot, God help me, I *will* crush it. I won't make any decisions on the other matter until after a thorough investigation into this goddamned Santa Olivia business. That's as good as it gets. Take it or leave it."

Floyd glanced at Loup.

She nodded reluctantly.

The general turned on his heel and strode toward the ropes. He uttered a brief word to the bewildered referee, climbed through the ropes, and paused at the announcer's platform to bark an order before taking his place in the stands.

"*All right!*" The announcer's voice boomed over the square, the volume turned all the way up to override the crowd noise. "Ladies and gentlemen, I don't know what the hell's going on, but we've got ourselves a fight!"

FORTY-NINE

I couldn't get a guarantee, Mig."

"It's okay, kid." He lifted Loup's chin, smearing her face with Vaseline. "It was always a long shot."

"McArdle, water," Floyd said brusquely.

Kevin squeezed a stream of water into Loup's mouth. She swished and swallowed.

"Mouth guard." The coach shoved it in place. "Okay. Ready?"

"Ready," she agreed.

The bell rang.

They came out of their corners—quick, quicker than human. Not as quick as either could move. The crowd gasped.

The crowd didn't matter.

They circled each other, each trying to take the other's measure. Ron Johnson's green eyes weren't calm anymore. They were fierce and bright, eager. He essayed a few testing jabs, confident in his height and reach.

Loup deflected them with ease, gauging his pace out of habit.

And then he *moved*, faster than lightning. Lashed out with a stinging right hook that landed square on her left ear, setting her entire head to ringing. It nearly knocked her off her feet.

But it didn't.

He looked mildly surprised.

She connected with a sharp jab to the center of his chest, sending him staggering. Followed up with a flurry of body blows, stalking him, chin tucked low. He caught his balance and absorbed the punishment, going to a clinch.

The harried referee intervened. "Break it up! Break it up, now!"

They skipped apart.

It went that way for the rest of the round. Johnson used his reach to try to keep her at bay, moving constantly. It felt strange and exhilarating to fight someone who moved at the same speed as her, but it was frustrating, too. Loup slipped and ducked and caught his long-armed jabs, trying to get inside his reach with limited success. Still, when the bell rang, she was ahead on points.

The crowd that had been so noisy was eerily quiet, stunned into silence. In the corner, Floyd wore a grim look.

"We've got a problem," he said to her.

"What?" Her head was still ringing. Miguel leaned over the ropes and pressed an ice pack to her ear while Kevin rinsed her mouth guard.

"You're too goddamned fast and too goddamned short. The judges can't keep score when you're in tight working his body. You land six shots, they see two."

"You want me to slow down?"

"No!"

"You gotta go for the knockout," Miguel said. "I told you, it's the only way. Go for it with everything you've got."

"No." The coach shook his head. "He's too big, too strong, and damn near as quick as you. Not yet. We've got to stick to the strategy. Your only hope is to outbox him. Keep it up, wear him down. Work his body. Try switching leads. But at some point . . . I'm afraid Mig's right."

"Okay." Loup nodded. "Just tell me when."

Nothing changed in the rounds that followed. She tried switching leads and fighting as a left-hander, but it bought her only a few seconds of confusion on his part and slowed her down a fraction. Johnson's height and reach worked to his advantage. He tagged her a couple of times; not solid hits, but they were showier than hers. His height made them easier to read, while her steady assault on his torso went overlooked.

In the fifth round, Johnson feinted for the first time, caught her by surprise, and opened a gash in her right eyebrow.

"Fuck!" Miguel swore. "Fuck, fuck, *fuck!*"

"It's okay." Floyd pinched the split and smeared coagulant on it. "You okay? She okay?" he asked the medic.

"I'm okay," Loup said.

The medic examined her pupils, checked the wound. "I guess she's okay." He sounded uncertain.

"Okay." Floyd grabbed her shoulders. "Just keep it up. Don't get careless; don't underestimate him. It's early. Remember, you're *winning* this."

Loup nodded.

It didn't feel like it and she knew it damned well didn't *look* like it. Johnson had gotten wary earlier, but now his confidence was back. His eyes gleamed. For the next two rounds, he launched a blistering, all-out offense, trying to open the cut above her eye wider. It wasn't skilled and it wasn't fancy, but it was brutal.

Remembering the first time she'd seen Kevin McArdle fight, Loup was careful. He'd had a similar injury, and it had forced a technical knockout. She fought two rounds of pure defense, protecting herself and failing to score points, visible or otherwise.

At the end of the seventh, the crowd had gotten over its initial shock. The soldiers were cheering. The Outposters were quiet.

Loup gazed at Ron Johnson in the opposite corner, watching his chest rise and fall, the sheen of sweat on his skin. "Coach? He's starting to get tired."

"Good." He wiped her gashed eyebrow, applied a new layer of coagulant. "You?"

"No. Just hungry."

"Then so is he. Keep it up."

In the middle of the eighth, Johnson's assault began to falter. Loup went back to pressing him: circling, darting, peppering his torso. It might not have showed where the judges were concerned, but all those body shots had to take a toll.

"Keep it up."

It was in the tenth that the tide turned at last. Johnson was slowing. His footwork turned leaden and his punches lost force. He dropped his guard in an effort to protect his belly, and for the first time, Loup landed a head shot, throwing an uppercut that landed on his chin and snapped his head back. It would have knocked out anyone else.

When the round ended, the Outposters roared.

She *wasn't* tired, but the sound filled her with a rush of energy anyway, buoying her. Suddenly, the crowd mattered.

"All right, child." Floyd gave her a hard, tight smile. "Cry havoc and let slip the dogs of war."

"What?"

"Turn it loose, Loup," Miguel said. "Hit him with everything you've got."

She stood for the beginning of the eleventh round. The ringing in her head hadn't gone away. Her fists ached as though she'd been pounding a brick wall. The gash in her right eyebrow stung like hell and her left ear was hot and throbbing.

She felt good.

Johnson didn't go down easily. He was strong and quick and fearless. But he was tired, and he was fighting an opponent who'd done nothing but train for this moment for years. Loup threw blistering combinations at him, driving him off balance, driving him staggering onto the ropes.

The crowd went wild.

The referee intervened. Loup stepped back. Johnson stood upright, moved slowly into position. The referee gave them the go-ahead. Johnson raised his guard. Loup feinted, then threw a blazing left cross that powered through his guard and knocked him down.

The referee began a count.

Johnson got up.

Loup knocked him down.

He got up again, slowly. Wavered on his feet. One eye was

swelling and his nose looked crooked. His good eye looked clear and fearless and ruefully surprised.

Loup knocked him down again.

This time he stayed down.

The noise in the square was deafening. It was a wild, jubilant roar of exultation; no words, just a deafening chorus of ecstasy. People turned to one another, laughing, weeping, and embracing. In her corner, Loup leaned on the ropes, letting Miguel and Kevin and the coach tend to her, removing her mouth guard, giving her water, wiping away blood and Vaseline. They were all shouting, too.

". . . did it, you fucking *did* it!"

". . . never seen anything *like* it."

In the opposite corner, Ron Johnson's handlers were hovering over him. He'd gotten up on his own and seemed to be dazed, but okay. She hoped he was.

The noise washed over her. She closed her eyes briefly and hoped that Pilar would hear it and know it meant that she was okay, that she'd won.

She thought about Tommy, lingering over his memory.

When she opened her eyes, she saw the Santitos and everyone pressing close to her corner of the ring, eyes filled with tears. Loup smiled and reached out to them. They pressed closer, touching her gloved fist.

The judges made the decision official. In the center of the ring, Loup and Ron Johnson stood on either side of the referee. He raised Loup's arm in victory. The cheers rang to heaven. And then the general descended, accompanied by four MPs. They surrounded her.

The crowd's mood shifted precariously.

"You've got to say something to them," the general muttered. "You agreed to this, child. If they riot, their blood's on your hands."

"Okay."

In her corner, Miguel was holding her robe. He had tears in

his eyes, too; so did Floyd and Kevin. Any other time, it might almost have been funny—three big, grown men in tears. Miguel helped her into the robe, tied the sash for her.

"Thanks," Loup murmured.

All three nodded without speaking.

She walked to the front of the ring and waited for the crowd to quiet. They did, gazing up at her. The soldiers in the bleachers were quiet, too. There was only the ringing in her head, the rumble of the generator, and a faint, high-pitched noise the lights emitted. She wished she had Jaime to give her something clever to say. He and Jane had always come up with Santa Olivia's best lines.

"I've gotta go with these guys," Loup said simply. "It's okay, really. Please don't try to stop them, they're just doing their job. I chose this. Okay?"

The crowd was silent, ominous.

"Seriously. Don't worry about me. Just take care of each other, you know?"

There was a scuffle of activity behind her. Loup glanced back to see Father Ramon striding across the canvas, the skirts of his black cassock flaring. He placed his hands on her shoulders as though to claim her for the church and addressed the crowd in his deep, resonant voice.

"The child speaks the truth. Go in peace."

It tipped the scales. The crowd didn't disperse, but they didn't riot, either. They stayed peaceable, wide-eyed and wondering as the MPs moved to escort Loup from the ring.

"Thanks, Father," she whispered.

He crossed himself without irony, perhaps for the first time in thirty years. "God be with you, Loup."

FIFTY

In sight of the crowd, the MPs were courteous.

Out of sight, that changed.

"Cuff her, goddamnit!" The general's voice, vicious with anger and betrayal. "She's *dangerous!*"

They wrestled her up against the side of an armored vehicle despite the fact that Loup offered no resistance, wrenched her arms behind her back, and bound her gloved wrists together with a durable plastic strap. Opened the rear door of the vehicle and shoved her into the cargo space.

Don't trust, don't believe. But don't fight them, either.

The nightmare had begun.

Loup levered herself upright, bound arms strained and aching. A soldier in the backseat trained a pistol on her, the open mouth of the barrel like an unblinking eye. She tried smiling at him. He didn't return the smile, only stared, eyes shocked and fearful.

Voices conferred.

The vehicle started.

They took her to the base, which Loup had expected. No one asked her any questions. She'd thought there would be questions. Instead, there was a cinder-block building with harsh, glaring lights and narrow cells. They shoved her into one, stumbling, and left her there.

It was hot, stifling hot.

There was a metal shelf she supposed was a bed, and an empty bucket she supposed was a toilet. A locked door with a tiny window.

Nothing else.

"Fuck," Loup muttered. "This sucks."

Her head ached and stung. Her arms and shoulders ached. She pulled, testing the plastic cuffs' resistance. Due to the awkwardness of securing them over the gloves, there was a little bit of slack. With an effort, she managed to wriggle her arms past her hips and butt, squirming and contorting, pulling her legs through the loop of her bound wrists.

Arms in front, better.

Much more comfortable.

Loup raised her wrists to her mouth and gnawed through the plastic strip joining the cuffs until it gave. Better still. She undid the laces of one of her boxing gloves with her teeth, a painstaking process. Unlaced the other. Eased her bruised, aching hands free.

Sighed with relief.

That was as good as it got, at least for now. She slid out of her robe and folded it carefully, then sat, waiting in the stifling heat.

No one came.

After what might have been one hour or three, she gave up on waiting. The combination of unrelenting light, heat, and hunger was making her battered head swim, and a deep exhaustion was settling into her muscles. Loup lay down on the metal shelf, pillowed her head on the folded robe, and fell into an uneasy sleep.

She awoke some hours later to the sound of the door clanging open and lurched to her feet without thinking, full speed. Two soldiers burst into her cell, training pistols on her.

"Get down! Hands behind your head!"

She obeyed.

"Okay. Get up slow, keep your hands there."

She did that, too.

One gestured with his pistol. "Sit. Hands behind your head." Once she'd complied, he turned to a third man. "Okay, doc. Have a look."

A man in a white doctor's coat entered. He examined Loup,

prodding and pinching the muscles of her arms and legs with impersonal interest. She endured it, fighting a surge of anger. He shone a flashlight into both her eyes, examined her swollen left ear. Wiped the split in her eyebrow with something that stung, then took out a suture needle and thread and closed the gash with three neat stitches.

"Good enough," the doctor said to the guards.

"Hey!" Loup called after them as they turned to go. "The other guy, Johnson. Is he okay?"

The doctor turned back, looking surprised and human for the first time. One of the guards shook his head at him. He hesitated, then gave Loup a faint, barely perceptible nod.

And then they left, locking the door behind them.

It was something, anyway. She was glad to know it. And at least they hadn't cuffed her again. She lay back down on the hard metal, head pillowed on Pilar's robe, and slept.

After that, people came and went at irregular hours. It was impossible to say what time it was with the lights always glaring. No one spoke to her except to bark orders. After the first couple of times, she found herself listening for them even in the midst of fitful sleep and managed to be ready for them, sitting upright with her hands behind her head before they entered her cell.

There were doctors, different doctors. Poking and prodding, shining lights into her eyes.

They gave her water.

No food.

How long that lasted, she couldn't say. Two days, maybe three. By the time someone *did* come to fetch her, she was weak and dizzy. They cuffed her hands before her, led her to a stark room, and shoved her into a chair.

"Hey, now!" A man with a clipboard protested. "No need to be rough. My God, look at her, she's just a kid."

"Did you see the fight, sir?"

"No."

"You should have."

"Nonetheless." He frowned and pointed. "Wait by the door." The soldiers obeyed, standing at attention. He pulled up a stool, perching in front of Loup. He wore glasses that reminded her of Jaime and he had a kind, intelligent face. "Now, how do you pronounce your name, honey? Is it Lou or Loop?"

"Lou."

"I'm Derek." He gave her a friendly, open smile. "Guess I missed a hell of a fight, huh?"

"Yeah."

"You look a little peaked. You want something, honey? Maybe a sandwich, a glass of milk?" He didn't wait for her answer. "Clayton, go fetch me a lunch tray." The soldier went, grumbling. Derek consulted his clipboard. "It says here that your mother's name was Carmen Garron. Is that right?"

The prospect of food made her polite. "Yes, sir."

"And your father?"

"Martin."

"Martin what?"

Loup shook her head. "I don't know. Tommy said he didn't have a last name."

"Tommy." Derek glanced at his notes. "That was your older brother?"

"Yes, sir."

"What else did he tell you about your father?"

She told him everything she could remember, reckoning there wasn't any reason not to. The army already knew. He nodded and took notes, encouraging her. In the midst of it, the soldier Clayton came in carrying a tray. It held a plate with a barbecued pork sandwich on a white bun, steaming fragrantly; a pile of fries; and a glass of milk so cold that the glass was sweating. He set it down on a nearby table.

"Smells good, huh?" Derek smiled at her. "I just have one more quick question for you. Tell me about the Santa Olivia conspiracy."

"The what?" The smell was giving her sharp hunger pangs.

"Santa Olivia." His smile didn't falter. "Whose idea was it?"

"Mine."

"Loup, it's okay." He put a reassuring hand on her knee, frowned slightly and withdrew it. "Honey, I don't blame you. What kid wouldn't want to be a folk hero? Especially a kid with your abilities. But whoever put you up to it wasn't doing you any favors. You could be in big trouble for assaulting a serviceman and destroying government property. Just tell me whose idea it was."

Loup sighed. "Mine."

"Who helped you?"

There wasn't going to be any sandwich. "No one."

He kept asking and asking, never angry, just gentle and persuasive. The sandwich bun turned pink and soggy with juices, the fries grew limp. After a while, Loup grew tired and stopped answering.

"All right." Derek regarded her with sorrow and disappointment. "I'm sorry, Loup. I can't help you if you won't help me." He beckoned to the soldiers. "You can take her back now. Loup, when you're ready to talk, just ask for me. I'm trying to be your friend."

She stared at him without blinking. "Yeah, right."

The soldiers returned her to her cell. They left the cuffs on her. This time, Loup was too tired to do anything about it.

She lay down and slept.

FIFTY-ONE

The next time they came for her, Loup was too tired to stand. It was like a dream, a bad dream, and she couldn't quite wake up. Soldiers yanked at her, prodded her. "C'mon, c'mon! Let's go!"

"Can't," she mumbled.

They swore and took her anyway, cutting her plastic cuffs and slinging her arms over their shoulders, dragging her.

In the stark room, they put her in the chair.

She fell asleep, listing sideways.

"Goddamnit!" Shaking, prodding. All kinds of commotion, barely registering. Men in white coats, lifting her eyelids and shining narrow flashlights into her eyes, shoving thermometers into her mouth, pinching the skin on the back of her hand. Feeling her pulse, listening to her heartbeat and her breathing. Shouting orders, calling for others.

The general's voice, querulous. "What the hell's *wrong* with her?"

"Fuck if I know, sir. Her temp's awfully low. Respiration and heart rate are abnormal."

"Abnormal how?"

"Steady, but slow. Very slow."

"Sir?" Another voice, one she knew, steady and calm. "Has she been deprived of food, sir?"

"What the fuck are you doing here, Johnson?"

"Just trying to help, sir. Has she?"

"Not for long. Only a few days."

"It's enough for our kind. She's going into hibernation."

"The *fuck?*"

One of the doctors spoke. "Humans don't hibernate."

"Call it what you like." The calm voice said. "Her metabolism is slowing down. It's a protective mechanism. We can control it to some extent with biofeedback, but she hasn't been taught the techniques. You ought to have an expert on staff to advise you. You're not going to get anywhere by starving her."

"So?"

"So *feed* her."

There was arguing.

Loup drifted out.

The taste of chicken broth awoke her—rich and savory, spooned between her lips. She swallowed without thinking, opened her eyes.

"Good?" Ron Johnson gave her a steady look. His nose was swollen and he had two black eyes, one worse than the other.

"Uh-huh."

He fed her another spoonful. "Thought you'd rather this than a glucose drip. It's better for our kind."

"Yeah." Loup swallowed. "Thanks." Her body came alive, seizing on the proteins and fats in the broth. She shuddered, took the bowl from him, and drained it, gulping down broth, noodles, and bits of shredded chicken and sundry vegetables. He refilled it from a steel vat without asking and handed it to her. She drained the second bowl. "Thanks," she repeated. Johnson nodded.

"So she's all right?" The general asked.

The doctors moved in with their thermometers and stethoscopes. "Seems to be. Vitals are returning to normal."

"All right, Johnson," the general said grudgingly. "You have my thanks. Dismissed."

"Yes, sir."

Loup was sorry to see him go. In the ring, he'd promised to help her if he could. She didn't know if she trusted him. He could be trying to trick her like I'm-trying-to-be-your-friend Derek. He'd killed her brother and they both bore the marks of their epic battle. But in a place filled with strange men, he was the only one she felt close to.

They took pity on her and didn't question her that day, only brought her back to her cell. That night—or whatever time it was—along with a bottle of water, there was another bowl of chicken soup, tepid and greasy. She drank it all.

The next day, the guards who came to fetch her informed her that they were taking her to the showers. They still cuffed her hands in front of her.

If it hadn't been for that, Loup might have believed them. She'd been confined in that hot, stuffy cell for at least four or five days, wearing the same sweat-stained top and trunks in which she'd fought an eleven-round boxing match, and she was pretty sure she stank to heaven by now.

But there were the cuffs.

"Ladies' shower room!" one of the guards said cheerfully, opening the door onto a barren cinder-block room with a drain in the cement floor. "All the modern luxuries."

The other began unwinding a large hose from a wall-mounted fixture. "Stand right over there."

She sighed.

It took both of them to handle the hose and the water pressure was so strong and relentless that even Loup couldn't keep her feet. They laughed, blasting her full in the face until it felt like she would drown, unable to draw a breath. She got her back against the wall and raised her bound arms in front of her face, deflecting the worst of it until they finally turned off the water.

"Whaddya think, Joe?" one asked the other, tapping his fingers suggestively on his belt buckle. "Clean enough to fuck?"

Loup got up, soaked and dripping. Her eyes glittered.

"Ahh, let's just get her to Room C," the other said uneasily. "They're expecting her."

She relaxed. At least she *was* cleaner.

Room C was another stark, windowless room. No chairs, no

nothing, just a ceramic tile floor. And it was cold, incredibly cold. There were vents on every wall blowing frigid air into the room.

They left her there.

No one came.

Her soaked clothing was plastered to her body, cold and clammy. Bit by bit, the cold seemed to creep into her bones. Loup shivered. By the end of an hour, she was colder than she'd ever been in her life.

She tried exercising to warm her blood, skipping in place. At first it helped, but then she began feeling weak and dizzy again. Three bowls of soup in four or five days wasn't enough to sustain her for long. She gave up and sat on the cold ceramic tiles, feeling them leach more warmth from her body, wrapping her bound arms around her knees, sodden and shivering.

At last, men came.

There were two of them this time. They brought a folding metal chair. Hauled her to her feet, shoved her into the chair. They shouted questions at her faster than she could answer through chattering teeth. They threatened her, told her that her friends would be in trouble if she didn't cooperate. That was the hardest one to resist.

Don't trust, don't believe. Remember that they'll say anything.

Loup stuck to her story.

In the days that followed, little changed. A doctor came and removed her stitches without speaking to her. They gave her food at irregular intervals, enough to keep her from drifting into what Ron Johnson called hibernation. Never enough to make her feel wholly restored. At least it meant she seldom had to use the bucket.

On some days she got the hose, the frigid room, and the shouting interrogators.

Others, nothing.

It felt like days, anyway. Loup spent them sitting motionless on the steel shelf, her knees drawn up, Pilar's robe draped over her shoulders. The feel of it comforted her despite the heat. If she closed her eyes, she could block out the glare of the harsh overhead lights and pretend that the redness behind her eyelids was due to afternoon sunlight streaming into a cozy room with a sewing table and a daybed, the satin robe spread over its cushions.

It helped.

Other than that, life sucked.

FIFTY-TWO

By Loup's best guess, it was another two or three weeks before they tried a new, improved gambit.

They treated her nicely.

A pair of guards escorted her to a room that looked like she imagined a nice hotel room did, the kind of thing you saw in the old-fashioned magazines that Katya and Pilar liked to page through. Three rooms, really; there was a sitting room with a couch and a table for two, a bedroom, and a bathroom. The temperature was perfectly comfortable. The lighting was soft and low, and all the linens looked pristine. The gleaming bathroom counter held an array of toiletries and a fluffy white bathrobe hung from a hook on the door.

"Go ahead, sweetheart." One snipped her plastic cuffs. "Make yourself at home. Derek will be with you in about an hour."

They locked the door behind her, sliding a bolt in place.

Trick or no trick, Loup didn't much care. She made a beeline for the bathroom.

It took ages to unpick the remnants of Miguel's French braid, tangled and matted. She combed her hair out with her fingers, reluctant to dirty the actual utensil. Stripped off the filthy clothes that had been soaked and dried on her skin too many times.

Turned on the shower.

It steamed.

Barring the revelation of sex, that shower was one of the most sensuous, luxuriant experiences of her life. Loup shivered with pleasure at the touch of warm water against her skin, the slippery delight of soap lathering beneath her hands. She washed her hair three times, herself twice. Turned off the water and climbed out of the shower with reluctance, wrapping herself in the thick terry-cloth robe.

Brushed her teeth three times.

Combed her wet hair.

Waited for Derek.

It felt strange, like she was some mistress waiting for her lover. Loup supposed she ought to put her clothes back on, but the terry-cloth was clean against her clean skin. She damn well wasn't putting her dirty, stinking clothes back on until she had to.

The door opened.

A soldier in desert fatigues wheeled in a tray filled with covered dishes that smelled very, very good, followed by I'm-trying-to-be-your-friend Derek in some kind of officer's uniform.

He smiled at her. "Good evening, Loup."

She shrugged.

"Thanks, Ted," he said to the soldier, who saluted and left. The bolt clicked shut behind him. Derek turned back to Loup, his gaze filled with sympathy. "You've had a rough time of it, huh?"

"No shit."

He lifted one hand. "Look, I feel bad about it. I do. Between you and me, I think General Argyle's overreacting, okay? And I think you're a smart girl. I'm here to make you an offer. Are you going to like all the terms of it? No. Should you listen to it?" He nodded. "Yes. Because you don't have a lot of options. Because after the way our first meeting went, I had to fight like hell for this opportunity and I don't think it's going to happen again." He lifted one of the dish domes, revealing a plate of steak, mashed potatoes, peas, and carrots. "Can we at least be civil?"

Loup eyed the food. "Sure."

She was braced for the trick, ready for him to take it away, but he didn't. He uncovered a second plate and served them both. Setting the table for two, opening a bottle of wine and pouring two glasses.

"To your health." Derek clinked his glass to hers. "You could be very, very valuable to us, Loup."

She waited for the trick.

He smiled at her and began to cut his steak.

The food was good. Loup ate quickly and precisely, clearing her plate. Feeling the warm glow of it in her belly, nutrition coursing through her veins, revitalizing her. Derek smiled at her again and scraped his leftover mashed potatoes onto her plate. She ate those, too.

"So," he said, refilling her wineglass.

"So," Loup echoed.

Derek leaned over the table, his glasses reflecting the light. "I can offer you a future. A very good one."

She gave him a skeptical look. "Yeah, I've noticed so many women in the army."

"There used to be before the policy was changed." He shook his head. "But I'm not talking about the army. Have you ever heard of the Secret Service?"

"No."

"They're men and women who provide security for the president and other important political figures."

"Bodyguards."

"That and more." Derek nodded. "Usually, a visible presence. But on some occasions, something less obvious is required. The world is changing, decades of isolationism ending. We're sending diplomats into delicate situations where they cannot afford to offend their hosts. A highly skilled bodyguard who doesn't *look* like a bodyguard would be most useful. One who could pass for a pretty aide or personal assistant." He smiled. "Do you see where I'm going?"

"Yeah."

"You'd travel the world." He waved one hand in an expansive gesture. "Stay in hotels ten times nicer than this, eat meals that put this to shame."

Loup smiled wryly. "Yeah, sure. Just like that."

"No, of course not. You'd still have to go through extensive training. Two years, at least. But I think you'd like it." He leaned forward again, eyes earnest behind his glasses. "It's a fledgling program. We're working with the Feds. There would be others like you in it, Loup."

She gave him a sharp look.

"You'd learn more about yourself, about what you are." Derek took the opening and pressed. "Biofeedback techniques to moderate your metabolism, ways to prolong your longevity. How does that sound?"

She shrugged.

He smiled. "I saw your eyes light up. It can't be easy, being the only person like *you* that you know. I don't pretend to understand, but I know it can't be easy." He steepled his fingers, touched them to his lips. "I took the liberty of making a few calls. The Feds are interested in you, very interested."

"What's the catch?" she asked.

Derek's expression turned serious. "Before I tell you, hear me out. You're in more trouble here than you realize, Loup. It's not just the Santa Olivia business." He shook his head. "That's just a tempest in a teapot. I imagine it will blow itself out in another month or so. It's the *excuse* it provides that's a problem."

"Excuse for what?"

He took off his glasses, wiped them on his napkin. "Coercive interrogation methods are based on the premise that three elements in the subject's response render it effective: debility, dependency, and dread. The three Ds. You're lacking the latter." He put his glasses back on and glanced at her puzzled face. "Subjects being questioned—that's you—have to be afraid, Loup. That's the conventional wisdom. In certain circles, it's a matter of intense interest. You've given them the perfect excuse to test the theory." He ticked off the reasons on his fingers. "You're incapable of feeling fear. You're a citizen of no country; but if you were, you'd be recognized as a legal adult. And you've freely admitted to committing acts of insurrection against the U.S. government."

Loup blew out her breath, impatient. "So . . . what? You're saying in a month or so, they won't care about the stupid questions they keep asking me? But they're gonna keep hosing me down and asking them anyway?"

"Exactly." Derek nodded. "Just to find out if you have a breaking point."

"That sucks," she said flatly.

He shrugged. "I didn't make the rules."

She eyed him. "So what's the catch?"

"Loyalty." Derek raised his hands as though to ward off an unspoken protest. "Loup, I can get you into this program. I can make this all go away, smooth over any problems. But I need a good-faith gesture from you. And I swear to you, it goes no farther than this room. No one gets punished; no one gets hurt. All it means is that I can report to Washington that you're one hundred percent committed." He lowered his voice. "Whose idea was the Santa Olivia business?"

"Thought you said I was a smart girl," she said wryly. "I was smart enough to figure out how to beat the guy who killed my brother. You don't think I'm smart enough to come up with a few stupid pranks on my own?"

"Just give me a name, one name." His tongue flicked out to lick his lower lip. "Father Ramon Perez. Was he in on the conspiracy?"

Loup sighed.

She got up from the table, went into the bathroom. Took off the clean, fluffy bathrobe and hung it neatly on the hook. Regarded her filthy clothing with distaste, then put them back on. She glanced at herself in the mirror.

Her wide-eyed reflection looked back.

I've gotta tell you, the whole cute and deadly thing gets me, too.

Too bad. She would have made a great secret agent bodyguard.

Loup walked back out, resigned. "At least the guys with the hose are honest. Take me back."

Derek didn't smile. "I won't make this offer again."

"Yeah, right." She shrugged. "Whatever."

FIFTY-THREE

Cell.
    Hose.
Questions.

The cycle seemed to accelerate after she turned down Derek's offer. Loup couldn't be sure; she could never be sure of anything involving time in that place. But it felt like they questioned her at least three times during the day that followed.

Never letting her sleep.

Never letting her rest.

Get used to it, she thought.

It wasn't easy, but it wasn't hard, either. Not exactly, not in the way normal people felt and thought. It was pain and discomfort, and she endured it. What else was there to do?

Mack would have understood.

Ever see a dog get hurt? That's what they do. Hole up and wait to live or die.

Loup prepared to hole up and endure for as long as it took. Her choice. This had been her choice. No matter that the repercussions were worse than she'd guessed. She'd made her choice and she would endure. She didn't think they'd kill her and she'd rather live than die, but she wasn't about to betray any of the Santitos, even if they kept her here for years.

Thinking that thought, she managed to fall asleep.

It was the darkness that woke her. For the first time since they'd put her in the cell the glaring lights were off. It was pitch-black, and someone was unlocking the cell door. She scrambled upright, putting her hands behind her head.

"Shh." Ron Johnson entered the cell almost soundlessly, a

flashlight in one hand and a rucksack in the other. He lowered the rucksack to the floor and pressed a finger against her lips. No flinch. "You want to get out of here? You've got about thirty seconds to decide."

Her heart hammered. "To where?"

"Mexico." His gaze was steady. "You've got kin there."

"My father?"

Johnson shook his head. "Sorry, no. None of the original kin lived much past forty. Cousins. Aunts, of a sort."

She stared at him, trying to read his expression behind the flashlight's beam. If he lied, he lied like her, without fear of being caught. She couldn't tell. "Why?"

"Long story. If you want to do this, I'll tell you on the way." He looked at her without blinking. "It's not a trick, but I can't prove it. All I can say is trust me. And it's not a sure thing. If we get caught, you're in twice the shit and I'm fucked."

"And you're only gonna make this offer once, right?" Loup asked wryly.

Johnson nodded. "First and last chance. I'm getting transferred out of here in three days. It wasn't easy to set this up."

Tommy's voice echoed through her memories. *Be careful!*

"Oh, fuck it. Fuck *careful*." She hopped off the bench. "Let's do it."

He was already moving, inhumanly quick. He set the flashlight on the shelf, unzipped the rucksack, and hauled out a set of fatigues, tossed them to her. "Put these on."

She stripped off her grimy boxing gear, put on the fatigues. Johnson stashed her old clothes in a plastic bag, handed her a pair of boots. They were too big, but she laced them tight around her ankles.

He handed her a cap. "Hide your hair. Brim low. Lower." He adjusted it. "Okay, good." Loup began folding the robe. He touched her wrist. "Leave it."

"But—"

There was sympathy in his glance. "We've got to leave a little mystery behind, Santa Olivia. Only way we're going to get away with this on my end." He pulled out one last item from his rucksack, a rustic woven basket. Placed it on the metal shelf, draped the blue and white robe over it. "See?"

Loup took a deep breath, fighting a disproportionate sense of loss. She stroked the satin fabric once in farewell. "Okay."

"Good girl." He put his hands on her shoulders. "Stay close beside me. If we encounter anyone, keep your head down, don't make eye contact. Don't talk to anyone." His mouth twitched in a faint smile. "Try not to walk like a girl."

"Okay."

Dim emergency lights came online a few seconds after he opened the cell door. Johnson shoved the flashlight into his belt and strode purposefully down the hall. Loup stuck close to his side, trying to match his stride and gait. At a security door, he swiped a card through a slot and a light turned green.

They headed deeper into the detention center.

A guard hurrying in the opposite direction came toward them, talking into a handheld radio. Johnson gave him a curt nod, the brim of his own cap low enough to shade his eyes. Loup kept her head down and concentrated on matching his stride. The guard nodded in reply and kept moving, still talking into his radio. He seemed more distracted than concerned. They turned a corner, then another.

Halfway down the next hallway, Johnson yanked open a utility door. "Move," he said. "Fast. It won't be long before someone thinks to check on you."

She plunged into darkness, feeling her way down a set of stairs. The door closed behind them. It smelled like dankness and corroding metal. A second later, Johnson switched the flashlight back on, revealing pipes overhead.

"Where are we?" she asked.

"Boiler room." The flashlight's beam tagged a high slit of a window, then went dark. "Over there."

Somewhere an alarm sounded.

Loup groped her way toward the window. It was propped open. She could smell fresh air.

"Give me your foot," Johnson's disembodied voice said. "I'll boost you."

She put her foot in his cupped hands.

He hoisted her effortlessly. "Stick tight to the side of the building. Don't move."

Loup nodded and wriggled out the window.

It was nighttime. The air was warm and dry. The sky was vast and filled with stars. Loup got to her feet and breathed deeply, raising her face involuntarily to gaze at the stars.

"Shit." Johnson's head and shoulders emerged from the window, but no more of him. "I'm stuck."

The rising and falling alarm took on a new urgency. Loup grabbed his shoulders and hauled hard. For a long moment there was resistance, then something gave way and he came slithering out.

"You okay?" she whispered.

He got up, rubbing his left shoulder. "Yeah. C'mon."

They sidled around the building, sticking close to the cinderblock walls. The alarm grew louder. The floodlights that had illuminated the front yard the night Loup had arrived were dark, but there were emergency searchlights sweeping back and forth across it.

"See those?" Johnson pointed. "We've got to dodge 'em."

Loup tugged her cap down firmly. "Okay."

He gave her a tight smile. "On my go."

Ron Johnson ran like something shot out of a cannon. Loup followed in his footsteps, feeling the effects of a month's incarceration and malnutrition. Adrenaline surged in her veins and her heart pounded in her chest. Years of training, shot to hell. The searchlights swept swiftly across the concrete. He dodged and veered with effortless grace while she struggled to keep up, awkward in her oversized boots.

Behind them, there was shouting. A squadron of men trotted

across the yard, the sweeping searchlights throwing their shadows in stark patterns.

Johnson made one last dash and cleared the yard. He crouched
in the shadow of a bush until Loup caught up with him.

"Okay." He straightened. "Walk like you've got a purpose,
soldier."

The alarm's siren continued to rise and fall. Ron Johnson set
out with a brisk, purposeful stride. Loup settled in beside him,
keeping her head lowered.

They crossed the base. Outside of the detention center, systems were operating normally. No one stopped them, no one
questioned them. Once a jeep careened past them, but it didn't
even slow down.

At the outskirts of the base, Johnson touched Loup's arm. She
glanced up at him.

"Perimeter's half a mile west," he said softly, lips close to her
ear. "We're going over the fence. I've got a jeep waiting on the far
side. But we're going to have to move fast to outstrip rumors. Can
you manage?"

She took a deep breath. "Yeah."

They ran into the night, into the desert. Warm, arid air
washed over them. Johnson set a hard, steady pace—too fast for
conversation. Loup felt her lungs burn and muscles strain as she
drained reserves of energy she hadn't known her body hoarded.
Her booted feet thudded on the hard-packed dirt, stumbling over
rocks and clumps of wiry grass. The lights of the base and the
sound of the siren grew fainter behind them.

Out of the starlit darkness, a chain-link fence loomed, topped
with razor wire.

Johnson halted. "Good girl."

She gazed at the glinting razor wire, breathing hard. "How—?"

"Like this." He rummaged along the base of the fence and
came up with a piece of carpet, then clambered up the fence and
laid it over the razor wire. "Try not to put your weight on it."

"Okay." She pushed through her tiredness and forced herself

to climb. It took a lot of concentration. Her legs trembled. At the top, Johnson steadied her while she straddled the carpeted razor wire. She wavered, feeling the sharp points beneath her threatening to pierce the thick carpeting.

Another, louder alarm siren joined the first.

"Base's on full alert now," he said laconically. "Better hurry."

"No kidding." Loup drew her other leg carefully over the wire. She clung to the chain links, catching her breath and letting her arms support her weight. Johnson used her to steady himself as he crossed the razor wire. "How come you're doing this, anyway?"

He pulled the carpet loose with a grunt, massaging his wrenched shoulder. "Because I should never have gotten in that ring with your brother. It wasn't right."

And then there was no more time to talk.

He steered her toward a waiting jeep concealed in a thicket of scrub. "Here." In the rear of the jeep he unsnapped a canvas cargo cover and tossed the carpet inside. "Get in. Make yourself small. Not a sound."

Loup met his eyes. "What's your name? Your real name?"

"John."

"John Johnson?"

His mouth twitched. "The government's not real creative." He pulled a bottle of cheap whiskey from his rucksack and swallowed a mouthful, then spilled some on his uniform. "Get in and shut the fuck up."

She crawled into the cargo space and curled into a ball. He pulled the cover taut and snapped it back into place.

Minutes later, the jeep coughed into life.

They jolted over rough terrain, a difficult drive rendered harder by the fact that Johnson was driving without headlights. Inside the cargo space, Loup braced herself. At last the jeep lurched onto a smooth surface. Johnson turned on his lights and drove faster. From time to time, other headlights swept past them. Loup curled herself tighter beneath the canvas. It made her think about that night in the cemetery after Tommy's death, lying on the ground, her body coiled around a knot of pain.

And Pilar, easing it.

She wished she could have brought the robe.

Then there was only the steady roar of the engine vibrating through the floorboards, the stink of diesel fumes. She wondered what it would mean to be in twice as much shit if they were caught. Beatings, maybe.

So what.

Betrayal would be worse. If Ron Johnson—*John* Johnson—was playing some game to fuck with her head, she was going to do her damnedest to make him pay for it. It was one thing to be lied to by fucking I-want-to-be-your-friend Derek. It was another thing to be lied to by her own kind.

The jeep slowed and began making turns. The sound of the engine reverberated differently. They weren't out in the open any longer. In fact, she could hear voices and the faint strains of music.

Outpost. They were in Outpost.

Someone hailed the jeep with a shout. It slowed, then stopped, the engine idling. Footsteps approached.

The beam of a flashlight played over the jeep. Loup hugged her knees to her chest, making sure no part of her showed or cast a shadow, trying not to breathe. Her heartbeat seemed unnaturally loud.

"Where you headed, soldier?" an MP's deep voice asked.

"Meetin' a girl, sir." Johnson sounded confident and a little slurred.

"You drinking and driving?"

"No, sir!"

"Uh-huh. Hand it over." There was a faint liquid slosh. "Go on, have fun while you can. Stay in radio contact. Right now the base is in lockdown, and all hands might be recalled for a manhunt. We've got a big-time runner."

Johnson sighed. "Yes, sir!"

And then the jeep was moving again, taking another series of turns. Loup let out her breath. If it was a trick, it was an elaborate one.

The jeep halted, engine idling. There were footsteps and a grating sound, then footsteps returning. The jeep lurched forward and halted. The engine cut out. Another grating sound. More footsteps. She tensed, wary and uncertain.

Johnson unsnapped the cargo cover.

Loup uncoiled, quick as a snake and ready for anything.

"Whoa!" He stepped back, flashing an unexpected grin. His green eyes glittered. "It's okay. We made it."

"Made it where?"

"You'll see."

She clambered out of the cargo space. John Johnson busied himself with his rucksack. The jeep's headlights were still on, illuminating the space. They were in a garage, an ordinary residential garage, with a homely door leading to the house and stairs leading to a basement. A sense of emptiness and abandonment pervaded the place.

But outside those walls . . .

Loup's blood quickened. "I don't know this place. But we're in Outpost, aren't we? *Aren't we?*"

"Yeah. On the outskirts. There's an old smugglers' tunnel here in the basement. The army dynamited it ages ago, but they did a half-assed job. There's people on the other end been working years to clear it. If we're lucky, it won't fall on our heads. Did I mention the part where we might get killed?" He came to face her. "Loup, I know what you're thinking. Don't."

"But—"

"*Don't.*" Johnson raised his voice. "They've got a watch posted on everyone you ever fucking knew in this town. You can't go back; not now, not for a damn long time. After you disappear, they're going to be watching harder. Did you hear that MP back there? Once they figure out you got off the base somehow, there's going to be a full-scale manhunt. You'll get caught and anyone you contact is going to be taken in for questioning. Maybe disappeared. Understand?"

She sighed. "I guess."

"Don't give me I-fucking-guess!" He shook her until her cap fell off. He was strong enough to do it. "Just understand, okay?"

"Okay," Loup said mildly. "It's just that I wish I could see—"

"I know. I do. We've had people watching you." Johnson sighed and loosed her. He picked up her cap and shoved it into his rucksack, producing a second flashlight in its place. "You won't be needing this. Come on." He turned off the jeep's headlights and headed down the basement stairs, turning on his flashlight.

"What people?" Loup asked, following.

"People. Friends, allies." He searched for a trapdoor, found it. Wrenched it open. A series of rusted metal rungs descended into darkness. He glanced at Loup, then fished in his pockets and handed her a couple of wrapped protein bars. "Here, eat these. You'll need the energy. We can't afford to slow down."

She obeyed, tearing open one of the bars. "What friends?"

"Your father and his brethren, the original kin, they always had allies." Johnson watched her eat. "Ordinary enlisted men who helped them escape, sympathetic scientists. The ones who made it to Mexico were able to make contact once they were safe. The network's grown ever since."

Loup chewed and swallowed. "Where do you come in?"

"Human GMOs are considered government property," he said. "Some of the same people who helped your father and kin are trying to help us. And you." He gave her a hard smile. "We're trying to change things from the inside out. You can be a part of it."

She took another bite. "What's a GMO?"

"Genetically modified organism. That's what they call us."

"How'd you know about me?"

"Your father. If we could have gotten you out years ago, we would have. But it wasn't worth the risk as long as you were safe."

Johnson smiled again, wryly. "You changed that when you decided to fight me three years ago."

Loup tore open the second bar. "You were sure it was me?"

"As soon as I heard." He played the flashlight's beam down the long shaft. "That's when they started working in earnest on the other side of the wall. They had to be careful as hell so the army wouldn't notice. Could have really used another month or two. There's a path, but it's not easy and the whole structure's unstable."

She shrugged. "If you knew, how come you didn't train harder?"

Johnson snorted. "Because I didn't think there was a chance in hell you could beat me. You ready?"

Loup crammed the last bite into her mouth. "Yeah."

He nodded and handed her a flashlight. "Follow me. Once we're in the tunnel, put your feet where I do, and don't touch a fucking thing."

"Okay."

FIFTY-FOUR

They descended into darkness.

The shaft was sunk deep, maybe eighty or a hundred feet below the surface. Down and down they climbed, rust flaking from the rungs. The air was hot and stifling, worse than Loup's cell, and the farther down they went, the worse it got.

"Okay." Johnson's flashlight beam moved sideways. "I'm down. Watch your head."

Her feet touched something solid. Cement. She tested, let go of the rungs, and moved away. Her head brushed the ceiling and dirt sifted down.

"You have to crouch."

"Got it." Loup turned, keeping her head ducked. She played her flashlight's beam over the tunnel. It was low and narrow and stifling, but it looked intact. "This isn't so bad."

"Here, no. The bad stretch is outside of town. This way."

He set out at a steady, crouched jog. Loup followed. She felt better for having eaten. The dirt walls passed in a blur. "Hey, Johnson? What's gonna happen to you?"

"Nothing, hopefully." His voice sounded muffled in the tunnel's close confines. "I'll be questioned. But there'll be a handful of people willing to swear they saw me somewhere else tonight."

"Friends and allies?"

"Some. Not all." He chuckled. "Doesn't hurt to have an identical twin. We've been planning this for a long time."

"What about *my* friends?"

"As long as you stay away, they'll be okay. No way any of them could have gotten you off the base." Johnson gave her a quick glance over his shoulder. "And that Santa Olivia business, that's a nice touch. Everyone's already in an uproar. When they find that empty cell with the basket and the robe . . . You think soldiers aren't superstitious? They'll talk. It'll muddy the waters, confuse things."

"What about Coach Roberts?"

He was quiet a moment, jogging without comment. "I don't know. He and General Argyle go way back. I think he'll be okay."

"What about Mig?" Loup asked. "Any chance he'll get his ticket north?"

"Miguel Garza?"

"Yeah."

"Some." Johnson shot her another quick look. "You care? I had the impression he was kind of an asshole."

"He is," she agreed. "But he's a good guy, too. He just doesn't know it yet."

He slowed, came to a halt. "Yeah, we do that."

Loup fetched up behind him. "Do what?"

"Show people what they could be if they dared." John Johnson's beam picked out the dimensions of the collapsed tunnel ahead, the sunken walls and fallen ceiling propped with crude planks, bits and pieces of salvage. "It's complicated. Here's where it gets bad. Follow me."

He led.

She followed.

It *was* bad. Three hundred yards' worth of tunnel had been dynamited, had collapsed in on itself. It had been cleared enough for a single person at a time to pass, but the entire structure groaned and quivered, tenuous. Johnson picked his way through the tunnel, stepping over piles of dirt, sidling past supporting planks. The air grew closer and his breath came hard and shallow.

Loup stepped in his footprints, emulating him.

There were other footprints.

"Who—?"

"Shh."

She went quiet. It felt like a single misdrawn breath would bring everything crashing down on their heads. Timbers creaked. She avoided touching them. In one hard-packed section, there was a hole so narrow they had to squirm through it like worms, wriggling in the dirt.

"Fuck," Loup muttered, crawling on her elbows. "Are you *trying* to kill me?"

"No." He flashed a white grin, helped pull her out. "Come on."

Step and step, sidestep and sidle. Feet placed exactly there and there and there. Touch nothing, move onward in an eternal crouch. Wood shivered, dirt filtered, shifting. The beams of their flashlights crisscrossed, making patterns in the hot, dusty air. At one point, Johnson aimed his overhead.

"We're under the wall."

"Shit!" Loup breathed.

"Yeah."

Timbers creaked and groaned.

And then the tunnel opened, became solid once more. Cement floor, dirt walls. All solid, holding. John Johnson shifted back into a steady jog, his back hunched, his rucksack over one shoulder. "Almost there."

They reached another shaft. Johnson aimed his beam up it and whistled softly, once, then twice. The second time, there was an answering whistle.

"Okay." He stowed his flashlight and began to climb. Loup followed, her heart beating fast. Up and up they went. The air grew cooler and easier to breathe.

Johnson reached the top and spoke to someone. A low voice answered. He clambered out of the shaft.

Loup took a deep breath and followed fast, scrambling to her feet.

She was in a warehouse filled with piles of dirt and rubble, unused boards. A trio of battery-powered lanterns lit the space.

A lean young man she didn't know gave her a broad smile. There was a car, another figure standing beside it. Smaller, shivering, arms wrapped around herself. Her face was uncertain, filled with hope and fear.

Pilar.

"Loup?" she said in a small voice.

Loup stared, disbelieving.

"Told you we had people watching you," John Johnson said behind her. "I wouldn't quite say our kind mates for life. But when we fall, it tends to stick, even at your age. I guess it helps keep us alive." He nudged her. "Go on."

She took three steps forward, still not daring to believe; but then Pilar was there, flinging her arms around her neck, burying her face against her shoulder. She was shaking like a leaf, her voice broken and her words half-incoherent. "Oh, God, I was so scared, I didn't know, I didn't know if I should trust him, I didn't know if I was gonna end up raped and murdered and left in the desert to die, and then that tunnel, that fucking tunnel, I thought I was gonna die in that tunnel, but I just, I just, if there was a chance . . . I just don't want to spend my life without you . . ."

On and on, the words poured out of her.

Loup wrapped her arms around Pilar, held her tight, tighter, absorbing her terrified shudders. Her heart soared, impossibly full and glad. "It's okay," she whispered, pressing her cheek against Pilar's bowed head. "It's okay. I'm here."

Finally, the shaking stopped.

"You okay?" Loup asked.

"Uh-huh." Pilar lifted her head and nodded vigorously, then demonstrated by kissing her with head-spinning fervor and a lot of tongue.

Someone made a throat-clearing noise.

Loup extricated herself, holding Pilar's hand. "How?" she asked simply. "You said they were all being watched."

"Yeah." Johnson grinned. "They are. And she was. But some

little pissant of a Salamanca pitched a fit about the army spying on his girlfriend. Convinced them she hadn't seen you in almost a year, didn't want to have anything to do with you. He got them to call off the dogs. Seems your heroics, um, threatened his manhood."

The young man laughed.

"Rory kind of freaked out after the fight," Pilar agreed. "I *did* tell him the truth. He didn't want anyone to know."

"Why?" Loup asked softly, gazing at John Johnson. "I understand about the guilt. Tommy. But you didn't have to do this. Take this risk."

He returned her gaze, level and unblinking. "I cost you someone you loved. I wish I could bring your brother back. I can't. But this I could do."

"Thanks."

"Sure." He nodded. "By the way, this is Christophe. Henri's son; your cousin. He's working in league with the Mexican government. He'll take you to meet people, talk to important people on the other side of the wall. Maybe make a difference. No one born in an Outpost has ever gotten out before."

"Hi." Loup greeted Christophe. "Thanks."

He inclined his head. His expression was somber, but there was a twinkle in his eyes, which were as wide and dark as her own. "My pleasure, *prima*," he said in softly accented English.

Johnson cleared his throat again. "Loup . . . I've got to run. And I need the uniform back. Laundry keeps tabs. Do you mind?"

"Umm . . ."

Pilar tugged her hand. "C'mon, baby." She smiled, all dimples. "I've got stuff you can wear."

"Okay." She let Pilar lead her to the far side of the waiting car, where she rummaged through a satchel crammed full of clothing. "I can't believe you're here."

"Me neither." She handed Loup a pair of faded jeans. "These oughta fit. They're, um, kind of tight on me. When that guy

came, Johnson, and told me he could take me to you, I thought it
had to be a trick, that it was gonna be something awful, but I just
had to try, you know?"

"That was really, really brave of you," Loup said honestly, un-
lacing her boots, stripping off the camouflage pants, and pulling
on the jeans.

Pilar flushed. "Yeah, well, you're worth it." She ducked her
head, picking through an array of crumpled shirts, settling on
a pink cotton camisole. "Here. This one's pretty small, too." She
watched Loup put it on. "Cute. I like seeing you in my clothes."
She traced the line of Loup's collarbone, her expression softening. "You're awfully thin, baby."

"Yeah, sorry. They didn't feed me enough."

"Loup, I'm not *complaining*, for God's sake." Pilar cupped her
face, kissed her tenderly. "Just let me fuss over you, okay?" She
brushed her fingertips over the faint pink line bisecting Loup's
eyebrow. "That from the fight?" Loup nodded. Pilar's eyes were
bright with tears. "From now on, I'm gonna take good care of
you, I promise."

Loup laughed.

"Don't laugh! I'm serious."

"I know, I know."

"I am," Pilar said adamantly. "I'll get a job, I bet I can get a job
bartending. That guy Christophe, he said so. I'll work all day and
take care of you all night."

"What am I gonna do all day?"

"I don't care." Pilar shook her head. "Play on the beach with
all the other little werewolves and chase your tails. I don't care."

"Pilar, you're kind of delirious."

She sighed. "Yeah, I know."

"Just don't ever leave me again," Loup said seriously. "Promise?"

"Never." Pilar kissed her, over and over. "Never, ever, ever."

Someone coughed.

"Okay, okay!" Loup called. She folded the fatigues and slid

her bare feet into a pair of flip-flops Pilar handed her, brought everything back to Johnson. He stowed the gear in his bag, then thrust out his hand.

"You take care." His handshake was firm.

"You, too," she said.

It felt strange to see him go, climbing back down the shaft. None of it seemed quite real. But it *was* real. Wherever she was, it wasn't a cell. The warehouse was real, the car was real. Impossible but true, Pilar was real. The young guy, Christophe, he was real. Kin, the son of a man her father had considered a brother.

Johnson reached the bottom of the shaft and whistled. Christophe whistled in reply, then wrestled the trapdoor closed.

"Okay!" He gave them both a grin. "We have to make time, too. Be gone by sunrise. You ever see sunrise from a convertible?"

They shook their heads.

"I never even rode in a car before today," Pilar added.

"Oh, *man!*" Christophe's grin widened. "I'm going to show you the world!" He went over to the cargo door and flung it open. Warm, dry air blew through the warehouse. "Cities and mountains and nightclubs, oceans and palm trees and coral reefs. You ever ate a fish grilled fresh off the boat?"

"Are you kidding?" Loup asked.

He beamed. "A little."

She laughed. "What about the important people we're supposed to meet?"

"Oh, sure." He nodded. "That, too. But it's not the fun part."

"Umm . . . what are we gonna live on?" Pilar asked.

Christophe shrugged. "You want to get a job, I can get you a job in Huatulco. Plenty of bars. Loup, you have a little bit of money owed you. Martin's stake in a fishing charter business. I don't know why, but all the original kin were crazy for fishing. Me, I just like eating them." He flashed another grin. "Right now, you're both guests of the government of Mexico, and I'm your lucky escort."

"Yeah?"

"Oh, yes." He nodded again. "And I will take you to meet the important people, the boring government officials, so we can make the world a better place. We have a long ride ahead of us and I will tell you more. But also, I am happy to be your guide. I will teach you to speak good Spanish and consult in important matters like buying bikini bathing suits, so you can lie beneath the palm trees and rub each other with suntan lotion."

"Bikinis," Pilar murmured.

Loup eyed her. "You'd look good in one."

"*You* would."

"Both of you will," Christophe said cheerfully. He opened the passenger door of the car. "So? Are you ready to see the world?"

Loup gave Pilar an inquiring look.

"What?" Pilar turned pink. "You're asking *me*?" She summoned a dazzling, heart-stopping smile, eyes still bright with tears, squeezing Loup's hand in hers. It made her so happy it almost hurt. "In case you hadn't noticed, baby, I'm pretty much ready to go anywhere as long as it's with you."

"So?" Christophe repeated. "Are you ready?"

"Yeah," Loup said. "Yeah, let's go."

The stars were still out. The convertible purred softly, running without headlights as they drove out of the abandoned border town, all three in the wide front seat. The dim road stretched before them.

"If you look back, you can see the lights of Outpost," Christophe said.

Loup turned and knelt on the seat, gazing behind them. The wall was a hulking gray presence receding in the distance. Beyond, she could see a faint stain of brightness in the night sky. Not much, but it was there. Pilar turned too, gazing over Loup's shoulder. A backwash of hot wind made her hair swirl, silken and tickling. Loup thought about everything they were leaving behind—the church and Father Ramon and Sister Martha and Anna. Mack and all the Santitos. The cemetery where her mother and Tommy were buried. Coach Roberts. Miguel Garza and his uncertain quest.

"Do you think we'll ever see them again?" Pilar whispered in her ear.

"Yeah, I do." She thought about the empty cell with the basket and the robe. Santa Olivia's last mystery. "We've got to believe it, that's all."

"Okay."

They turned back to face the road. Christophe hummed to himself, tuneless and good-natured, concentrating on driving in near-darkness. Pilar stifled a yawn and settled her head on Loup's shoulder.

Overhead, the stars began to pale.

They drove onward toward dawn and the future, leaving Santa Olivia behind.

ABOUT THE AUTHOR

Jacqueline Carey is the author of short stories, essays, the novels *Banewreaker* and *Godslayer*, and the nationally bestselling Kushiel's Legacy series. Carey lives in western Michigan.